Vivien Brown lives in Uxbridge, on the outskirts of London, with her husband and two cats. After a career in banking and accountancy and the birth of her twin daughters, she gave up working with numbers and moved into working with words and has never looked back.

 @VivBrownAuthor
vivienbrownauthor.wordpress.com

Also by Vivien Brown

Lily Alone
Five Unforgivable Things
No Sister of Mine

Be Careful What You Wish For

Vivien Brown

One More Chapter
a division of HarperCollins*Publishers*
The News Building
1 London Bridge Street
London SE1 9GF

www.harpercollins.co.uk

This paperback edition 2020

First published in Great Britain in ebook format by
HarperCollins*Publishers* 2020

A catalogue record for this book
is available from the British Library

ISBN: 978-0-00-837417-4

Printed and bound by CPI Group (UK) Ltd, Croydon, CR0 4YY

Set in Birka by Palimpsest Book Production Ltd, Falkirk
Stirlingshire

To my dad, Wilfred Alexander Smith
1920–1993
Loving father, loyal friend
Hard to believe, but you would have been 100 this year

Prologue

I close the door behind me and lean against it, taking deep breaths while I wait for my heart to slow down, my hands to stop shaking, and my head to tell me what to do next.

I wish it was all just some sick dream, revenge acting itself out as it has so often done before, satisfyingly, harmlessly, as I sleep. But I know this was no dream. This is real. Horribly, frighteningly real.

I didn't mean to do it. I really didn't. I only meant to unnerve her, unsettle her, to drip some small fluttering of fear into her life. It was a game. That's all. A game where one player doesn't even know the other exists. A game only one player can win. But I never intended things to go this far. I am not a violent person. It was just a reaction, a spur of the moment thing. I had no idea anybody was there.

But she was.

And she still is.

I left her there, in the dark, lying motionless on the floor. Alone. There is water, and silence, and far too much blood.

Nobody knows I was there. And nobody knows she is there . . . except me.

I'm a good person. He used to tell me that, a long time ago. How good I was. How precious. That I was his angel, the light of his life. Until she took him away.

What would he think of me now, if he were still here? If he knew what I had become? A murderer?

A cold fear falls over me. He can't help me now. Nobody can help me. I am alone, and I just want to hide away, to close my eyes and wait for it all to go away. But it's not going away, is it? Oh my God, what have I done? And what am I supposed to do now?

Chapter 1

Prue Harris plonked her bulging suitcase down beside her on the pavement, just missing a muddy puddle, moved her camera bag across to her other shoulder and stretched her aching back. She took the crumpled sheet of paper from her raincoat pocket and looked again at the address she had scribbled down. Belle Vue Court. Yes, this was definitely the place. She stared up at the ugly three-storeyed block in front of her. The big black front door, with its peeling paint, was flanked by rows of doorbells, one for each flat, with a little white card beside each one announcing the name of the occupant. Prue struggled up the three wide concrete steps, her battered old case thumping against her heels, wishing she had thought to buy herself one of those modern waterproof ones with wheels and a long handle, and searched for flat number 9.

Madalyn Cardew, it said, in fading ballpoint pen, on the card. Yes, that must be her, although in the few emails they had exchanged so far she had only ever called herself Madi. It was only now that Prue realised she had not even known her

3

surname. How strange, for a woman to be handing over her flat, and everything in it, for a whole month without even having exchanged full names! In fact, she knew very little about Madi Cardew. What she looked like, how old she was, even if she had a husband or a family. Just that, like herself, Madi had wanted, or needed, a bit of time away from her normal day-to-day life, had been desperate for some time alone in a new environment far from home. Beyond that, no questions had been asked. Prue valued her privacy and Madi, no doubt, did too.

The keys had arrived by registered post the previous day. Prue had suggested that Madi leave them in the care of a neighbour, so she could pick them up when she got here, which was exactly what Prue herself had done with her own keys, handing them over to her friend Sian that morning, but Madi had quickly made it clear that she did not have those kind of neighbours. Most were out all day and, even when they were in, they tended to keep themselves to themselves. And hiding the keys under a plant pot somewhere was far too risky. This wasn't a cosy Norfolk village. This was London, and it was just not that kind of place.

There were three keys on the ring and Prue tried them, one at a time, in the front door. At the turn of key number three it swung open and she walked into a large square hall. A dim light came on automatically, highlighting the dust as she took off her woolly hat and stood on a strip of dirty coir matting to stamp her feet and shake the rain from her shoulders.

She closed the heavy door behind her and absorbed the sudden silence. Well, she was here. Wet and weary, with her arms feeling like they were about to pop out of their sockets after lugging her case all the way from the station, but here. So now what? The hallway was deserted and she stood for a moment, taking in her new surroundings. The wallpaper was ancient, the stippled kind, with a dull cream-coloured paint daubed over the top and the scuffed skirting boards finished in a pale shade of green.

Despite a collection of numbered boxes set out in three tiers to hold the post for each individual flat, there was also a teetering pile of what must be unwanted junk mail strewn across the front of the long rectangular table, giving the impression that it was down to the residents to pick everything up off the mat and sort it, and that the leftover stuff with no obvious recipient had probably been there for a long time and might never be read at all. It was a strange and not very private system, very open to theft, and one that would have worried her a lot had she been expecting any post of her own. Still, she noted that the box marked 9 was empty, although policing its contents, or lack of, was really not down to her. A few curry house and pizza takeaway leaflets were pinned haphazardly to a corkboard up above, and a battered pink baby buggy lay pushed up against the wall.

Flats 1 to 3, each one identified by a large brass number on its door, led off the hall, one to each side and one at the back. Ahead of her was a steep narrow staircase with thin grey carpet fraying at the edges which she assumed must lead up to the others. With three floors and three flats on each, it didn't take a lot of calculation to work out that flat 9 was likely to be on the top floor, and there was no sign of a lift.

Prue sighed. As she started up the stairs, bumping her case step by step behind her, she asked herself why she had brought quite so much stuff with her, and why she was here at all, whether her rather hasty retreat from Norfolk and the distance she was putting between herself and Joseph Barton would make any real difference to the way she felt. Or, perhaps even more importantly, to the way *he* felt.

It was the beginning of March, not the ideal time of year to take a holiday, but waiting for warmer weather was not an option. She had needed to escape now – right now – before anyone realised what she was doing and tried to stop her, and the house swap site she had stumbled across on the internet had provided what had seemed like the perfect solution. Besides, she was hopeful that London would have plenty of attractions on offer whatever the weather. Art galleries, department stores, museums, and she was determined to take a look at Buckingham Palace while she was here and watch the changing of the guard, just like Christopher Robin and Alice. Enough to do, surely, to distract her from the aching feeling, part bewilderment, part shame, that had overwhelmed her and that she knew was going to be so hard to shake off.

She arrived, a little breathlessly, on the top-floor landing. Perhaps being here, with time on her hands, with no work to go to for a whole month, and no car, she could try to work on her fitness. Walks in the beautiful London parks, or along the banks of the Thames, held a lot more appeal than tramping over the familiar muddy fields at home and she was so looking forward to the liberation of a wellie-free life for a while.

She looked around for flat 9. It was, she was pleased to see, the one at the back of the building, which she hoped would mean less traffic noise, and perhaps a more interesting view. The front offered nothing more than a busy street, more buildings just like the one she was standing in, and rows of bright streetlights which, for a girl used to the sparsely lit country lane outside her own home, would have almost certainly kept her awake at night, flooding the place with far too much unnatural light.

She quickly found the right key and opened the door to the flat – *her* flat – wondering briefly what the third key was for. She would take a stroll around later and get her bearings, but for now she found herself standing in a tiny lobby area with a few coat hooks on the wall, all of them occupied, and a couple of pairs of well-polished leather boots lined up neatly in the corner. She dropped her case on the carpet at her feet, kicked off her damp shoes and walked through into what turned out to be the living room.

She was not quite sure what she had expected, but this was definitely not it. The room was stylish yet warm and cosy, the sofa enormous and squidgy, in a deep shade of red, with a sprinkling of big multi-coloured floral cushions that matched the flowing floor-to-ceiling curtains. A stunning mix of bright white walls, red table lamps, purple rugs, and enormous theatre posters in frames completed the décor. There was some sort of golden statuette in the shape of a mask on the mantelpiece, with various knick-knacks to each side of it, and through an open archway she could see a white wood kitchen, complete with a small pine table and chairs and lots of shiny stainless steel accessories. It was posh, and pristine, and plush . . . not at all how she had imagined the interior of a London flat in such an ordinary block to look, but she breathed a sigh of relief. It was so different from the casual shabbiness she was used to, but exactly what she needed. A challenge, a change. She loved the flat already and felt instantly at home.

Prue walked over to the window and parted the curtains. The rain had stopped, and a dim late-afternoon light wafted in. She had been right about the traffic. From this side of the building she could hardly hear it. And, to her delight, she could see a little patch of faded grass down below, with a wooden bench set up beneath the one and only tree, and despite it looking a bit sparse and unkempt, it could be the perfect place to sit with a coffee and a book, if the sun ever came out, which it surely must at some time during her stay.

There were three more doors, all closed. Opening the first, Prue found a sumptuous, shiny-white bathroom. From the empty holder attached to the tiles above the sink it looked as if the only thing Madi had taken with her was her tooth-brush. Everything else had been left behind, with several half-empty shampoo and bubble-bath bottles lined up along the side of the bath and a small cupboard on the wall revealing a selection of hairsprays, headache tablets, cough medicines and plasters. There was an unopened packet of ash blonde hair dye too, which provided the first clue to what Madi might look like or wanted to look like at least. Two fresh towels, in a pretty lemon colour with a scalloped edge, had been left for her on a chair next to the radiator, which, like the water when she tried the tap, was wonderfully hot.

The second door led her into a small double bedroom, simply furnished and clearly not in use, although there was an old teddy lying on the pillows and a handful of old *Rupert* annuals and a lamp shaped like a car on a shelf by the bed. The third door took her into what must be Madi's room. For the first time since she had arrived, Prue felt like an intruder. This was no hotel room. This was Madi's private space. The bed was a large king size, with a pretty rose-patterned duvet and heaps of small pink cushions, most of which Prue knew she would have to chuck onto the floor in order to get into bed. She half expected to lift a pillow and find Madi's pyjamas hiding underneath. Posh satin ones, if the rest of the flat was anything to go by. A book sat on the bedside cabinet with a bookmark sticking out of it, as if its reader had just left the room and would be back at any minute. How could anyone do that? Know they were going away for a month and leave a book behind, unfinished? Prue certainly couldn't, and had brought a good six or seven new novels with her, as well as the romance she had been so engrossed in on the train and couldn't wait to get back to.

On the top of the chest of drawers, Madi's perfumes and various items of jewellery, some laid out on a flower-painted china tray, some curled into trinket boxes with no lids, had been pushed aside, making room for a vase of purple tulips whose petals were already starting to droop, and providing space for Prue to put some of her own things. The perfume bottles were all expensive brands. She took the lid off one and sprayed some onto her wrist, lifting it to her nose and enjoying the fresh citrusy aroma that reminded her, just briefly, of her gran, standing in the kitchen years ago, leaning over a bubbling pan of lemon marmalade as a young Prue sat at the table, sticking labels onto the waiting jars. She still missed her gran every day and couldn't imagine a time when that would ever stop.

Most of the necklaces looked like they were real gold and, picking up a ring and holding it towards the light, she felt sure the gorgeous green stone must be an emerald. Why hadn't Madi taken them with her, or at least put them away safely somewhere? She felt ridiculously honoured that this stranger trusted her enough to leave such things lying about so casually, and more than a little guilty that she had carefully stowed all her own valuables away in a locked cupboard under the stairs before she'd left, and had brought the key with her. But then, everyone's idea of what was most precious to them was different, wasn't it? Prue's biggest worry as she'd packed to leave the village had been for her gran's old cat, Flo, definitely the hardest thing of all to leave behind, but Madi had assured her she would look after her as if she were her own. Jewels could be easily replaced, certainly if you were as rich as Madi appeared to be. Pets really couldn't. Prue had inherited the cat along with the cottage, but she had to admit she had grown increasingly fond of her this past year and was missing her already.

Peering inside the chest, she found that the top two drawers had been emptied for her, although the lower ones still held brightly coloured headscarves and neatly folded piles of nightwear and T-shirts. Similarly, a section of the wardrobe stood empty except for a few padded hangers, while the rest contained a range of boldly patterned dresses, smart jackets and trousers, two loose kaftan-type garments in Chinese designs that probably served as summer dressing gowns, and some very nice handbags and high-heeled shoes. Prue touched the soft lacy collar of one of the dresses and peered at the label. A good make. Size fourteen. Too big for her to borrow, not that she ever would, but already she felt she was beginning to know just a little more about Madalyn Cardew.

There was a photo next to the bed, a black and white shot in an ornate silver frame. A man, good-looking, probably about thirty years old, smiled up at her. Husband? Boyfriend? Brother? She couldn't help noticing that the photo was a bit fuzzy, the exposure not quite right. And why, she wondered, if the picture was important enough to stand by her bed, had Madi not taken it with her, just as Prue herself had brought a few favourite family photos along with her, tucked into the little pocket inside her purse? She was being too inquisitive, of course. She had no business asking such questions, or snooping into Madi's life. It was enough that she had free run of the place, that she had found somewhere private and comfortable to hide away and lick her wounds.

A combination of adrenalin, excitement, and curiosity had taken her over for a while but now she just felt tired. She needed normality. To eat, make a cup of tea, unpack and watch some TV before climbing into Madi's bed. No, it was *her* bed now, for the next month anyway.

Perhaps, for the first time in days, she might manage to sleep well. Nobody knew where she was, not her parents, not her boss, not even Sian, so nobody was going to turn up

11

unexpectedly at the door. She didn't have to switch on her phone or her laptop, or open her emails, or even step outside, if she chose not to. She had left everything that mattered behind in Norfolk, for a whole month. Her home, her job. And Joe, of course. Oh, how her cheeks burned with embarrassment just thinking about Joe. She would never forget the look on his face the last time she'd seen him. That mixture of stunned shock and unmistakeable pity. That face still came to her in her dreams. Maybe, if she was lucky, she'd left the dreams behind in Norfolk too. One way or another, she'd find that out tonight, but she wasn't hopeful. Sleeping alone, in an unfamiliar bed, without Flo's fluffy little body pressed against her and her gentle purring close to her ear, would probably be difficult enough as it was.

Her memories and her humiliation, of course, had come with her to London, like unwanted extra baggage she had dragged behind her alongside her battered old suitcase, and couldn't quite manage to let go of. From some things, it seemed, it was never possible to escape.

Chapter 2

MADI

Madalyn Cardew pulled into the side of the road and peered out through the grimy windscreen. If she had realised how muddy the roads around here were going to be she wouldn't have put her car through the carwash before leaving London. She'd have brought some sturdy boots too, instead of leaving them behind in the flat. Still, there must surely be some decent shops around here where she could buy replacements, she thought, not at all convinced that there were.

The small white sign, almost hidden among the bushes and bearing the words 'Shelling. Please drive carefully' as she entered the village, had reassured her that this was the right place. Her satnav had brought her straight here, without even one wrong turn, even though it was so far off the beaten track, with the hedges scratching at the doors as she'd made her way, gingerly, down that last narrow lane, that being reminded to drive carefully seemed laughable.

She had expected the village to be small and quiet, and it

13

was. It looked like exactly what she needed, a quiet out-of-the-way bolthole, somewhere she wasn't known and would not be recognised, yet this place was so Sunday-afternoon sleepy it looked practically comatose. There was not a soul about as she stepped out of the car and locked it, carefully avoiding the muddiest bits of road, and made her way round to the rather ragged pavement outside the tiny stone cottage which she assumed must be Prue Harris's. She looked up and down the road for a parking meter, but there wasn't one. No yellow lines either, so she hoped it was all right to park where she had, but there was a little black Mini already occupying the narrow driveway, mud-spattered as all the vehicles around here seemed to be, and she had no option but to leave her car parked outside the gate.

The gate was low, partially rotten, and creaked on its hinges as she walked through and tried to snap the catch shut behind her, finally managing it on the third attempt. The winding cobbled path led through a small square patch of garden to a pillar-box-red front door, with a tiny net-curtained window in its centre. Terracotta pots containing a few fading daffodils stood, not quite as straight as they might, to each side. *Snowdrop Cottage.* The name was carved into an oval wooden sign above the knocker. Yes, this was it. Not that there was even a single snowdrop to be seen, but it was March already and, if they had been there at all, then they were probably long gone by now. Madi would be the first to admit that, having no proper garden to call her own, she was far from an expert when it came to flowers. Still, she'd bought a bunch of tulips by way of a welcome, and left them at home in the bedroom. She knew virtually nothing about Prue or her tastes but hoped she would like them.

Madi felt in her coat pocket. The keys! Of course, she still didn't have them. *'Turn left out of the gate,'* Prue's email had instructed, *'and take the lane up to the left when you see the church. You'll find the new vets' surgery up ahead of you. Just ask for Sian.'*

She retraced her steps down the path and turned left, as instructed, taking in the large stone-built house next door with its frilly net curtains and sturdy oak door, and the smaller, more modern pair of semi-detached houses beyond it. Every building different. As luck would have it, the little church was built at the top of an incline and the lane beside it seemed to have stayed relatively dry, all the rain and hence the mud having run straight down and accumulated in a giant squelchy mess at the bottom. Presumably the church services were over for the day as there was nobody about, but it sounded as if someone was still inside, practising their bell ringing, as a mix of disconnected chimes rang out haphazardly from the tower, not quite making anything resembling a tune. Madi picked her way around the mud, staying close to the hedge at the side, and slowly made her way to the surgery.

An old dog gazed up at her as she entered, its front paw bandaged, its elderly owner sitting with his knees wide apart, hunched forward and flicking through a magazine with a photo of a tractor on its cover. There were no other animals, or people, waiting, but it was a Sunday, so it was quite surprising to find the place open at all.

'Hello. Can I help you?' The girl behind the reception desk

looked up from her computer screen, put down the biscuit she had been nibbling and wiped her fingers on the front of her green tabard.

'Yes, I'm looking for Sian.'

'That's me.' The girl's face cracked into a smile. 'Oh, you must be Prue's visitor!'

'Yes. Madalyn Cardew.'

'I'm sorry, I'd expected you to be . . .' The girl didn't finish her sentence, just looked away for a moment, leaving Madi wondering just what it was about her that was so obviously not as expected. 'You'll be after the keys, right? Hang on a minute and I'll walk down with you, show you around the place. How to work the fire and stuff like that. Prue's left you a few bits – milk and bread –but you'll probably be wanting to visit the shop for supplies in the morning, so I can show you where that is too.'

'There's no need. Honestly.' Madi tried to be polite but she really didn't need some stranger accompanying her every-where. 'I'll find my own way around. And I have food. So, if I could just have the keys . . .'

'Right-o. If you're sure.' The girl stood up, went to a back room and came back with a wax jacket, then rummaged about in the depths of its enormous pockets before finding the key ring and brandishing it aloft. 'Got them! This big long one is for the front door, and the smaller round one for the back. Not sure about the little tiny one. I'm sure you'll figure that out though if it's anything important. Just shout if you need anything else, and welcome to Shelling! I think Prue's left you a note on the table and my number's on there, along with some others you might need. Oh, and the dustman comes on Tuesdays. Just pop your rubbish in the bin round the side. Recycling goes in a separate green one, but you'll see that. I can sort you out a newspaper delivery while you're here, if you'd like. My parents own the shop. Oh, and Mum does hair too, if you're interested . . .'

'Thank you. Very kind of you, but no thanks.' Madi stepped over the dog's outstretched paws and made a hasty escape back down the lane. All she really wanted was to collect her bags from the boot of the car, get inside the cottage and close the door on the world. No shop. No papers. And definitely not someone to do her hair.

The cottage felt chilly. She kept her coat on as she wandered from room to room which, as it was only a simple two-up two-down, didn't take very long. The living-room furniture was old and shabby but looked comfy enough: a cream sofa covered with an oversized throw, one armchair facing a bit-too-large TV, and a coffee table piled with books and magazines. A few cat hairs floated up into the air and made her sneeze as she lifted and plumped a big flat cushion and replaced it on a squashy pouffe in front of the fireplace. Flo's domain, obviously.

The kitchen, she saw once she'd switched on the light, was of the oak cupboards, range cooker, scrubbed wooden table in the middle kind, with a plain roller blind pulled right down over the back window. There was a small plastic cat flap low down in the door, with the dried marks from muddy paws on the doormat at its base. A separate pantry housed baking essentials, packets and tins on deep shelves, and there was a small fridge and a freezer tucked in, side by side, underneath. Despite its old-fashioned, traditional appearance, Madi was pleased to see a microwave and a washing machine, and an internet hub in the corner of the worktop so she wouldn't have to rely on a mobile phone signal if she did decide to communicate with the outside world. A bathroom, small but adequate, led off the kitchen, housed in what looked to be a more modern extension. A bowl of blue hyacinths, just coming into bloom, sat on the windowsill above the bath, their heady scent drifting through the kitchen and right out as far as the living room.

Upstairs there was a tiny single bedroom without a bed, just a desk with a computer, trays of papers, a printer and a small wooden chair. Across the way was a more spacious double, the bed swathed in a thick duvet that felt like duck down, with a crocheted bedspread folded across the foot end, and two big fluffy pillows. She was already tired from the journey, and the bed certainly looked inviting. It was the longest she had been behind the wheel of a car for months and the effects of her treatment were still leaving her feeling constantly washed out and listless. No bath or shower up here though, or even a toilet, so she made a mental note not to drink too much before bedtime if she was to avoid nocturnal trips down the steep stairs every time she needed the loo. Still, the cottage had a certain rustic charm about it. It served her purpose. It would do.

She gripped the banister tightly as she tottered back downstairs. Perhaps her usual heels were a little out of place here, so it was a good job she'd brought flats. It was not as if anyone of importance was going to see her. She could relax and let her appearance take a back seat for once. She was glad she'd thought to bring trainers, baggy jumpers and blouses and a couple of pairs of jeans, even though she was still annoyed with herself for coming into the depths of the countryside and not thinking to bring boots.

The note Sian had mentioned was lying on the kitchen table, held down by a smoothly polished pebble. Madi skimmed through the typed list of phone numbers, the instructions for rubbish removal repeating what Sian had already told her, almost word for word, and the details of the wi-fi code. There was a note about the immersion heater and how best to time it for hot water without having to leave it on all day, and a long section detailing how and when to feed the cat – a cat that Madi realised was, so far, noticeably absent. Scribbled at the bottom, as if as an afterthought, was a single sentence in what must be Prue's handwriting. '*Sorry, no central heating,*' Madi read. '*But once the fire is lit, the place soon warms up. Thick walls!*'

Oh, yes, the fire. Sian had offered to come and help her light it. Staring at the fireplace with its rather intimidating black and glass stove and huge wicker basket piled with old newspapers and chopped-up logs, she thought perhaps she should have accepted after all. To a townie like her, working out how to light it was as alien a concept as rubbing two sticks together and hoping to make a flame. Why couldn't it just have a button to press? Something that said *Off* and *On*, with a dial to set the temperature? She felt the cold far more than she'd used to when she was younger, especially in recent months, when she'd lost so much weight. Damned illness. Other than the occasional cold, and that highly inconvenient sore throat that had kept her off stage for three days right in the middle of a touring run of *Hamlet* in 1988, she'd never had a day's illness in her life before this, and she didn't like it one bit. She'd rather be fat, healthy and working than skinny and scared, and stuck here recovering with nothing useful to do, any day of the week.

She rubbed her hands together and cupped them around her nose and chin, blowing into them to warm them. It was a good job she'd spotted that thick duvet on the bed and a hot water bottle on the table beside it. She might be needing both of those downstairs during the evenings, and her dressing gown to snuggle into, if her fire lighting skills failed her. And as for the range cooker, all she could say was that the microwave would probably be getting a lot more use than it was accustomed to. Hopefully the village pub she had spotted on her drive in might do meals, or there might be some sort of café or coffee shop somewhere, if she could just build up enough enthusiasm to go out and face people. Cooking had never really been her thing.

It didn't take long to settle in. Carefully she carried her bags upstairs, one at a time, and squeezed her few clothes into the wardrobe alongside Prue's, pleased to see that the full-length mirror was attached to the inside of the door and not the outside, so she wouldn't have to keep seeing herself walk past, or even use it at all if she didn't want to. She put her sponge bag of basic toiletries aside, and the dreaded box of pills, ready to take downstairs with her, and stowed her empty bags under the bed.

She took a look out of the bedroom window, catching her first glimpse of the back garden, which was neat and surprisingly green, its rounded lawn dotted with crocuses, deep flowerbeds packed with shrubs, and a pair of matching leafless trees, all encased within a low stone wall. Down at the end stood some kind of outhouse, like a tool shed, but with its windows all blacked out, and next to it a round garden table with a couple of all-weather chairs. There was a washing line too, reminiscent of one her mother used to have, stretching the length of the garden and propped up in the middle with a long wooden pole, a few plastic pegs clipped closely together at the end nearest the house. It had been many years since Madi had pegged anything out to dry, happy enough to let her tumble dryer do the work, but if there wasn't one here, well, she was prepared to give it a go, assuming the weather picked up. Right now, it was cold. Madi walked round closing all the curtains in an attempt to trap whatever little warmth there was, and to isolate herself from the silent, rapidly darkening evening outside.

There were lots of photographs hanging on the uneven white walls. More than she had ever seen in one place, barring a gallery. They were in the living room, in both bedrooms, even in the kitchen and on the stairs. Many were what she assumed to be local scenes, showing farmers at work in misty fields, reeds poking their heads out from shimmering water, sunset over a deserted beach, and a group of three, hanging close together, of a small tabby cat with huge green eyes that she assumed must be the elusive Flo.

Above the fireplace was a large portrait of an old lady, her skin gently wrinkled, her hair tightly permed, her eyes twinkling as if lit from within. Madi liked it. The photo, and the woman herself, had real character, the sort of character that came with being old but still mentally alert and cheekily lively, and that she would have loved to capture onstage, and still might one day, if all went well. As a kindly yet knowing Miss Marple perhaps, with some clever make-up, and layers of padding bundled up inside her dress. She wondered who the woman was. Possibly Prue's mother or grandmother, but she decided it was none of her business and went in search of something to drink and, if she was to have any hope of getting the fire going, a box of matches.

There was no sign of any alcohol, not that she should be drinking much anyway while she was taking her medication, but she'd always believed a little of what you fancy did you good. Oh, God, the pills! Even after leaving them right next to her on the bed as she'd unpacked, she'd still managed to leave them upstairs. She'd become so forgetful lately, so easily distracted. Putting things down somewhere and then finding them somewhere else. Losing things altogether. She'd lose her head if it wasn't screwed on. Bloody cancer had a lot to answer for. But what if it was something else? Thinking back, it might even have started before her cancer was diagnosed. There had been that night when she had left the tap dripping in the bathroom, with the plug still in the sink. If she hadn't got up to use the loo and found it just in time, she would have flooded the place, and quite possibly the flat beneath hers as well. It might have been nothing, the sort of thing that happened to anyone when they were tired, but you heard such stories, about people getting forgetful as they got older. Putting the kettle in the fridge or getting on the wrong bus . . . How on earth would she ever cope with work, having to learn lines again, if that was what was happening to her?

She shook the thoughts away and looked at her watch. Four thirty. A small sherry or a glass of chilled wine would go down beautifully right now, and sod the pills, but she'd just have to make do with something a little less exciting. She boiled the kettle, standing close to it and breathing in the heat. She found a jar of instant coffee in the pantry and a bottle of locally produced full fat milk in the fridge. She would have preferred her usual skimmed but at least the label told her it had been pasteurised and she hadn't been confronted with a jug of something still steaming, straight from the cow.

The coffee warmed her as she slumped down on the sofa with the matches in her hand ready to have a go at the fire. Was it a mistake coming here? Back in London, she had started to feel that the walls of her flat were closing in on her, she had spent so much time cooped up in there lately, but all she was doing now was swapping one lonely existence for another, miles away, and bringing all her fears and her sadness along with her. She missed her old way of life, and her old body. Feeling fit, working, keeping busy. She missed the bustle of the theatre and the excitement it brought into her life. But most of all she missed her son.

Still, getting better had to take priority now, and that meant taking it easy, letting her body, and her mind, recover for a while, so she could bounce back and have all of those things again. Time, that was all she needed. And they did say a change was as good as a rest, didn't they? She pulled off her wig, closed her eyes and tried to decide what to do with herself for the next month.

Chapter 3

*I*hadn't expected her to be there.

  I was sure I'd heard the door slam earlier, her feet on the stairs, the bumping of bags, her car driving away. Usually that meant a few days, a few nights, at least, when the place would be empty. She's a creature of habit. And tidy. I'll give her that. No dirty mugs left in the sink, no stuff scattered around the floor. Just the lingering smells of furniture polish, good coffee and posh perfume.

  I suppose I'm a creature of habit too, in my way. I never go in during the day. I prefer the evenings, or the dead of night. Never when I might be seen. Or heard. No noisy shoes on the creaky stairs. No dirty marks left behind on her immaculate carpets. And I never put the light on. No need to. I can feel my way around that flat as if it's my own.

  It's been different lately though. There had been talk of her not being well, a hospital stay, an operation, but she keeps herself to herself, that one, so nobody really seemed to know for sure. I had wondered if it might be serious, if she was going to die like he did, at the back of some stage somewhere, and how I might feel if she did.

But she survived it, whatever it was. Came back, holed up, stayed at home a lot more. Which curtailed things for me, for a while, until she started venturing out again. No visitors though. Or none that I'd noticed. No flowers either, which you'd expect, wouldn't you? If someone's sick? Except the tulips. I found them this morning, in the dark, touched the petals, felt a couple of them fall.

But then I heard her, shuffling about in the bed. The rustle of the pillows. I had no idea she was there until then, and it unnerved me a bit, I can tell you. I was sure the place was empty.

There was a raincoat on the back of a chair. Damp, its belt trailing on the carpet. I brushed against it on my way out. Could have tripped over it. Not like her, that. She's usually so tidy. So I hung it up for her, on a hook. I like to do little things like that when I'm here. Oh, don't get me wrong. I'm not trying to help her out or anything like that. I just like to make her wonder. How this has happened, or that. It makes me smile, to think of her wondering. Just a little game I play. Seeing how far I can go, to worry her, maybe even scare her a bit. Like that time I put the plug in and left the tap on, just dripping, that was all, but what fun if it had flooded the place, knowing she would rack her brains, struggle to remember how it could have happened. How she had made that sort of stupid mistake. Well, who else could it possibly have been? She lives alone, and she knows, just as I do, that there's nobody to blame but herself.

Still, this morning, I should have just left. Stopping to move the coat was a stupid idea, when she was showing signs of waking up, nearly catching me. It was bad enough the door clicking the way it always does, no matter how gently I pull it closed behind me, but there's not much I can do about that. But I know I'll have to be more careful. The coat could have stayed where it was. There will be other occasions. Other chances. It's not worth taking risks.

She has no idea about me. Utterly oblivious. And I'd like to keep it that way.

Chapter 4

Monday mornings in London were nothing like those at home. A strange clicking sound had woken Prue while it was still dark, her eyes flying open in semi-panic. She had half expected to see someone leaning over the bed, it had been so real. She lay still and listened, hardly daring to move, waiting for her heart rate to slow back down, but there was nobody there. Of course not. Just the creaks and clatters of the walls and floors and plumbing system of what was still an unfamiliar building talking to her in its own peculiar way, no doubt. Coming from an old cottage like hers, she was only too aware of any number of those, although they had all faded into their own kind of regular routine in time, so she no longer heard them.

Once she was awake though, she couldn't get back to sleep. The growing rumble of passing traffic throbbed through her head, even though she was sleeping at the back of the building and had pulled her pillow over her ears. And then various clunks and slams as the other residents got up, ran showers, turned on radios and TVs, banged doors and clomped noisily down the stairs on their way to work. Prue was more used to the chug-chug sound of occasional tractors trundling by, the chink of milk bottles being left on the step, and the old cockerel's crowing call from a nearby farmyard so much a part of her life that she hardly noticed it any more, all in all a much quieter, more solitary start to her day.

But then, since losing her beloved gran, that's how her life had seemed lately – more and more solitary. If it wasn't for work, having to drive to the local newspaper office every day and then head out to see the people making the news, even if only briefly, and mostly through a lens, she knew she could quite easily hide away indoors and not speak to another living soul for days. As long as she had one of her cameras for company, and a book to read, and her cat, she didn't really need anyone else. Oh, she had thought she did, had started to imagine how her future might be as half of a proper couple . . . but that was not an option any more. If it ever had been, of course, apart from in her own head.

Her parents were nearby, of course, although constantly busy. And she had friends – good friends she'd had since school – but most had moved away from the village now, for exciting new jobs and adventures and marriages, and only kept in touch occasionally, largely by email. There was still her best friend Sian, and Joe and his older brother Ralph, all of whom she had known for ever, all still living in the village, the four of them thick as thieves, as Gran used to say, since their early days at primary school. She remembered them all doing their homework together, Ralph reluctantly helping the others because he was three years older, having fun at various birthday parties, playing games of Twister or Monopoly on snowy stay-indoors days, watching kids' TV or listening to music in each other's bedrooms.

She allowed herself a nostalgic moment, picturing them all together as kids, curling up and rolling side by side down a grassy slope, turning faster and faster, racing their way to the bottom, and then crashing into each other, all squealing loudly and her giggling so helplessly that she'd wet her knickers. It was a flash of memory that made her smile, before reality crept back in. Joe. Oh, God. Joe. No, she really didn't want to think too much about Joe right now, or that night in The Brown Cow just a week ago when she had got things so horribly wrong.

It was going to be hard staying friends with Joe – the comfortable, easy-going kind of friendship they had had before. Since he'd rented the small ground-floor-extension flat in her parents' old house, they lived within yards of each other and she ran the constant risk of bumping into him, unexpectedly and often. How would she cope with that? She couldn't bear the thought of him avoiding her, pitying her, perhaps even laughing at her. But she had stepped over a line, and stepping back behind it again, as if nothing had happened, would be pretty much impossible, for both of them. She had not only lost him as a boyfriend, and quite probably as a friend too, but embarrassed herself, publicly and spectacularly, in front of just about everyone she knew. Short of either staying indoors for ever or packing up and moving away permanently, she had no idea how to deal with that. Still, this month away would help, even if it really was just a temporary solution. She was running away. She knew that. And she also knew that, once the dust had settled, and with all her remaining annual leave used up at work, she would have no alternative but to go back.

She stretched out her arms and legs, yawning. Thankfully, there had been no dreams, just a long lovely slip into oblivion that she had needed even more than she had realised. Sticking a foot out from under the covers she was surprised at how warm the bedroom was. Perhaps she should think about modernising the cottage, putting in some central heating with instant hot water any time she needed it, and one of those hot towel rails in the bathroom. Having lived here for just a few hours, she could already see what a difference they made.

The tulips on the chest of drawers had lost a few more of their petals overnight but they would probably last another day. She might buy herself some more when she went out. She did love fresh flowers. And fresh air, fresh bread, the fresh fruity tang of homemade jam. All the joys of a village existence she had known all her life and had never walked away from before. She hadn't even gone to university, so sure had she been that the life, and the job, she wanted could be found right on her own doorstep. But, of course, she would be able to find real fresh bread if she wanted it. This was London, not Timbuctoo.

She had only brought a few basics with her, food-wise. Biscuits to eat on the way, a sandwich she'd eaten last night before bed, a couple of bananas already turning black, some chocolate, and the last two mini boxes of cereal from a variety pack that had been hanging about for months in the pantry. Any more would have been too much to carry on the train and she knew London would be choc-a-bloc with shops, many of them probably open late into the evenings. Madi had told her to help herself from the kitchen cupboards and, as promised, had left her some milk and a few other bits and pieces in the fridge, including a bottle of white wine, which she probably wouldn't drink, but it was a generous gesture and one she wished she had thought to reciprocate.

After a long hot shower, a bowl of cereal and a cup of tea, she went looking for her raincoat. It was odd, but she could have sworn she had left it drying on the back of a dining chair but now it was hanging on the coat hooks by the door. How could that have happened? She shook away a shiver of unease. She'd never had a problem with her memory before. It must just be the new surroundings, so much to take in, or she'd been more tired last night than she'd realised. The coat was still slightly damp but she pulled it on, locked the door behind her and headed down the stairs to get some air and start exploring the neighbourhood.

It was a lot easier going down the two steep flights than it had been going up, and Prue quickly found herself back in the dusty communal hall. The postman had already been and someone must have sifted through the letters as there were now three in the box marked 9 that hadn't been there before. Should she forward them on to Madi at Snowdrop Cottage, or just leave them alone? She and Madi hadn't discussed things in that much detail but, thinking about it, she would probably quite like to have her own mail sent here. A month was a long time to risk ignoring anything that might be important. What if there was a bill she'd forgotten to pay, or a photography commission she'd kick herself for missing out on? She'd have to email Madi later and make some arrangements. It would give Prue the excuse to ask after little Flo as well. The poor thing might be feeling a bit uneasy, finding a stranger tucked up in her mistress's bed, especially if Madi threw her off onto the floor or shut her out on the landing. Not everybody liked the idea of an animal, and its shedding fur, sharing their bed.

It was a bright morning. Prue had done her homework before leaving Norfolk and had printed off a street map covering the immediate area. London was a huge place, pretty daunting for a girl like her, and the last thing she wanted was to get lost. She'd looked up the local bus routes too, to find out what landmarks might be within easy reach. But first she fancied a stroll along the main road outside and a peek down a few of the side turnings, to get her bearings and track down the nearest shops and cafés.

She closed the front door and hovered for a moment on the steps. Should she try to the right first, or to the left? A bus was coming into view. A real, red London double decker, so different from the little green local bus that came through the village just twice a day, and went into town and back again on Saturday nights. She gazed at it in awe, whipping her small digital camera out of her pocket and taking several photos in quick succession and from different angles as it came closer. Although the bus was red she could already imagine how it might look in black and white, an iconic, unchanging image of a city she had only ever seen in pictures. Oh, wow! There was going to be so much here in the capital that she would love to capture, as a reminder, a record. Who knew when, or if, she would ever spend time here again? Next time she came out she would bring her bag with her proper camera, and some of her lenses, although just the thought of it made her shoulder ache after yesterday's struggle with the suitcase.

She watched the bus sail by, the occupants mostly staring ahead or busy reading papers, just one small face pressed against the glass and sticking its tongue out at her as it passed. She laughed and stuck her own tongue out in reply, then stepped down onto the pavement and set off in the same direction.

There was a row of shops on the first corner she came to. An off licence, currently closed, but it was only half past nine. A newsagent's cum post office and card shop, with a pillar box outside. A small Co-Op, with a lottery advert on the door. An old-fashioned hairdresser's with a price list stuck to the window, offering cheap cuts for pensioners and half-price perms on Tuesdays. And, across the road, a kebab place with faded pictures of its meal choices, showing that they did chips and burgers too. She didn't stop, but it was good to know that anything she was likely to need in a hurry was within yards of her door.

Five minutes later she came to the first of several coffee shops, dotted among lots of larger shops and offices. She went into the third one, which looked cleaner and brighter than the rest, and bought herself a cup to take away, baffled by the enormous range of what, when it came down to it, was just coffee by different names, in varying strengths and degrees of milkiness, and shocked at the prices. She chose a bun with icing on top to go with it, the filling effect of her meagre portion of cereal having already worn off. A black iron gate to her left led through to a small square park, hidden away behind the buildings, mostly laid to grass with some cut-back rose bushes in neatly weeded beds and a series of wooden benches placed at regular intervals along the circular path. She sat down on one at the far end and shared some crumbs from her bun with a hungry pigeon and a couple of sparrows brave enough to venture right up to her feet.

She had always loved animals. From the old spaniel, Molly, who had been such an important part of her childhood, but now long gone, to her parents' latest dog, a little white poodle called Noodle. And there was Flo, of course, the twelve-year-old sweetheart of a cat she had taken on after her gran died. In between, there had been a pair of green budgies, Chirp and Cheep, that they'd kept in a cage in the kitchen, and a goldfish who came home in a plastic bag from the funfair and never did get itself a name. It had only lived for a few weeks but had been given a proper shoebox funeral in the garden, just the same. And, of course, all the village pets that had come through the doors at her dad's old vets' surgery tacked on at the back of their house, and the farm animals in need of visits, when she had spent her school holidays helping her dad out around the place or, to be honest, mostly just getting in the way.

Prue was no scientist. She loved English and art. From the day she had been given her first camera, she had known she wanted to become a photographer and that's exactly what she'd done, even if so far it was only working for the local paper, with the occasional wedding job at the weekends. Much to her dad's disappointment, she had never wanted to study chemistry or biology and follow in his footsteps to become a vet but, slowly and surely, as her friends spent more and more time hanging about at the surgery with her after school and in the holidays, it became clear that her school friend Ralph Barton did. Her dad had taken Ralph under his wing, given him work experience and paid him to help out during his holidays from uni, sat with him for hours at a time, helping with revision and essays and practical tasks, then taken him on as his assistant. By the time Ralph was qualified, her dad had been more than willing to accept him into the business as a junior partner, getting him ready to take over one day when the joys of retirement started to beckon, which couldn't be that far off now he was in his sixties.

It had caused a lot of jealousy between the brothers when their father had invested so heavily in Ralph's future, mortgaging the family home to help Ralph raise the money to bring the practice into the modern world with a website and brand new premises. Prue could see that Joe had felt sidelined, as if his own accountancy career, and perhaps even he himself, was regarded as less important when measured against his big brother. Perhaps if their mother had still been alive it might have been different, but she had died when the boys were still at school. Their dad just didn't seem to have the same natural intuition when it came to his sons' feelings, finding it easier to concentrate on the practical side of things, as if chucking his money around, buying bigger and better Christmas presents and bikes and computer games, and then ploughing so much cash into the vets', could somehow compensate for the loss of a mother's love.

Prue had seen Joe's initial hurt turn to anger and resentment as he moved out of his dad's home and took on the tenancy of the small self-contained flat that had once been the surgery behind her mum and dad's house. Her heart had gone out to him. As an only child, and an only grandchild, she had never had to vie for attention, never had to share, certainly never seen herself as second best, and she found it hard to imagine how it must feel. Poor Joe.

He'd lived away from the village long enough, he'd said, what with uni and then that job up north that he'd left only a year ago. Why had he come back home? Certainly not to spend more time with his brother and his dad. Had something gone wrong with his job? His life? Prue wondered why he had never explained, or even tried to. Still, he was back in Norfolk now, where he insisted he belonged, and he wasn't going to let his family problems drive him away, even if it meant living alone. She'd foolishly allowed herself to believe that she might be the reason he had come back home, that his heart was telling him he belonged with her, but of course that wasn't true. She knew that now.

Why was it that her thoughts always came back to Joe? Because she loved him, she supposed. Or had thought she did. She had felt safe with him, and comfortable, but that wasn't love, was it? It was friendship and familiarity, and gratitude. An acceptance of what she had and a fear of letting that all go if she were ever to take that scarily dangerous step and reach out for something more.

They had been friends for as long as she could remember. Her and Joe, Ralph and Sian, their own little gang of four, until, somewhere along the way, as they all got older, things had started to change. Sian and Ralph had fallen for each other. In an innocent, teenage way at first, but it was clear sometimes that they just wanted to be by themselves, just the two of them, leaving Prue and Joe behind, forced to find a way to rub along together, more and more often, without their partners in crime.

In time, with teenage hormones doing their thing, Prue had begun to look forward to being alone with Joe. She'd started to notice his eyes, his hands, what he was wearing, the smell of him, the feel of him. There had been a gradual, gentle move towards the holding of hands, tentative experimental kisses on the way back from school, out of sight, on the corner, before she turned into the lane that led her home. How much of it had happened simply because the others were doing it, she could never be sure, but they'd gone to the cinema together too, her and Joe, sharing tubs of popcorn, her head resting sleepily on his shoulder on the way home on the bus, and sometimes, once they were old enough, he would ring and ask if she fancied a drink and they'd meet in The Brown Cow, have a game of darts, a bag of crisps, a laugh. Looking back now, she couldn't help wondering if that was all it had ever been to him. A laugh? A casual thing. Not the romance she had imagined it to be. Needed it to be. Not the real thing at all.

The bun was gone now, every crumb pecked up greedily from the path, and the birds flew off, their eyes fixed on an old man who had just arrived on the next bench, providing another likely source of food. Prue screwed up the paper bag and dropped it inside her empty cup, popped the lid back on and took it to an overflowing rubbish bin. It was no good dwelling on what was gone. She was twenty-four, and she had let too many years slip by. There was no her and Joe. Not any more. Not in the way she had wanted anyway. She had watched him go off to uni, been proud of him, and excused his long absences and his long silences as necessary if he was to do well, work hard, study hard. Had he played hard too? She would never know. She had believed only what she'd wanted to believe, seen only what she'd wanted to see, and heard . . . well, what? She had certainly never heard him say he loved her. Because he didn't love her, and he probably never had. That was so blindingly obvious now.

She went back out through the gate to the street and spotted another bus approaching. Without any time to work out where it might take her, she ran to the stop and jumped on board. What was the point of being in London and telling herself she was going to change her life if she couldn't act on impulse and just hop on a passing bus and see where she ended up?

'Sorry, love.' The driver sniffed at the fiver she held out towards him. 'We don't take cash these days. Oyster?'

Prue shook her head. She hadn't had time to think about getting herself a travel card, but no cash? Really? How could a bus not take cash?

'Or a contactless card'll do. Got one of those?'

She rummaged about in her purse, feeling her face redden, wishing her research into bus routes had expanded into working out how to pay, but thankful at least that there was no queue behind her waiting impatiently to board. She found her bank card and touched it on the round yellow pad the driver was pointing at. The beep noise seemed to satisfy him. He nodded, and she walked down the bus and found herself a seat as he drove back out into the traffic, narrowly missing a cyclist who stuck two fingers up in the air as he clung to the handlebars one-handedly and wobbled out into the centre of the road.

The man sitting in front of her was tall, his head bent over a newspaper, his dark brown hair skimming his collar at the back. She caught her breath. He looked so much like Joe she had to fight the urge to reach out and touch him. But as he turned his head to look out of the window she saw that he really didn't look like Joe at all. He was about ten years older for a start, and dark skinned, and he was wearing glasses. Prue shook her thoughts away. Silly, silly, silly . . . Joe was miles away, and she couldn't conjure him up at will, much as she might like to.

She turned her attention away from random passengers and towards what was going on outside the window, lifting a finger and wiping a little patch of the glass clean. Was that Trafalgar Square looming up at her? Yes, it was. The big stone lions, the fountain, and all those people! This was where she would start her first London adventure. Checking that her compact camera was still safely tucked in her pocket, she jumped up so excitedly that she almost tripped over her own feet, and rang the bell.

Chapter 5

MADI

When Madi woke up, to the sound of a far-off cockerel announcing the morning, it was still dark. She turned over onto her back, her scar sore where she had rolled onto her side in her sleep, and lay for a while, listening to the unfamiliar creaks of the old cottage.

When she was sure she was not going to be able to get back to sleep, she made her way slowly down the stairs, pulling her dressing gown tightly around her against the chill, and went into the kitchen, hoping to find that the cat had returned. The bowl of food she'd left on the floor was empty, so at least the little truant was around somewhere, not run off in disgust at the new living arrangements or trapped in someone's shed. Well, you heard such stories about animals going missing when an owner moved house or went on holiday, and she'd hate to be the one to have to explain to Prue that she'd let her down and lost the poor little mite.

The water that emerged from the hot tap was, if anything, even colder than the water coming from the cold one and she remembered, too late, about the immersion heater. Oh, well, no bath or shower for her this morning. At least there was a kettle, so she could enjoy her first coffee of the day and make herself some porridge.

Madi ran her hand over her head. With nobody here to see her, and the curtains still closed, she had not bothered wrapping one of her many coloured scarves around it this morning or resorted to hiding beneath that nasty, itchy wig. Her fingers played with the short stubbly covering of new hair that was starting to emerge and she couldn't help wondering what colour it would turn out to be. It had been a very long time since she had last seen her natural chestnut colour, having veered between various reds and browns and even the occasional blonde over the years, depending on changing fashions or her mood or what role she was playing at the time. At sixty-two, the chances were that it would end up grey, of course. Or, at best, a sophisticated shade of silver. Still, having hair back at all was a relief, and there was always the dye bottle to fall back on again if what nature decided to provide needed a helping hand.

As she sat at the kitchen table, a clack of plastic at floor level alerted her to the return of the missing cat.

'Ah, so you must be Flo,' she said, lowering her hand and feeling pleasantly surprised when the little tabby walked towards her, tipped her head and started rubbing it round and round against her fingers, her tail pointing straight upwards as she arched her back and purred loudly. 'Well, I can see we're going to get along just fine, aren't we, sweetie?' She tried to remember which cupboard held the clean cat bowls and found them on the third attempt. Her memory, quite worryingly, wasn't as good recently as it had once been. 'Now, let's find you some breakfast, shall we?'

The first day in any new place always felt a bit unsettling. Not knowing where things were, or how things worked. She'd moved around a lot as various theatrical productions she'd been involved with had toured the country. It was a life she had chosen long ago and had grown used to. Two or three nights in one town, then maybe a week or two in another and, if she was lucky, a few days back at home in between. Different dressing rooms, different guesthouses and hotels, different rules. A changing circle of colleagues and crew members and friends, some of whom she would come across often and some she would never meet again. Her face and her name on the posters outside greeted her at every theatre they went to, sometimes in a leading role, sometimes (and more frequently as she grew older) just as one of the supporting cast, but she always made a point of keeping a programme to add to her vast collection. She had even been in a TV soap once, although only for a dozen or so episodes, and still had the *Radio Times* to prove it.

This, she told herself, peering through the curtains at the lane outside, was going to be just the same. A new place to explore, a new bed to sleep in, new people to meet, and then home again to touch base and await whatever opportunities might follow. Was there any call for a damaged ageing actress without a full head of hair? She hoped so, but it had become all too easy lately to look at life more pessimistically. Just four months ago she had been utterly oblivious to what was going on inside her own body, those horrid little rogue cells gathering together and ganging up on her, determined to do their worst. But she was rid of them now and, despite the surgery and the chemo, she was still here. She had survived and, apart from occasional visits from Betty next door to check she was doing okay or to get her heavier bits of shopping in, she'd done it alone. And from now on it was all about recovery, regaining her strength and her positivity, making time for herself for a change. She fought back the tears that so often threatened to overwhelm her. What good would it do to cry? It would change nothing and, besides, the worst was surely over now. Life could only get better.

She had told nobody of the seriousness of her illness, just blamed a bad bout of flu, withdrew from the play she had been rehearsing in favour of an understudy, and slipped out of the loop for a while. The last thing she needed was pity. Best that nobody knew. Not even George. *Especially* George.

While she was here, just as if she was acting a part, she did not have to reveal anything of her real life or her true self if she chose not to. In Norfolk she could be anyone she wanted to be. In this little corner of the world, she could be whole again. No cancer, no scars, everything still in its place. That, more than anything, was what she needed right now. That anonymity, that normality, the chance to re-adjust to her new self, before going back to face whatever life decided to throw at her next.

One thing she could not do, try as she might, was lie to herself. As soon as she took off her dressing gown and opened the wardrobe to select an outfit for the day, the full-length mirror reminded her of that. It still came as a shock, seeing her newly altered body, so unfamiliar, so lopsided, her scars still raw and so difficult to look at. The easiest thing, the safest thing, was simply not to look at all, to select something to wear, something loose and all-concealing, cover herself up and shut the door on the mirror as quickly as possible, but she couldn't do it. Every mirror she approached seemed to compel her to look into it, as if it was forcing her to confront the truth.

The cat was rubbing around her legs now, almost tripping her as she stepped into her trousers. She bent down and picked her up, holding the thin little body close and listening to her purr. 'It doesn't bother you, does it, sweetie? What I look like, whether I have one breast or two, as long as I give you cuddles and fill your bowl.'

People were a different matter though. In a business like hers, appearance was everything. It was a world of costumes and camouflage, make-up and make-believe, where its players came on stage for a while, fooled the audience into believing just about anything and then left again through different doors, a world where nobody was entirely who they seemed. Perhaps that was the best way to live, given a choice. Just pretending all the time. Avoiding real life altogether, because real life, as George would no doubt say, sucked.

She wondered, briefly, where George might be at this moment, what he was doing and who he was with. It had been almost five months since she had last seen him, at the small party she had held for her birthday, backstage in her dressing room straight after coming off stage. She hadn't

47

known about her cancer then. The lump lurking in her left breast had not yet made itself known, and life was still busy, hectic, normal. George had wanted to take her out for dinner, said there was something he wanted to talk to her about, but she had already made the arrangements. Assorted bottles of booze and a cocktail shaker were lined up beneath her mirror, the lights positioned around it sparkling off the glass, and the cast were elated after a successful opening night. George had hovered in the corner, out of place, and had left early. As far as he was concerned, he told her afterwards, it was yet another snub, proof that she preferred the company of her fellow actors and had never put him first. Oh, how wrong he was. If only she had taken the time to notice his distress and give him the love and attention he needed, but she had been caught up in the buzz all around her and it had never occurred to her that there might not be a chance the next day to put things right.

When she had called him in the morning, he had told her that Jessica had left him. That everyone he had ever loved always left him. The sting in his voice left no doubt that he was talking about her. His hurt ran down the phone line like treacle she had no idea how to wade through. Her heart went out to him but she couldn't find the words she needed to say how sorry she was. She knew only too well the pain of being abandoned, but that didn't mean she had the answers, or that she had ever had the right to abandon him too. But she had had her career to think about . . .

Remembering their argument still hurt but reaching out across the void between them just seemed to get harder and harder as time went by. He had ignored her calls over the following weeks, and she knew that if she had tried to get in touch later, while she was ill, she would just have looked needy, come across as a sick woman desperate for sympathy and for her son to come back and look after her, and the irony of that, after all the years when she should have been there to look after him, was far from lost on her. No, it wouldn't have been fair. She'd had to deal with this on her own, even spending Christmas by herself, lying low, doing very little, as she recovered from her mastectomy. He had sent a card but no invitation to meet, and there had been no festive phone call. Clearly, he found it hard to forgive, but not telling him about her cancer felt like the right thing to do and being alone to face it was quite possibly exactly what she had deserved. But now she was on the mend, maybe . . .

She carefully positioned her wig on her head and pulled a chiffon scarf over the top, tying it securely under her chin, still not comfortable or confident enough wearing the damned thing to trust it to stay in place. She dreaded to think what she must look like, but going out without it would feel a whole lot worse. She picked up a deep canvas shopping bag she found hanging on a hook in the kitchen and popped her purse and keys inside it, deliberately leaving her handbag with its mobile phone and diary and everything else that marked her out as Madalyn Cardew, escapee, behind. On the dresser, she told herself, trying to imprint exactly where she had left them onto her memory, desperate to retrain it before she mislaid anything else. It had happened too often in the last six months or so. It must be a sign that she was getting old, that perhaps a little part of her mind was starting to slip away and might never come back. She shivered at the thought and peered into the bag again, just to make sure she really had picked up the keys.

The morning was looking bright and clear as she opened the front door and stood, breathing in lungsful of country air, on the step. It was time to walk around the village and see what it had to offer, and to locate the shop the girl at the vets' had mentioned yesterday so she could stock up on food, perhaps buy a newspaper or a magazine, and a bottle of wine or something a tad stronger to ward off the cold until she figured out how to light that damned fire.

'Good morning.' The voice, coming from behind her, took her by surprise.

'Oh, hello.' Madi turned to see a short and dumpy woman, her tightly permed hair framing a round suntanned face, standing and looking at her from the pavement. 'It's looking like we're in for a nice day.'

'Nothing like a bit of spring sunshine after a long cold winter. I'm Faith Harris, by the way. Prue's mum.' The woman lifted the gate and pushed it open, a lot more expertly than Madi herself had done the day before and, without waiting for an invitation, ambled up the path towards her. 'Prue did say someone would be staying here for a while, but she left in such a hurry, I'm afraid I didn't get the chance to find out anything more. Not even your name . . .?'

'It's Madalyn, but call me Madi. Everyone does.'

Faith held out a hand and Madi took it. 'Nice to meet you, Madi.' She stood silently for a moment, her arms folded over her bosom. 'This was my mother's cottage, you know. I grew up here, lived here all my life until I got married. Then Mum left it to Prue in her will. Well, I didn't need it, and I think she wanted to give Prue her first step on the ladder, a taste of independence, you know? Always close, those two.'

'Ah. The elderly lady on the wall in the lounge? I thought as much.'

'You've been looking at the photos then? All our Prue's doing. She's quite a talented photographer, isn't she? But, yes, that's her gran over the fireplace. Verity Bligh. One of a kind. She passed on last year. Eighty-three. Not a bad age, I suppose, but I would have liked to have her around for longer. I still miss her.' She sighed deeply. 'I don't know what she would have made of all this business . . .'

'Business?'

'Well, Prue running off like that, I mean. Hardly a word to any of us. No forwarding address, and she's not answering her phone. Taken time off from her job, and everything. It's really not like her at all. I'm quite worried about her, to tell you the truth, and so is Joe, of course. I don't suppose you know where she is?'

Joe? Madi had no idea who Joe might be and didn't think it her place to ask. She bit her tongue. If this Prue didn't want to be found, it wasn't for her to give the game away. 'Sorry. No.'

'Right. Well, if you do hear from her, would you let me know?'

Madi gave a non-committal nod.

'Anyway, I mustn't keep you. Nice to meet you, Madi, and if you fancy a chat or a coffee, I'm just down the lane there.

Orchard House. Not that we've got an actual orchard, or even one apple tree these days, but these old names stick, don't they? Like the snowdrops here.' She pointed at the name on the cottage door. 'You've probably seen that there aren't any. Still, any morning will suit me, if you want to pop down. I'm working up at the new vets' surgery in the afternoons. Well, not every afternoon, but still helping out when needed. My husband's the vet, you see. The senior partner.'

'Yes, I know the place. I went there for the keys when I arrived. I met . . . Sian, was it?'

'Ah, yes, Sian. Lovely girl. Prue's best friend, ever since they were at school together, and even she doesn't know where she's gone. Or, if she does, she's not telling. Kids, eh?' She let out something that sounded halfway between a huff and a snort, and retreated back through the gate, waving over her shoulder but not looking back.

Madi waited until she had walked off to the right, gone around the corner and out of sight before following her as far as the gate and then turning the other way. Best to keep her distance for now and avoid another grilling about something that really was none of her business.

She walked slowly, enjoying the peace and quiet. So, Prue was young then? A kid, her mother had called her, although judging by the best friend she had met yesterday, she guessed they were probably both in their early to mid-twenties. A lot younger than she had imagined Prue to be, from the outdated look of the cottage, but the fact it had until recently belonged to her elderly grandmother explained a lot.

This time, she didn't take the turning by the church that

led up to the surgery, but carried on past it, back in the direction from which she had driven into the village the previous afternoon. She remembered passing a small row of shops, although they had looked closed, it being a Sunday, and a sleepy-looking pub, The Brown Cow, caught in the lull between lunchtime and evening drinking hours, with only a couple of cars in its gravelled car park. Today things were different. There was a delivery in progress at the pub, with all the banging and crashing of barrels and trap doors, and someone cursing as they dropped a box of crisps. Alongside it was a small antique shop that Madi made a mental note to investigate later and, strangely, for such a small village, an estate agency. She stopped to look at the photos and read the cards in the window, amazed at just how cheap property was around here, when compared to the exorbitant prices she was used to back at home.

At the end of the row, the village shop was definitely open, with piles of goods lined up on the narrow pavement outside. From buckets and mops to bags of potatoes and with an ice-cream advertising plaque, a lottery sign and a rack of newspapers attached to the wall, it was clearly one of those places that sold anything and everything. Madi peered in through the window and was amused to see a pair of eyes looking right back at her. She was about to walk past, leaving any shopping until her return journey, but a head appeared at the open doorway and a hand beckoned her in.

'Ah, you must be Prue's friend. My daughter, Sian, said she'd met you. Come on in and rest your legs a while.'

Madi smiled. The jungle drums had clearly not been slow

to beat out news of her arrival and, having only walked a hundred yards or so from her front door, her legs were not yet in need of a rest, but she went inside anyway.

'Now, my dear, let me introduce myself. Patty Martin, that's me. Shopkeeper, postmistress, dog walker, mobile hairdresser. You name it and I'm probably it. I run the local branch of the W.I. as well, if you're interested. We're always happy to welcome guests.'

'Well, you certainly keep busy!'

'I try. Not one of those who can sit about doing nothing. Idle hands and all that! I help out in our little lending library too, when I can. Not that it's the sort of library you're probably used to, but we do our best. Donated books mainly, stored in a corner of the village hall, but it can be a lifeline to the older folk, and those that live on their own. We open twice a week, Wednesdays and Saturdays, just for an hour or so in the afternoons, if you fancy borrowing something to read while you're here.'

'Thank you. I'll keep it in mind. Maybe just a newspaper for now?' Madi went back to the still open door and pulled one down from the rack. 'And I was going to wait until I came back past later to pick up a few other bits . . .'

'Of course, but if you want to do your shopping now I'm happy to hang on to it for a while until you collect it.'

Madi nodded. 'Okay.' It would have seemed rude somehow to say no.

'Just grab a wire basket from over there. Shout if you can't find what you want. It can be a bit of an Aladdin's cave in here until you get used to the layout. Not enough space, but

I pride myself on offering a wide choice.' The woman slid back behind her counter and picked up what looked like a piece of half-finished crochet. There were no other customers in sight.

Madi wondered how a place like this could possibly make any money but she was grateful it was here, nonetheless, saving her a drive to the nearest town.

'Sorry, I didn't catch your name,' the woman said five minutes later as she totted up Madi's purchases on an old-fashioned till and piled them up at the end of the counter. 'Or if our Sian told me, I'm afraid I've already forgotten it!'

'It's Madi.'

'Nice to meet you, Madi dear, although I'm sure I've seen your face somewhere.' She tilted her head as if trying to remember something. 'You've not been to Shelling before, have you?'

'No, never.' Madi smiled to herself. It was good to know she wasn't the only one who struggled to remember things sometimes.

'Oh, well. Never mind. It'll come to me, I'm sure. Now, I'll keep this little lot safe until you walk back, don't you worry. And you know where I am now, so don't be a stranger. Always nice to have someone new to chat to.' She smiled, switching to a ridiculous American accent and adding, 'Have a nice day,' as Madi went back out into the street, the empty shopping bag still swinging on her arm.

Chapter 6

It's not her feet I hear on the stairs. Too fast, no high heels, too light a tread. No, there's definitely someone else there. Coming. Going. Living.

It's not like her to have someone stay the night, so something's changed. Has she taken in a lodger? A carer? Perhaps I was wrong about her getting over her illness. Perhaps she's sicker than I thought. Or maybe it's a man! I try to imagine her having a love life. A sex life. Finding someone new, at her age, and after all this time. It's not something I want to think about too deeply. It conjures up images I'd rather not explore.

But if she has . . . what then? Will she marry? Move away? Leave the flat empty? I have imagined many things, but never that. There is nothing I would like more than for her to leave, but something tells me she's here for the duration. Or would like to be. The memories tie her down, just as mine do. We are where he wanted us to be. Kept close. Linked. Like a prized stamp collection, or a tea set, all the pieces having to stay together or they will be incomplete, lose their worth, their usefulness, their reason for being.

There's only really one way out, of course. And only one way to win. *And that's to drive her away, to be the last man standing. Or the last woman, should I say? One down, two to go. It's either her or me now. I'm not sure if she realises that. If she even knows who I am. But one thing's for sure. I know who she is, and I'm going nowhere.*

Chapter 7

PRUE

There was another letter for Madi in the tray in the hallway and it looked important. Not that you could always tell, but this one had the NHS logo plastered right across the top, and they had used first class post. Prue picked it up and shoved it into her coat pocket for safety.

She walked quickly to the nearby shops to buy a bottle of milk and a box of Coco Pops, and then went straight back up to the flat. Whatever sightseeing plans she had for the day were pretty vague and there was nothing to stop her putting off her trip for an hour or so while she sat down and sent an email to find out what she should do about the letters, and any more that might turn up. Leaving them in a public hallway where anyone could take them or tamper with them just felt wrong somehow. It would be a nice gesture to check that Madi was settling in okay anyway, and emailing would give her a chance to ask about Flo, whom she missed really badly every time she thought about her.

She dropped the letter on the coffee table with the others,

dug out her old laptop and tried to switch it on, but the battery was dead. She pulled out the cable from its case and plugged it into the mains, then, while the system was firing up, which took ages these days, she went on a hunt for the wi-fi code that Madi had been unable to remember but had assured her, in her last hastily written email before she left, must still be there, written on the original installation sticker on the back of the router. Prue found it on a high shelf in a corner of the kitchen, the blue light at the front reassuring her that everything was in working order, and hurriedly grabbed a pen and scribbled the code down on a sheet of paper from a narrow pad headed *'Shopping List'* which she spotted stuck to the side of the fridge.

There were eleven unopened emails waiting on the screen, none of which she had any intention of dealing with. Work, junk, work, Sian, Mum, more work . . . They could all wait. What was the point in hiding away and wanting some time alone if she then went straight back to communicating with the very people she was hiding from? She scrolled down the list until she came to one of Madi's brief messages, and clicked the Reply button.

Dear Madi,

I hope you have arrived and settled in and that every-thing in the cottage is OK. My main reason for getting in touch is to ask what you would like me to do with any post? There are already a few letters waiting for you. Should I send them on? Similarly, I assume you might receive some for me, so we could perhaps exchange them every now and

then? Just in case anything might be urgent. Can you let
me know that Flo is all right too? Give her a big cuddle
from me. Your flat is beautiful, by the way, and I am loving
London. We must swap more often!

Very best wishes
Prue

Of course, it was unlikely that she would receive a reply straight away. In fact, Madi might well be avoiding emails in just the same way she was. It had been made clear that she was looking for a place to escape to, although she had never mentioned what she was escaping *from*, and keeping in touch with a stranger was probably way down her to-do list. Prue switched the laptop off again, afraid she might be tempted to start reading her own mail and get dragged back into real life before she was ready. She wound the cable up and opened the laptop case to stow it away. Inside was a smaller cable for charging her phone. Should she? She had deliberately kept it switched off since she'd left Shelling but she really should at least glance at it in case of any missed calls or messages. What if there was some emergency? Her dad taken ill? Her boss telling her she was being made redundant? Joe ringing to say he had made a terrible mistake and that he did want to marry her after all?

She pulled the phone out of her bag, flicked it on and stared at it. No need for a charger. It had not been touched for days, so it still had plenty of life in it. And three missed calls. All from her mum. Nothing from Joe at all. She closed her eyes and sighed. This was exactly what she had wanted to avoid. Thinking about Joe, waiting for him to call, hoping he would apologise, worrying that he might be waiting for *her* to apologise. They were supposed to be friends, and friends should be able to deal with anything. Anything but *that*, obviously. They should be able to laugh it off, kiss and make up. Well, maybe not kiss. Not any more. She didn't often swear but oh bugger! She had come here to get herself away from all that misplaced expectation and the sickening feeling of disappointment, and it was time she pulled herself together and got on with her life the way it was destined to be from now on. Without him in it.

She clicked on her messages. One voicemail. Mum again. She knew exactly what it would say. *Where are you? Why did you run away? Are you eating properly? When are you coming home?* Maybe she should just hear her out, get it over with. But no. She had come here to free herself of that life for a whole month, to get away from all their sympathy and their questions, no matter how well-meaning, and that was what she was going to do.

She wrote a two-word text. *I'm fine.* Then she added a row of crosses as kisses, pressed send, quickly turned the phone off again and made a promise to herself. She would try to look at it just once a day, and her emails too, last thing before she went to bed, to reassure herself that nothing dramatic, nothing life or death, had happened and that she could sleep easy, but that was all. Minimal contact, and definitely no letting slip where she was so they could come after her and try to take her back. A month away from it all meant just that and, apart from being separated from Flo, she was really looking forward to it.

Be Careful What You Wish For

Considering that it was still early March, the weather was surprisingly good. After a cup of tea and a bowl of cereal, Prue headed back out, taking the street map she had printed off before she had left home, a rolled-up mac in case of rain and her favourite camera in her big professional camera bag. It would be heavy to lug about all day, but she fancied taking some proper photos today. Not just snaps, but good photos of a London she had yet to explore, maybe taken from some unusual viewpoints and angles. Real hang-on-the-wall photos, if only she had any wall space left where she could put them. And where better to start than at the palace? She had promised herself the full Christopher Robin changing the guard experience and, if she was lucky, there might be horses. She had always enjoyed photographing horses. And the royal family, although the chances of spotting one of the princes chugging up the drive, or the Queen pottering in her garden, were admittedly remote.

As she pulled the front door closed behind her, a young man, probably no older than eighteen or nineteen, came hurrying up the steps from the street, one arm stretching out towards the door as if he was trying to catch it before it banged shut. His head was bent down over his phone, a thumb prodding at the keypad, his music so loud she could still hear it despite the headphone buds stuffed into his ears.

'Oh, just too late,' he said, looking up at her accusingly as the door closed and switching the music off. 'I'll have to find my keys now.' He started digging around with one hand in the depths of his jacket pocket, still clutching his phone in the other, pulling out a paperback book and an open packet of extra strong mints.

'Sorry,' Prue said. 'Didn't see you in time. But . . .'

'Yes?'

'Well, I don't know who you are, do I? I can't hold the door open for just anybody and let them in, can I?'

'I suppose not. Not that I know who you are either.' His glare seemed to have toned down now into something more resembling a look of curious annoyance. 'You don't live here, I do know that much.'

'Well, that's where you're wrong, because I do. For the next month anyway. I'm Prue. Flat nine.'

'Ah, so you're staying with the actress, are you? I'm Aaron. I live with my mum, in flat six, right underneath yours.' He located his keys at last and inserted one in the lock, stuffing the book back into his pocket and a mint into his mouth. 'I heard a rumour she'd been in hospital, that another of the neighbours had been looking in on her, but I've not seen her about lately. Not heard her telly so much either, which you do sometimes, with floors and ceilings as thin as ours. Your turn now, is it? To be nursemaid? How is she anyway? All right?'

'I don't know actually. And I'm not staying *with* her exactly, or here to look after her. She's gone away for a while – a sort of holiday – and I'm here until she gets back. I'm Prue Harris, by the way.'

'Hi, Prue. Flat-sitting, eh? Makes sense, I guess, not to leave the place empty. Friends, are you? Or family?'

Prue hesitated. This stranger was rather nosey, and it wasn't always a good idea to divulge too much. 'Something like that,' she muttered. 'But I must get on. See you again maybe?'

'Maybe.' He yawned, showing a row of not quite even teeth. And then he was through the door and gone. It closed behind him with a slam.

So, Madi had been ill. Maybe she still was. That might go some way towards explaining her need to get away. She could be convalescing. Clean fresh country air, and a quiet peaceful life. There was nowhere quite like Shelling to provide all of that. And he'd said she was an actress. What with the theatre posters on the walls and the colourful, flamboyant clothes, that came as less of a surprise. She had spotted some sort of a trophy thing on the shelf over the fire too, although the date on it told her it had been awarded many years ago. Slowly, Prue was finding out a little more about Madi, and getting the impression that Madi was probably a good deal older than she was. The only real mystery now was the photo by the bed, and who the man in it might be. She smiled to herself. She was turning into a right little Miss Marple. All she needed was a magnifying glass and a little notebook to complete the transformation. And she'd thought that Aaron was being nosey!

By the time she arrived home soon after five, the strap of her camera bag having dug what felt like an inch-wide ridge in the flesh at her shoulder and her feet aching, all she really wanted was a strong coffee, a few chapters of her book and a long hot bath in which to lie back and enjoy both. Thank God for Madi's super-efficient heating system, with hot water more or less in constant supply.

She threw everything down on the coffee table in front of the sofa and kicked off her shoes, before turning on the taps in the bath and walking back to the small kitchen to flick on the kettle, its blue light shining through the see-through window at the side as the water began to bubble. She had eaten a good lunch, a tuna sandwich and a salad, on a bench in St James's Park, again sharing her crumbs with the birds, and had brought a jumbo sausage roll home in a paper bag, a simple meal which would be quick and easy to warm up later in the microwave. No need to go out again tonight, which suited her just fine. Being alone on the streets of a big, strange, impersonal city after dark was a step she did not yet feel quite ready for.

While she waited for her bath to fill, she couldn't resist a quick look at the photos she had taken, flicking between them on the viewer, her trained eye instantly knowing which were worth doing something with and which could be deleted and, most importantly, recognising the two or three she could feel really proud of. There was one of the front of the palace, taken through the black railings of the gate, the camera tilted upwards, capturing the moment a pigeon, wings still outspread, had landed on the famous balcony. Another was of a guardsman yawning, clearly caught completely off guard, words she knew would make a fantastic caption and which she couldn't help laughing about. And the horse. Oh, how she loved her photo of the horse. Not that it was doing anything especially unusual or earth-shattering. It was just the expression on its face, the ears upright and alert, the eyes somehow worldly and wise. She would try cropping that one and zooming in, to see if she could pick out the different shades of light falling on the fine lines of its hair.

Before she realised it, the water had almost reached the top of the bath, the surface smothered in big airy soapy bubbles from one of Madi's potion bottles, and the whole lot was in danger of flowing over onto the floor. She could just imagine what Aaron and his mother in the flat beneath would say had she let that happen, with rivers of steaming bathwater flooding through those terribly thin floors he had talked about.

She turned off the taps, ran her hands through the water to check the temperature, pulled out the plug to let a few inches of water escape, then added a drop more cold. The kettle had boiled and she made her coffee, put the mug and her book down on the little flat area in the corner of the bath, then stripped off and lowered herself into the deliciously warm and soothing water. Ah, bliss!

Prue picked up her book and turned to the place where her fluffy pink bookmark protruded between the pages. She hadn't read since she'd been on the train and it took her a page or two to get back into the story. It was one of those Regency romances, where ladies in long slim dresses chatted to friends in elegant drawing rooms and swooned over handsome heroes. Not everyone's cup of tea, she knew, but it was easy reading, providing a little escapism, taking her back to a time when young ladies knew very little of the realities of life or love and rarely spent any time alone in male company, when chaperones were the norm and convention was everything. A long way from the sort of novel young Aaron was reading, which she had noticed was one of the later Harry Potters, or the rather serious-looking biography of an aging actor she had never heard of that was still lying next to Madi's bed. A long way from real twenty-first-century life too.

She reached the end of Chapter Ten. The hero had just spoken to the master of the house and had been permitted to ask for his daughter's hand, which he was now doing on bended breeches-covered knee.

Prue lay back, letting the warm water slosh up over the back of her neck and into her hair, laid the book down again and closed her eyes. Proposals. Not her favourite subject at the moment. And, oh boy, how very different these things were nowadays. She remembered the way Ralph Barton had proposed to her friend Sian, hiding the ring in a little pouch under his dog's collar as they walked across the fields, and producing it at just the right moment, mid-picnic, the sun streaming down, grass stains on his knees, and a bottle of champagne tucked away in the hamper, surrounded by ice packs, to mark the moment she said yes. Even the dog had been given a sip of bubbly as they celebrated.

She would never know if that was what had put the idea into her own head. Was it Sian and Ralph planning their wedding, or the newspapers sending her out to photograph an elderly couple, both widowed, who had found each other again and had just got engaged more than sixty years after they had first met as teenagers? Or was it simply the date on the calendar? Of course, that had been the clincher. The 29th of February and its age-old tradition presented a unique opportunity, a reason to be brave that only came around every four years. Waiting for Joe to do it himself, or having to wait another four years for her next chance? Both options had seemed too uncertain, too fraught with potential error, so why wait?

Joe was not a planner. He was a ditherer, the sort who drifted through life without long-term plans, but that didn't mean he would be averse to someone else doing the planning for him, did it? He would be surprised, maybe a bit shocked, but she had hoped he would be secretly pleased too. Pleased to know how much she wanted to be with him, for them to make a future together. They might even be able to arrange a double wedding with Sian and Ralph, the four of them back doing everything together again, just as they always had when they were kids. It might help to mend the rift between the brothers that had kept them at arm's length ever since their dad had ploughed so much money into the vets'. A vision of herself as peacemaker, of the two brides swathed in white lace, and the foolish romantic notion of happy-ever-afters had driven her on.

How stupid she had been. How naïve. You couldn't make someone love you just because you wanted it so badly. You couldn't get down on one knee in the middle of the village pub, accidentally flashing your knickers because your new bought-specially-for-the-occasion dress is too short, and ask a question like that in front of all your friends and neighbours and embarrass someone into saying yes. The look on his face had said it all. He was more than shocked. He was appalled. And the only person left feeling embarrassed was her.

Joe had not come after her when she ran outside. Only Sian had done that, wrapping her arms around her in the car park, muttering words that Prue had not really taken in. Words about fish in the sea, and his loss, and heartless bastard, all merged together in the fog of hurt that had settled over her, and had still not fully lifted.

Prue sighed and slowly lowered herself deeper into the water, bending her knees and dipping her head back so her whole face went under. She breathed out, a steady stream of tiny air bubbles breaking the surface, until her lungs were empty and she had no choice but to bob back up again. Wash him away, Prue, she told herself. What did they sing in that old film? *Wash that man right out of your hair.* She slicked her wet curls back over her scalp and sat up, reached for her now almost cold coffee and drank it in one big gulp.

'Don't do it, Adeline,' she said, staring at the cover of her book. 'Don't say yes. Men aren't worth the hassle. You'll be better off on your own.'

Chapter 8

MADI

Madi had been living in Shelling for four days when she finally forced herself to check her emails and social media pages. Much as she was relishing being alone, she did have to keep her future in mind, and her future revolved, just as her past and present always had, around her work. There could be news from her agent, offers of a part in a play, maybe even some messages from fans. Those were few and far between these days, but they never failed to lift her spirits.

There were none of those waiting for her when she logged on that Thursday afternoon. A couple of junk ads offering her the sort of products only a mastectomy patient might need leapt out at her. How did they know these things? Sometimes it felt as if Big Brother really was watching her, or more likely watching everybody, these days. Even at home sometimes she got the shuddery feeling that someone else was there. A fleeting shadow on the wall, an unexpected creak of the floorboards, a tiny flutter of a curtain when the windows were all closed. Of course, it was just her imagination. There was nobody there. Nothing to be scared of. Her home was her castle, her sanctuary, and always had been. Jeremy had made sure of that. She was just feeling jumpy lately. It was what came of living by herself, and getting older, she supposed, her memory playing its silly cruel little tricks, the cancer forcing her to face the biggest fear she had ever had to face, and the restless nights and crippling tiredness that resulted from all that. And with her son nowhere in sight, it all made her suddenly aware of her own vulnerability and how alone she was in the world.

But the world itself went on without her. There was news of Sally Wendover, her biggest rival and one-time nemesis, landing the role of the nurse in a new production of *Romeo and Juliet*, which had Madi grinding her teeth together in a mixture of frustration and barely suppressed jealousy. That could have been her, if the bloody cancer hadn't intervened. Sally had beaten her to the lead role of Juliet too, more than forty years ago when Madi had been too distracted elsewhere to fight for it, and she had never quite forgotten or forgiven her for that.

The email from Prue was short and to the point. Did she want to have her post sent on? It wasn't something she had thought about, but you never knew. It was still possible, even in this digitally prominent day and age that a career opportunity might turn up in an old-fashioned letter. And, of course, it would be Mother's Day soon, while she was still here in Norfolk, so there might – just might – be a card.

She sent a quick reply, promising a post exchange once a week at least, and added a word or two of reassurance about Flo, who had jumped up onto her lap as she typed and had fallen asleep there, preventing Madi from doing anything much for the next hour at least. She switched everything back off and leant forward, carefully, to pick up one of Prue's many magazines. It was one of those lifestyle ones, with celebrities she had never heard of plastered across the cover. Not a real actress amongst them, just unknown faces from this so-called reality TV that the young ones seemed to enjoy. It was a page or two before the end, in the odds and sods section, otherwise known as minor showbiz news, that she spotted a tiny picture of Sally Wendover, clutching a bouquet in one hand and a man's arm in the other. The bloody woman got everywhere.

She threw the magazine down without reading any more of it. She ran her hand over her head. Was her hair growing yet? Did it feel any longer, any thicker, any softer than it had the day before, or the day before that? She liked to think so. At this rate, by the time she went back to London, she might be on the way to looking half decent again and could start thinking about abandoning the wig, in favour of a fashionably short pixie cut. Then she would give that Sally a run for her money, and no mistake.

The knock at the door made her jump and sent Flo skittering off her lap and towards her cat flap, which she shot through as if the devil himself was after her. Madi stood up and reached for her wig, positioning it squarely on her head and checking in the small wall mirror before opening the door to reveal the imposing figure of Prue's mother smiling back at her.

'Mrs Harris . . .'

'Oh, it's Faith, please. I'm sorry to disturb you, Madi, but I've been worrying about you stuck here all by yourself. You haven't popped down for that cup of tea, and I thought you might just be a bit . . . well, shy, I suppose. It's my day off from work and I'm at a bit of a loose end. Are you busy now?'

She wasn't, of course, but admitting to that would mean she had no excuse to refuse. 'Well, I was about to take a walk. Get some air in my lungs while the sun's still shining.'

'I could come with you!'

Madi took one look at the little woman's eager expression and gave in. She nodded. 'Okay. Why not? Just let me get my coat and scarf.'

Faith Harris waited patiently on the step. At least she wasn't one of those people who barged their way in, whether invited or not. Madi pulled on her coat and wrapped a thin headscarf around her head as usual, then grabbed her door keys.

Faith nodded towards Prue's car, standing idle on the drive. 'Battery'll go flat,' she muttered, shaking her head. 'She should have left me the key, so I could start it up or move it. Sorry it's stopping you from parking.'

'No problem. Mine seems fine where it is, in the road.'

'True enough. It's not as if we get much traffic going by.'

Madi closed the door and, without discussing any sort of route, they both seemed to turn naturally to the left, walking side by side in the direction of the church and the pub. The bells were ringing again, not especially tunefully, as they had been on the afternoon she'd arrived.

'That'll be young Donny,' Faith said, raising her eyebrows. 'He's not very good, is he? That's why he practises so often I assume, in the hope of getting better.' She laughed. 'It could take a while.'

Madi laughed too. 'Everyone has to start somewhere, I suppose, no matter what it is they're trying to master. How old is he? This Donny?'

'Thirteen, I think. Or fourteen. He comes out of school and his mum's not back from work yet, and there's time to kill before his tea. Same for a lot of the kids around here. It's not as if we have much to entertain them. No cinema or bowling alley or anything like that. They get bored, and probably not overly keen to get stuck into their homework!'

'No youth club?'

'There used to be, until the man who ran it moved away. It died a death after that. There's football practice once a week though, for those who are interested, and the school has a chess club on a Tuesday, but the other days young Donny's up there in the tower, regular as clockwork. After the service on a Sunday too sometimes. He does try hard, poor lad.'

'And his mum?'

'Gloria. Works at the estate agency along the way there. Well, she owns it actually. Her and her husband Jim. He does all the viewings and the legal stuff and she takes care of the admin, making appointments, typing up the details of the properties. My Prue usually takes the photos for them. She knows how to bring out the best in a place, especially with the interiors, getting the light right and all that. To be honest, I'm not sure how they've stayed in business in a little place like this. It's not like people move in or out of the village that often, and there's a lot of competition from the bigger agencies in town, and then there's the internet . . .'

Madi let her talk. It was certainly something she seemed

good at. Village gossip was not high on Madi's list of interests, but it did help to know a little about the place and the people in it, now that she was living here. Who to make friends with, who to avoid. She felt almost sorry for Donny, with nothing to do except ring the bells, and pretty badly at that. And for his parents, struggling to keep a business afloat in the back of beyond. It couldn't be easy trying to keep yourself entertained or to make any sort of living in a quiet little place like Shelling. She hadn't seen the whole village yet, except on a map, but she was fairly sure she'd be able to walk the entire outskirts in no more than ten minutes. She doubted there were more than fifty houses, fifty families, at most. Stay long enough and she would probably know them all by name, just as they all no doubt did. It wasn't surprising they knew each other's personal business too. It must be hard to keep secrets when you lived so closely with your neighbours. But then, she lived just as closely with her own neighbours back at Belle Vue Court and could honestly say she knew very little about any of them. Nor did she particularly want to. She smiled to herself at the irony. How different London was to this tiny country community where even a strange car passing through would probably be noticed and commented upon. She wondered what they made of her, what the rumour mill was saying about her and her reasons for turning up out of the blue like that.

'So, Madi,' Faith said, changing the subject abruptly. 'What is it that you do?'

'Do?'

'For a job, I mean. Unless you're retired, of course, but you don't look old enough.'

God, the woman was blunt. 'Thank you. I'm sixty-two so I am pretty much old enough, I suppose, technically, but I'm not in the sort of industry that has a retirement age as such. We tend to go on until we drop.'

'Oh? Which industry is that then? Because you look like a teacher to me. Maybe a headmistress. Am I close?'

Madi laughed. 'What is this? Twenty questions? Animal, vegetable or mineral?'

Faith looked confused for a moment. 'I'm sorry, am I being overly inquisitive?'

'Not at all,' Madi lied. 'But, no, I'm not a teacher, head or otherwise. I'm an actress.'

'Oh.' Faith's arms began to flap wildly, and her voice shot up an octave. 'Oh! How exciting. Have you been in anything? Well, of course you have. Silly me. What I mean is . . . well, have you been in anything I might have seen? Heard of? You know, anything famous?'

'Is Shakespeare famous enough for you?'

Faith giggled. 'Well, I might not know a lot about the theatre but even I've heard of him! Do tell me everything . . .'

'Everything?' The two women reached the turning that led up to the church and the vets' but walked on past it and headed towards the shops. Madi did her best to suppress a grin. 'About Shakespeare?'

'Oh, you know what I mean. About you. Your career. Stage or TV? Who have you met, and who have you acted with? Are you terribly well known? But then you probably use a stage name, don't you? Not Madi at all.' She grabbed Madi's arm as if some sort of magic stardust was going to rub off.

'Oh, we've never had an actress in Shelling before. The most famous resident we've ever had was a novelist – or so she said – who lived just a couple of doors along from me for a few months, but nobody had ever actually heard of her. Her books weren't even in the library. The proper library in town, I mean, of course, not our little cupboard affair in the hall! Oh, Madi, do tell all . . .'

Madi had only just begun to present a very potted history of her career so far when they reached the village shop and Patty Martin came bustling out onto the pavement, almost as if she had been waiting for them to appear.

'Oh, how lovely to see you both,' she said, beckoning them in. 'Business is quiet today and I was just about to put the kettle on. Do come and join me. I could do with the company.'

'We'll have to carry on our little chat later, Madi,' Faith muttered under her breath, as they followed Patty into the shop. 'Patty can be terribly nosey.'

'What's that?'

'Nothing, Patty dear. A cup of tea will be just the job. Do you have any bikkies?'

Patty turned and gave her friend a look of sheer disdain. 'Faith Harris, this is a grocery shop. We have biscuits galore, in any flavour you care to mention. But we'll let Madi choose, shall we?'

'Oh, you two have met then, have you?' Faith said, looking a little peeved.

'We have. Now, come through to the back and I'll pop the *Closed* sign up for half an hour. The customers can always rap on the glass if it's important.'

The back room was small but cosy, with two shabby armchairs, which Patty insisted her visitors sit on while she took the wooden chair at a desk piled high with papers. She reached up and took three cups and a large brown teapot down from a cupboard above the sink in the corner and put the kettle on to boil.

'So, how are you enjoying life in our little village?' she said, turning her attention to Madi.

'It's lovely. So peaceful. Charming, in fact.'

'Well, that's nice to hear. Charming . . . I like that. Are you planning on staying long?'

Madi heard Faith sigh beside her. 'Just a few weeks. I shall be off back to London when Prue returns.'

'Ah, yes, Prue . . . Poor soul. How that Joe could humiliate her like that, and in public too, I just don't know. Idiot man doesn't know a good thing when he sees it.'

'Patty!' Faith leant forward in her chair and put a restraining hand on Patty's arm. 'Madi doesn't need to know about all that. And it's my Prue's business, not ours.'

'It's hardly something you can expect to keep a secret, dear. Not when half the village witnessed it. It's leap year, you see, Madi, and there are, of course, certain age-old traditions attached. Come the 29th of Feb, in the middle of a busy Saturday night in the local pub, young Prue got it into her head to propose, with absolutely no guarantee, or even the teeniest hint, that the young man in question would say yes. Took a bit of a leap of faith, or more like a leap in the dark, if you'll excuse the terrible puns, seeing as we're talking leap year here, but unfortunately landed flat on her face.'

'Ah, I see.' Madi could feel the tension stretching out between her two companions, and thought it might be time to steer the talk in another direction. 'It's a shame it didn't go well, but as Faith says, it's not really anyone's business but theirs, is it? Now, what was it you said about biscuits, Patty? I must admit I have a fondness for a nice custard cream.'

Patty got to her feet. 'I'll go and see if we have any. Won't be a tick.'

As soon as she had disappeared behind the beaded curtain that separated them from the shop, Faith shook her head and whispered, 'It would never have worked out anyway. I'm glad he turned her down. She can do so much better. I'm sorry it seems to have upset her so much, though she'll get over it soon enough. Hurt pride, I think, more than anything. Do you know where it is she's gone? I know you said you didn't but . . .'

'No. I'm sorry. Why don't you just phone her? I'm sure if she wants to speak to you, she will.'

Faith sat back in her chair, frowning. 'Don't you think I've tried?' she said, just as Patty arrived back, brandishing an extra-large pack of custard creams, and poured the tea.

'Do you remember,' Patty said, beaming at Madi and clearly unaware of what she had walked back into, 'when we last met I told you I thought I knew you from somewhere?'

'Aha!' said Faith, eager to take over the conversation again. 'There we are, Madi. Patty recognises you. You have a fan!'

'A fan?' Patty looked bemused. 'I only meant that I'm pretty sure I've seen Madi in the big supermarket in town. Do you work there, dear? On the tills, or one of the counters?'

Faith laughed. 'I hardly think so, Patty. Madi doesn't spend her days slicing bacon in Tesco's. She's an actress. She's done Shakespeare, you know.'

'Oh, really? I've never seen any Shakespeare. But now you come to mention it, you could be right, Faith. That could well be where I've seen her. *In* something.'

Madi took a sip from her tea and watched them discussing her as if they'd forgotten she was even in the room.

'I know!' Patty squealed, almost sloshing her tea into her lap. 'It was that soap opera on the telly a few years ago. Now, what was it called? The one set in a coffee shop by the sea. It was only on a few weeks and they stopped showing it. You were a bit chubbier then, weren't you, dear? And your hair was a different colour, but I'm sure it was you.'

'Don't be ridiculous, Patty,' Faith butted in. 'Madi does plays. Proper plays, on the stage. She wasn't in any soap.'

'Actually, I was.'

Four eyes swivelled her way.

'Oh, how thrilling. A real TV star in our midst.' Patty piled the biscuits onto a flowery plate and held it out towards Madi, her hand shaking with excitement. 'Please, take two. Oh, isn't that what they say when they're filming? With one of those little clapperboard things. Lights, camera, action. Take two!'

They all laughed.

'Oh, do let me do your hair while you're here, Madi. I can put a sign above the door then. *Hairdresser to the stars.* Like having a royal warrant! I could do you a nice perm or add a few highlights. It's looking a bit dull, if you don't mind me saying. In fact, let me take a look at it now.'

Before Madi could stop her, Patty stood up and whipped the scarf from her head. 'Oh,' she said, the dismay obvious in her voice, as she knocked the wig a little too vigorously and it tilted off centre. 'It's not your own.'

There was a stunned silence as Madi adjusted her headwear and tried not to cry.

'Oh, Patty, we all know that actresses wear wigs, don't we?' Faith said, coming quickly to her rescue. 'Stage names, make-up, costumes. Why not wigs? All part of the mystery, eh? I bet these superstars hardly ever go out as themselves. Helps protect them from being recognised and pestered.' She chuckled. 'Autographs another time, eh? Now, come on, Madi, let's be on our way before it gets dark.'

'Thank you,' Madi said, as the two of them made their escape and turned back towards home, their planned walk forgotten.

'No problem. Is it cancer?'

Madi nodded. 'Breast.'

'My father had it. Cancer, that is. His was in the lungs. Smoked all his life, so not surprising really. This was nearly ten years ago, and treatments probably weren't as good as they are nowadays. He went quickly though. Didn't suffer too long. Yours?'

'I had surgery, lost a breast, then chemo. The cancer's all gone though, or they hope so anyway.'

'That's good. Losing a breast must be hard, but at our age you have to wonder why we still need them.' She shrugged, then put a hand on Madi's arm and patted it. 'At least you're still alive, and that's what counts, eh? To me . . . well, I often think losing your hair must be the most upsetting part. Not a problem for my old dad as he was bald as a badger anyway, but it's different for us girls, isn't it?'

'Yes. It is.'

'In your line of work, too. It will grow back though, good as ever. Don't let it get you down, not now you're over the worst of it all. Still, I feel for you. It must have been tough . . . and I won't be gossiping about you, rest assured.'

'Thank you.'

They had reached Madi's gate.

'See you again soon, I hope. The offer's still open, for tea at mine. I can't promise custard creams, but I do make a mean Victoria sponge.' Faith took a pen from her handbag and scribbled something on a tiny scrap of paper, which she tore off the corner of a used envelope. 'My number,' she said, hovering long enough to make it obvious she expected to receive Madi's number in return. As soon as Madi had, reluctantly, supplied it and Faith had written it down, Faith gave a little wave over her shoulder and wandered away, leaving Madi alone on the path. 'Just let me know when you're coming, and I'll have that sponge rustled up and in the oven toot sweet!'

Madi slid the scrap of paper into her pocket, the edge of her scarf slipping out as she withdrew her hand. It hadn't seemed worth the charade of tying it on again, now that the cat was out of the bag. She didn't believe for a minute that her health, or her dubious celebrity status as an ex-soap actress, would remain secret for long. But did it really matter? She was who she was, wig and all, and if people couldn't deal with that they probably weren't worth knowing.

Chapter 9

PRUE

For the second time in a week, Aaron was coming in just as Prue was going out, Madi's letters in her hand, her own address in Shelling now written across the front, ready to post on to her. This time she held the door for him and they stopped for a few moments to chat.

'We seem to be making a habit of this,' he joked.

'Ships that pass in the night.'

'I don't know about that.' He looked at the time on his phone, which was wired direct to his ears as usual, and switched off whatever it was he had been listening to. 'It's quarter past nine in the morning.'

'Just an expression. So, what gets you up and about so early?'

'Early?' He laughed. 'I've been up and about for hours. This is bedtime for me. I work nights at a supermarket. You know, stacking shelves, sweeping up, all the things that have to go on before the shop opens up again in the mornings. I finish at eight, stop for a bit of brekkie, then get the train home. You?'

'Oh, I'm on a month's leave. Free as a bird, just looking forward to exploring. No plans, just wanting to get out early and make the most of the day. I work for a newspaper when I'm at home. Just a little local one, but it keeps me busy. I'm a photographer.'

'Cool.'

'Well, I won't keep you from your sleep. At least I'll be out most of the day so you won't have me stamping about making noise through your ceiling.'

'Wouldn't bother me if you did. There's always noise in a place like this. Traffic and stuff. But I can sleep pretty much anywhere, and earplugs are a wonderful thing.'

She watched him lope up the stairs, his long skinny legs taking them two at a time, then she stepped outside and closed the front door behind her.

Despite the building being split into nine flats, Aaron was still the only other resident she had spoken to. She could only assume that everyone else either kept themselves to themselves or went out to work, probably long gone by the time she surfaced each day, and not back until after she'd settled herself back in for the evening. Perhaps it would be different at the weekend.

She spent a pleasant Friday morning wandering around the Science Museum, particularly enjoying the photography exhibits. She tried to imagine how hard her job would be if she had to lug those huge old-fashioned cameras around the countryside now, fiddling about with boxes and curtains and plates, or putting reels of film into the camera and taking them out again in the dark, mixing up chemicals and waiting for hours before she got to see the results of her labours. She had loved developing her own photos when, as a kid, she'd first started experimenting and learning, and the little shed in Gran and Granddad's cottage garden had provided the perfect darkroom in which to do it – so much more fun than taking the film to be developed at the chemists' – but she rarely used it nowadays. The arrival of digital photography and all the amazing software that enabled her to crop and filter and enhance her pictures had changed things beyond all recognition, even in the few years since she had first shown a flair for her craft.

The Natural History Museum was just around the corner so, after a sandwich and an ice-cream eaten out on the grass, she went inside and lost herself in the magical world of stuffed animals and dinosaur bones and the internal workings of the human body for a few hours, before buying herself a souvenir wooden pen, and a silly T-Rex T-shirt she had picked up on an impulse and would probably only ever wear to sleep in, and heading back towards the tube.

Cooking for one was never a particularly appealing prospect so she stopped at the takeaway place along the road from the flat and treated herself to a kebab and a can of Diet Coke, hurrying back before the food had a chance to go cold.

Much as she had wanted some time alone, it occurred to her as she munched her way through the greasy slices of lamb and mound of shredded lettuce that she was starting to feel a bit lonely. If not for Aaron and a few random strangers she'd spoken to briefly when she was being served in various shops, she really hadn't had any kind of interaction with anyone since she'd left Norfolk and the thought of going out at night in the city by herself was still too scary to contemplate.

She picked up her phone and switched it on. It still had a couple of bars of power before she needed to recharge it. She had told herself she would only use it at bedtimes, and even then only for emergencies and to check for important messages, but now she'd eaten and, with nothing to do but read or watch TV before going to sleep, she could do with hearing a friendly voice. Before she could change her mind, she ran through her most recent contacts and pressed Sian's number.

'Prue!' Sian's voice squealed down the line with excitement.

'Yep, it's me.'

'I thought you'd disappeared off the face of the earth! Your mum's been pestering me day and night to tell her where you are. Not that I have any idea. She's even been badgering the lady staying at yours. Who seems very nice, by the way.'

'Does she? I'm glad.'

'*Does she?* You mean you don't know? Prue, she has the run of your cottage. I thought she must be a friend or something.'

'Nope. Never met her in my life.'

'Now I am curious. I must say, I did wonder how you might know someone like her. Not that she isn't lovely, because she is, apparently, or so Mum tells me. I thought maybe you'd met her through work, taken her picture or something. She's not . . . well, not like us, is she?'

'Isn't she?'

'Oh, stop it. You know what I mean. She's kind of . . . poised, I suppose is the word for her. Posh, even. An actress, so I hear. And she must be at least sixty.'

'She's just looking after the cottage for me, Sian. It's an arrangement that works for both of us. We don't have to be bosom buddies.'

'Well, according to Mum, this friend of yours – or not, as the case may be – has had breast cancer. Like, recently, I mean. Mum reckons that's why she's here, getting over it.'

'Ah, that explains a lot, I suppose.'

'Does it? If you say so. So, go on, tell me then. Where are you? And who are you with? I know you haven't eloped with Joe because I saw him just yesterday. Looking even more grumpy than usual, I might add.'

Prue swallowed hard. 'How is he?'

'To be honest, I didn't stop to ask. Stupid man. How could he treat you like that? You're meant to be his girlfriend. Okay, so maybe he's not ready to get married yet . . .'

'If ever.'

'Well, yes, you could be right, but he still could have been a bit kinder with his answer. Asked for time to think about it or something . . .'

'He obviously didn't need time to think about it. He doesn't want to get married. Or not to me anyway.'

'His loss, babe. Rest assured, I shall make it clear just what I think about him at every opportunity.'

'And how long can you keep that up, what with him being practically family? You know, I quite liked the idea of us marrying brothers, becoming sisters-in-law. I think I got a bit carried away with the old "gang of four" thing, but that's not a good enough reason to do it, is it?'

'Probably not. Nice idea though. We could have had

matching dresses and bouquets and had babies on the same day and everything. But what's done is done, and I'm not going to say any more about it, except that if he doesn't love you, he should have just said so and let you go long before now. He's been keeping you dangling on a string for way too long. Years! Just makes me even more glad I was lucky enough to get the nice brother . . . who's just come into the room and says hello, by the way. Now, tell me all. Where are you staying, and how long for?' She giggled down the line. 'And if it's somewhere brill, can I come and stay too?'

Prue gave her friend a quick rundown of the flat, the area, how she'd agreed to swap homes with Madi, and her plans to chill out for a few more weeks and take lots of fantastic photos.

'And your mum? Can I tell her any of this? You know I'm bloody hopeless at keeping secrets. She'll see through me in a heartbeat if I try to lie to her.'

'I'll tell her myself if that makes it easier. Just the basics, mind. Not the actual address. I really do need to put a bit of space between me and Shelling at the moment. I need some time to think, and her turning up would ruin all that.'

'To think about what?'

'Oh, you know. Life, the universe and everything. Where I really want to be, what I really want to do. If I don't have Joe tying me to the village, I can start looking at my own future now, instead of a joint one, can't I? The world's a big place, and I can't see myself taking photos for the *Gazette* for ever.'

'I've always said your talent is wasted there. Not that I want you to leave. The village wouldn't be the same without you.'

'Living just up the lane from Joe? Trying to just be friends? Watching him take up with someone else, as he's bound to eventually? I might even get asked to photograph his wedding one day. It'll be hard. Well, weird anyway.'

'Oh, never mind him. You can't let him drive you away from your lovely little cottage. And Shelling's as much your home as his. Just grin and bear it, or totally ignore him if you need to. But, as for a job . . . your pictures are really great, Prue. You could be doing stuff for the glossy magazines or have an exhibition or something. Proper art, instead of Farmer Giles's prize pig or Auntie Nelly's golden wedding.'

Prue couldn't help but laugh. 'I actually quite like going out and taking photos of people's special moments, giving them their fifteen minutes of fame. But I know what you mean. It would be good to do more, to stretch myself a bit. Maybe while I'm in London I might find some inspiration. There's certainly a lot here to point my lens at!'

'And men? Are there lots of them in London too? Have you met anyone . . . suitable? Or sexy? A little fling would do you a world of good.'

'Sian, you are terrible! It's less than two weeks since I split up with Joe. Give my battered heart a bit longer to recover, please! And I'm not sure men are what I need right now.'

'Nonsense. It's like falling off a horse. The sooner you get back on . . .'

'Oh, stop it! Now tell me, how's Flo? The only one in my life who I know really loves me just as I am. Have you seen her?'

'No, I haven't. Why would I, unless she gets sick? But loads of people love you, and don't you forget it.'

'I'll try not to. Now, I have to go. I have a bath to run and a book to finish.'

'It's a hard life! I'll say night night then. And don't forget to talk to your mum, so I don't have to.'

Prue sat for a while after the call had ended, tucked her feet up beneath her on the sofa and finished her Coke. Her hunch about Madi being a lot older was right then. She hoped she was settling in and that the villagers were showing her a warm welcome. That was one thing Shelling did well. Unlike London, where, she was beginning to realise, weeks, or possibly even years, might go by, living in a block like this, without even your closest neighbours knowing who you were or anything about you. God help her if she got ill, like Madi, or fell over and knocked herself out or broke a leg or something. What would happen to her then, she wondered, when absolutely nobody, not even her own family, knew she was there?

Chapter 10

*I*t's a woman in there. And young, by the sound of things.

It's so tempting. All I have to do is find myself in the hallway at the same time, make it look like I've bumped into her by accident, say hello.

Curiosity satisfied.

Cover blown.

No, it's best I keep my distance. Our paths will cross soon enough, I'm sure. No need to force it.

I'm fairly sure she's in there on her own – there's been no sign of the actress for days now – but I'm still not sure who she is. What connection there is between them. A fellow actress? A niece? A daughter, even? I think it unlikely, but it wouldn't be the first secret that woman's kept.

I could go in there while she's out, have a poke about, but it's a risk, not knowing where she's gone, how long for, when she might come back. Her habits are still a mystery. She is still a mystery. And I've never dared do it in broad daylight before. But it's tempting, just the same. And I've never been one to resist temptation . . .

Chapter 11

MADI

The first batch of redirected mail arrived on Saturday morning, the young postman knocking and handing it to her with a cheery 'G'morning' rather than just dropping it through the letterbox in the door. Madi could see without opening it that the top envelope was from the NHS. What now? Surely, with her chemo sessions over and her medication sorted out for the next few weeks, there couldn't be anything else they needed to tell her? She felt half inclined to ignore it, but that probably wouldn't be wise, so she sat herself down with a cup of strong tea and forced herself to open it.

It was funny how cancer took over your life, she thought, as she realised with relief that the letter had nothing to do with her treatment at all. Normal life went on just as it did before. The world didn't stop turning. Of course, there were other reasons the NHS might be getting in touch and this was simply a reminder that she hadn't given blood for a while and that current stocks of her blood type were running low. Not that she was probably allowed to give any now, what

95

with all the drugs whooshing round her system, and so recently after surgery. No doubt one department hadn't communicated that information to the other.

The rest of the mail was junk which she ripped up and threw in the bin, before picking up her tea and opening the back door to the garden, stepping over Flo, who had taken up temporary residence on the step, and going outside. It was a nice day, quite sunny considering it was only mid-March, but still a bit chilly as she wandered down the narrow path, ducking under the swaying washing line, and towards the small glass-topped table and tucked-under chairs. It didn't look as if they had been used much over the winter as she had to take a tissue from her cardigan pocket and give one of the chairs a wipe to take off some of the grime before she could sit down, her hands clasping the mug for warmth as she turned her face up towards the watery sun and suppressed a shiver.

It was a rare luxury to have a garden to sit in, and this one was neat and looked well maintained. The grass, a bit patchy but generally recovering well after the winter, was leaf-free, having obviously been swept or raked recently, but there was a mound of dry brown leaves, probably blown together by the wind, under the table, and it was only as her feet found them that Madi realised she was still wearing her slippers.

She looked at the small shed, curious to know what it might contain. Garden tools and lawnmowers didn't usually warrant darkened windows, and she had an inkling it could be some kind of darkroom for young Prue's photography. She'd never seen inside one before. She really shouldn't be so inquisitive, but perhaps that little third key on her keyring might open the padlock she could see hooked round the door. One tiny peek surely couldn't do any harm.

'Hello there!' A voice from behind her made her jump. She turned to see a man of about her own age smiling at her over the low stone wall that divided the cottage garden from the much bigger one next door. 'Sorry if I'm disturbing you. Just wanted to introduce myself. Tom Bishop, your neighbour. Well, for as long as you're here anyway. Won't get in your way, I promise, but it's always handy to have someone you can ask if you need anything, isn't it? Happy to oblige, that's all.'

Madi stood up and walked towards him. 'Thank you. I'm Madalyn Cardew.'

He looked at her for a moment, tilting his head as if deep in thought. 'The actress?'

'Well, yes, actually, but how did you . . .?'

'Oh, I'm a great theatre lover, me. Not that I get to go much these days but when I was younger . . . Anyway, I still like to keep up, read all the interviews and the reviews. Never forget a name, me. Faces I'm not always so good at, but I'm sure I saw you once. Now, what was it in again? Ah, yes, I remember. It was *Hamlet*, and you were Ophelia!'

'Gosh. That takes me back. I've taken that role twice. Which one did you see? Was it the one at Chichester, or the modern version where I floated down the river in a crochet bikini?'

'The former, I believe. But I think I'd have been even more likely to remember if I'd seen the bikini version!'

Madi could feel herself blushing. Ridiculous at her age!

'I'm just amazed you remember me at all, after all these years. I'm not exactly Dame Judi, am I?'

'Fine acting leaves its mark, my dear. You don't have to be famous for that. Performance is everything, not who you might or might not be. And I've got the memory of an elephant, me. Some would say the ears as well!' He laughed and made to walk away.

'Oh, wait. Please. Would you like to come over, for a cup of tea maybe? A slice of cake? Not home-made, I'm afraid, but . . .'

Tom stopped and grinned. 'Thought you'd never ask!' he quipped, and strolled down to the bottom of the garden to a small gate that she hadn't noticed until now, buried in the wall, and stepped through from his garden into hers.

'I'm afraid these chairs are a bit mucky,' she said, getting up. 'It's none too warm and, as you can see, I'm in my slippers, so I think we'd be better off indoors. Perhaps . . . your wife . . .?'

'No, she won't be able to join us.' He shook his head. 'If that's what you were going to suggest. She's not here at present. Nor likely to be, I suppose, if I'm honest about it. It's a long story.'

'Fair enough.' Determined not to pry, Madi simply led him along the path and into the kitchen.

'Oh, dear, it's a bit chilly in here, isn't it? It was warmer outside!' Tom rubbed his hands together and blew on them in an exaggerated manner. 'Seems to me you haven't quite got to grips with the heating. It can be tricky, that fire.'

'You're right there. I've managed to get it lit a couple of times, in the evenings, but it soon goes out again. I've been making do with hot drinks and a blanket.'

'Well, that won't do, will it? You get that kettle on and I'll take a look, shall I?'

'You know about fires?'

'I do. More used to putting them out than getting them started, mind. I was a fireman, man and boy. Retired now, of course. Still, these log fires aren't that tricky once you get the hang of them. I've got one similar, so I know the ropes. Now, where are the matches?'

It didn't take long for Tom to not only start the fire but give Madi instructions so she would be able to manage it herself in future. 'Simple when you know how,' he said, smiling at her as he sat down opposite her at the kitchen table and spooned sugar into the mug of tea she put down in front of him. 'Sugar for you?'

'Two please.'

'Any problems with the fire, or anything else for that matter, just knock and ask,' he said, sipping his tea, 'I'm usually in, except in the afternoons. That's when I visit her, you see. Barbara, my wife.'

'Visit?'

'She's got dementia. Can't really live at home any more. She's not far from here though. Nice place. Very friendly. It's one of those care places. And they do. Care, I mean. We've been lucky.'

Madi didn't think that having dementia sounded particularly lucky at all, but if he was able to stay positive and cheerful, who was she to knock it? 'I'm sorry.'

'Don't be. We had a good life together, and it's up to me to make sure she still has a good life now. As far as possible, anyway.'

She busied herself slicing the cake she'd bought at Patty Martin's shop. 'I hope you like ginger,' she said.

'Love it. Barbara used to make a lovely gingerbread. More like a scrunchy biscuit than a cake though. At Christmas, when the kids were small. They'd try to make houses out of it with icing to stick the pieces together, but they usually fell down. Tasted good though. Not that Barbara remembers any of that nowadays.'

Madi shivered. Her own memory problems seemed to have subsided since she'd been in Norfolk, but the dread of what they could lead to still worried her.

'Can't be easy,' she said. 'And the children? How many do you have?'

'Just the two. Both girls, both married and moved out. Got their own lives, their own families. They come when they can, try to do their bit, but it's not fair really, is it, to drag the grandchildren over here to visit a confused old woman?'

'Old? Surely she can't be more than . . .'

'She's sixty-eight, same as me. Yes, it took her way too early. But she's old to them. Not the sort of jolly grandma who can walk them to the swings in the park or teach them to bake cookies, you see. It's a crying shame but there it is. Nothing we can do about it. Now, let's change the subject, shall we? You don't want to hear my woes. What brings you here to our little corner of the world? Young Prue didn't tell me much, just that you'd be here for a few weeks, looking after the place, and the cat of course. Where is little Flo, by the way?'

'She was here not ten minutes ago. Gone out mousing,

probably. She left one in my shoe this morning! Dead, I'm pleased to say.'

'Ah, the joys of country living.' Tom laughed. 'Not from around here, are you? London, I'll be guessing.'

'That's right, London's my base, but I do travel around a fair bit. The nature of the job. Here, let me top you up.'

Tom lifted his empty mug and held it under the spout as Madi poured the last of the tea.

'Must be exciting, the theatre. From the inside, I mean. The rehearsals, the first nights, taking all those wonderful bows when the audience love what you've given them. Roar of the greasepaint, smell of the crowd and all that! It's something I wish I'd done when I was younger. I've only ever really seen things from the other side, the public side. You know – buy a ticket, watch the show, clap and go home.'

'Never too late. There's always amateur dramatics, local groups, whether it's acting you fancy or helping out behind the scenes . . .'

'Oh, I think it is. Too late, I mean. Can't commit to anything these days, you see, with Barb how she is. And I'd never get to grips with learning all those lines off by heart. I wouldn't say no to a bit of a backstage tour though, next time you're in anything local. Or is that too much to ask?'

'Not at all. Just not sure where I'll be working next. Or when. I've had . . . well, a spot of illness myself, you see, and had no choice really but to take some time out.'

'Sorry to hear that. But you'll be back, I'm sure. I imagine it's your life, isn't it? In the blood, so to speak.'

'You're not wrong there, Tom. Although I wish sometimes

I'd spent a bit more time and attention on some of the other things in my life, the more important things.'

'Family?'

Madi nodded.

'Did you not have children?'

'I did, yes. A boy. George. Hard to believe, but he's almost forty now. Where did the years go?'

'And his father?'

'Where did he go, do you mean?' She shrugged. 'Didn't even stick around for the birth.'

'I'm sorry. That can't have been easy.'

'It wasn't. Oh, he did the decent thing moneywise, was very generous in fact, I'll give him that, but as for anything else we were persona non grata, written out of his life as if we'd never existed. He never asked to meet his son, and only saw me when work threw us together from time to time. He had another life to protect, you see, and a reputation, and we didn't fit into that. George had to spend a lot of time with my parents while I was working. And I never had the kind of work that let me come home every night to bath him and put him to bed. I often didn't see him for weeks at a time, but travelling about from theatre to theatre, staying in boarding houses, trying to get someone backstage to keep an eye on him while I was on, that's no life for a kid. He was better off with his grandparents. Or so I thought at the time, but maybe I was just being selfish, not willing to give it all up. The stage sort of gets under your skin.'

'I'm sure it must. But he doesn't blame you, does he? You had to make a living, after all. For him, as much as for you.'

'I'm afraid he probably does blame me, yes.' Madi fought back a tear and turned to look out through the window, hoping Tom wouldn't see it.

'Oh, dear. You never remarried, I take it?'

'Not even the once actually. Turns out George's dad had been married to someone else all along. Which I should have known, or at least guessed. The naivety of youth! Or perhaps I preferred not to know, not to ask. But I think that made it worse somehow, him being married. My parents didn't approve of my lifestyle, my bad choices as they called them, and not only having a baby out of wedlock but adding adultery into the mix as well was a couple of steps too far, if you know what I mean. Oh, they loved George, sure enough. No doubt of that, and they're both long gone now, but I can't help wondering what they filled his head with and how much of it is still in there somewhere.'

'And did he ever want to find his father?'

'Too late, I'm afraid. He died, of a heart attack, backstage, when George was only six. So he never got the chance.'

'Oh dear.'

'In a way, I'm glad. Oh, not that he died. I did love him while we were together. Or thought I did. But it was probably for the best that George never got the chance to track him down. I'm not sure he would have been welcome, if you know what I mean. A dirty little secret well buried, as far as his so-called father was concerned . . .'

'He knows who his dad was though? I do think it's important for all of us to know where we came from, don't you?'

'Oh, yes, I told him his father's name. His real name, anyway.

103

Jeremy, which is what I always called him. Not the stage name that everyone else knew him by, just in case he blabbed it at school or something.'

'He was famous then?'

'Yes, he was, in theatrical circles anyway, which just made everything harder somehow. More important to keep the secret. But I was honest about him being a lot older than me, and that he was already married. I suppose I painted him in as bad a light as I could, to stop George wanting to ask too many questions, but I'm not sure it worked. He soon figured out who his dad was, as soon as he was a teenager and old enough to get access to a computer. It was easy enough to read about his brilliant career and to find photos of him on the internet. He knew what I was telling him was true, and that his father probably did have a wife somewhere, although Jeremy always kept his family life well out of the limelight. Obviously, there was no mention anywhere of him having a son. His father had clearly written him out of his life, disowned him and abandoned me, but, of course, I still ended up being the bad guy.'

'All long ago, Madalyn. You did what you felt was best for your son, and for you. And he's a grown man now. Able to see things from an adult perspective, understand why you had to do what you did.'

'True.' She knew only too well how George saw things, which was why she'd not set eyes on him for so long. It was time to change the topic of conversation, before she let too much hurt rise back up to the surface. Crying in front of this kind stranger, who had more than enough pain of his own to deal with, would be unthinkable. 'Now, where's that cat? Let's see if she wants to finish this last drop of milk, shall we?' She emptied the contents of the milk jug into a bowl and laid it on the floor, carefully avoiding Tom's gaze.

'Well, I'd best be off.' He took the hint quickly and looked at his watch. 'I've taken up far too much of your time. It's been good to chat. See you again perhaps, Madalyn, before you head off home?'

'Yes, I hope so. And do call me Madi. Everyone does.'

'I will. Thank you, Madi, for the tea and cake.' He pulled the back door open, ready to go back the way he'd come, through the garden. 'Ah, look, here comes Flo. And not a mouse in sight, you'll be glad to hear.'

Madi sat quietly after he'd gone. She lifted Flo up onto her lap and enjoyed the warm weight of her as the little cat purred contentedly with her eyes closed and her paws gently padding up and down on the soft edges of Madi's woolly cardigan.

Goodness, what was she thinking telling so much about herself to someone she had only just met? But then, he had been more willing to talk about his own troubles, and in such a natural, uncomplicated way too. In fact, the way he had talked, it was hard to see them as troubles at all. Life had thrown a curve ball and he had learned how to adapt and deal with it. Perhaps she had been looking at things the wrong way all along. Nothing was going to change the past. She had been dealt a hand and it couldn't be undealt. But she could certainly work out what to do about it from now on.

She waited until Flo had had enough pampering and had

headed off up the stairs to leave yet more hairs all over the bed and retrieved her mobile from her handbag. She had resisted going anywhere near it all week, but perhaps it was time. If having cancer had made one thing clear to her it was that you never really knew how long you had left, that something could come along and hit you full pelt at any time. It was all too easy to put things off until tomorrow, but there might never be a tomorrow. And now the worst of it was behind her and her call could not be misinterpreted as a cry for help, it was time to start mending fences.

She scrolled down her contacts list. Casting agents, theatre offices, fellow actors, doctors, George . . . Her thumb hovered over his name.

Home number? Of course, he might have moved house since his split with Jessica. They could have decided to sell up, and he could be living alone in some little bedsit or hotel room by now. Or even with another woman, but knowing her son as she did, that didn't seem likely. Still, Madi realised with a jolt of guilt, maybe she didn't know him that well at all any more. How had she let things come to this?

Mobile number? He probably wouldn't have changed that, unless he wanted to stop his wife – or his mother – from calling. Maybe blocked her somehow. It all came down to how badly he wanted to avoid her, and how willing he might be to leave the door open and see if she made any effort to come through it. Only one way to find out.

As it was the weekend there was no reason to think she might be disturbing him at work. After a childhood like his, he had told her on the day he got married ten years ago that he knew only too well the importance of drawing a line between work and family, of taking proper days off when his marriage and his home life would take precedence, and work was nothing but a dirty word. She had thought him arrogant at the time he'd said it. Unrealistically romantic. As if he was merely trying to make a point, and at her expense, but maybe he had been right all along. Whatever had gone wrong between George and Jessica – and she had a fair idea what that was – it would not have happened because of any want of trying on his part.

It threw her when the answerphone message kicked in. 'Hello, this is George Cardew. I am not available right now. Please leave your name and number.'

She didn't, of course. That was not the way she wanted to make contact again after so long. Not with an impersonal message that he might decide not to respond to. She sat, nursing the phone after she had hastily rung off, just staring ahead of her into space. She would try again, of course. Another day, another time. And he would see her name in his missed calls, so there was always the chance he might call her back. In the meantime, however, it had been lovely – no, better than lovely – just to hear his voice.

Chapter 12

After a whole week of mooching around alone, eating too many takeaways and feeling mildly sorry for herself, Prue made up her mind: it had to stop. What a shame it would be to go home after a month in London having achieved nothing but wandering aimlessly about and gazing at a few sights she had already seen a hundred times on TV. So what if she had nobody to talk to, nobody to go out drinking with, no structure to her days? All of that belonged to her normal, everyday life. It was what she had wanted to run from, to test the waters away from Shelling for once, away from the slog of nine to five and the safe haven of familiarity and routine, and most definitely away from Joe Barton. She needed to make the most of the remainder of her time in London. She had had such grand ideas about all the things she could do . . .

When she opened the door on Monday morning, Aaron was loitering on the landing, one arm raised as if he was about to knock, and his phone, for once, nowhere to be seen.

'Oh, hi,' he said, a bit awkwardly. 'I didn't know if you were in. It's my day off – night off, whatever, so I don't need to sleep all day – and I was wondering if . . . well, if you were thinking of going out with your camera anywhere today.'

'I was, yes. Down towards the river somewhere, maybe. Why?' She hesitated, not quite sure where the conversation was going. 'Did you want to come?'

'If you don't mind.' He seemed suddenly more animated than she had seen him before. 'Not if you'd rather not. I mean, we hardly know each other, so I'd understand if you'd prefer to be on your own. But I'm quite interested. In photography. Well, all art really. And I might be able to help in some way. As a local, I mean. Knowing the best places to go, depending on what it is you want to see . . .'

'Okay.'

'Okay? You mean I can?'

'Don't see why not. To be honest, I don't know anyone else here and it might be nice to have some company. Give me half an hour though, eh? I was just popping out for some supplies. Meet back here at ten?'

'Cool. And thanks. Want me to bring anything?'

'Not that I can think of. Your lunch maybe? It's what I'll be doing. I'm watching the pennies a bit and it's cheaper than having to eat out somewhere.'

'Like a packed lunch, you mean? I've not had one of them since school!'

She laughed. 'Well, it doesn't have to be in a Thomas the Tank plastic box, but just a sandwich and an apple or something? And a bottle of water, or a flask.'

'Right. I'll get onto it. See you later.' And he was off, bounding back down the stairs like an over-eager puppy.

She followed him down, at a slower pace, and walked to the shop where she quickly bought some bread, cheese, bananas and a couple of bottles of juice. She stopped to check Madi's post tray in the hall on her way back. Nothing today. By the time she had rustled up a cheese and pickle sandwich and packed a few things in her rucksack, it was still only ten to ten. She didn't want to have to do it but she'd promised Sian, so she switched her phone on and sent a proper text to her mum. She knew she should call, but texting was just so much easier, with no chance of being interrogated or pressure being applied to make her go back.

Am in London. Swapped homes with Madi. Promise to be back in three weeks. Don't worry about me. All is fine. And please don't pester Madi for the address. She has been sworn to secrecy! Love you x

That would have to do. She didn't want to be too accessible, but now, if some disaster did happen to strike, she was at least traceable. That text had put her mind at rest, and hopefully would do the same for her mum. She wondered, not for the first time, if this level of anxiety was one of those inherited things, if worrying about some ludicrous scenario that might never happen, instead of dealing with the here and now and just enjoying life, was something her mum had passed on to her through her genes. No, it was highly unlikely that she was about to end up unconscious on the bathroom floor, but if she did, there was a chance now of being saved. Eventually. Because if she wasn't calling home regularly, how was anyone meant to know when to worry enough to raise the alarm? She gave herself a mental slap. God, she'd be checking she had her best knickers on next, just in case she got run over!

Before her thoughts could take her any further down that route, Aaron was back at the door, and the two of them set off down the road towards the tube.

'Thanks again for this,' he said.

'That's okay.'

'I hope you don't think I'm some kind of stalker. It's just . . .'

'Aaron, it's okay. Honestly. If you're keen on learning about photography, I'm more than happy to have you tag along. You can take a turn with Camilla yourself later if you'd like.'

'Camilla?'

Prue laughed. 'Sorry. My camera. I've always named them. They spend so much time out and about with me, I've always thought they deserved names of their own. My first was an old Box Brownie that used to belong to my grandad. I was about six and I called it Brownie, of course. No real imagination in those days. But Camilla's my biggest and my best. Where I go, she goes. So, where will that be today? You're the local interest expert. Take us somewhere I might not have found for myself. By the river, but off the obvious tourist route. But pretty, just the same.'

'You don't ask for much, do you?' he joked. 'But for you, and Camilla here, I'll put my thinking cap on.'

* * *

They ended up at Strand-on-the-Green, tucked away under Kew Bridge, strolling along the footpath beside the Thames, the sun shining on the water. Every few paces Aaron had to stop and shorten his stride so she could keep up.

'Wow. Beautiful houses.' Prue gazed up in awe. 'I wonder what these cost?'

'If you need to ask you probably can't afford them.'

'And look at that little island over there!'

'Something to do with Cromwell, I think, hiding out there in the Civil War. My dad told me about that. He used to bring me here, on our Sundays. You know, the classic divorced parents thing. A burger, a film, feed the ducks or visit a park somewhere before being deposited back at Mum's like a parcel. This was one of my favourites. There's something calming about the river, isn't there? And sort of constant, when everything else around you is changing.'

'You're quite a thinker, aren't you?'

'Not really. Thick as shit actually, which is why I work nights stacking shelves.'

'I'm sure that's not true. The thick bit, I mean. You shouldn't put yourself down, you know, or you'll find other people will too. You just need a bit of confidence in yourself.' That was a joke, coming from her. Miss Underconfident herself! If only she knew how to take her own advice.

They stopped for a while, Prue pointing her camera at a lone bird floating by, adjusting the lens to bring it into focus. 'You didn't want to go to uni?'

'Never an option. Mum needs me working, to help out with the bills, and the thought of running up all that student debt worried the hell out of her. And me. I wasn't good enough at anything anyway. Bit of this, bit of that. I liked history, wasn't bad at art, could manage basic maths and a few words of French, but I didn't shine at any one thing, and average grades don't count for much.'

'How old are you?'

'Nineteen. You?'

'Twenty-four, although sometimes I feel more like fifty! Like I'm stuck in a rut I'll probably chug along in until the day I retire. I do enjoy my job and I was lucky enough to inherit a little house, but the downside is that it ties me to the village I was born in. I really have nothing to complain about, but I sometimes feel like I haven't achieved anything, struck out and done anything for myself yet, you know?'

'Ah, but you said *yet*, so there's still hope that you might!'

'I suppose so. In theory, anyway.'

'So, you didn't go to uni either?'

She shook her head. 'No excuses really. Mum and Dad would have supported me, and I did get the grades. But the thought of leaving home, leaving . . . well, the people I cared about. My gran wasn't well and I wanted to be there for her. And I knew that when she passed away I wouldn't have to worry about saving up for a home or trying to get a mortgage, and there was a perfectly good job already lined up and waiting for me . . .'

'Sounds so easy. I wish someone would just give me a house and a decent job.'

'Oh, God, I must sound so up myself. I know there are people worse off than me. Much worse off. And I'm sorry about the divorce, having to split yourself between two parents like that. Mine are stuck together like glue, rock solid, to the point of turning to stone. The classic happy family, although they stopped after having me and never made the regulation 2.4 children. Still, I know I should be grateful. I'd just like the chance to get out and spread my wings a bit now, that's all.'

As she said the words, a swan opened its massive white wings wide and skittered across the water, and they both laughed.

'There you are. If he can do it, so can you!' Aaron lowered himself onto a patch of grass and reached for the camera. 'Can I?'

'Yeah, sure.' She unhooked the strap from around her neck and handed him the camera, watching him balance it on his knees. 'Do you know how . . .?'

'Show me.'

Heads close together, Prue sat beside him and spent a few minutes explaining the workings of the camera and twisting at the lens, showing him how best to frame the shot and capture the right light.

'You're good at this, aren't you?' he said. 'Show me some of your pictures.'

She scrolled through some of her recent shots, bringing them up on the screen for him to see.

'I like this one. And I really love this . . .'

'Thanks.' Did he mean it or was he just being kind? She pulled away from him, suddenly feeling awkward at their closeness. 'Ready to have a go now?'

'Yeah, okay. Probably be rubbish though.'

'There you go, putting yourself down again.'

'Sorry.' He swung the strap over his head and lifted the camera to his eye. 'Oh, great. A boat!'

'Take your time, Aaron. Look for the right shot. Nobody's interested in just another photo of a boat. Try to find something different, a unique angle. The way it moves through the water. Its name on the side. That man at the back, trying to hang onto his hat . . .'

'You know what I'd really like to do?' he said, after he'd taken twenty or so shots and declared himself disappointed with them all. 'Come back when it's dark. Oh, not right here necessarily, but just by the water somewhere. Can we?'

'Together? In the evening?'

'I don't mean like go on a date.' He looked embarrassed. 'Unless you fancy it, that is.'

'Aaron, I like you, of course I do, but . . .'

'Yeah, yeah. I know. Age difference, and all that. Don't worry. It was just a thought. No, I meant to take pictures really. See how the river looks with all the lights reflected in it, the boats moored up, what the birds are getting up to when there are no boats going by and disturbing them . . .'

'Nice idea. Black and white can work really well if it's reflections you're after. Adds a sort of moodiness.'

'Yeah, that sounds cool. Moodiness! I like that. So, can we?'

'I suppose we could. I haven't actually seen London at night yet. Wasn't sure how safe I'd be, on my own.' Prue pulled one of her drink bottles from her rucksack and twisted at the lid.

'No need to be worried about that if I'm there.'

'Okay.'

'Cool.' He pulled out his own water bottle and took a swig. 'Could I take some of you?' he asked, the camera still in his hands.

'Me?'

'Yeah, why not? I like pictures of people, don't you?'

'I do, yes, but I'm no model.'

'So? It doesn't have to be like a fashion shoot. It's art, isn't it? And we're looking for something different. The right angle, the right light . . .'

'You've got me there!'

'Proves I've been listening. So, can I? Take some of you? Just sitting, looking at the river? You can always delete them if they're crap.'

'Only if I can take some of you too.'

'Fair enough.'

They took turns posing and photographing each other, moving along the path and then back up onto the bridge, to find new locations, new backdrops, until Prue declared it must be time for lunch and they went in search of a bench.

'So, why are you here?' Aaron took a big bite of his doorstop sandwich and carried on talking through it, crumbs falling straight at the feet of a waiting duck. 'Why come to London, and what's the connection with the actress?'

'Escape. The same thing I think she was after too, so we agreed to swap for a while.'

'Swap what? Lives?'

'Well, homes. I'm not sure actually swapping lives would have worked. I can't act for toffee and I don't suppose she'd really be up for photographing prize marrows!'

117

'Your job's really that exciting, is it?'

'Well, there's the occasional parsnip.'

Aaron smiled. 'You're funny, you know. As well as pretty.'

Prue felt her cheeks turn pink.

'No boyfriend back at home, pining for you?'

'Not any more.'

'I sense a story there.'

'One for another time maybe.' She pulled her coat collar up, aware of the sudden turn in the weather. 'Look at those clouds. I think it's going to rain.'

'Can I try a photo? Of the clouds?'

'Of course. Here's me worrying about getting wet and you're still looking for the perfect shot. We'll make a photographer of you yet.'

'I hope so. I'm really enjoying all this. It beats my phone any day. It might have all the megapixels and the zoom and everything, but really it's still just point and click. Where's the fun in that?'

It was four o'clock by the time they got back to Belle Vue Court. The rain had come down hard as they'd exited the tube and Prue's shoes were soaked through.

'I'd best try and get a bit of sleep,' Aaron said, yawning, as he led the way up the stairs. 'Not used to staying awake all day. I'm more of a night owl really. Have to be, working late shifts.'

'I'll look through the pictures you took, maybe edit them a bit and then you can come and look at them. I could email the best ones to you, if you'd like to keep them. Or we could become Facebook friends and I'll send some that way.'

'Cool.' He took out his phone, the first time he'd looked at it all day, and tapped in all her details – name, mobile, Facebook, email. 'Harris, eh? Like the tweed? Oh, I know my materials! Mum used to do sewing. Dressmaking, alterations, stuff like that. Surprising what you pick up. She doesn't do it now though . . .' He hesitated but didn't explain. 'And I'm a Jones, by the way. Common, I know, but at least everyone knows how to spell it! So, I'll see you again soon, Prue Harris. But next time, we'll go after dark, right? I'll check my shifts.'

She watched him open the door to flat 6, catching a glimpse of a woman's outline silhouetted in an internal doorway, the sound of a radio and the unmistakeable smell of roasting chicken spilling out into the hall as he disappeared inside, before she walked up the final flight to the top of the building.

The landline phone was ringing as she opened the door, a persistent chirruping sound that echoed around the empty flat. She hadn't even noticed that the flat had a landline until now, and it took her a minute to track the handset down, tucked away on a windowsill behind the living-room curtain.

'Hello?' she said, tentatively, not sure she should even be answering it, but it was too late. The caller had just hung up.

Chapter 13

They've been out all day. Together. I heard them laughing as they came back. It didn't take her long, did it? Trying to get her claws into him. Who is she anyway? The actress doesn't have a daughter. I'm almost sure of that. I'd know, wouldn't I? It would have been mentioned somewhere, in all the stuff that gets written about her. About all famous people. Or semi-famous, in her case. Not that they know everything, these celeb-watchers. They never found out about her back then, did they? Who she was. Her relationship with him. That she even existed.

It's amazing what you can keep secret, if you really want to.

But, from what that solicitor said, it's perhaps not so easy to keep secrets after death. She had to be told, I suppose. His widow. It was her inheritance, after all. Her life turned upside down. His mess was her mess now. Personal. Financial. It must have been so hurtful, so humiliating, for a wife to be treated that way, to discover the truth, and then to have to keep it all in place. His little house of cards. But she said nothing. Did nothing. Never said a word to me, or to them. And it's too late now to ask her why.

Still, it's odd, this girl, some young relative or whatever she is, swanning in like she owns the place, spending all day with a boy so much younger than her, a boy she hardly knows.

Doesn't she realise who he is?

Obviously not.

Chapter 14

MADI

Madi put the phone down, hanging up on the twelfth ring, just before she knew she would be met with her own voice asking her to leave a message. Of course, Prue would be out and about somewhere at this time of the day, making the most of her London jaunt. Either that or she might feel reluctant to answer someone else's phone. They had not swapped mobile numbers so Madi would just have to try again later, or maybe send an email and hope that Prue was checking her inbox regularly.

She was no animal expert but the more she looked at Flo the more she convinced herself something was wrong. She was definitely off her food and she hadn't been outside at all today, just stayed curled up in her usual place on the pouffe in front of the fire, which wasn't even lit. Madi couldn't help but wonder how much longer the little cat's bladder could possibly last out, and whether she'd be mopping the floor by the evening.

She put out a tentative hand and stroked Flo's back, an action which had always resulted in her rolling over to expose her tummy and producing a considerable amount of loud contented purring, but neither happened. Flo simply opened her eyes and stayed put. Should she try to pick her up? What if she was in pain? Should she wait until she'd contacted Prue? No, it was no use. She really couldn't just sit here, doing nothing. There was a vets' surgery just yards away up the lane, and the least she could do was to pop along there and ask for some help.

This time, as she opened the doors, it wasn't young Sian sitting at the reception desk but Faith Harris, wearing an identical green tabard to the one Sian had worn on the day Madi had arrived in the village.

'Madi!' she exclaimed. 'How nice! Come to arrange our date for tea and cake?'

'Erm, no, although we must do that soon. It's your daughter's little cat. I'm a bit worried about her. She seems very sorry for herself today.'

'Oh dear. Can't have that, can we? Here. Let me just pull up her records and we'll get one of the vets to come and see her. My husband's out on a call and I have no idea how long that might take, so it will probably be Ralph. You won't have met him yet, I assume? He's Sian's young man. Well, fiancé now, I should say. Anyway, he's a very capable vet, our Ralph. Been a godsend to us, he has. It might actually mean that Stuart can retire in the not too distant future now Ralph's here to take the reins. Now, let me see.' She clicked away at the keys on the computer on her desk, shaking her head before trying again. 'Oh, bring back a proper appointments diary, I say. We used to have a lovely big black leather one in the old days, but you can't escape technology now, can you? Right.

He has one more appointment booked in for this afternoon, then I can ask him to come down to you, unless any emergencies crop up before then.'

'Perfect. I might be worrying about nothing but . . .'

'Better to be safe than sorry, especially with an elderly cat. Flo's twelve. Did you know that? And she is family.'

'Yes, I suppose she is!'

'Now, tea? Have you got time for a cup? As I say, we've only one more patient due in, so I've got time to put the kettle on.'

'Okay, yes. Why not?'

'No cake, I'm afraid, but I can rustle up a digestive.' She lifted a concealed flap at the end of the counter and ushered Madi through. 'Come on. Come and take a seat back here in the staff room. Stay in the public area and you'll probably get the biscuit snatched out of your hand. He's a bit of a tinker, this little terrier who's coming in. And, besides, the chairs out there are too hard.'

Faith busied herself making tea as Madi took a seat and studied her surroundings.

'You've made it very comfy. And the photos on the wall? Are they . . .?'

'Yes, all my Prue's work. Good, aren't they? I keep telling her she should have done more with her talent. Portraits maybe. There's money in that, isn't there? Not stuck in a little newspaper office, but there we are. She didn't want to leave the village, or leave that Joe Barton more like, not that hanging around for him has done her any good. But, still, you can't tell other people what to do, can you? Especially your own children. Much as I might worry, you can't live their lives for them, can you? Have you got any children, Madi?'

There was something so forthright, so open, about this woman that Madi found it hard to take offence.

'Just the one. And I've never had much luck telling him what to do either. He's his own man, that's for sure.'

'And is he an actor too?'

'God, no! It's the last thing my George would want to do. He blames the theatre for everything, that one. It's what kept me away so much, you see, when he was growing up. Not really the ideal life as far as family goes. No, he's an accountant. Small businesses, tax, that sort of thing . . .'

'Same as Joe. He's an accountant too. Or a trainee one, more like. Oh, here's Mr Simpkins with young Toby. Back in a tick.'

Madi couldn't help but wonder whether Mr Simpkins was the name of the terrier and Toby its owner, or if it was the other way around. Some people did give their pets ridiculous names. There had been a big mouthy parrot once that an eccentric old actor had kept in his dressing room. It had sworn like a trooper at everyone who came in, yet he had called it The Duchess. She smiled at the memory as she sipped at her tea, pleased to realise just how good her memory still was when it came to the long ago. Faith dealt with the incoming client and his dog, ushering them straight through to see the vet, then came back to join her.

'Now, where were we?' she said, plonking herself down in the opposite chair. 'Ah, yes, kids!'

'Well, mine's hardly a kid any more. He's thirty-nine.'

'A mother's work is never done, is it? Still a worry, long after they've grown up and flown the nest.'

Madi nodded, concentrating on her tea to avoid having to

explain anything more about her own mother–son situation, but it was only a matter of minutes before Toby and Mr Simpkins re-emerged into the reception area and Faith went back to sort out their bill and help carry a giant bag of dog food outside to their car.

'Phew! Another day over . . .' A tall, slim man, who Madi assumed must be Ralph, appeared at the staff room door, still wearing his white medical coat and running a hand through his floppy sandy-coloured hair. 'Oh, sorry. I expected you to be Faith. I didn't realise we had a guest.'

Madi stood up and held out her hand. 'Madi Cardew. I'm staying at Prue Harris's place and I came in just for some advice really, but Faith insisted I stop for tea. I'm a bit concerned about Prue's cat. She's very . . . lethargic is the only word I can think of. And not eating.'

'Little Flo? Can't have that now, can we? Have you brought her in?'

'Sorry, no. I didn't really know how to. If Prue might have some kind of cat carrier . . .'

'No worries. I'll come to you. Only the best for our Flo. I've known her since I was a teenager, when she belonged to Prue's gran. We're all quite fond of her. Do you mind if I just have a quick sit down first? I've not stopped since lunch.'

'Ah, Ralph,' said Faith, joining them and pulling on her outdoor coat. 'You've met Madi, I see. I hope you don't mind if I dash off now, but I have a few errands to run, so I'll leave you to lock up and make arrangements about Flo. There's tea in the pot. And I'll see you soon, I hope, Madi. You've got my number.'

The place seemed to fall very quiet as soon as Faith had

gone. 'Ah, a moment's peace,' Ralph said, settling himself down with an enormous mug of tea and balancing four digestives on his knees, without the benefit of a plate. 'I'm Ralph Barton, by the way, as I'm sure you've gathered. Sian has mentioned you, so I know enough not to bore you with the same old questions. Good to meet you anyway, and I'm sure we'll soon have our Flo back fighting fit.'

'I hope so. I can't help but feel responsible for her while Prue's away. And I have no experience of pets at all. If anything were to happen to her while she's in my care . . .'

'Well, I'll do my best to make sure it doesn't.' He gulped his tea down and smacked his lips, popped the first biscuit into his mouth whole and slipped the remaining three into the pocket of his white coat. 'Right, I'll just grab my bag and fetch the keys, and we can walk down together. A little something to keep me going until dinner.' He laughed, patting the pocket.

'Do much more of that and they'll turn to crumbs!'

'No chance. These'll be long gone by the time we arrive. Food doesn't last long when I'm around.'

Ralph pushed a few buttons on the alarm pad on their way out, turned the key in the lock and pulled at the door to make sure it was locked. 'Can't be too careful,' he said. 'Not when we have drugs and cash on the premises. You may think this is a safe village, and it generally is, but crime gets everywhere these days. The estate agent had his car nicked a week or two back.'

'That would be Donny's dad?'

Ralph laughed. 'I see you're getting to know a bit about the village already. Met young Donny, have you?'

'Not yet, but I've heard him.

'Ah. The bells, the bells . . .' Ralph went instantly into a bent-over Hunchback of Notre Dame impression, which set Madi off giggling. 'No, seriously though, Donny's a good kid, but from his efforts so far I'm not convinced he has a future in campanology. Just not enough going on locally to keep him occupied, and there are so few kids his own age living in the village, but at least while he's up there in the tower he's not getting into any trouble. That's how crime so often starts among the young, isn't it? Boredom.'

'I suppose it is. Although in London we have more than enough things for kids to do, but still have such high crime rates . . .'

'True.'

They had reached Snowdrop Cottage and Madi let them in.

'So, here's my little patient.' Ralph crossed straight to Flo, still curled up on her pouffe, and got down onto his knees beside her.

Madi watched as he gently ran his hands over her, stretching out each paw to check for damage, lifting her ears and feeling around her abdomen. He put on some disposable gloves, took a thermometer from his bag and inserted it in her rear end, checked and disinfected it and put it away again, then pulled off his gloves and slid his fingers into her mouth and over her teeth. 'Her temperature's up, and her face is quite swollen,' he said, turning back to Madi. 'And she's not at all happy about me touching her mouth. I'm pretty sure what we have here is an abscess. It's no wonder she hasn't wanted to eat.'

'Can you do anything?'

'I certainly can. Her teeth are in quite a bad way too, but that's largely down to her age. Lots of plaque building up. I'm going to have to take her into the surgery, I'm afraid, and lance that abscess before it bursts. We don't want her running the risk of a dangerous infection. We can sort out a little op to clean up her teeth later. Can you look after her while I pop back for a carrier?'

'Yes, of course. Is it serious? Should I contact Prue and get her home?'

'Depends. Is she somewhere she'll want to rush back from, or would we simply be spoiling things for her? I don't know what you've been told about my idiot of a brother, but I think Prue probably needs this time away, from him and the village, and all of us. Gossip is not a nice thing to have to deal with. And neither is rejection, especially when it's been done so publicly. I could knock Joe's block off, to be honest with you, but what's done is done. And, poorly though Flo is right now, I can promise you she's not about to die. So, let's keep shtum and allow Prue to enjoy her holiday, shall we? I'll take good care of Flo and I'll let you know if things change.'

Madi sat on the carpet and stroked the cat lightly with the tips of her fingers until Ralph returned ten minutes later with a plastic carrier. There was only the smallest of plaintive objections from Flo, who was clearly not feeling her usual self, as he lifted her in and closed the grille.

'I'll take a proper look and get the abscess treated as soon as we're back at the surgery.'

'But you'd finished for the evening.'

'Ha! A vet's life can't be run by the clock. Animals get sick at all times of the day and night. Sian will come in and assist. It's very much a family business, or two families really, and it certainly helps that we all live so close to the surgery! We'll make Flo comfy for an overnight stay, and we'll take it from there in the morning. And don't worry, Madi. All will be well.'

But, of course, she did worry. How could she not? She must have woken at least three times during the night, aware of Flo's absence beside her on the bed, her dreams taking her to places she would much rather not have gone. Was this what it was like, to share your life with another being? It had been so long since she had had to worry about anyone but herself.

It was only as she dragged herself up in the morning and sat at the table with a bowl of porridge and a coffee, still wearing a baggy nightie and without her wig, that she realised, for the first time since she'd arrived here, that she hadn't so much as glanced at herself in the mirror this morning. Any mirror. She knew she didn't look the way she used to, and might never do again, but there was nothing she could do about that. The constant checking of her scar and her lopsided profile and her stubbly head could do nothing to change anything. Only time and nature and specialist underwear could work that kind of a miracle. Even her paranoia about forgetting or losing things, and the dread of succumbing to some awful dementia-type illness like Tom's poor wife, had finally begun to subside. She had lost a breast, but that was all. As Faith had said, what real use was a breast anyway, at her age? Of course she wasn't losing her mind as well. It was all just black thoughts, too much time sitting alone and feeling sorry for herself, her mind playing cruel tricks. She had even wondered, for a while, if there was some crazed fan out there somewhere, watching her, stalking her, making her feel so uneasy about something vaguely threatening that she couldn't even put her finger on, but that was just ridiculous. She wasn't famous enough for any of that nonsense, and how on earth could someone on the outside be making things happen inside her flat? No, she had just got herself into a state, had not been 'quite herself' for a while, and understandably so, what with a nasty lump growing inside her and a cabinet full of drugs addling her brain. It was clear now that she had simply imagined it all. It was time to put it all behind her, and to start thinking positively. Slowly but surely, she was on the mend. Now all she wanted to know was whether the same could be said about Flo.

Phoning wouldn't do. On the dot of nine, Madi walked up the lane and was the first through the doors of the surgery as Sian opened them up for the day.

'Hello, Ms Cardew. Here about Flo? You can come through and see her if you like. Visiting hours are pretty flexible. Get well cards are fine, but I must tell you that we don't allow flowers or grapes.'

It took Madi a moment to realise Sian was joking.

'She's had a good night. Ralph's drained the abscess and started her on some antibiotics. She's even managed a little bit of food this morning.' Sian yawned, leading Madi through to a small room at the back of the building and to a row of wire cages, most of which were empty. Flo was right at the end, curled on a blanket, and lifted her head to look through the bars at them as soon as she heard their voices. 'We can show you how to administer those yourself, ready for when you take her home.'

'Home? Already?' Madi pushed a finger through the bars and ran them over the little cat's back, carefully avoiding her head. Amazingly, Flo began to purr.

'Later today, I should think. As long as you keep her indoors for a few days. We can provide a litter tray if Prue doesn't have one. If that's okay?'

'It does worry me, to be honest. I don't know anything about looking after a cat, not a sick cat anyway. It was fine when she was taking care of herself, coming in and out through her flap, with me just putting down some food and water twice a day, but this is different, trying to keep her in, getting medicine down her. It's quite a responsibility, when she belongs to someone else.'

'Would you like me to call Prue?'

'Oh, no, don't do that. I'll manage somehow.'

'Ah, Madi, good morning.' Ralph Barton had come in behind them. 'I see our patient has perked up since yesterday. Thanks to you spotting something was wrong, we got to it quickly, and she's going to be absolutely fine. I couldn't help overhearing you just now, but really there's no need to trouble Prue. If you feel uneasy, we can always keep Flo here for a while longer, or Prue's mum would take her in, I'm sure.'

'No, I'll do it. Poor little thing needs to be in her own home, where she feels safe. Show me what to do, and I'll give it my best shot.'

'I'm sure you will. Pop back later, say around two, and we'll sort out everything you need. And, there's no charge, obviously, because Flo's . . .'

'Family!' they all said together.

Chapter 15

I'm getting tired of this now. Sitting here, day after day, wondering. Where is the damned woman? The interloper doesn't really interest me. Not in the same way. I hear her skipping about, in that carefree way young people do. Thundering down the stairs as if everything is so urgent, so important, as if everything has to be rushed.

I prefer to take my time, do things slowly. Carefully. Give everything more thought. I like to bide my time. Do things properly, do things thoroughly.

Revenge. Best served cold, so they say.

I can wait. I've waited this long to bring her down, so what's a bit longer? Not too much longer though. My patience isn't everlasting. It may stretch, but only so far, and one day it's going to snap.

Chapter 16

PRUE

Prue could hardly believe she had been in London for ten days already. Ten days of near solitude as she passed the occasional fellow resident in the hall, exchanging curious nods, wandered the streets by herself, and spent her evenings with only the TV or a book for company. Thank God for Aaron, or she just might start to believe she was never going to have a proper conversation with anyone again.

She had decided to leave her camera behind for once and hit the shops. The real shops, rather than the little local parade she had been using for supplies. Shops that didn't close their doors at lunchtime every Wednesday for 'half day closing' as they always had, and still did, in the village back home.

Oxford Street stretched out in front of her as she emerged from the underground at Marble Arch. It would be Mother's Day on Sunday, the first she had ever spent apart from her mum. She wouldn't be able to turn up on her doorstep with the usual bunch of daffodils and a box of her favourite coffee creams, but if she was quick enough she could find her a nice present, wrap it and get it into the post in time.

It was fun exploring the big department stores, riding the escalators, taking armfuls of clothes into assorted changing rooms and parading in front of mirrors. By two o'clock she was laden down with bags and her stomach was telling her it was time for a very late but desperately needed lunch.

She sat in a burger bar, at a small table in the window, working her way through a super-sized meal and a huge strawberry milkshake, and watching the crowds go by. Men in business suits, women trying to negotiate the bustling pavement while pushing prams and shopping trolleys, Japanese tourists huddled in groups taking selfies. So many people, and mid-week too. She could hardly imagine what this street must be like on a Saturday, or in the days leading up to Christmas.

For a fleeting moment she missed the village, its quiet lanes and sleepy pace of life, the uninterrupted green spaces and big open skies. When she peered upwards out of the window now, all she could see were buildings and streetlights and a dull all-over greyness that could have been anything from air pollution to dirty windows to clouds. But being here was new and different – and different was exciting. When had she ever done anything truly exciting before? She had finally managed to prise herself away and climb out of her rut. She must not forget that, even if it was only a temporary escape. And, most importantly, she was away from Joe. Joe, who she had foolishly believed was her future, but she was beginning to realise was the one thing that had been dragging her down and anchoring her so securely to the past.

She had tried to move on from him once before, to test the romantic waters with someone else, and it had worked for a while. Joe had been gone for months, years, head down and working hard for his degree, and his calls and visits home had become less and less frequent until they had dwindled almost to nothing. She should have known then that he was not as into her as she was into him, that he was in no hurry to rush back to her, but she had made excuses for him, to other people and to herself, kidded herself that he was doing it for the right reasons, solid career-building reasons, and that everything would change and be okay again once he was back for good. But he hadn't come back, heading straight off to Leeds with one of his uni roommates as soon as he graduated, grabbing the first job he was offered.

That was when she had given in and succumbed to the charms of another man. Luke. They'd met through work, on a photo-shoot. His sister's wedding. He had been dressed to the nines – grey suit, white shirt, shiny shoes, pink rose – and he had looked good, even more so when viewed in soft focus through the lens of her camera. He was what she would call photogenic. The camera loved him. And people did too. He was tall, handsome, funny, and more than a little drunk. He had deep brown eyes and slightly-too-long dark blond hair, and one of those sexy little-boy-lost smiles no girl could resist. And he was alone. No plus one. Until he had caught her eye and taken the camera from her hand, put it down on a table and led her onto the dancefloor. For an hour or so she had melted into his chest, moved with the music, wrapped up in his arms, stopped being the photographer and become . . . What had she become? Happy, carefree, besotted . . .

Luke didn't live locally. They had tried to make it work. Five months of exhausting and expensive train trips, long lonely drives, meals in restaurants that had to be cut short because one or other of them had work in the morning and a long journey home, weekends in hotels that had been wonderful while they lasted, but always ended in the same way. Distance, absence, and neither of them sure enough or brave enough to make the move the relationship needed if it had any chance of survival.

It was Prue who ended it. She could picture him now, the sad puppy-dog eyes that showed regret but no sign of actual tears, the final wave as she drove away. Back to Shelling and familiarity, and to waiting, as she always had, for Joe Barton to come home and claim her.

She finished her food and screwed up the paper bag, sucked hard on her straw, aiming for the final mouthful of milk and making a loud slurping noise that had the man at the next table looking up at her and laughing. She laughed back.

It was time to head back to Madi's flat and wrap up her mum's present. She'd found her a lovely silky square scarf, in a swirl of purples and reds, which reminded her, in some crazy way, of Madi's décor. It was just the sort of big bold scarf that her mum would never have bought for herself, especially if she had seen the price tag, but would love anyway. And it would be easy to fold and wrap, and light enough not to cost the earth to post. Time to break the mould and be spontaneous, unexpected, surprising. She liked the idea of that. A new, surprising Prue Harris.

She spent the evening transferring her most recent photos onto the laptop and editing them, cropping and trying out various effects and filters, until she was happy enough to choose one as her new desktop background, and to earmark another couple for a competition she had been thinking of entering.

Tired from all the walking, and with her shoulders aching from carrying so many bags and hunching over a screen, she closed the software down and decided to get ready for bed, but not before trying on her purchases again. Yes, she had given in to another pair of dark blue jeans, a couple of plain T-shirts, and a pack of M&S undies, because she needed them for practical, day-to-day life, but she had bought a few other things too. Things that she would definitely call surprising. A long skirt with an uneven hankie-shaped hem that skimmed her knees at the front and almost reached her ankles at the back. A bright red top with zips on the shoulders – she had never worn anything quite so red! A pair of soft brown leather trousers which she was on the verge of convincing herself to take back in the morning until she realised how much of a rebel they made her feel, and that being a rebel was a whole new experience she felt suddenly ready to embrace.

Curled on the sofa and back in her cosy pyjamas, she put her romance novel aside and started on a psychological thriller, the tension building up as she turned each page until she worried that the dark and disturbing images it was conjuring up in her mind were getting a little too scary and might keep her awake. A cup of tea, a couple of slices of toast and a comedy programme on TV soon settled her thoughts back to normal levels, and she took herself off to bed with no further thoughts of Joe or Luke, just Madi's mystery man gazing down at her from the photo frame beside the bed as she turned off the light. There was something about his face that seemed familiar. Something about the eyes, although it was impossible to tell if they were brown or blue. If only it had been a clearer image, better focused, or even in colour, she just might be able to work out why she thought she recognised him.

When she woke, later than usual, the sun was already slanting its way in through a gap in the curtains. She pulled them back and looked out over the small garden down below. Somehow, what with the typical chilly March weather and her being out and about during the daytime, she still hadn't found her way down there to investigate, but the wonky wooden bench still stood there beneath the tree, looking for all the world as if nobody ever used it. Maybe today she could try sitting outside for a while. If she wore her coat and took a hot drink with her, she might manage an hour or so reading in the fresh air. It was the thing she missed the most in winter, that daily dose of warmth on her skin as she sat and listened to the birds and lost herself in a good book.

She never had identified what the third key on Madi's keyring was for, and was banking on it opening a back door or a gate somewhere downstairs that would lead her out to the garden. Unless, of course, it wasn't communal land at all, but belonged to one of the ground-floor residents. In which case, she would go out to that little park where she'd fed the birds and read there instead.

She dressed warmly, ate a leisurely breakfast and then took her mum's present down the road to the post office. She had been right about the weather. There was a definite change for the better. She checked for post in the box in the hall on her way back, found nothing, then ran up both flights of stairs to make herself a coffee and collect her book.

Within minutes she was back at the foot of the stairs. Just as she had hoped, there was a small door hidden away in a corner behind the staircase, and the key fitted. The hinges creaked as if, just like the garden itself, the door was rarely used. Stepping through, clutching her mug and with her book tucked under her arm, she found herself standing in a shaded concrete side alleyway badly in need of a sweep, with a smattering of discarded cigarette ends around its edges. A crazy-paving path led around a corner to the back of the building and out onto the grass, which was going brown in places and was full of weeds. Prue wondered who was responsible for looking after it, or if nobody bothered. It certainly hadn't been tackled for a while, and there was nowhere obvious to store a lawnmower or any garden tools.

She stepped back and closed the door behind her, retraced her steps along the path, then picked her way across the grass to the bench. Even though she was at the back of the building, she had been overly optimistic to have expected peace and quiet and the tweeting of birds. The traffic hummed and roared in the background. The bench was solid enough, but was littered with fallen leaves and encrusted with bird droppings, so at least she knew there were birds, somewhere. She put her coffee and book down on the edge of the path, took a tissue from her coat pocket, and did her best to clear a space to sit down.

It was such a shame that everything had been left untended. Yet this could be a lovely little haven in the middle of a bustling street if someone took the time to work on it. It wouldn't take a lot. Cutting the grass, killing off the dande-lions, a little trim of the overhanging tree branches, a few more chairs and a table, some shrubs and flowers in pots, a little bird feeder hanging from the tree . . .

But it really wasn't her problem. In another three weeks she would be gone and Madi would be back, and for all she knew Madi was not the type to enjoy gardening or sitting in the sun. Aaron had said she was an actress, so it was highly likely she spent a lot of time away from home anyway. And there were, after all, eight other flats in the building. All those people, including at least one child if the buggy she'd spotted in the hall meant anything at all . . . did none of them care about the outdoor space they were so lucky to have? Somewhere they could sit, chat, read, have a barbecue, kick a ball or watch their kids ride a bike?

Sipping her coffee, which had already gone cold, Prue was so lost in thought that, at first, she didn't hear her name being called.

'Hey, Prue! You going deaf, or just ignoring me?'

She looked up to see Aaron hanging out of the window of the flat below her own and laughing at her.

'Sorry. In a world of my own.'

'Mind if I come down and join you?'

'Course not. It's your garden, not mine.'

The window banged shut and he disappeared from view, bounding out through the garden door a few moments later.

'It's ages since I've been out here,' he said, plonking himself down on the bench beside her.

'Careful. I haven't wiped that bit.'

He lifted his bottom, inspected the seat of his jeans and sat down again. 'Too late to worry now,' he said. 'They're due for a wash anyway! So, you've found our own little Kew Gardens then?'

'Hardly.'

'It is a bit rundown, I suppose.' He looked around it as if he hadn't really noticed before.

'Does nobody ever do anything with it?'

'*With it?*'

'You know, maintain it, look after it, plant anything . . .?'

'Not so you'd notice. All too busy, I guess. Or all waiting for someone else to do it. That's the problem with shared space, isn't it? Like if one of the lightbulbs goes on the landing, or the hall doormat needs a shake. Everyone waits and hopes someone else will take care of it, or that if they leave it long enough it'll somehow happen by magic.'

'And it never does?'

'Oh, there is a sort of part-time caretaker. He's a cousin, I think, or maybe it's a nephew, of the landlord. Comes in a van from time to time and hoovers the stairs, washes the front step, runs a cloth over the banisters, that sort of thing, and the grass gets cut maybe three or four times a year if he remembers to bring the mower and it's not actually raining on the day he comes . . . but day to day we're pretty much left to our own devices. A bit different from your place, I presume?'

'The village, you mean? Well, yes, it's all cottages and houses, no flats, and most people make sure their gardens look neat and their nets are washed, if you know what I mean. There is a certain pride in keeping everything nice.'

'Sounds idyllic. Like something off the lid of an old chocolate box, like the one my mum keeps her buttons in.'

'Does she? My gran used to do that too, but hers were in a biscuit tin. In fact, I've still got it, not that I ever do enough sewing to need buttons, but I can't throw them away.'

'Funny, isn't it? How people can come from totally different backgrounds, but there's always something exactly the same?'

'We're all the same under the skin, I suppose.' Prue finished her coffee and put her mug down. 'So, not working tonight?'

'No. I decided to take a few days off. I had leave owing and I wanted to be around, and wide awake, to do our river trip.'

'You still want to do that?'

'Of course. You?'

'Sure. I'll be glad of the company.'

'Bodyguard, you mean?'

'Yeah, okay, tease me, why don't you? But there's nothing wrong with wanting to stay safe. A country girl like me, not used to the dangers of city life . . .'

'To be honest, I think I'd be more worried about the dangers of country life. All those winding roads with bloody great tractors trundling towards you, and bees and stinging nettles, not to mention the rampaging bulls.'

'Ha! It's not all like that, I promise you. Not in Shelling anyway.'

'So? How about Saturday then? For the photography lesson. We could head out in the afternoon, before it gets dark, and go down to the embankment. South Bank maybe, watch the entertainers, and the people going by, and the boats, take in a couple of bridges? Go up on the London Eye too, if you fancy it, and take some aerial shots.'

'Not too sure about that. I'm not good with heights. Can't even manage the rollercoaster at the fair.'

'Well, that's heights *and* speed, to be fair, and the Eye's hardly superfast!'

'Well, maybe,' she said, without committing herself either way.

'Oh, go on. Be bold for once. I dare you!'

Prue laughed. 'We'll see.'

'And I know I said it's not a date, but we will need to eat something at some point, if you can bear my company for that long.'

'I'd like that.'

'Right. I'm going now. Out to meet some mates for a drink while I don't have a night shift to worry about, and I'm sure you want to get back to your book. What is it, by the way?' He leaned down and picked the book up from the path. 'Hmm. Thriller, eh? And I had you down as a Mills & Boon kind of a girl.' He stood up and dropped the book into her lap. 'See you Saturday. I'll come up and knock for you. Five-ish okay?'

Prue nodded and watched him walk away. Mills & Boon? All hearts and flowers, and hunky heroes. Was that really the image she gave off? She felt a bit insulted until she remembered she had actually been reading a romance not too dissimilar to that just the other day. Nothing wrong with romance though, as long as she saw it for what it was. An escape, a fantasy. She was only too aware that real life wasn't much like the way things were depicted in mushy novels. It didn't always come with happy endings, for a start.

Chapter 17

MADI

'And how is our Flo this afternoon?'

Since word had got around Madi had had a constant stream of callers, asking after everyone's favourite little cat and offering what help they could, including twice-daily visits from the young vet Ralph to administer Flo's meds and check on her progress. This time it was Tom Bishop from next door, standing on her front step, carrying a box of Jaffa Cakes and a tin of tuna.

'Much better, thank you. She's up on my bed, having a nap.' She nodded towards the box in his hand. 'But I'm not sure cats eat Jaffa Cakes.'

'Oh, no. The tuna's for Flo. Nice and soft, while her gums are still sore. The cakes . . . well, they're for you. Well, actually I was hoping you might like to share them with me, over a pot of tea . . .'

Madi laughed. 'I know. Just having you on. Come on in.' She went into the kitchen to fill the kettle, and Tom followed. 'So, how are things? How's your wife doing?'

149

'No change. But then, there never is really. But how are you? I see you're . . .' He gestured towards her head.

'Not wearing my wig? No, I've decided to brave it out, be the real me, while I'm indoors at least.'

'Good girl. That's the right attitude. And may I say that it did you no favours, that wig. You look much better . . . more natural, more real . . . without it.'

'Thanks, but you didn't see me when I was totally bald. As a coot, as they say. Not a pretty sight anyway, I can assure you. But now my hair's starting to grow back, I'm feeling a lot more positive. Things can only get better.'

'They can indeed. And are *you* better? You didn't say a lot before, about your illness, your treatment. Cancer, I'm assuming, and chemo. Is it gone now? The cancer? For good?'

'No one can ever promise that, but it's looking hopeful, yes. Should be able to think about getting back to work when I go home.'

Tom took the tea she handed him and they moved across to sit at opposite ends of the sofa. 'And is that what you want? To work? I'd have thought maybe you'd like to do something different now. You know, take a world cruise or do a bungee jump or something. One of those life-affirming, getting-your-life-back moments you read about people doing. Or just take it easy and enjoy being alive?'

'I am taking it easy, while I'm here, but I can't do nothing for ever. Work is all I know.'

'And that's a good thing? Doesn't sound like a very good reason to go straight back to it. Not to me. How old are you, Madi, if you don't mind me asking?'

'Not something I could keep secret if I tried, in my profession. A quick internet search would tell you all you wanted to know, right down to my shoe size, even my bra size, I shouldn't wonder, although that won't work in quite the same way it did before, will it? One cup or two!' She smiled, feeling proud of herself at being able to make jokes about it all, and after a moment's hesitation Tom smiled with her. 'I'm sixty-two,' she went on, coming back to his question. 'Not quite ready for the scrap heap just yet.'

'I wasn't suggesting you were! But certainly young enough to live out a few dreams. Tell me, what have you always wanted to do?'

Madi shrugged. 'Act.'

'Oh, come on. You've already done that, a thousand times over. Nothing left to prove. What else?'

'Learn to swim.' Madi sipped at her tea and took a Jaffa Cake from the packet Tom had just opened and waved in front of her. 'Something I never got around to. And see the pyramids, I suppose. Finish a *Times* crossword without cheating. Be a better mother . . .'

'And what's been stopping you?'

'From what?'

'From doing all those things? There are lots of swimming classes for beginners, for older people, even women-only classes if that's your bag. And we're not far from the sea here. What's to stop us going for a splash right now, if we wanted to?'

'It would be freezing!'

'True. Maybe not the sea then, or not today anyway. But

the pyramids? A holiday to Egypt? How hard can that be to arrange? Plenty of specialist singles tour operators out there if you're worried about going on your own. And what better time to perfect your crossword skills than on a long lazy holiday? Or buy a book to help you learn. As for the better mother thing . . .'

'That's the one I really can't do much about, isn't it? I was a poor mother while my son was growing up, and now I'm paying for it. I haven't seen him, or spoken to him, in months.'

'And why is that?' Tom offered her another Jaffa Cake and she took it, nibbling at the edges so she could save the orange filling until last. 'Because it's never too late, you know. You need to fix these things while you still can. There might come a day when you realise your chance has gone. When something happens to him, or to you . . .'

'You're talking about your wife?'

'Exactly. Not that we had any unresolved arguments to settle, but you never know when it might be the last time you see each other or spend time together, being happy, enjoying a normal life . . . the last time it's possible to say what you want to say and know it's been heard and under-stood. You always think there will be another day, another opportunity, and then suddenly there isn't.'

'Yes, I could have died, I know that, but I didn't want to burden George with my illness. He has troubles of his own. They couldn't have children. Or he couldn't, apparently. And his marriage was breaking up. Probably has by now.'

'Even more reason to talk. Sounds to me like you stopped communicating just when you needed each other the most.'

'And what advice could I give him? About hanging on to a relationship, making a marriage work? I never married. His father was married to someone else. Hardly role models, were we? And my only pregnancy happened by accident.'

'We all make mistakes. No son should judge his mother because of something she did, or didn't do, years ago, before he was even born. It's what you do now that matters.'

'And what is that exactly? Rock up at George's door with one boob, no hair, and say I'm sorry with a bunch of flowers? His wife was . . . is . . . desperate for a baby. They found it difficult, impossible. I think, in the end, that future non-existent baby she couldn't get out of her head meant more to her than he did, and she's probably already found herself a conveniently fertile bloke to give her what my George couldn't. And then she'll dump him, when she's got what she wanted, just like she's dumped George. The power of the maternal urge, eh? Another thing I'm not qualified to understand.'

'You're very hard on yourself, Madi. And on her. Do you know that?'

'I'm a cynic, Tom. People do what they have to do, to get what they need. Look after number one. It's what I did for all those years, palming my only child off on my parents. I always thought it would be just for a while, that I'd come back and be a real mum, that we'd fall into each other's arms and live happily ever after, but then I'd get offered another show, a leading role in a play . . . Like you said earlier, you never know when it's going to be too late, do you? When the chance to put things right has gone by? Maybe she'll go back to him. George's wife, Jessica. Maybe she'll get pregnant by someone else and he'll take her back, take the baby on, because he loves her and it's what she wants more than anything, and because it's the only way he can ever be a dad . . .'

'Madi, you don't know if any of this is true. What about IVF? Adoption? There are any number of solutions that don't involve her sleeping with some random stranger. Their marriage was under strain obviously, but you don't even know if it's definitely over. Or why. Anything could have happened in the months since you last spoke to your son. A reconciliation. Counselling. Medical intervention. A miracle conception, even. And you'll never know unless you make that first move and break the ice.'

'I did try. Just the other night. I tried to call but it went to answerphone.'

'And? What message did you leave?'

'I didn't. I chickened out.'

Tom sighed. 'Oh, Madi, what am I going to do with you? You know, if he was here, your George, I'd bash your stubborn heads together. Still, there's only so much nagging I can do. The rest is up to you, so I'll back off now and we'll change the subject. Have another Jaffa Cake before I eat the lot, and let's check on Flo, shall we? It is what I'm supposed to have come round for. Feeling poorly or not, I bet if we open this tuna, the smell will have her down those stairs like a shot!'

Flo appeared, right on cue, as soon as the tin was opened.

'She knows which side her bread's buttered!' Tom said, draining off the liquid and forking the fishy contents into a saucer. 'What a life, eh? A comfy bed, a sunny garden, her own entry door, not to mention people falling over themselves to come and visit her, and even her own personal physician on call. This cat is pampered to within an inch of her life!'

'Sounds pretty idyllic, when you put it like that.'

'She's certainly on the mend, isn't she? Do you think maybe you could bear to leave her for a few hours later and join me for a meal? Oh, only local. The Brown Cow do a fantastic steak and kidney pie. Best for miles around. Chips or mash, a pile of peas, homemade gravy. What more could you ask for?'

Madi hesitated. She had been meaning to give the village pub a try ever since she'd arrived, but somehow she hadn't got around to it yet. The thought of all those regulars sitting at the bar, their eyes turning in her direction as she walked in alone, hovered at the back of her mind. Silly really, for an actress used to being watched by strangers, to feel almost shy about drinking or dining alone. She'd done it often enough before, but going with Tom, having a companion to sit and chat with over a meal in a quiet corner, sounded wonderful. The trouble was, he was a married man. She knew, better than anyone, where a relationship like that could lead. The trouble it could cause. And what would the locals have to say about it, she wondered?

'I don't know, Tom. Your wife . . .'

'Barbara has nothing to do with this, Madi. Look, I'm not asking you out in a romantic way. Friends, okay? You're away from home, away from work, and you spend your days, and your evenings, in this cottage by yourself. I think you might be lonely. I know I am. Nothing more.'

'You're right, of course. I just wouldn't want anyone to get the wrong idea.'

'As long as *we* have the right idea, it's none of anyone else's business, is it? I don't hold with village gossip. It can be hard to avoid listening to it sometimes, but I don't create it, or abide by it. It's my life, and my Barbara would want me to live it, and enjoy it, while I can. So, are you coming, or not?' He winked at her. 'Could be your last chance. My hurt pride just might mean that I never ask again.'

Madi took her time deciding what to wear. Tom was a married man, a friend, and this was not a date. She kept telling herself that, trying to convince herself that dressing up was not necessary, that Tom would not be expecting her to look overly glamorous, just for an evening eating pie and mash in a small village pub. Not that she had the sort of clothes with her to create a glam look even if she wanted to. No, trousers it would have to be, and a nice top. Just a hint of make-up, and she would discard her flat shoes for the one good pair of heels she had brought with her. She stood in front of the bedroom mirror and toyed with the idea of not wearing the wig, putting it on and then taking it off again several times. Tom had said she looked better without it, but she knew he had only said that to boost her confidence. Her half an inch of pale stubble might look okay when sitting at home sipping tea, but out for a meal? No, she would feel more like her old self with a decent head of hair. Long hair. It would make it less likely that she might be stared at, talked about, pitied.

He arrived right on time, ignoring the doorbell and tapping gently on the glass in the front door. He was wearing jeans. Good, very dark, blue jeans, with a leather belt looped through at the waist and a crisp white shirt tucked in, open at the neck. She was so glad she hadn't forced herself into a dress. This was *not* a date, and keeping things casual started with looking and feeling casual. So far, so good. She saw him looking at her head, but he said nothing, just smiled and nodded, making it clear that the choice was up to her. So far, even better.

He took her arm as they walked down the lane, tucking it carefully into his own.

'There's sometimes a singer, on a Saturday night,' he said. 'I rang to book us a table, in case they're busy, but I didn't think to ask.'

'That would be nice, if there is. I'm looking forward to the meal anyway, with or without, but I do like a bit of entertainment.'

He laughed. 'I should think you do, in your line of work. Ever done any yourself? Singing, I mean. Musicals maybe?'

'I'm no singer, believe me. I did try it out, at drama school, as we all did. Tried a bit of everything actually. Comedy, tragedy, mime, dance . . .'

'But you settled on straight acting?'

'It's where my heart is, I suppose. Not that I don't enjoy an occasional go at something lighter, hence my ill-fated foray into soap for a while, but I prefer something challenging. And the older I get, the more I'm offered the more interesting parts. You know, the sinister old woman, the evil murderer, the old battle-axe. I even played a female King Lear once. A rather modern version, obviously! But singing? No.'

The pub was warm and noisy and packed with people as they pushed open the door and Tom led the way to the bar.

There were paintings of all shapes and sizes on the white-washed walls, all of which appeared to depict cattle or horses or sheep, and there were long red candles in waxy wine bottles on the tables, and a real fire glowing in the grate.

'What would you like to drink?' Tom asked, having to raise his voice above the hubbub. 'Or would you rather go straight to the table and order a bottle of wine?'

'Wine, I think. But just a glass. My pills . . .'

'Righto.' He spoke to the girl behind the bar and Madi saw her check her reservations book before picking up two menus and leading them to a small table in the far corner.

'Thanks, Sally,' Tom said, waving the waitress away and pulling Madi's chair out for her to sit down. 'I chose this one because it's nicely tucked away, so we have more chance of hearing each other speak. And you get a good view of the garden too, with the fairy lights on. A few hardy folk do go and eat out there, under the canopy, even at this time of year. Probably so they can smoke, of course, but at least they can do it in pretty surroundings.'

Madi picked up her menu and studied it. 'I thought you said pie!' she said. 'I'd imagined a choice of maybe two or three pub staples, but I didn't expect this. There's more choice here than you'd see at a lot of top London restaurants. Crab, mussels, venison, black turkey – I'm intrigued to know what that is – and roast lamb . . .'

'All good local fare, Madi. You can't live off the land and be this close to the sea without benefiting from the freshest, best-tasting local food going. Please don't tell me you've been eating all that frozen and tinned stuff Patty sells in the shop. What a travesty! I must introduce you to a fantastic butcher I know. Brings his meat over in a van. To Shelling and all the other villages around, twice a week, so you don't even have to go to him. And his turkeys are something else . . . well, they're pretty much our national dish around here! I know you probably can't eat a whole one, but I'm always willing to come over and share. In the interests of not wasting good food, obviously. As for the lamb . . . well, you must have noticed all the fields of fluffy little white sheep around these parts.'

'Oh, don't. I don't like to think about that. Give them a face or a name, and I have an almost immediate urge to turn vegetarian.'

'Well, don't do it tonight!'

'I won't, I promise. Now, what do you recommend?'

'The pie. Like I told you when I invited you to join me, it's the best.'

'Really? With all this choice, you're going for pie?'

'Always been my favourite, a good steak and kidney. And since my Barbara isn't able to make it for me any more, the Brown Cow version is the next best thing. I'll probably have the spotted dick after as well. With custard.'

'You're thinking about pudding already?'

'I like to plan ahead, Madi. Know what it is I'm leaving enough room for.'

'In that case . . .' Madi turned the menu over and studied the desserts list. 'I'm going to leave room for a chocolate fudge sundae.'

'Atta girl!'

* * *

159

The evening flew by. Tom had been wrong about the singer, who never did materialise, but that just made it easier to talk, which they did, in abundance.

They were struggling with the final mouthfuls of dessert, Tom loosening his belt by a notch and Madi glad she'd picked trousers with a hidden elasticated section of waistband at the sides, so useful with her weight fluctuating up and down as it had in recent months, when Tom reached out a hand to stop someone passing by on his way to the gents.

'Hello, Ken,' he said. 'Long time no see.'

The man stopped and grinned. 'What? All of three days, you mean? Didn't spot you tucked away over here or I'd have been over to say hello sooner. Never have liked drinking alone.'

'Alone? Ken, you know just about everyone in here. Don't you pretend you've been sitting on your own sobbing into a pint! Madi, let me introduce you to Ken Barton, an old buddy of mine, who, despite what he might have you believe, has a million friends and likes to make up a good story.'

'Not so much of the old. You're a good five years older than me, remember? Nice to meet you, Madi. The lady staying at Prue's, I assume?' He held out his hand and shook hers firmly. 'I've heard all about you from my son Ralph. The vet.'

'Oh, of course. He's been so incredibly kind, looking after little Flo.'

'He's a good lad. Sensible head on his shoulders. Can I buy you both a drink? A coffee maybe, and a brandy to go in it?'

Madi made to object but held her tongue. What harm could a drop of brandy do? A little of what you fancy . . .

Ken returned a few minutes later, with a drink in his hand and another man in tow.

'Madi, this is Stuart.' Tom did the introductions as Ken pulled up a couple of spare chairs. 'Ralph's business partner and fellow vet, and of course young Prue's dad. And one of those many drinking friends our Ken here swears he doesn't have!'

'Pleased to meet you, my dear. Not often we get any new faces around here.' Stuart sat down heavily and turned his chair to face her. 'And my wife tells me you're quite famous. Star of stage and screen, I hear.'

'A huge exaggeration!' Madi could feel herself reddening. Her hand went to her hair, as if to check it was still there. 'But where is Faith tonight? Not with you?'

'Oh, she and her friend Patty are up at the village hall. Well, it's more of a large wooden shack, to tell you the truth. Still, it serves its purpose well enough. Big enough to squeeze us all in when needed, although it can get mighty chilly in there, with no proper heating system. They're getting set up for one of their W.I. events tomorrow. It's one of those produce affairs where women flaunt their best fruitcakes and daffodils and what have you. I'm sure half the competitors buy the stuff in Tesco's and pass it off as their own, but it's all good fun, isn't it? They even have men's categories nowadays. Supposed to bring in a cake made with apples, or a homemade wine. Stuff and nonsense. You won't find me in the kitchen. And I prefer the real deal myself.' He lifted the glass of whisky he'd brought over with him and downed it in one.

'Well, I always enter. I've made a lovely mango wine this

year. From pulp in a tin, obviously. We don't grow a lot of mangoes around here! You should pop along there, Madi,' Ken chipped in. 'Starts around twelve. I believe. You might enjoy it. Being as it's fine weather, and Mother's Day as well, there should be a good turnout. Bring your coat though. As I say, it can get a bit draughty. They do lunches too, and a mean cream tea, at the back of the hall, with scones and all. Worth going, just for that.'

Madi sat back, savouring the brandy-laced coffee the waitress had just delivered to the table, and listened to the three old friends chatting. Having just told Tom about her time playing King Lear had put her in mind of some unusual cross-gender castings and it was not difficult to imagine them as the three witches from Macbeth, heads close together, hubbling and bubbling away nineteen to the dozen.

Mother's Day! She had temporarily forgotten about that. Well, she wouldn't be getting anything from George this year, that was for sure. If he had even thought of sending a card, it would be at the flat, stuck in the tray in the hall, unless Prue had already sent it on. And that meant she wouldn't see it until at least Monday or Tuesday. No, she might as well go along to the hall and support the local produce show. It would kill two birds with one stone as well, as she still hadn't sampled Faith's famous Victoria sponge cake, which she felt sure would be on offer, and probably taking pride of place among the winning entries.

Chapter 18

PRUE

The lights twinkled on the water as Prue and Aaron stood side by side in the pod and the Eye rose up and over in a wide, slowly circling arc, so slowly in fact that Prue could hardly detect any movement at all.

'See. I told you it was worth doing,' Aaron said, skipping over to the other side to get a better look at the Houses of Parliament and Big Ben, the tower still enveloped in scaffolding while its restoration works went ahead. 'Nothing to make you feel sick. Just brilliant views. Lots of things to take photos of, right?'

She had to agree that any initial reservations had been totally unfounded, and this was indeed a great vantage point from which to see London in a whole different way. Her camera had hardly left its position clamped to her eye since they'd set off.

'It's great. Thanks.'

'What for?'

'Being my guide. Looking after me.'

'You don't need looking after, just pointing in the right direction.'

'Maybe.' She spotted someone walking on the embankment below, dressed from head to toe in garish yellow tartan, trying to keep his kilt down in the wind, and she couldn't resist taking a few sneaky close-ups with her zoom. That image would make a wonderful greetings card, if only she was any good at writing funny captions.

'Heard anything from home?' Aaron asked, following her gaze and laughing at what he saw.

'Just a thank-you text from my mum. For her present. Not that she was meant to open it until tomorrow, but that's what she's like. Can't resist delving straight in. No patience. She did try calling earlier but I only have the phone on for a little while at a time so I must have missed the call.'

'Why?'

'Why what?'

'Why don't you keep your phone on? I never turn mine off, unless the battery dies.'

'Ah, but I'm trying to escape from people, not leave myself open to them morning, noon and night. I want to be in some sort of control. Who I talk to, and when.'

'This is about your ex, I guess?'

'Got it in one. The last thing I need is Joe Barton calling me, thinking he can get hold of me whenever he wants to, messing with my head.'

'Is that what he does? Messes with your head?'

'I'm beginning to think that's all he's ever done. Telling me how special I am one minute, then cold as a bloody fridge the next . . .'

'The man's a prat. Not worth thinking about.'

'Oh, believe me, I am trying, really hard, not to think about him.'

'And succeeding?'

'Most of the time.'

'It's his loss, you know. He was probably regretting your break-up as soon as it happened.'

'Oh, I don't think so. But let's not have any more talk about Joe, okay?'

'Okay. How about you then? Prue. Where does that name come from? I don't think I've ever met a Prue before.'

'Short for Prudence. As in careful, which I suppose I am. My mum's called Faith, and my gran was Verity, meaning truth. All good, old-fashioned, God-fearing names. A family tradition.'

'I like them. All of them.'

'Well, Aaron's pretty Biblical too, isn't it?'

'Sure is. Although not in my case. I was actually named after my mum's favourite auntie, Nora. Spelt backwards, see? Or as close as she could get it and still end up with a real name. Would have been so much easier if I had been born a girl!' He gazed out across the sparkling water. 'So what names do you have lined up for your own kids? And don't tell me you haven't thought about it. Most people have. You girls, especially. Like knowing what sort of wedding dress you want to wear before you've even met the right bloke.'

'We do not!'

'Okay then. For the first time, as you've never given it a moment's thought before, what names would you choose?'

'Boy or girl?'

'Both.'

Prue pretended to ponder the question, although she did, just as he'd suggested, already know the answer. 'I've always liked Bobby, actually. For a boy, or with an i at the end for a girl. But that probably had a lot to do with it sounding good with Barton after it. Now I'm never going to be Mrs Barton, I may have to think again.'

'Oh, good grief. I was right! You have been planning it for ever! And I thought the wedding-dress thing before you're even engaged was bad enough, but choosing baby names to fit with your potential, possible, might-not-ever-happen, future surname . . . that's crazy.'

'I suppose it is. Maybe that's what I am. Or was. Crazy.'

'More like blinkered, or stuck in a rut. Blimey, Prue, did you ever do anything in life that didn't revolve around this Joe character? Whatever happened to having a life of your own?'

'I do have a life of my own. A cottage, a job . . .'

'The cottage was handed to you on a plate, and the job bores you rigid but pays the bills. Hardly earth-shattering stuff. No wild thoughts about travelling the world, or going up in a hot-air balloon?'

'I told you I'm scared of heights. And that includes flying.'

'So you did. And may I remind you that you are currently hanging four hundred feet above London in nothing but a glass bubble? What about an adventure? Like zipping round a track in a racing car?'

Prue shuddered. 'God, no. That sounds just as bad as a rollercoaster. I don't do speed.'

'Is there anything just a tiny bit scary that you would

consider doing? It's great for the rush it gives you, you know, that flash of fear!'

'Sorry, Aaron, but I'm strictly a two-feet-firmly-on-the-ground sort of a girl. I'll tell you what I'll do though, to prove I'm up for a challenge. Find me some jellied eels or one of those East End cockle and whelk stalls I've heard so much about and I'll try one, okay?'

'Just the one?'

'Well, I might not like it.'

'Prue, you are such a daredevil! And I'm not sure there's a lot of that stuff about these days. I think you might be basing your ideas of London cuisine on something you've read in one of your books. Set in Victorian times, by the sound of it. How about cod and chips if you're after something fishy? Not exactly caught in the Thames, but will that do you? And if you're really serious about trying something a bit racy, we can ask for a pickled egg on the side.'

She couldn't help but giggle. Aaron might be a lot younger than her, and there was absolutely no romantic spark between them, but he *got* her. He shared her sense of humour and he wasn't afraid to poke fun at her. In just a few days she felt as if she knew him almost as well as she knew herself, and a whole lot better than she had ever known Joe Barton. Why couldn't Joe have been more like Aaron? More open, more fun, more real?

As their pod reached ground level, they stepped out and headed along the embankment and up the steps to Westminster Bridge. Leaning on the stone wall, Prue aimed her camera at the boats moving through the water below, clicking quickly

167

to record a sequence of shots taken just seconds apart. 'There might only be one good one among this lot,' she said. 'That's the beauty of digital. No wasted film. Try as often as you like to capture the perfect image and just delete the rest.'

'Maybe that's what you should have been doing with your men.'

'What men?'

'Exactly. Just homing in on the one was always going to be a gamble, wasn't it?'

'Two. I've had two boyfriends, I'll have you know.'

'Right. Sorry. But two? Really, Prue? You should have gone out with loads of them by now. Played the field a bit, tested the water. You know, try before you buy. It's what I've always done, not that I'm in any hurry to find The One, but it's fun looking, and I'm pretty sure it's the only way to recognise perfection when it finally arrives. Then you can just delete the rest! And that includes that loser Joe.'

Prue knew he was joking, but she had to admit he was probably right. She was twenty-four and she had had precisely two boyfriends. One a best friend she had hoped for more from but it had never been offered, and the other, if she was honest about it, probably nothing more than an exciting experiment, to test herself, to see what it would be like with someone else. Dating, kissing, sex . . .

She shook her head, trying to dislodge the image of Joe, on the few occasions they had slept together, his pale face next to hers on the pillow, his clothes neatly folded on the chair by the bed, his shoes lined up in parallel with his socks tucked inside, the kiss on the top of her head as he crept away early in the morning. Like an old married couple, following a routine, going through the motions. Her inheriting her own place, and him moving out of his dad's, should have given them all the chances they needed to be alone together, to make the most of each other, but it hadn't happened. Nothing had changed. There had always been something hesitant about Joe, always something missing, but she had been too naïve, too trusting, too needy, to work out what it was. But she knew now. Looking back, and with this newly permanent distance stretching out between them, she knew what had been missing. It was passion. Raw, uncontrollable passion. The sort she had read about in novels, seen in films, had glimpsed very briefly on those sexy hotel weekends away with Luke. But she hadn't loved Luke. He had taken possession of her body for a while and brought it to life but hadn't quite reached her heart. And passion didn't really work without love. Perhaps the perfect man, if he existed somewhere, would give her both . . .

'Come on, dreamy. Let's go and find something to eat, shall we?'

'What? Oh, yes, let's.' She hooked her arm through his as he led her off down the street. 'Not fish and chips though. I fancy something more . . . exotic.'

'Pizza?'

'Yes please. That sounds perfect.'

'I've been thinking about your garden.'

'What garden?' Aaron swallowed the last strip of stuffed crust and wiped his mouth on the back of his hand. 'Oh, you mean that scrappy lump of old grass out the back of the flats. What about it?'

'Haven't you ever wanted to do something with it? Smarten it up a bit? We're coming into spring now, warmer weather, sunny afternoons. It's somewhere you could sit, read, get some air, a tan . . .'

'Never really thought about it. I live a fairly nocturnal life, remember? I'm asleep most of the time the sun's up.'

'You make yourself sound like some kind of vampire! How about the other residents? Your mum?'

'Dunno. I suppose they might make use of it, if it was there, all prettified, but sorting it out looks like hard work to me. I'm not sure any of them would be up for that.'

'Wouldn't your mum like it though? It would be a great Mother's Day gift.'

'What? Me, cutting the grass for her? By tomorrow? Not quite the same as a nice bunch of roses and a box of Milk Tray, is it?'

'Start a garden for her this Mother's Day and you could be picking her flowers from it by the next one!'

'Ha! I don't think so. I work in a supermarket, remember. I can get whatever I want to give her, all ready made, and with staff discount . . .'

'It was just a thought.'

'And a good one, but I'm no gardener, and neither is my mum, much as I think she might have liked to be.'

'I still haven't met your mum, by the way. Not even just passing on the stairs. I don't even know her name.'

'It's Suzy. And she doesn't go out much.'

'What does she do? Work-wise, I mean.'

'Telephone stuff, from home. Nothing too exciting, but it suits her.'

'You should bring her up to me one day for a coffee and a chat.'

'Yeah, maybe. Not to talk her into some sneaky weeding and planting plan though. We have a bloke who comes to do that sort of thing, remember? Well, maintenance generally, like I told you, not that he does a lot out there. Simon, I think he's called. Why don't you catch him next time he's round and see what he says? To be honest, I don't even know if we've got a spade anywhere. He carts it all about with him in the van. What is all this about anyway? You'll be gone in a couple of weeks, so why bother?'

'I just thought it might be nice, that's all. To make a difference, leave something behind, you know. To remember me by.'

'In other words, you're bored. You're looking for something to do.'

'You could be right. I like green things. Gardens, trees, plants. I like being outdoors. Walking Mum's dog. Photographing the wildlife. Fields are my thing!'

'Well, that so-called garden of ours is a bit small to be classed as a field, but I'm not going to stop you, if you want to have a go. And I will remember you, by the way. When you've gone. I won't need a garden for that, believe me.'

'Thanks, Aaron.'

'You're welcome.'

'So, where to next?'

'Isn't it getting a bit late for a country bumpkin like you? When you've got to be up for the milking?'

'Oh, very funny. No, I want to make the most of it while I'm here. Noise. Bright lights. Stuff . . . going on. There'll be plenty of time for the quiet life and early nights when I get back home, believe me.'

'Okay. What about some fruit machines then? Noisy and bright enough for you? We'll see if I can make a gambler of you.'

She laughed, pulling out the linings of her coat pockets to show they were empty. 'When you don't have it, you can't lose it. Get me a bag of pennies and I'll be happy as can be.'

'Oh, I do like a cheap date. But are you? Happy, I mean?'

'Never happier.' She leaned across the table and kissed him, lightly, on the cheek. His skin was rough with the beginnings of stubble, and he smelled of soap and tomato sauce. 'So what are we waiting for? Let's go and make a killing.'

'Fifty pence says I win more than you.'

'You're on.'

Chapter 19

I *don't like not knowing where she is, or when she's coming back.*
There are still so many things I need to know; things only
she can tell me. I just have to work out when, and how – and
if – she is ever going to do that. But why should she? Unless I
can find a way to make her.

It's not easy looking for clues. Alone in the dark, padding
about with bare feet, not wanting to leave any trace. What would
I expect to find anyway? It's not as if I need evidence. She was
the one. I know that now, only too well.

But I've done it again anyway. Crept in here, while the place
is empty. The girl went out, and I came in. At least the nights
fall early at this time of the year. Darkness and silence cover
my tracks.

This is her territory, her space, and being here gives me a
special sense of satisfaction. Keep the enemy close, that's what
they say. And while she's away . . . well, she's never going to
know, is she? Until I decide to tell her.

The flowers have gone, but there are necklaces, lying neatly,
side by side, in a tray. Not in their usual tangle. As if she's sorted
through them, rearranged them. Deciding what to take with her,

perhaps, and what to leave behind? One by one I pick them up, run my fingers over the chains. I can't help wondering where they came from. Whether he bought her this one, or that one? All of them? None of them?

I've never done it before. I've rearranged things, hidden things, even turned on a tap once, but I've never taken anything away. But this time, I will. Just the one. She won't miss it. Not one, among so many. And if she does, she'll tell herself she's lost it, put it down somewhere and forgotten where, the way she so often does. Especially since I've been playing my little games. Working my magic. She'll expect it to turn up again, but it won't. Not this time.

I have so little that was his. I'm just taking something back, that's all.

I pick up a thin chain, with what feels like a pearl hanging from it. I lift it to my face, feel its roundness against my skin, its smoothness. He used to say I was precious, his pearl, his little gem. I thought then that it meant he loved me best. More than anyone. I believed I was the centre of his world.

No, not this one. Not the pearl. I lay it down again. He would never have bought her a pearl. He knew how much that would have hurt me. It would be too cruel, and he was never deliberately cruel.

But this next one . . . a locket. Thick, flat, oval. I wonder what's inside. His picture? A lock of his hair? Or nothing to do with him at all? I try to prise it open with my fingernail. Whatever it holds, I will remove it, destroy it or keep it, depending on what it might turn out to be, leave her just an empty shell. But it's locked tight, holding its secrets close. I take it anyway.

Whatever it contains, it will be precious to her. That's what lockets are for, holding the mementoes, the memories you want to cling to, the ones you never want to lose. But she didn't even take it with her. That's how little he means to her now. Left on a cupboard, lost in a pile of tat. She didn't have to take him from me. She robbed me, and now I am robbing her. I slip the chain over my head, around my neck, clasp it to my skin. Her loss, my gain. It feels good to turn things around that way, to turn the tables, take something from her for a change.

Men let us down, don't they? I know that only too well. They make promises, they give and they take away. But it's usually a woman behind the betrayal, a woman who leads them on, leads them astray, makes them do it.

I hate you, Madalyn Cardew. All the years I have been without him I didn't know who to hate, and now I do. Slowly, drip by drip, I will make you suffer. You have to pay for what you've done.

Chapter 20

MADI

Madi stood on the step and watched the villagers piling out of the lane that led down from the church and turning towards the cottage, heading for the hall beyond. She had thought about joining them for the service, perhaps sitting quietly at the back, but she'd chickened out at the last minute. Religion never had been her thing. Now she pulled the front door shut behind her and hurried down the path to catch up with Faith and Patty as they rushed past, ahead of the pack.

'Oh, Madi, how lovely! Are you coming to the Shelling Show? We can always use an extra pair of hands.'

'Leave the poor woman alone,' Stuart chipped in, coming along behind them. 'She's here as a visitor, a guest, not to help you two make the tea!'

'Oh, I don't mind at all. I'm usually happier with something to do.'

'And how's our little Flo this morning? I keep meaning to drop by with a bit of fish or something.' Faith slowed her pace a fraction and put a hand on Madi's arm. 'I do feel bad that we've left you to take care of her. I had half a mind to ring Prue and tell her to come home. All this running-off nonsense makes no sense at all. And Flo is her cat . . .'

'There's no need, really. Flo is doing fine, and I don't mind taking care of her. As I said, I like having something to do. And she's company for me.'

'Company? Feeling lonely, are you? We can't have that,' Patty said, pulling a packet of mints from her pocket and offering them round. 'And if it's something to do that you're after, I'm sure we can think of all manner of things to entertain you and keep you out of mischief, can't we, Faith?'

They had reached the door to the village hall and Faith was too busy fumbling in her bag for the keys to reply.

'Take no notice.' It was Tom, already waiting outside with a bottle of wine tucked under his arm and a square cake tin in his hands. He had clearly dodged the church service too. 'They mean well,' he whispered, following the women inside. 'They'll have you manning the library or joining the choir if you're not careful.'

'Oh, God. I have a friend – well, a neighbour really – who works in a library. Betty. The way she talks about it, you'd think it was the most exciting job in the world!'

'Each to their own. And you can always use me as an excuse if they try to rope you into anything you don't fancy. Say we've already arranged something. A drive to the sea, maybe. Which is still on offer, by the way, with or without the swimming. You're not the only one who needs a spot of company every now and then.'

'How is Barbara? You not visiting her today?'

'I probably will later. She'll have the kids there this afternoon, and I don't want to miss seeing them. Might even tempt them back over here for a while later. They can't come often but they won't miss Mother's Day. They're good girls, both of them.' He looked around at the various tables placed around the edges of the hall, read the category cards, and deposited his wine on one table and the cake, which he had now pulled out of its tin, on another.

'They look lovely. Did you make them?'

'Of course. With my own fair hands. Thought I might as well have a go at the men's categories this year. Give old Ken a run for his money. Not that there'll be many entries, but it's a bit of fun, isn't it? And we usually get to taste everything, once the judges have been. You must be sure to try my elderberry wine. Brings hairs to your chest. Or is it tears to your eyes? One or the other!'

I could do with a few new hairs, or just a proper chest, come to that, Madi thought, smiling to herself, but she didn't say it out loud. The last thing she wanted was to make poor Tom feel as if he'd put his foot in it.

Tom went to a small desk that had been set up at the front and paid his entry fees, collected the cards he needed, filled in his name and placed them next to his entries, face downwards.

'The judges only turn them over after they've decided the winners, so it's all anonymous,' he explained. 'Not that I'm likely to be picked, but you never know your luck.'

'I suppose today will be my chance to meet a lot of new people, won't it? Everyone gathered together in one place,

179

taking a peek at the newcomer. I should have put my best wig on.'

'You have more than one?'

'Just joking. Best to make fun of myself. So much better than others doing it for me.'

'Madi, stop it. Nobody is going to make fun of you, with or without the wig. And, for the record, I much preferred seeing you without it.'

'One person at a time isn't so scary, but I'm not quite ready to face the world at large just yet, Tom. Step by step, eh?'

'Whatever you feel comfortable with. Now, let's see if those scones are ready yet, shall we? It's the real reason I've come, you know. Faith's strawberry jam is to die for. And I could murder a cup of tea.'

As people came streaming into the main hall, bearing boxes and bottles and vases, Madi followed Tom through to the small kitchen area where two enormous kettles were already on the boil and Patty was furiously transferring scones from tins to plates and dolloping jam into bowls.

'Not quite ready yet,' Faith trilled. 'Give us five minutes and we'll be open for business.'

'Right-oh.' Tom took Madi's arm and led her through an open doorway and down an alleyway at the side. 'It'll be a madhouse in there for the next half an hour while the exhibits arrive, with everyone vying for the best positions and having a nose at the opposition. Let's wait out in the sunshine for a while, shall we? But tell me if you start to feel cold.'

'Don't worry, I will.' She pulled her collar up around her neck but, despite a breeze that was rustling the leaves, it was really quite pleasant out. In her rush to catch up with the other women, she had left her headscarf at home, but there was nothing quite like a wig to keep things . . . well, she'd like to say warm and snug, but sweaty would be a better description.

There was a small garden area behind the old wooden hall, with a collection of weathered tables and chairs arranged haphazardly on the grass. A couple of fat pigeons rose up from where they had been pecking at the ground and flew away as they approached. 'They'll be back soon enough.' Tom laughed. 'Once we start dropping crumbs.'

Within moments, Patty came flying out too, opening up a folded tablecloth and smoothing it over the nearest table. With her greying hair and white apron, and her arms flapping around like frantic wings, she looked like an over-sized pigeon herself.

'Here, let me help you.' Madi took the pile of linen from under Patty's arm. 'I'm sure you've got lots to be getting on with, and I can do these.'

'Oh, thank you, Madi. Two cream teas, is it? Or I can make you a sandwich, if you prefer.'

'It's okay. You don't have to wait on us.' Tom waved her away. 'I'll come in and order at the counter like everyone else. When we're ready.'

Madi moved around the garden, covering each table with a cloth, then they chose their seats, close to the shelter of the hedge, and sat down. 'She means well.'

'Oh, I know, but I do find her a bit . . . irritating is too strong a word. Just so *busy*, I suppose. The woman never seems to slow down. It's like she doesn't have an off button.'

Madi laughed. 'But we are ready, aren't we? For scones and a cup of tea. In fact, I'm famished! You should have let her bring them.'

'Famished? Didn't you have any breakfast?'

'I did, but it's getting on for lunchtime, isn't it? Must just be the country air making me hungry. Or the beginnings of recovery. My appetite's certainly coming back anyway, with a vengeance!'

'That's a good thing, isn't it?'

'It is, so long as I don't stuff myself to the point of obesity.'

'Madi, I somehow can't see that happening. You strike me as a woman who knows how to look her best.'

'All those years in the public eye, I suppose, where appearance is all. Can't go on stage without the right costume, every hair in its place, the full make-up . . . I've spent my life putting on a serious face or a tragic face or a laughing face, no matter how I might feel inside. I've lost weight for a part, padded up for others. It's all a façade. A charade. Sometimes I forget who the real Madi Cardew is.'

'And have you found her now?'

'That's why I'm here. To escape for a while, to let myself breathe. And it's working, Tom. Or I hope it is. There's something about having cancer that changes your view of life, you know. Brings things into focus. The things that have been pushed aside, forgotten.'

'Like?'

'Like people. Friendships. Even Patty there. You shouldn't mock her, you know. She's tried so hard to be nice to me. Welcomed me into the village. Okay, she can be a bit . . . in your face, but she's a good woman. She's genuine, if you know what I mean, which I have to say a lot of actors aren't. It's all me, me, me. And I've been guilty of that too, I'm sure. Suddenly my acting life seems a bit superficial, a long way removed from reality. And here . . . well, this is real life, isn't it? A village show, open fields, a sick cat, scones and jam . . .'

'Okay, I get the hint.' He stood up and felt in his pocket for his wallet. 'Scones it is. And a sandwich or two. And tea with two sugars, right? See, I remembered. Sit and enjoy the peace and quiet while you can. The hordes will be joining us out here soon enough.'

He was right, of course. He had no sooner disappeared inside than a string of villagers began to wander into the garden, nodding hello as they rushed to bag a table before they all filled up. Ralph and Sian stopped to ask after Flo and to introduce Ralph's brother Joe who shook Madi's hand but looked far too distracted to stop and chat.

'Oh, don't mind him,' Sian said when he'd wandered back inside to get their tea. 'He can be a moody sod when he wants to be. Not really his thing, this, but their dad wanted them both here in case he won the wine contest. I'm surprised Joe came, to be honest, as he and his dad are hardly speaking these days, but old habits die hard and I think he was hoping Prue might turn up.'

'Not likely. As far as I know, she's still at my place, and will be for another two weeks at least.'

'Ah, but he doesn't know that. She never did tell him where she went. Or for how long.'

'Poor boy.'

'Oh, don't feel sorry for him. It's Prue who drew the short straw, and he might be my future brother-in-law so I know I shouldn't say it, but she's better off without him, believe me.'

Madi watched them walk away, stopping to chat to just about everyone else who crossed their path. Being the local vet was bound to get you recognised, Madi thought. And liked.

'Excuse me.'

The boy standing beside her laid one hand on the back of Madi's chair and waited for her to turn to face him.

'Oh, hello.' He was probably about thirteen or fourteen but short for his age, and a bit on the chubby side, and he was wearing a shirt and tie that didn't quite seem to go with the scuffed trainers (the toes of which he was busily kicking into the grass) or the unruly hair badly in need of a comb. She gave him her best smile, noticing how anxious he looked, and tried to put him at his ease.

'Sorry to disturb you, Miss, but they say you're famous.' He lifted his hand from the chair and nibbled at his nails. His cheeks were very red, and he was gazing at her quizzically, as if trying to put a name to the face. She half expected him to produce an autograph book any second now, if only to work out exactly who she was by reading her signature.

'No. Not famous. Known maybe, among people who go to the theatre, but far from famous. I'm Madalyn Cardew, and you can call me Madi. Miss is for schoolteachers.'

'Right. I'm Donny.'

'Ah, we meet at last! I've heard a lot about you, Donny. And I've heard you in the bell tower, of course.'

His eyes lit up. 'Have you?'

'Hard not to, Donny, while I'm living so close to the church.'

'Sorry. Is it too loud?' He lowered his eyes. 'I'm sort of teaching myself, so I haven't worked out how to do it quietly yet. But I will.'

'I'm sure you will. Now, would you like to sit down? Perhaps I can tempt you to a scone, once they arrive? I'm sure we can spare one.'

'Oh, no. Mum'll be here later. She doesn't like me to have too many snacks, and she'll be wanting me to eat my dinner when we get home. After she's done the judging. Not that she'll eat much herself tonight, after tasting all those cakes!'

'A cup of tea then, or a lemonade or something?'

'No, you're all right. I just wanted to ask . . .'

'Come on, sit. You're making the place look untidy.' She pulled out a chair and pointed to it, and Donny reluctantly sat down. 'Now, what was it you wanted to say? It's okay, I don't bite!'

'I had this idea, you see, Miss. About doing a show. Oh, not like this one, with cakes and things.' He threw his arms out to encompass the hall and its surroundings. 'A proper show. On a stage. Music and comedy and stuff.' He stopped and took a breath before spilling his ideas out, so thick and fast she could hardly keep up. 'Bells aren't the only thing I play, I'm learning the guitar as well, and I've written some lyrics for a song. Or I could just read them out like poems. Or my mate Sean could sing them. He can sing okay. Or thinks he can. And tell jokes. And there are these girls from school who pretend to be The Supremes, in the playground at break times. You know, that girl group from the old days. They can't be the Spice Girls or Little Mix cos there's only the three of them, but they're quite good, I think, even though only one of them is actually black . . .'

'Donny, where is all this going? What is it you wanted to ask me?'

'Well, seeing as you're famous . . . well, *known* anyway . . . I wondered if you could help me. You know, tell me how to make a show. Practising it, and getting the right sort of costumes to wear, and how to get people to come and see it. Because I do think it's important that people come, if we go to all the trouble of doing it, don't you? I thought maybe we could use the hall here if it's free, and give the ticket money to charity . . .'

'What's all this then?' Tom had returned, carrying a tray laden with cups and food, which he placed carefully on the table. 'Did I hear something about charity?'

Donny went to stand but Tom put his hand on the boy's shoulder and eased him back down. 'Don't go on my account, lad.'

'Donny was just running an idea by me,' Madi explained, picking up a knife and spreading a good-sized splash of jam onto a big fat scone. They looked so inviting, the sandwiches could wait. 'A very good idea, as it happens, about putting on some sort of a performance here in the hall, for charity, but I'm afraid I won't be staying here long enough to be much help. Maybe it's something you'd like to be involved in, Tom? You did tell me how much you fancied getting into amateur theatre in some way.'

'Me? I wouldn't know where to start!'

'How hard can it be? A group of eager teenagers who just need a bit of adult guidance, that's all. And what a great way to keep them occupied, and off the streets.' Tom didn't look convinced. 'And away from the bell tower!'

'Ah, now you're talking.' He winked at her. 'There is a small stage in there, as it happens. And a little back room that could work as a changing area. We did have a panto once, years ago, that went down very well. *Cinderella*, if I remember rightly. My wife helped make the costumes. All the brainchild of our old postmistress, Aggie – a sweet old thing she was – but somehow the impetus got lost after she died. God, that must be all of twenty years back. How time flies . . .'

'Would you, Mr Bishop?' Donny said, eyeing the bowl of cream with undisguised interest. 'Only, it's not something we can do on our own. And my mum and dad are always too busy, and not really into that sort of thing at all.'

'I don't know. I've never . . .'

'What was it you were saying to me, Tom, about living your dreams, about grabbing the here and now? Go on, give it a try. The smell of the greasepaint, remember? Something you've always wanted to do. I'll help you get started, while I'm still here.' She gazed at him as he wielded his spoon, plonking a large helping of clotted cream onto his scone. 'And why are you putting the cream on first?'

'I always do it that way. Don't tell me you're a jam-first girl?'

Madi took a big bite, the jam dribbling out from under its cream topping and down her chin. 'Just proves how different we all are,' she said, swallowing her first mouthful and rootling in her bag for a tissue to clean her face. 'We don't even say it the same way. It's scone like stone, not scon like gone! But there's room for all sorts in this world. Go on, Donny, help yourself to one. I won't tell your mum, if you don't. And from the way Mr Bishop here is smiling, it looks as if we may have something to celebrate.'

Chapter 21

PRUE

When Prue heard noises down below and peered out of the bedroom window, she was pleased to see there was a young man making a start on cutting the grass. This could only be the famous Simon, who by some miracle had turned up the very day after she and Aaron had been talking about him.

Well, there was no time like the present to get out there and introduce herself, even if she was still wearing her pyjamas and hadn't yet got around to brushing her hair. It was only when she was dressed and halfway down the stairs ten minutes later that her nerves began to kick in. She really wasn't all that good at talking to complete strangers, and, to be honest, she hadn't given any thought to exactly what she was going to say. 'Hello, I don't even live here but I have this great idea for transforming this overgrown tip into a garden' did sound a bit presumptuous, if not totally mad.

She stopped on the middle landing, half hoping that Aaron might emerge from the door of his flat and go with her, but all was quiet, so she plodded on alone. There were muddy footprints across the floor down in the hall and the door to the back was propped open, a long electrical lead snaking its way out from the socket under the stairs. Prue could hear the drone of the electric mower getting louder and then softer as it struggled to work its way up and down the grass.

She went outside and stood for a few moments watching, the young man totally unaware of her presence behind him as he guided the mower around the bench at the base of the tree and carried on his way, with no attempt to move the bench or mow the patch of grass underneath. As he reached the end and turned back, flipping the trailing cable over his shoulder to keep it out of the way of the blades, he saw her.

He let go of the trigger on the handle and the machine shuddered to a halt. 'Hello,' he said, leaving the mower where it was and wiping his sleeve over his forehead as he walked towards her. 'Can I help you?'

He was tall, fair-haired, about her own age or maybe a couple of years older, and his skin had that weathered look that so many of the men back home had, that marked them very much as someone used to working outdoors.

'I don't know. Maybe you can.' Prue took a deep breath and ploughed on. 'My name's Prue Harris and I'm staying in number nine. Madi Cardew's flat. You might know her?'

'Of course. Everybody knows Madi. Or *of* her, anyway. Used to be on the telly, you know. I heard she was ill. Not seen her for a bit. Oh . . . she hasn't died, has she?'

'Oh, God, no. Nothing like that. She's just gone away for a while, and I'm here instead.'

'Well, that's good. That she's okay, I mean. So, what can I do for you?'

'The garden . . .'

'Yes?'

'Well, I was wondering if you . . . or the landlord, I suppose . . . had ever thought of making it more usable, if you know what I mean.'

'Usable?'

'More user-friendly. Not just a scrap of tatty grass. Make it somewhere the residents could actually enjoy.'

'What, flowers, you mean?'

'Flowers, yes. Shrubs. Maybe a little paved area to have barbecues on. And seating.'

'They can bring their own chairs out if they want to sit.'

'No, I meant proper outside seating, that could stay out here in all weathers.'

'You've got the bench . . .'

Prue walked over to it and gave it a gentle shove. It wobbled and she could feel a splinter from the rough wood at the back slice straight into her finger. 'The wood's rotting. I bet it's never had any preservative on it. And one leg's shorter than the other!'

He grinned. 'It's not exactly perfect, I agree. Bit of a Long John Silver, with legs like that! Here, let me take a look at that finger. It's starting to bleed. I keep a first-aid box in the van.'

'My finger's fine. Or it will be, once I get a needle to it. It's only a splinter.' She instinctively popped the finger into her mouth and sucked. 'And it was just an idea. Doing up the garden. It could all come to nothing.'

191

He nodded. 'I'm Simon, by the way. The landlord's my uncle. I do all the odd jobs around here, and at two other blocks he owns. Oh, not full-time, mind. Usually only at the week-ends, or after work. I do have a real job too, but I'm on leave this week.'

He tested the bench for stability, brushed away some dead leaves and sat down at one end, beckoning Prue to join him.

'It wouldn't have to cost a fortune,' she said, returning to the subject of the garden. 'I just wondered if your uncle might consider it as an investment. You know, keeping the place looking nice, and his tenants happy. In fact, I'm hoping the other residents might all chip in a few pounds or give up an hour or two of their time, at least to get things started. It is for their benefit, after all. Not that I've met many of them yet, so I know I'm jumping the gun a bit. I'll need to get some discussions going, but I'm happy to get my hands dirty and do some digging and planting. I might need help with the heavy stuff though.'

'I want to say you've thought this through pretty well, but I kind of get the impression you haven't. Not properly.'

Prue blushed. 'I did say it was just an idea. To be worked on.'

'Well, let me get on and finish the grass while I have a think about it, eh? A cup of tea would be nice. And a biscuit, maybe?'

'You do know I'd have to go up two flights of stairs?'

'True.'

'And back down again, carrying hot tea? And me with a poorly finger.'

'Ah, but a man can't think well on an empty stomach, and you do want me to think, don't you?'

'I suppose I do.'

'And our Madi must have a tray up there, to help you carry. So . . . hot and strong, please. And no sugar. I'm sweet enough already.'

She laughed at the sheer cheek of the man. 'That is such a corny line!'

'Still made you laugh though, eh?'

Prue went back inside and sorted out the tray of tea and biscuits, carrying it carefully down the stairs and out into what she had trouble making herself call the garden.

'Ah, lovely, thanks.' Simon pushed his hair away from his eyes and grabbed the bigger of the two mugs, blowing on the surface before taking a swig. 'I've got a mate,' he said, 'that does carpentry. I reckon he could make you a couple of basic benches if that's what you're after. Maybe a table or two. It'll cost you though, even if I ask him nicely and he gives me mates' rates. And, to be honest, I can't see my uncle coughing up. He's not really what you'd call the generous sort. There was an old girl before, used to own a couple of the flats. She might have been more on your wavelength but she died, I think. Not sure who took over, just that my uncle's mad as hell he can't persuade them to sell. Not owning the whole place bugs him!'

'I suppose it would.' Prue gazed up at the block in front of her, where most of the windows remained closed and the rooms behind them showed no obvious signs of life, although she was sure she saw the edge of a curtain twitch in the ground-floor flat, then just as quickly go still again. 'So, what else? Any more suggestions?'

'You'd need some decent paving for under the benches, so

you could lose some of the grass, which would certainly make this mowing lark a bit easier for me. And somewhere for that barbecue of yours to sit too. Plants are the easy bit.'

'I'm biting off more than I can chew, aren't I?' Prue sipped at her tea and lowered her gaze to the mangled lawn beneath her feet. 'Stupid idea . . .'

'No, it's not. And I can see where you're coming from, but you're going to need to get a few of the others . . . well, preferably *all* of the others . . . living here to get behind it, if you really want something done.'

'I know, and I'll work on it, but I don't have very long. I'm only here another couple of weeks.'

'Can't really see why you're bothering then. Not if you won't be sticking around. And it's not as if it's even planting season yet, is it?' He gulped down the rest of his tea and put the mug down on the path. 'Still, you know where I am if you want any help. I'm a builder by trade, so I can probably help out with the slabs and stuff if you do go ahead. Here, let me give you my number.' He pulled a pen out from the inside pocket of his jacket and hastily scrawled a row of digits on Prue's arm, just above the wrist. 'Sorry, no paper!' he joked as she tried to pull away. 'Just remember to copy it down before you wash it off, eh?'

And then, stuffing a biscuit into his mouth, he went back to his mowing.

Prue sat for a while and watched him, until she'd finished her tea. 'This mate of yours? The carpenter?' she said, as Simon drew near enough to hear her. 'Would he be up for a bit of bartering, do you think?'

He cut the engine again. 'Bartering? Like beads and pebbles, you mean?'

'Of course not. No, it's just that if there's no money for the garden stuff, maybe we could trade favours in some way? He's not getting married or anything, is he? The carpenter? Or has a new baby maybe? Only, I'm a photographer and I could do a free shoot, in exchange . . .'

'Not that I know of. But it's not a bad idea. I can ask around for you. Some free paving slabs, wood, plant pots . . . who knows what people might be willing to swap for a good set of photos? I don't suppose any of the other residents have anything to offer as well, do they? Any secret skills? I know my mum and dad are after someone to make them an anniversary cake. Something special for their twenty-fifth.'

'No idea, but leave it with me and I'll find out. I do know that Aaron's mum in flat six is into sewing . . .'

'Suzy, you mean?'

'Oh, do you know her?'

'Yeah, but I doubt that she's up to much sewing somehow.'

'Do you? Why's that?'

'You haven't met her yet then?'

'No. Why? Is there something I should know?'

'Only that I wouldn't let her near you with a needle if I was you, not even to get that splinter out of your finger.' He looked up towards the closed window of flat 6 and lowered his voice. 'Poor woman had some kind of accident a few years back. She's totally blind.'

* * *

'Why didn't you tell me about your mum?' Prue had invited Aaron up to look through the photos he'd taken by the river, now that she'd finished editing them.

'What about her?'

'I was talking to Simon, the odd-job guy.'

'Oh, yeah? Simon, eh? On first-name terms with the hired help!'

'Stop it. And don't change the subject. He told me about your mum, that she's blind.'

'Oh, that. Yeah, it just didn't come up, I guess. She is who she is. My mum. Anything else isn't really relevant, is it?'

'Maybe not, but I just thought you might have said something, when you were talking about her. The sewing, the buttons . . .'

'She doesn't do any of that stuff now. Can't, obviously. We've still got the box though, of buttons. Ones she cut off my old baby clothes, her wedding dress before she binned it, and Nan's. And one or two that came off my grandad's old shirts. Not the sort of thing she'd ever throw away.'

'I can understand that. So, how did it happen? Losing her sight? Simon said something about an accident?'

'It was a car crash. Five years ago now. She was over the limit – the speed limit *and* the alcohol one – and drove headlong into a tree. Her head hit the windscreen. Hard. Blunt trauma, they call it. She was lucky to survive it at all, I suppose. It was touch and go for a while.'

'That's awful. Was anyone with her? Your dad?'

'No. It was after they'd split up. He didn't really want to know. Said she wasn't his problem any more. It drove a wedge

196

between us for a while, my dad and me. I hardly saw him during the first year or so after it happened, but it wasn't his fault, was it? Although, to listen to Mum, it was. If only he hadn't got mixed up with this other woman, if only he hadn't left, then she wouldn't have been there, would she? Driving at night, by herself? That was her logic anyway. But it wasn't Dad's fault. He didn't make her get behind the wheel after too many gins. So I sort of forgave him eventually. Missed him, really. The Sunday meet-ups, the burgers and all that, even though I was too old by then for an afternoon at the swings. No, it was my nan who swept in and took over while Mum was in hospital and after she came home. There was nobody else, really. Only me, and I wasn't up to the job. Not then. Mum doesn't have any brothers or sisters, you see, and the few friends she had just kind of shied away after . . .'

'That's a shame.'

'People can't deal with it, can they? Don't know what to say, so they don't say anything. Anyway, Nan practically lived with us for a long time, made sure I kept going to school, ate properly. She went back to her own place for the odd day or two, weekends mainly, just to keep it going really, but she more or less gave up any life of her own for us. I don't think we'd have coped without her.'

'They're great, aren't they? Grandmothers? In times of crisis. I still miss mine.'

'Yeah. Me too. She died just six months ago. Her heart. Mum thinks it was the worry and the strain of it all, but she's like that, my mum. Everything has to be someone's fault.'

'She blames herself for your nan dying?'

'Oh, no. She blames Dad, and his fancy woman. Lauren, she's called. He's married to her now. The wicked stepmother! You can imagine what Mum has to say about that.'

'It can't have been easy though. A divorce, and then the accident. On her, or on you. God, I can't imagine what it must be like, losing your sight. And with a teenager to take care of too. I guess it explains a lot about you not really knuckling down at school. Too much going on at home.'

'Exams seemed like the last of my worries.'

'Have you always lived here?'

'No, we came here after the divorce, when our old house had to be sold. The previous tenant of the flat here had just died, which was lucky. Well, no, I don't mean lucky that she died. She was a nice old lady, from what I've heard. Some sort of dancer, in her day. But it was good timing for us, stopped us being homeless! The block had been owned by my grandad way back, see, but Nan sold most of it off to some property company bloke after he died. She had to, to clear his debts I think. He was a bit of a gambler on the quiet, my grandad, although he died before I was born, so I never actually knew him. He had no head for money, apparently, even though he'd earned a shedload of it over the years. Lost most of it on dodgy stocks and shares, days at the races, being over-generous to his friends, that kind of thing.'

'If I'd known there was gambling in your genes I'd have kept you away from those fruit machines!'

'Pennies don't count. And I'm sure we must be the only people to have ever walked away from one of those arcades in profit!'

'It felt like a good time to stop. While we were ahead. I can't have your mum blaming me for you losing your life savings.'

'What? All fifteen quid? No, seriously though, Nan sold the block, or most of it, just before prices went sky high. If only she'd hung on, we'd probably be millionaires by now! She held on to three of the flats though – the bigger, better ones at the back – including ours, and Madi's here.'

'Ah, your nan was the mystery owner Simon mentioned to me. His uncle's none too keen on not owning the whole block.'

'I think she got quite a lot of pleasure from knowing that! Anyway, the flats were her nest egg, as she called them, and she always said they'd be Mum's inheritance eventually. And mine, I guess. She said Grandad owed us that much, for all the good he'd been when he was alive. I don't think theirs was the happiest of marriages, and he was away a lot working, but I guess this was her security, her retirement fund, not that she ended up with much of a retirement, running about looking after us. It was only meant to be a temporary thing at first, us living here, but then Mum had her accident and she couldn't go out to work any more, and there wasn't any compensation or anything, seeing as she'd caused it herself, so we're still here. We own our flat now, of course, since we lost Nan. And the other two she'd hung onto. Mum spent ages with the solicitor, going through Nan's papers, sorting out about the rents and everything, but she won't sell. Or can't. I'm not sure which. She doesn't talk about it. But they were her dad's after all, so there's a bit of sentimental value attached, and she doesn't have much else that was his.'

199

'Quite a story.'

'The true ones are always the best.'

'So, Madi's your tenant! Well, yours and your mum's. This flat is technically yours.'

'Yeah, the best flat in the block too. Mum isn't happy about that. The penthouse, she calls it! Which is a bit of an exaggeration. Thinks we should be living in it. She never even speaks to Miss Cardew now.'

'Seems a bit extreme, falling out over something like that.'

'Tell me about it!'

'And is it? The best flat?'

'Oh, definitely. Top floor. Beautifully decorated. Nice fittings. Well, look at it. We could be in The Ritz! But it's not something to get jealous about, is it? And I quite like our flat. I can't see Mum moving, not any more. But Mum feels safer staying put, because she knows her way around in our place. By feel, or sixth sense or something. Never bumps into anything unless I move things about.'

'Do you think she'd . . .?'

'What?'

'Like to get out a bit more, get involved with my plans for the garden? I know you said she works, doing phone stuff, so she does at least get to talk to people, but still it can't be much fun being stuck indoors on her own so much. There must be something she could help with. And, if she part owns the place, she might feel more invested in it than some of the tenants.'

'Well, I could ask, but she's not really one for other people. She does come out with me sometimes. For a walk or whatever, in the evenings when I'm not working, but it's not like she can enjoy a film or a museum, or even read a book any more, and there's nothing that really motivates her these days. She does a bit of cleaning in the flat, but it's hit and miss. I usually have a quick wipe round after she's finished and do the bits she's missed.'

'How old is she, Aaron?'

'Erm, let's think now. Forty-four, I think. No, forty-five.'

'God, really? That's way too young to be a hermit. Let's see if we can get her out and doing something again. Does she like plants? Flowers?'

'Only the ones that smell nice. Not a lot of good otherwise, are they, if you can't see them? Or eat them!'

'We could do a sensory garden!' Where had that idea sprung from? Now it had popped into her head, she just had to run with it. 'Wind chimes for sound. Plants with strong scents, and ones she can rub between her fingers, like herbs, lavender . . .'

'You're getting carried away again. You're leaving soon, remember?'

'But *you're* not. Oh, come on, let's put all that artistic talent of yours into something useful.'

'What artistic talent? You make your plans if you must, and I'll do what I can to help you, but don't count on Mum. She's a tough nut to crack.'

Chapter 22

MADI

The darkroom was a big disappointment. It had wooden workbenches running around three sides, and a cupboard high on the back wall that dropped dead spiders all over Madi's shoulders when she forced open its rather creaky door. There were a few old dusty chemical bottles inside, a sink with old-fashioned rusted taps, and a line of string running across from one corner of the ceiling to another, with pegs that must have once held the photos as they dried, but otherwise nothing of any interest. But if it was cleaned up a bit, it might make a useful space.

'Caught you!'

Madi felt herself stiffen, her heart rate shooting up in fear. If she hadn't realised almost immediately that it was Tom's voice behind her she would quite likely have jumped right out of her skin, and probably grabbed the nearest of the potion bottles as a weapon to defend herself. He had obviously come through the gate between the gardens while her attention was otherwise engaged and was now standing in the doorway.

'Oh, sorry!' Madi took a deep breath and turned round, allowing herself a moment for the panic to subside. 'I know I shouldn't be nosing around, but I only wanted a quick peek. You won't tell Prue, will you?'

'Depends. Have you stolen anything? Broken anything?'

'Of course not.'

'Nothing to tell then, is there? Come on, lock up and let's get out of here. The cobwebby look really doesn't suit you.' He lifted a hand and eased a strand of something brown and sticky out of her hair. 'And I have other plans for you today, assuming you're free?'

'And what might they be?'

'I thought a trip into Norwich. I have to go to see my optician, and I could do with the company and perhaps we could do a spot of shopping and lunch, if you're up for it. You worry me, the way you stay in so much. If you won't fling yourself into the sea or fly to Egypt, then at least have a day away from Shelling. It may be home, and I love it dearly, but it can be a bit stifling after a while.'

'Well, okay, but only if we take my car. It's been sitting outside so long I worry it might not start if I abandon it any longer. And if you're having eyesight problems, I'd feel safer if I drive!'

'Fair enough. You're the boss.'

'Am I?'

'It's what I always used to say to Barb to keep her happy. Let her believe she was the one making all the decisions, the one in the driving seat.' He laughed. 'Which you actually will be, on this occasion!'

'When were you thinking of setting off?'

'Half an hour suit you? Long enough to get changed, and to put on your face or whatever it is you ladies do.'

'This face is the only one I've got, unfortunately.' Madi could see Tom was about to say something, but quickly put up her hand to stop him. 'Don't you go contradicting me. All that soppy flattery's the last thing I need. Let's call a spade a spade. I am what I am. Over sixty, and not looking my best just now.'

'I was only going to say that lunch is on me.'

'That's all right then. I'm sorry.' She pulled the shed door shut and turned the key in the padlock, keeping her back to him while she swallowed back her embarrassment at misreading things again. 'And thank you. That would be lovely.'

Madi enjoyed the drive. She hadn't been behind the wheel since she'd arrived and the weather was picking up nicely, the sun throwing shadows onto the lanes as the overhanging bushes brushed against the roof of the car.

'Not visiting your wife today?'

Tom shook his head. 'I'm taking a chores day. Optician, a visit to the bank, a spot of much-needed clothes shopping. I only seem to have five socks left with no holes in them and no two of those make a matching pair.' He lifted his trouser leg a few inches to reveal a dark grey sock, then flashed a navy one from underneath the other.

'Stop it.' She laughed. 'I need to keep my eyes on the road, especially until we get off these narrow lanes.'

'They can be a bit scary, I suppose, if you're not used to them. Let's just hope we don't meet a bloody great giant-sized tractor coming the other way.'

'Now you are worrying me.'

'Plenty of passing places. And we can always swap seats if you feel the need.'

'I'm a perfectly competent driver, thank you.'

'I'm only teasing you, Madi. I hope you know that.'

'Of course. Now, is it left up here?'

'Yep. Then just follow the signs.'

'I must find a car wash too. Just look at the state of the windows. And you should see the wheels . . . yuk!'

'I did notice, as I got in. Almost got mud on my socks. At least then I'd have had a matching pair. In muddy brown! Anyway, let's not waste time in car washes. I can do it for you any time. I enjoy it actually. Messing about with a big bucket of suds and a squishy sponge. A real man's job is that, second only to barbecuing sausages!'

Madi gave the windscreen another squirt and set the wipers onto high speed for a couple of swipes, which seemed to do the job at least well enough to see out. 'Okay, you're on.'

'Glad to be of service. I just wish I'd offered sooner. That mud's probably ground in by now. I'll probably need a fish slice to scrape it off!'

'Just not the same one you use for turning the sausages, eh?' Madi joked, feeling herself relax as they turned out onto the main road.

Tom pointed out various landmarks as they drove along, regaling her with stories of his youth, places he'd worked, pubs he'd eaten in. It felt as if she was getting her very own guided tour, with insider knowledge only a local could provide.

'You love this place, don't you?' she said.

'What? The A47?'

'No, Norfolk! It's so clearly home.'

'Has been my whole life, and I can't see that changing.'

'Have you given any more thought to young Donny and his theatrical dreams? All he needs is a bit of direction and support. An adult to take charge if need be, and help pull the thing together and sort out a bit of publicity. Find some sponsorship, even. I really think you're the man to help him, you know.'

'Something to give me an interest in life and stop me brooding at home alone, you mean?'

'No, I don't mean that at all. And I'm hardly the one to say that, considering it's what I've been doing myself for the last few months. But it will give the local kids an interest, won't it? And benefit the whole village, if you can bring a really good performance together.'

'I know. And I am considering it, Madi.'

'And what would your Barb say about it, do you think? She's the boss, after all. The one who makes all the decisions, you said . . .'

'I think she'd have been all for it actually, but she's not here, is she? And it'll be me in the driving seat. Without a co-driver, or even a passenger.'

'You'll have Donny.'

Tom raised his eyes and sighed. 'That's what bothers me.'

'Oh, don't be mean. He seems like a nice lad. And he's nothing if not keen.'

'He's keen on bell ringing and look how that's turned out.'

'True. But he's very willing to learn. If only there was someone able to show him what to do.'

'Are we still talking about the bells?'

'Possibly not!'

'Oh, okay, Madi, I give in! But before I can show him the ropes, you're going to have to show them to me.'

'But I don't know the first thing about bell ringing. Let me loose with those ropes and I'd probably end up strangling myself!'

'You know perfectly well what ropes I meant.' Tom laughed, and Madi laughed with him. She was going to enjoy this day out.

While Tom had his eye test, Madi set off for a wander around the shops. He would be at least an hour, he'd said, or probably longer if he had to choose new frames, so they had agreed on a place to meet up for lunch later.

It had been a while since she had felt any need to buy new clothes. The cancer and its aftermath had left her feeling very down for a time. She had lost weight and was now slowly regaining it, so even choosing the right size would have been a challenge, and there had been no need to dress up while all she did was lie around at home, recovering from each chemo session, not at all sure how to come to terms with her new shape, let alone dress to accommodate it. The big bold colours she had always favoured seemed somehow inappropriate now that fading into the background held a lot more appeal than being centre stage. So she bypassed the fancy dresses and glittery tops and bought black, and grey, and comfy. And new boots, flatter than she was used to, but so much more suited to country life.

The café was easy enough to find and she arrived early. She found a table tucked away at the back and balanced her shopping bags around her on the floor, ordered a coffee and picked up a menu.

Every time the door to the street opened, she glanced up, hoping it would be Tom. After four or five false alarms, she wondered if she might look a bit needy, sitting here alone and watching the door. Like a woman stood up on a blind date. Not that anyone was watching her or would care even if they were. This was not Madalyn Cardew, semi-famous actress, out on public display. This was an almost unrecognisable version, looking plainer and thinner than she had for years, quietly minding her own business in an out-of-the-way café, with nothing about her likely to draw anyone's attention at all.

Only, she wasn't minding her own business. Not any more. Because there, at a table for two in the opposite corner, if she wasn't very much mistaken, was Prue's ex-boyfriend, the one who had led her on and turned her down and driven her away from home because of it. The one Madi had met very briefly in the garden of the village hall just before his father had won first prize for his wine. What was the lad called again? Joe. That was it. And yes, that was definitely him. And he was not alone. She watched as his hand reached across the table and closed around the long slender fingers of his companion, a pale, thin, but rather gorgeous young man whose face he seemed unable to take his eyes from.

Ah! Well that explained a lot, didn't it? Not that it was any of Madi's business, but she couldn't help feeling sorry for Prue, who, presumably, had no idea.

Joe looked up as the door opened yet again, and so did she. And this time it was Tom. He walked straight towards her, smiling, totally oblivious to who was sitting just a few tables away, but Joe had spotted him all right. When Madi next looked his way, Joe's hand was very much back on his own half of the table, clutching his cup far more tightly than was strictly necessary, and he had turned his chair by a few degrees so all Tom would see if he should happen to look their way was his back view, pretty much indistinguishable from that of any other office worker taking an early lunch with a friend.

'I wonder if they have any pies?' Tom said, picking up the second menu and reading through it eagerly. 'Oh, and I've ordered a new pair, by the way. Glasses, that is. Not pies! Fancied a change . . . so I went for bright pink, with diamante arms.'

'Sorry. What?'

'You've not listened to a word I've said, have you?'

'Sorry.'

'So you said.' He looked at her inquisitively, but she didn't attempt to explain what had taken her attention elsewhere. 'Now, what are you having?'

By the time they had eaten and Tom was sorting out the bill, Joe and his friend had gone. Madi hadn't seen them leave, and presumably neither had Tom.

'So, where now?' she said as they stepped back out into the street.

'Socks. And lots of them!'

Madi laughed. 'I wouldn't mind a few pairs myself. I thought maybe pink, with diamantes.'

'So you were listening?'

'Of course. Just distracted for a moment, that was all.'

'Penny for them,' Tom said, stopping so abruptly on the pavement that Madi walked right into him.

'Oh, it's nothing. Come on, we're at M&S, so let's do socks. Sock it to me, Tom!'

'Now there's an offer a man doesn't get every day,' Tom said as they entered through the big glass doors. 'We can buy matching pairs. His and hers. But I bet mine are bigger than yours.'

'Tom Bishop, you have a rather naughty sense of humour, do you know that?'

'I'm only talking about socks, Madi.' His eyes glinted with mischief and he gave her an exaggerated wink.

'Were you like this with Barbara?'

'Like what exactly?'

'Joking all the time, going out for lunch, shopping for socks?'

'Not all the time, but yes, we tended to do most things together.'

'I'm just a bit worried that I might be becoming some kind of substitute, that's all. You do know that's not what I need right now?'

'Me neither, Madi. Friends, okay? Like we said right from the start. In fact, why don't you come with me next time I visit Barb? Meet her for yourself, put your mind at rest that I am still a happily married man. Or as happy as I can be, in the circumstances. She'd like you, you know. Okay, so she may not remember who you are five minutes after you've been introduced, but that's just Barb. It's nothing to be wary of, or scared of. She's just Barb. *My* Barb.'

'I don't know. It would feel like intruding.'

'Nonsense. Any friend of mine is a friend of hers. Always been that way. Although she did take things a bit far the first time she met my mate Ken.'

'Ken, as in Ralph's dad, you mean? And Joe's?'

'Yep, that's the man. We were nothing more than kids back then, of course. I was just a teenager, trying to impress the girls, blagging my way into pubs, and he was a few years older. We hung about in the same groups, often found ourselves at the same football match or the same youth club. I met her first, or that's what I've always argued, although to be honest it was only about thirty seconds before he did. It was a disco, in a neighbouring village, just a small summer thing, and all over by about ten. And he was the one who walked her to the bus stop that first night, and shared a bit of a snog, so she told me later. Didn't last though. Well, how could it once I'd decided to make my move? A pretty girl, my Barb, back then. Still is, mind you. And it was me she chose.'

'And Ken didn't mind?'

'How could he? He'd only known her for a few hours. Hardly stealing the love of his life, was I? And he met his own wife soon after anyway. The lovely Janet. Gone now, sadly. I keep hoping he might hook up with someone else, but no joy so far. The boys became his life for so long that he just pushed any idea of another romance aside. Probably too late now, which is a shame. He's a good bloke. I don't suppose you . . .?'

'Trying to match-make now, are you?' She prodded his arm. 'No, leave me out of it. Men are off my agenda. Except for my son, and a bit of matchmaking there wouldn't go amiss if you can work some magic and get us back together, or talking at least. I'm not doing a very good job of it myself.'

'Have you tried, Madi? Really tried? Calling once, and hanging up without leaving a message . . . well, I think you may have to make a little more effort than that.'

'What size? Eight to nine and a half? Or ten to twelve?'

'Pardon?'

'Socks, Tom.' She held up two different packs, side by side.

'If I didn't know better I'd say you're trying to change the subject.'

Madi didn't answer.

'And I'm a ten, by the way. You know what they say. Big feet, big . . .'

She wanted to laugh, but this time her heart wasn't in it. What with fretting over Joe's secret, worrying that Tom was about to palm her off on Ken, and having to deal with George's obstinate silence, she sometimes couldn't help but think men were more trouble than they were worth.

Chapter 23

*S*o, I'm going to meet her at last. The visitor at number nine. *She's certainly made her mark on the young men around here. First Aaron, and now that boy who does the mowing. Flirting, spreading herself about. It can't end well.*

And now she's been shoving notes through doors, trying to get support for some scheme or other, inviting everyone into the flat she's taken over as if it's her own, and it seems she wants me there too.

I've never been invited in before. There's never been any occasion for it. The actress and I have never been friends. She keeps herself to herself, and so do I. Before that solicitor came, I would never have believed we had anything in common. How wrong I was!

But I'll have to be careful. Act like it's all unfamiliar, the inside of her flat, like I don't know where her fancy sofa is until I sit on it. If I turn up at all, that is. But I'd be crazy not to, wouldn't I? Although sometimes I think that must be exactly what I am. Crazy. To have kept my silence, let her carry on as if nothing ever happened. She needs to pay for what she did. The actress, that is. Not the other one, although she's shaping up to be no better.

She's still away. I'm hoping something might be said, about why she left, when she's coming back. If she ever is. Because it's time I confronted her. It really is. She thinks she's got away with it all this time, that nobody knows who she is. That's the trouble with the likes of her. She thinks the past can be put away in a drawer, like her posh knickers or her old theatre programmes. That it can all be written over, wiped clean. Thinks that nobody got hurt, except her. Huh! If only that were true.

I lost him too. And when someone dies before their time, there's usually someone to blame. Someone who set them on that path, someone who pushed them over the edge. She was faceless before, but not any more. Now I know her for who she is. For what she is.

She's the one. Not the only one, but the only one I can still do something about. The one I can never forgive.

Chapter 24

The handful of people who turned up at Prue's meeting were a varied bunch. She had picked a time when the other tenants should be back home from work, although guessing what their usual evening activities might involve had been a bit of a hit-and-miss affair. Too early and they could still be cooking or eating, too late and they could be getting ready for bed. Ideally, she would have liked to hold the meeting out in the garden itself, but it was dark and cold and they wouldn't be able to see much, so there didn't seem a lot of point. Inviting them into Madi's flat had felt like a bit of a cheek, but Madi had insisted when they'd first made their swapping arrangement that she must treat it as her own, and so she had. She just hoped they weren't the sort to spill their drink on the carpet or start nicking the silver.

The leaflets were easy enough to produce on her laptop, with the help of Aaron and his printer, and pushing them through the remaining doors in the block had only taken minutes. Now all she had to do was wait and see who turned up.

'We did say eight o'clock, didn't we?' Prue circled the flat again, too nervous to sit down.

Aaron was busy with his phone and didn't look up. 'You know we did.'

'But it's already five to, and nobody's here.'

'Exactly. It's only five to. It's not as if any of them have far to come, or buses to catch. They won't have to come out of their doors until eight, will they? Or maybe a minute to, if they want to be on time.'

'I suppose.'

She went through to the kitchen and re-boiled the kettle, fiddled with the cups, lining all the handles up the same way round, and rearranged the biscuits she had already put out on plates. When the bell rang it made her jump.

By quarter past eight, six strangers were dotted about the living room, among them Aaron's mum Suzy, who was nothing like the woman she had imagined. She was quite chubby but attractive in an almost girlish way and could easily pass for ten years younger than her mid-forties, despite the thin scar that ran across her forehead and poked out beneath the fringe of her short blonde hair, which was obviously dyed and, although she probably didn't know it, was noticeably darker at the roots. She walked carefully across the crowded space, holding her son's arm, and sat down next to him, one hand resting on his knee. Whether it was to lay claim to him or merely to anchor herself in an unfamiliar room Prue could not be sure. The others all seemed to know her but in a vague sort of way, which wasn't surprising if she had lived here for a few years but had spent most of them stuck indoors. Prue made a mental note to pay Suzy a visit soon, now that the ice had been broken, and try to get to know her better, especially as she apparently spent so much time alone.

The youngest amongst the others were Beth and Rob from number 2. They, it appeared, were the ones whose pink baby buggy spent so much time propped against the hall wall downstairs. Their daughter Carrie was spending the night at Beth's mother's, meaning they could actually both come out together, which they assured her was a very rare occurrence. Prue got the impression she was probably keeping them from their bed as they both kept yawning and she caught Rob looking at his watch on more than one occasion. They did love the idea of a garden though, especially as an outdoor play space for Carrie, who was just about to turn three, and most of their ideas revolved around getting a swing or a slide and making sure there was enough space to ride a bike.

Also from the ground floor was Stan, who was probably only about sixty but acted as if he was at least twenty years older. A miserable old bugger, he had clearly come along with the sole intention of complaining. All those people banging the garden door and throwing balls against the walls and windows, even though his were at the front and didn't even overlook the garden. The noise, the disruption, the smell from the barbecues . . . and for what? A poncey new garden they had all lived perfectly well without all these years. There was grass already. What more did they need? As she refilled Stan's cup Prue found it hard even to look at him for fear of doing something he could find fault with. Tea too hot, not enough milk, the wrong type of sugar . . .

'And as for the absent Miss Cardew,' Stan went on, 'I wouldn't bother asking what she thinks of it all. Never see the woman. She's away half the time.'

'Yes, what interest has she ever shown in the garden?' Suzy replied. 'Or in what the rest of us want? You're right, Stanley. She's too busy with her play acting.'

'I think she takes it a bit more seriously than that, Mum. She's done Shakespeare and all. Look, she even won an award.' Aaron picked up Madi's statuette from the mantelpiece, eager to come to her defence, and read out the words on the base. '*The Hamlet Society. Best newcomer. Presented to Madalyn Cardew, 1979.* Do you want to hold it, have a feel of it? It's very shiny, and engraved . . .'

'Huh! Why would I want to do that? Hamlet Society, indeed. Hardly the Oscars, is it? Put the damn thing down, in case you break it. Besides, that was more than forty years ago. What has she done since, eh? Off round the country, playing little theatres nobody's heard of. Such a waste, leaving this lovely flat empty so often when we—'

'Okay, Mum. Not now.'

An air of awkwardness descended.

Across the room, in Madi's best armchair, sat Miss Parker from number 3. She was a very small, quiet woman, probably in her eighties, with wrinkled skin and a long straight nose which somehow, in the absence of any first name being offered, lent itself to the obvious nickname of Nosey Parker, which had rapidly sprung into Prue's head and now refused to go away. Whether the woman was actually nosey remained to be seen as she said very little, just held her cup rigidly, inches above her lap, and turned her head this way and that, like a curious bird, towards whoever happened to be speaking. Which, once Suzy had said her piece and retreated back into silence, tended to be Betty.

Betty Bloomfield lived at number 8, right next door to Madi, although Prue had never seen her before, not even coming in or out. She gave the impression of being one of those women who lived alone, with nobody to talk to for long periods, and who then can't stop chattering away nineteen to the dozen the minute they are let loose among a captive audience. By the time she left, Prue knew all there was to know about Betty's job at the library (probably another reason she talked so much, having to be so quiet all day long), her attempts at line dancing, the crime book she was currently reading, the pills she was on, and her rather erratic thoughts on the government, the church and the weather. Had she actually said anything about the garden? Prue's head was aching too much to remember.

'So . . .' Aaron took the used cups through to the kitchen after everyone but he and his mum had gone, and left them all precariously piled up in the sink as Prue nibbled on the last of the biscuits. 'Any joy, do you think? Are you going to make anything of the garden, with that lot involved?'

'No idea. I just feel a bit shell-shocked, to tell you the truth. There were still three flats who were no-shows and I'm not sure, for all their turning up and having their say, that any of those who came actually volunteered for anything.'

'Betty did say she could lay her hands on some gardening books, for ideas.'

'Yeah, from the library. Which any one of us could go and borrow just as easily.'

'And Miss Parker sounded like she was up for the bartering thingy. As soon as you mentioned baking an anniversary cake her eyes lit up like candles!'

'If she's any good. Imagine if it turned out to be some soggy old lopsided sponge with gooseberry jam or something equally hideous sandwiched in the middle! How many planks of wood is that going to get us?'

'Well, she did invite you up for a tasting, so you'll know soon enough.'

They returned to the living room and Aaron immediately gravitated back to his mum.

'And that Stan was so negative about everything, I think he could be trouble,' Prue went on. 'I can just imagine us planting some flowers and him creeping out there after dark and pulling them all up again. And the couple, Beth and Rob, all they want is a kids' playground they don't have to walk down the road to.'

'Giving up then?' Suzy said. 'It was worth a try, but if nobody's interested . . .'

'Is that what you think we should do? Give up?'

'Depends how much you want to do it really,' Aaron said, cutting in. 'We can't let Stan's negative attitude rub off on the rest of us, can we, Mum?'

'He's always been a cantankerous old devil, stirring up trouble, that one. But I still don't really see why you'd bother, Prue, when Aaron tells me you'll be leaving so soon.'

They all fell silent, until Aaron stood up and nudged his mum to do the same.

'We'll leave you to have a think, Prue, about the garden. But, knowing you, this won't be the end of it.'

'No, you're right. Because when I start something, I want to see it through.'

'But you haven't started, have you?' Suzy said.

'True, but I've been thinking about it so much I can almost see it, and smell it! Of all the ideas knocking about, I can't get the idea of a sensory garden out of my head. Surely that's something you could benefit from, Suzy, something you could enjoy . . . Well, everyone could, and will, I hope. And I don't think it will take long to do, once we get started. I thought maybe at the weekend, if I can get hold of Simon.'

'And what about Carrie's swing?'

'I'm really not sure about that. I was hoping for something more tranquil, somewhere where everyone can relax, not have a toddler squealing and kicking her legs in their faces.'

'I don't think they'll be living here much longer anyway. Theirs is only a one-bed, and I should think the little girl's going to need a room of her own pretty soon, never mind a garden.'

'Maybe a sandpit then? Easy to cover over again if it's not needed in the future. A token gesture, to keep them happy for now? And it's relatively unobtrusive . . . and quiet! Can't go upsetting Stan now, can we?'

'Oh, no,' Suzy said, with more than a hint of sarcasm. 'Nobody must upset Stan. Never mind the rest of us . . .'

* * *

223

'She didn't like me, did she?'

Aaron shrugged. 'I'm not sure she likes anybody very much. You notice she didn't say a word to Miss Parker, or to Betty. She keeps her distance, pretends that because she can't see them she doesn't know they're there, but that's rubbish. And she certainly can't stand that miserable old bugger Stan. He can be difficult, but so can she. And she doesn't like change. I think that comes down to not being able to see things change, if you know what I mean. In her head, everything's still the way it was when she last set eyes on it. And that includes that scrappy bit of grass outside. Change them and they become alien things that she can't picture. So, no, I don't think it's you she's taken against. It's more what you're hoping to do. And the fact that she doesn't know you, or what you look like, doesn't help.'

Prue nodded.

'I think her main reason for coming to your meeting last night wasn't really to offer much in the way of help, but to make sure she knows what's going on and to veto any sugges- tions the others might come up with, just out of spite. She's always said Stan's a scheming old busybody, and you'd think that Miss Parker from down below us was some old witch the way she talks about her. It's just Mum, I'm afraid. Just the way she is.'

'She does sound quite bitter. Do you think it's some kind of depression? She's had to go through a lot, and without any real support network around her.'

'She's got me.'

'Of course she has. Oh, don't get all defensive. But a woman of her age needs . . . a life of her own. Friends. Fun. It's not really healthy is it, staying in all the time, not meeting anyone, relying on a teenaged boy . . .'

'Boy?'

'Okay, man. I meant man!'

'Right. Well, I only came up to say hello. I really need to get some sleep in today if I'm going to be anywhere near fit for work tonight. When are you going to see Miss Parker?'

'About three. She said to call in for afternoon tea. If I don't appear tomorrow you'll know I've come down with food poisoning.'

'Harsh, Miss Harris. Very harsh. Don't look a gift horse in the gob, as my dad always says. Free cakes. What's not to like? And if they're any good you just might have found the way to get your garden started. Oh, and don't forget to take photos. If I don't get to eat any of the baking, I can at least see what I've missed!'

Prue sat for a while after he'd gone. Aaron might only be young but he always seemed to know what to say to cheer her up, to make her feel good about herself, to make her laugh. If anything at all had come out of her escape to London, it was meeting him, making a true friend. Of course, she would take photos. He knew she would. Because she always did. Of everything. Photography was what she did, what she lived and breathed for. It had been her hobby, her job, her passion for a long time now. She could give up village life. She could give up Joe Barton, although to be more accurate it was he who had given her up, but even so . . . The one thing she could never imagine being without was photography.

She fetched her laptop and switched it on. She had a few hours to kill before her cake date at number 3. Paving slabs and lavender plants and the future of the garden could wait. There was something else she needed to do before she chickened out again. And that was to start planning her own future.

She couldn't waste any more of her life snapping prize vegetables and hanging around taking pictures at weddings, let alone dreaming about her own. It was time she took this thing seriously, developed her skills, her knowledge, her art.

She brought Google up on the screen, then started to type into the search box. *Photography courses.* She only hesitated for a moment before adding one more word. *London.*

Chapter 25

MADI

Madi and Tom sat down in Prue's kitchen with Donny and a couple of his mates after school on Wednesday, and started to make plans for the stage show.

'Don't they do any of this at that school of yours?' Tom asked. 'Drama lessons, end-of-term performances, that sort of thing?'

Donny raised his eyes and let out a big sigh. 'I wish! No, drama is all Shakespeare at the moment. They're holding auditions for *Romeo and Juliet*, but I can't see me in those old tights, talking in a language I don't even understand.'

'You should give dear old Will a chance,' Madi said. 'He tells a good story. And the language is actually quite beautiful once you really listen to it, and funny sometimes too.' She had always loved Shakespeare, but she had to admit it wasn't to everyone's taste. She blamed it on the teaching. Thank God she'd had a wonderful English teacher, bursting with enthusiasm and fire. Mr Shearn, probably long dead by now, but she knew she would never have become an actress if not for the seeds he had planted in her imagination and his dogged determination to push her to succeed.

'And the only concerts they want us to put on are piano recitals and horrible screechy stuff from the kids learning the violin,' Donny went on, 'or the choir doing hymns and some old Messiah thing.'

'Not quite what you had in mind?' Tom smiled as all three boys shook their heads vigorously.

'Right then. Let's make a list, shall we? What sort of things you want to do, how many performers, what props you might need, whose parents we can count on to help backstage . . . and a date, of course. We must pick a date and book the hall. Not just for the show but for the rehearsals too. I would suggest twice a week to start with, but we may need a few more nearer the day. How does eight weeks sound? Enough, do you think? So, the performance in May sometime? Or maybe we could do two nights, if there's enough interest. And tickets . . . how many should we print? And what sort of entry price should we charge?'

Madi could see Donny's eyes light up as if to say 'Wow! This is really happening.'

'So, get some sort of first auditions cum rehearsal scheduled then, shall we? Get all your young friends together and find out who's up for getting involved.' Tom's pen was flying over the paper in his notepad. 'How about next week? Say Wednesday or Thursday?'

'Couldn't we make it Monday? Or Saturday even? We could work at it for longer then, rather than after school.'

'Well, you're keen! Fine by me though. A bit short notice, but if you think they'll come. I'll see if we can book the hall.'

'Not bad for someone worried about having no theatrical experience,' Madi said, after the boys had gone. 'I thought you said you wouldn't know where to start.'

Tom grinned. 'Ah, but I'm not bad at making things up as I go along. They're a bunch of teenagers. How hard can it be?'

'That's the attitude. They'll do all the work. All you have to do is be the grown-up, take charge of the money and make sure everything's done properly. All legal, and safe.'

'Oh, God, I hadn't even thought about all that health and safety lark. You'd think, being a fireman for so long, that would have been top of my list, wouldn't you? Fire exits, public liability insurance, all that malarkey . . .'

'You'll walk it. Now, I was thinking about storage. There'll be props, costumes, and you may need to hire in some extra chairs. I was thinking maybe the little shed in Prue's garden. Would she mind, do you think?'

'The old darkroom, you mean? I can't see why she should. It hasn't been used for years, not since her grandad was alive. They used to spend ages in there when she was a kid. It's where her love of photography began, with the science side of it, all the chemicals. Strings of prints, hanging up to dry. Like their own little washing line, it was! The place might need a bit of a clean out after all this time, to fight off the spiders, but it's watertight, I think, so nothing's going to get ruined if it rains. Good idea there, Madi. I'll jot it down in the book.'

* * *

'You sure you want to do this?'

'Yes, of course.'

They were going to the care home to visit Barbara, and Madi noticed, as she climbed into Tom's car, that there was a big carrier bag already waiting on the back seat.

'Just a few bits,' Tom said, spotting the direction of her gaze. 'They feed her well enough, and keep her clothes clean, but there's nothing quite like extra treats from home. She's very partial to a bourbon biscuit but they hardly ever have them in the tin. And I've dug out a pair of warm slippers she'd hidden away in the wardrobe and never worn. Still had the label on them! The ones she's got now are looking past their best.'

'You are a very thoughtful man. She's lucky to have you.'

'It's nothing. Just keeping her feet warm and her tastebuds catered for! I wish I could do more.'

'Are you able to take her out? For a walk? Lunch? The theatre?'

'I can. There's no rules to say I can't, but . . . well, to tell the truth, a short walk's fine, if it's somewhere quiet, but anything more would just unsettle her. Scare her, even. A strange place, people she doesn't know. And watching a play would be pointless. She doesn't have the concentration. Not any more.'

'That's a shame. But I'm a stranger. Are you sure . . .?'

'Quite sure. You'll be entering her environment, not dragging her out into yours. It's safer. And you'll be with me. It'll be okay, honestly. She'll like you.'

They drove in companionable silence for the rest of the

way, Tom scooting along the lanes with enviable confidence, and pulled into the car park just before three.

'Just in time for tea!' he said, grabbing the bag from the back and running round to help Madi from the car.

'I'm not an invalid, you know. You don't have to . . .'

'Nonsense. It's the way I was brought up. Always hold doors open for a lady, lay my cloak over puddles and all that. And, besides, you're still recovering from fairly major surgery, not that anyone would know, to look at you.'

'Oh, don't remind me.' She crossed her arms and wrapped them across her chest, then realised what she was doing and started rubbing her hands up and down her arms as if she was cold, adding a little 'brrr' noise to emphasise the point.

'Ready?' Tom said, sliding a hand beneath her elbow and guiding her up the wide concrete steps to the front door.

There was a young woman at the reception desk, idly filing her nails. 'Oh, hello, Tom,' she said, peering up at Madi. 'And you've brought a friend, I see.'

'I have indeed, Clara.' Tom made no attempt to introduce her. 'And how is my princess today?'

'Oh, the same. She had chicken for lunch, and a little nap in her room. I think she's in the TV lounge now.'

'Kettle on?'

Clara glanced at the clock. 'Of course. Three o'clock, on the dot. You know that. And we've got a nice fruit cake today, courtesy of Olive, Harold's wife.'

'Right-o.'

The girl pressed a button to release the inner door, and Tom led Madi through into a long beige corridor. 'This way, Madi.

231

And don't get too excited. I've sampled Olive's cakes before and, believe me, you'll be glad I've brought the bourbons.'

The TV was on, but nobody seemed to be paying it any attention. Tom pointed to a woman sitting in a high-backed green plush chair facing the window, her fingers working away rhythmically at the arm as if she was trying to pick off some imaginary pieces of fluff. As they approached, Madi could see that Barbara looked a lot older than her sixty-eight years. Her hair was loosely permed but not well combed, and she was wearing no make-up.

Her face lit up as she spotted them. 'Hello,' she said, tentatively, staring at Tom as if meeting an interesting-looking stranger at a party, and holding out her hand to be shaken. 'I'm Barbara.'

'Hello, Barbara. My name's Tom.' His voice was low and gentle as he knelt down on the carpet bedside her and held tightly to her hand, not letting it go. 'And this is Madi.'

Barbara tilted her head up and studied Madi's face. 'I know you,' she said. 'I've seen you before.'

'Have you?'

'I've seen you on the telly. You were reading the news.'

'Was I?'

'Are you two married?' she said, looking from one to the other.

'I am,' said Tom, getting to his feet. 'But not to Madi. We're just friends.'

'Oh. That's nice.' She stared ahead of her, at something far away, outside the window, as Tom pulled two plastic chairs over and he and Madi sat down.

'Have you brought me anything?'

232

Tom picked up the bag from next to his feet and pulled out the biscuits. 'Look. Your favourites,' he said, his voice gentle. He must find this all so upsetting, but Madi could see the effort he was making not to let it show.

'They're not my favourites,' Barbara said, pushing his hand away. 'Didn't you bring any digestives?'

A staff member brought a tray and laid it down on the table next to Barbara's chair. 'Three cups,' she said. 'Just help yourselves from the pot. And there's cake, if you'd like some?'

'We'll pass on that, thanks, Claire.' Tom winked at the woman, who had to suppress a giggle.

'Can't say I blame you,' she said under her breath, and moved off to serve someone else.

'So, how are you today, Barb?'

'Good. The shower was cold this morning, and there was a blackbird. Who did you say you were again?'

'Tom. Remember? We've known each other a long time.'

'Have we?'

'Nearly fifty years.'

'It was the eighteenth of June,' she said, a slow smile spreading across her face.

'That's right!'

'I could have married Ken, you know.'

Tom poured a cup of tea and handed it to her, carefully. 'I'm so glad you didn't.'

'How are the girls?' she said, suddenly lucid. 'Not with you today?'

'Not today, love. Busy with the little ones, I expect, but I'm sure they'll be along to see you soon.'

'Do you have any children, Madi?'

'I do, yes. One son.'

'I had a son once.'

Madi looked across at Tom who shook his head and put his fingers to his lips as if to say, 'Just go along with it.'

'So, what have you been up to, Barb?' Tom tried to steer the conversation in a new direction. 'Been out dancing?' His eyes shone with mischief. 'Discoing the night away?'

'Don't be daft,' she said, tapping his arm. 'You know they only have the discos on Saturdays. You should come, Madi.' She turned her head towards Madi and whispered. 'There are some great-looking lads there. Between you and me I've got my eyes on one. His name's Tom . . .'

'Is she always like that?'

'Good days and bad days. That was somewhere in between, I suppose. She remembered your name, and she wanted you to go dancing with her. You've made a friend there!'

'But . . .'

'But she didn't recognise me, her own husband? Yes, I know. She gets confused. It's how it is, I'm afraid. But she liked the slippers, even though she had no idea it was her who'd bought them, and she did eat the bourbons in the end, so we did our bit to make her happy.'

'And the thing about having a son?'

'Miscarriage. Long ago, and no knowing what sex it was, but she likes to have something to cling to. Called it – *him* – Ian. Keeps him real. And surprisingly not something she forgets.'

'Oh, Tom. I'm so sorry.'

'Now don't you start or you'll get me going too. There's nothing I can do. Just accept things as they are and keep on being there for her. And I do need other things to do, to think about. Which is where young Donny's stage show comes in. That should keep my mind occupied and my hands busy for a while. Just what I need. Thanks, Madi. I wouldn't have even considered it if not for you.'

'I know I won't be here when it all finally comes together, but do reserve me a ticket, won't you? I'd definitely like to come back and see it. Well, to see you too, of course.'

'Front-row seat already has your name on it, Madi. Not quite the kind of production you're used to, but . . .'

'I'm looking forward to it, and we all had to start somewhere. You should have seen my first time on stage. No, actually, come to think of it, I'm glad you didn't.'

'Bad, was it?'

'Truly appalling. I was only nine, I forgot half my lines, and my long blonde wig fell off in the middle of a scene.' She lifted her hand to her head. 'Oh dear. At least that didn't happen today. God, I'd actually forgotten I was wearing the damn thing.'

'Shows your confidence is coming back. And it won't be long now until you can discard it altogether. You know I much prefer you without it anyway. More natural. More *you*.'

'Tom, you hardly know me. How can you possibly know what's the real me?'

'Oh, I have a pretty good idea. And I like what I see. And I meant it when I told Barb we were friends. Good friends, and I hope we can stay that way after you go back home.

Keep in touch. And you did promise me a backstage tour, remember?'

'If I go back to work.'

'Oh, you will, Madi. It's in your blood. I may not know you very well – yet – but I do know that much. You are an actress above all else. Well, apart from being a mother. But there's absolutely no reason you can't do both, and do them well. I have faith in you.'

'Talking of which . . . Faith. I keep promising I'll pop in and see her, for tea and cake. I don't suppose you'd come with me, would you?'

'Why? Not scared of her, are you?'

'Not at all. But I watched you sampling the wares at that village produce show and I know how partial you are to cake, that's all.'

'Oh, go on then. No time like the present. Let's go and knock on her door. Those bourbons were okay, but not enough to satisfy a growing lad like me. And Faith does make a great cup of tea.'

Orchard House was just as Madi had imagined it. Big and sprawling, surrounded by lawns and hedges, with an oak front door that creaked as it opened. Faith welcomed them both with awkward hugs and squeals of surprise, and they went inside, with Faith leading the way down a long hall with a high ceiling, past doors that opened into rooms that she could see were full of dark wood furniture, fat squishy armchairs and lots of floral printed cushions and curtains. In the kitchen, a threadbare rug was spread out on a tiled floor in front of the range, where a small white dog lay, tail twitching as he slept.

'Oh, don't mind Noodle,' Faith said, stepping over him and hurriedly pulling off her apron as she reached for the kettle. 'That's his favourite place. And he's had a tiring day, chasing rabbits! Not that he ever catches any. Now, shall we sit in here or would you prefer to get more comfy in the parlour?'

'Here's fine. No need to stand on ceremony with us, Faith. It's not as if I haven't been in this kitchen many times before.'

'Ah, but Madi hasn't, Tom. Now, let me pour you some tea, and then maybe Madi would like a little tour of the house? It's quite old. And quite grand once, in its day. They say the fireplace is original Victorian.'

'I'd like that.'

'So, where's Stuart? Still at work?' Tom took the mug he was offered and wrapped his hands around it, blowing across the top of his tea to cool it.

'Out delivering a litter of puppies up at Bradwell Farm. They'll be looking for homes for them, I shouldn't wonder. Fancy a puppy, Madi? A bit of company for you in London?'

Madi laughed. 'I don't think a puppy would really be suited to a top-floor flat. And I'm not at home enough to take on any sort of pet, I'm afraid. I'd struggle, even with keeping a goldfish fed and watered!'

'Ah, but you've been doing so well with little Flo. Ralph says you're a natural. How is she, by the way?'

'Better. More or less back to her old self, I'd say. And quite happily curled up on the bed when I left earlier.'

'That's good. I'm sure our Prue will be grateful. How is

she, by the way? Have you heard anything from her? She's living in your flat, I understand?'

'Yes, she is, but we don't stay in touch. It was purely a business arrangement. A swap that suited us both, that's all. And one that, sadly, will be over all too soon. I've loved being here in Shelling. It's been exactly what I needed, and I hope that London has proved to be what Prue needed too.'

Madi could see Faith bristle. 'She has a perfectly good life here . . .'

'Oh, I'm sure she does, but some time away never does any harm, does it? Helps put things into perspective, show us what's important.'

'I suppose so.' Faith turned her back and opened a cupboard, pulled out a large tin and opened that as well. 'Now . . . I do believe I promised you cake, and as luck would have it, I made one only this morning. A nice big slice for you, Tom?'

'You know me so well.'

'I should do, after all these years. And Madi . . . can I tempt you too?'

'It looks lovely, Faith. Yes, please.'

Madi looked up at the sound of footsteps crunching across the gravel outside the window.

'Oh, that'll be Joe,' Faith said, lowering her voice. 'Home from work. He rents our extension flat at the back there. To be honest, it's put me in a bit of a quandary, this business between him and Prue. I mean, if they're no longer an *item*, it could get a bit difficult, couldn't it? Having him living right here on our doorstep. I was wondering if maybe we should ask him to leave?'

'Seems a bit harsh,' Tom said, shrugging his shoulders and licking cake crumbs from his fingers. 'A man losing his home because of something he has, or hasn't, done in his private life. Oh, I know she's your daughter and all, but I'm not sure breaking up with her is really grounds for eviction, do you?'

'Well, you know me, Tom. I don't like any unpleasantness. And I want Prue to feel happy to come here at any time. This was her home, and always will be. I'd hate to think she felt uncomfortable coming here in case she runs into *him*.'

'You make him sound like the devil all of a sudden. I thought you liked him?'

'I did. I do.'

'Then let them sort it out between them. If you want my advice, don't get involved.'

'Is that what you think too, Madi?'

'None of my business, Faith.' Madi couldn't help remembering that glimpse of young Joe and his friend just days ago, and how she'd told herself that very same thing then. None of my business indeed. 'But I think Tom's right. Stay out of it. Meddling in our children's lives never ends well. If you don't want to end up doing the wrong thing, it's often best to do nothing. Say nothing.'

'Families, eh? Have you ever put your foot in it, Madi? Done the wrong thing, but for all the right reasons?'

'Too many times to mention! And once you mess up, it can be a struggle knowing how to put things right again. Best not to mess up in the first place.'

Madi could feel Tom's eyes on her. He knew exactly what she was thinking about. George.

'So, shall I show you around?' Faith bustled to her feet. 'Excuse the mess!'

'That would be lovely.'

After a leisurely tour of the house, which made Madi feel like a bit of an intruder as Faith insisted on opening every door, even the one for the toilet, and showing off what seemed like every last cobwebbed corner, it was time to go.

'Come on, Madi. I'm sure Faith has things to do, Stuart's dinner to cook . . .'

'Well, it was nice to see you both . . . together.'

Tom smiled. 'We've been out. Visiting Barbara,' he added, cutting off any further enquiry. 'You should come and see her yourself. It's been a long time.'

'Oh, yes.' Faith looked flustered. 'I will. It's just that . . . well, I find that sort of thing difficult. I wouldn't really know what to say.'

'I think you'll find she's the one who doesn't know what to say. Sometimes she doesn't even know her own name. But she's still Barbara, underneath, and you were good friends once.'

'I'm sorry, Tom. It's just . . .'

'I know. And I'll leave it up to you. Thanks for the tea. And the cake. It was delicious, as always.'

They walked back to Tom's car, Faith waving them off and then hurrying back inside.

'Come on, hop in. It may only be a few yards home and you could walk it almost as quickly, but we set out together and we'll arrive back together. Let the gossips have their day!'

He started the engine and pulled away from the kerb.

'I don't suppose, after all that cake, that you fancy dinner, do you? In the pub? Oh, not right away. Leave it an hour or so. My treat, naturally.'

He turned his face towards Madi's, waiting for an answer, his eyes drawn away from the road ahead. For seconds. Only seconds.

They both felt the bump. Tom slammed on the brakes and they leapt out of the car. Madi's hands flew up to her face and it was all she could do not to scream.

It was Flo, dear, sweet little Flo, lying on her side on the road, her paws outstretched, her tail curled limply behind her. And, if it was not for the trickle of blood slowly pooling around her head, she would have looked for all the world as if she was simply asleep.

Chapter 26

PRUE

M iss Parker's flat was cluttered and dark.

'You must call me Emily,' she said, once the initial awkwardness was over and Prue was sitting with a bone-china cup of weak tea on the small chintzy sofa by the window, the curtains three-quarters closed behind her.

'Thank you, and I'm Prue, as you already know. It's very good of you to offer us some help with raising funds for the garden.'

'Us? I thought you were here alone.'

'Oh, I am. No, I meant Aaron. You know, from number six. He's been very good, helping me out . . .'

'I see. Not with the cake baking, I assume.'

Prue wasn't sure whether to smile. Emily Parker had one of those faces that made it very hard to tell whether she was joking or deadly serious. 'No, of course not. That's where you come in, I hope.'

'Depends what this couple want, I suppose.' Emily handed Prue a thick piece of fruitcake and a small fork. 'I am rather a traditionalist when it comes to a celebration cake. Fruit or sponge, royal icing and a piping bag. I don't really hold with this new fad of piling cupcakes into towers or flavouring the sponge with lavender or roses or whatever. I'm happy to donate the flour and eggs and such like. Fruit too, if that's what they want. It's not as if any of that costs very much. It's the time that adds the value, you see. The care, the skill, that's where the real cost lies, but I am prepared to give of those freely too, in aid of the cause, so to speak. I have time on my hands, and I like the idea of a garden. I like flowers. Roses, in particular. Such a romantic flower . . .'

'Thank you. And I'm happy to let you choose some of the plants, if you'd like to. It is your garden, not mine, in the long-term.' Prue swallowed a mouthful of cake, rich with sultanas and cherries. It really was very good. 'I'll speak to Simon.'

'Simon?'

'He's the one who comes to cut the grass and clean the stairs . . .'

'Ah, yes. And his part in all this is . . .?'

'It's his friend who wants the anniversary cake and might be willing to supply some paving in exchange.'

'I see. I can't say I've ever been paid in concrete before.'

This time Prue did see the hint of a smile playing at the corners of Miss Parker's lips.

'Have you always been a baker, Emily? Because this cake is delicious. My mother makes cakes, but yours is in a different league. I can certainly tell you're no beginner.'

'Oh, thank you. Yes, I suppose you could say I was a profes-sional, of sorts. I had a little café, you see. Close to the West

End. Hidden away, but its reputation made sure they came. For speciality teas, home-made scones, a slice of cake . . . I didn't open in the evenings, when the riff-raff descend, looking for chips and alcohol, making all their mess and noise. Oh no, I preferred the more respectful afternoon trade. All the best people knew where I was. Popping in after a matinee, or when out shopping. Some of them quite well-known . . .'

'Oh, really? That sounds exciting.' Prue finished her cake, wiping a stray crumb from her mouth, and laid the empty plate down on the small, ornate table beside her. 'Anyone I might have heard of?'

'Oh, I don't gossip, dear. The secrets of the rich and famous are safe with me. And I knew quite a few, believe me. But, yes, I have always baked. Not so much these days, with nobody to eat it but myself, but I will relish the challenge. And a silver wedding, I think you said. Little bells, some silver ribbon. You see, I already have ideas. So, you speak to this Simon and his friend and let me know what's required. You know where to find me. I don't get out much these days. I'm always here.'

Prue found herself ushered quietly out, the door closed behind her. Stan was hovering in the hall, fiddling with the latest batch of pizza leaflets and tutting to himself over little Carrie's buggy, parked unobtrusively in the corner. He turned his back and pretended not to have seen her, which suited Prue just fine. Miserable old devil!

'I have to go home.'

Aaron had answered the door wearing nothing but pyjama bottoms.

'What?' He looked at her through sleepy eyes, not quite with-it enough to be sure what was going on. 'Slow down. Calm down. And say that again.'

'I have to leave. Today. Now.'

'But your month isn't up yet. And what about the garden? You haven't even told me about your visit to Miss Nosey Parker yet.'

'I'm sorry about that. Maybe you can do it. Take over the garden, I mean. Or we can just forget the whole thing.'

'What? Of course we can't.'

'Well, maybe I could come back. I don't know. For now, I just have to go. It's my cat, Flo. She's been in an accident, hit by a car.'

'Oh, no, Prue, I'm so sorry. Is she . . .?'

'No, she's still alive, but it doesn't look good. She's an old cat. Not strong, and she's been hurt badly. My friend Sian works at the vets'. She rang, thought I'd want to know straight-away. So I've grabbed a few essentials and I'm going to catch the first available train. I didn't really have time to pack prop-erly, so I suppose I'll have to come back, won't I? If only to collect my things. Do you think Madi will mind, me leaving stuff here, not tidying up or changing the sheets or anything?'

'I wouldn't worry about any of that for now. I can always go in and clean up if you like. Just leave me the key. Oh, no, actually, I think we already have one. For emergencies. Mum is the landlord, after all.'

'Thanks, Aaron.' She leant forward, not quite sure whether she should kiss him goodbye, but doing it anyway, briefly, on the cheek. 'Wish me luck. Wish Flo luck . . .'

'Of course.'

He stepped forward, his hands on the banister, and remained standing there, shivering on the landing, as she rushed off down the stairs and turned to give him a limp wave when she reached the bottom. 'Bye.'

'Bye.'

The walk to the station, the wait on the platform, the train journey in the dark, all blurred together, until several hours later she found herself back in Norfolk, Sian wrapping an arm around her shoulders and guiding her into a cab.

'How is she?'

'It's early days but she's doing well. She's a little fighter, that one, and your dad and Ralph will do everything they possibly can for her. You know that.'

'How did it happen? You said it was Tom Bishop and Madi in the car. Who was actually driving? Were they speeding?'

'No, just an accident from what I can gather. It was Tom driving, and he's really cut up about it. But Flo's alive, Prue, that's what matters. So come on, stop fretting. We'll be home soon enough and you can see for yourself.'

'Home? Oh, God, I can't even go home, can I? Madi's still there, in my house. We had a deal. I can't suddenly throw her out because I've come back early.'

'I'm sure she'll understand. Or maybe you could share for a while?'

'Sian, I don't even have a spare bed. I got rid of Gran's rickety old single and put my desk in there, remember?'

'Sofa? Or farm her out to your mum's maybe? We'll work

something out. She'll be okay about it. She's okay, is Madi. Nice. Caring. She's been really great looking after Flo, since the abscess.'

'The what?'

'Oh, no! I'm sorry. You didn't know about that, did you? Look, it was nothing serious, just a sore mouth, and we didn't want to spoil things for you, drag you back over nothing . . .'

'Well, it's not nothing now, is it?' Prue's mind was racing. 'If Flo wasn't her usual self, if she was feeling poorly, in pain, slow to cross the road . . . For heaven's sake, Sian! She's my cat. My responsibility. How could you not tell me? If you'd have called me sooner, I could have been here, taking care of her, then maybe it wouldn't have happened. Oh, God, it's my fault, isn't it? For going away, leaving her . . .'

'You can't think like that. These things happen. It's nobody's fault, and certainly not yours. Now, come on, wipe that miserable expression away. Flo won't want to see you looking sad. She'll just be glad her mummy's home.'

'You make her sound like she's my child, not my cat.'

'Same thing really. Flo's family.'

'Yes, she is, isn't she?'

They climbed out of the cab, Sian pushing Prue's purse away and insisting on paying the fare, and they hurried up the narrow lane towards the surgery. The bells were silent for a change.

'No Donny tonight?'

'It's football on Thursdays, remember? And besides, it's almost ten o'clock!'

'Is it? I'd lost track.'

'Actually, there's talk of our Donny taking up other interests, thanks to your house guest, so we may yet be spared!'

'I'm curious. And relieved! Tell me later.'

Once inside, Sian ushered Prue straight through to the back room and to the wire cage at the end where Flo lay sleeping on a blanket. Prue felt her heart lurch when she saw her, looking so small and helpless. 'Hello, sweetie. Have you missed me?'

Flo tried to lift her head, swathed in bandages so Prue couldn't even see her ears. One eye was swollen and almost closed, one leg held straight by some kind of splint-like contraption, and there was an IV line feeding her fluids.

'Oh . . .'

'It's not as bad as it looks. Her leg is fractured but her skull isn't, thank God.'

'But the blood . . . you said on the phone that there was blood.'

'She was quite badly cut, so your dad's had to stitch her up, and she's lost a couple of teeth, that's all. Her poor old mouth's taken a bit of a battering lately, what with one thing and another. She's still in shock, Prue, and she'll be very sleepy for a while, from the drugs we've given her, but she's been incredibly lucky, especially considering her age. Here, I'll open up, then you can stroke her. Gently, mind.'

Prue nodded, feeling her best friend's arms close around her. And that was when she finally allowed herself to cry.

Prue sat in her mum's kitchen the next morning, nursing a cup of tea.

'You were so late last night I must have nodded off waiting

for you. Your father says you were at the surgery until nearly midnight!'

'I had to make sure she was okay. Thanks for the bed though, not that I actually got a lot of sleep.'

'Well, you must have slept eventually or you wouldn't have got up so late. Still, it's good to have you back, love. I assume you'll be staying? Not swanning back to London again?'

'There was no swanning involved, Mum. I needed a break. A short break, to get my head together. I was always coming back.'

'Glad to hear it. And have you? Got your head together?'

'Getting there.'

'No pining over what's not to be? Because he's not good enough for you, you know. That Joe Barton. Never was.'

'Funny you never said that when we were together. In fact, I always thought you liked him. Letting him move into the annexe . . .'

'That was a business arrangement. A financial transaction. And when he fell out with his father we thought it would keep him near, stop him running off somewhere again, so that you two could . . .'

'Live happily ever after?'

Her mother huffed. 'Obviously not.' She stood up and went to the cupboard behind her. 'How about some breakfast? Cereal, or toast?'

'Bit late for that. It's more like elevenses time!'

'Cake then? I've got some nice cherry genoa, made yesterday. Or there's a slice of carrot left?'

'Is that your answer to everything? Cake? Whatever's

wrong in my life, in the family, in the world, it can be solved with cake.'

'Don't be silly. Food can be a comfort, that's all. Talking of which, what would you like for dinner later? I thought I might invite Madi along. I hear you've never actually met, which I find very odd, I must say, what with you letting her live in your gran's house.'

'*My* house, Mum. And I've been living in hers, so it seems pretty fair to me. But, yes, I would like to meet her. And to sort out who's sleeping where, now that I'm back. I'd best not leave it until this evening. I'll pop round in a minute.'

'Well, it was good to have you back in your old room last night. You know I always keep it aired, with clean sheets, just in case . . . so if Madi won't budge, you can always stay here until she's gone. Whenever that might be. She's got her claws right into our Tom, from what I can tell, so who knows how long she might hang around.'

'Mum! Tom's perfectly happy with Barbara. You surely don't think he'd . . .'

'Probably not, but you never know, do you? Poor Barbara's hardly in a position to challenge him, is she? She'd never know, would she? And men do have . . . needs. Who knows what goes on in other people's relationships? Just look at you and your Joe.'

'Well, he's not exactly *my* Joe any more, is he? If he ever was.'

'No, he's not, and it's time you held your head up high and showed him you're doing fine, that you don't care what he says or does. Running away isn't the answer. You should have stayed and faced him. You're a Harris, and we don't let people walk all over us, you hear?'

Prue laughed. 'You make it sound like we're lords of the manor or something. Lord and Lady Harris of Shelling and their spinster daughter!'

'Spinster indeed! And we don't need a fancy title to make us who we are, Prue. We're a good, hardworking family who belong here in Shelling. Don't let anyone drive you away, that's all I'm saying. Now, is roast chicken all right for tonight? And an apple pie for afters.'

'With apples from the family orchard?'

'Oh, you may mock, my girl, but you won't find a better pie than mine around these parts, whatever that landlady at The Brown Cow may say.'

'You can be a right snob when you want to be.'

'It's not snobbish to know what you're good at, to know your own worth. I just wish you'd remember that when it comes to your photography.'

'I've been thinking about that, as it happens. About taking it further.'

'About bloody time!'

It wasn't often Prue heard her mother swear. 'Yes, I suppose it is,' she said. 'But for now I'm off to see Flo, and then to call on Madi.'

'If she's not in, try Tom's place.'

'Stop it, Mum. It's not our business.'

'No, you're right. I'll say no more about it. Are you sure I can't tempt you to try the cake? You haven't eaten properly for hours.'

'I had some crisps and a lump of cheese when I got in last night.'

'Oh, that was you, was it? When I saw the crumbs all over the worktop I thought we'd had mice in the night!'

'We'd best hope Flo recovers quickly then, so she can come and chase them away. But, go on then. I'll have your last slice of carrot cake, and another cuppa before I go.'

It felt strange knocking on her own front door, but it would not have seemed quite right to use her key. For the time being, she had to regard this as Madi's home, not hers. And she should really move her car off the drive too, maybe start it up to make sure it hadn't given up the ghost, having been abandoned for so long. She hadn't given a thought to Madi's parking arrangements, not having been sure whether she would have come down by car or on the train, but that had to be Madi's little blue car parked in the road. She'd drive her own down to her parents' when she left here, and perhaps run the hose over it to shake off the mud and dust.

As she waited on the step, she couldn't help noticing the last of the tulips bent over in the front garden, and the long-dead remains of the daffodils in the tubs. The grass was slowly coming back to life after a dry winter spell, and would soon be in need of its first cut of the season. It might only be small, but she had missed her own garden, both front and back. Perhaps that was why she had been so instantly aware of the lack of one at the flats. Or one pleasant enough to relax in, anyway. There really was nothing quite like fresh air and flowers, and the tranquillity of dozing peacefully in a chair under a tree.

The woman who opened the door was nothing like she

had imagined her. She was shorter than Prue, and a good forty years older, but the flamboyant theatricality she had expected was nowhere in evidence. She looked ordinary somehow, in her loose shirt and jeans, her face make-up free and her feet bare.

'Hello?'

'Hi. You must be Madi.'

'I am, and you are . . .'

'Oh, sorry, I'm Prue.'

'Prue? As in Prue who lives here?'

Prue nodded. 'Yep, that's me. I'm so sorry to drop in out of the blue like this, but . . .'

'But you're back in the village . . . and you want your house back?' Madi looked suddenly crestfallen.

'Oh, God, no. We had a deal. It's just that . . .'

'Flo!' Madi's hand came up and cupped her mouth. 'How silly of me. You're back for Flo. Of course, you are. Look, come on in, please. Not that you need me to invite you into your own home, but we do need to talk, don't we?'

Prue followed Madi into the lounge. Apart from a cardigan draped over a chair and a box of chocolates open on the rug, nothing looked any different. But then, why should it? Madi didn't look the type to hold wild parties and trash the place.

'About Flo. I am so sorry. I was supposed to be looking after her, and I feel absolutely terrible about what happened. Tell me, is she okay this morning? Has there been any change? I didn't like to go down to the surgery hassling them, when I know how busy they must be. Especially when it was me in the car . . .'

'She's as well as anyone can expect. Better than that, in fact.'

'I'm glad. You don't know what a relief it is to hear that. I thought we'd killed her, I honestly did.' Madi wiped a tear from her cheek. 'Now, Prue, can I get you anything? A coffee? A biscuit?' They walked through to the kitchen. 'I'm not much of a cook, so I can't offer you anything more substantial, I'm afraid.'

'Coffee would be good, and Mum's already fed me up, thanks.' Prue shivered, looking back through the open doorway into the lounge. 'You haven't lit the fire, I see.'

'Never could quite get the hang of it. And the weather's on the up now. A thick woolly jumper and that lovely cosy duvet of yours are all I need.'

'Are you sure? I can light it now, if you like, and show you how.'

'Oh, Tom's already tried showing me, but I'm hopeless at technical things. I'll just forget again. And my memory's not at its best right now.' Madi filled the kettle and switched it on. 'You've probably heard about my illness and my op, not that it's a state secret. My mind's been a bit fuzzy for a while, all over the place. That's what's worried me the most, even more than the physical changes to be honest, but I'm getting there. Since I've been here I've even started finding my keys exactly where I last left them! Must be the country life doing its thing. De-stressing.'

'That's good. I'm glad you've settled in. And made friends, I hear.'

'Well, yes, I suppose so. Your mother's been kind, and Patty at the shop. Don't know where I'd be without her constant supply of frozen ready-meals! And Tom, of course. He took me to meet his wife, you know, which I thought might be awful but it really wasn't. So sad . . .'

'Yes, it is.' Prue took the mug of coffee from Madi's hands and they sat down at the small kitchen table.

'So, are you back to stay? I can always head home early myself, if that helps.'

'That hardly seems fair, especially if being here is proving good for your health. And I hear you're up to something with young Donny?'

'Hah, yes! The boy was keen to put on a show in the village hall and thought I might be able to help, but I won't be around as it comes to fruition, will I? No, I've been happy to start things off, but I've already passed the reins to Tom. The poor man needed a project, something to do . . .'

'Funny you should say that, because I've sort of started something back in London too, and it looks like I'll have to hand it over to someone else if it's ever likely to get finished.'

'Oh? Now I am intrigued.'

'It's the garden at the back. If you can call it that.'

'Oh, yes, it is a bit of a mess, isn't it?'

'Exactly. So I had this idea to make it into something more . . .'

'More like this?' Madi said, gesturing towards the garden through the kitchen window.

'Well, yes, I suppose so. A decent lawn, a paved area, some flowers, something to be enjoyed and shared rather than just tolerated or used as a place to have a smoke! Perhaps I was being too ambitious. It's not really my place to start changing anything, is it? I don't live there, and I won't be the one living with it in the future, but I do like something to get my teeth into, and I figured you like flowers by the beautiful tulips you left in the bedroom, so it felt like a way of paying you back. A surprise for you when you got back. Not that it will be now. And something with some scents and textures to it, you know, for Suzy downstairs . . . but I'd hate to step on anyone's toes, and I already seem to have annoyed the hell out of Stan.'

'Who hasn't?' Madi laughed. 'There are some people you can never please. Born grumpy, that one.'

'I suppose so. Anyway, now I'm back here I don't suppose I'll see it through. Aaron from downstairs has offered to help, but it's not really fair to leave him to it.'

'Ah, so you've made friends too! But why not let Aaron do it? If he's offered? And if you think it might help his mum. He's a nice lad, from what I've seen, and it'll be them, and the others, who'll benefit, won't it? And me too, while I'm still recuperating at home. So many books to catch up on, and a long summer ahead. I've spent so much time away over the years, I hardly ever had time to run the hoover round, do my washing and re-pack, let alone worry about the garden. Yes, I'm all for it, and I can always lend a hand when I get back. Not the actual digging as I'm meant to be going easy on the physical stuff for a while, but if it's money you need . . .'

'Thank you, Madi.'

'Sounds more like it's me who should be thanking you. And your garden here is lovely, by the way. The whole village is lovely. I'll be sorry to leave.'

'Then don't! It's only Friday. We still have . . .' She counted

257

on her fingers. 'Another twelve days of our agreement left, and I'll be perfectly happy at my parents' place until then. If Flo recovers enough, I might even go back to yours for a while. So, stay, please. It will be nice to get to know you properly. In fact, that reminds me, Mum wants you to come to dinner tonight. And I'd like that too. You can fill me in about the other residents at Belle Vue Court.'

'They're certainly a mixed bunch, aren't they?'

'As are the residents of Shelling!'

'Ah, but that's what the world's about. Variety. All part of life's rich tapestry . . .' Madi closed her eyes and tilted her head back, just enough for Prue to spot the join where her wig didn't quite sit squarely against her forehead. She sat upright again and smiled. 'Yes, I would love to come to dinner. And no, before you ask, there really is no need to invite Tom as well, just in case your mum has any ideas on that score. We are friends, and that's all.'

'And you can't have too many of those.'

'No, I don't suppose you can. Very pleased to meet you at last, Prue my darling. And to add another friend to my list.'

Chapter 27

*S*o, she's gone. The interloper. Full of crazy ideas, begging everyone for help, and then running off into the night before so much as a spade's hit the ground. Not to be trusted, that one, pretty much as I suspected all along. Garden, indeed! It might have been all right, I suppose, to help to create something soothing in an otherwise harsh and ugly world, but I'm not going to miss something I never had. Even so, promises should be kept. People should finish what they've started, see things through to the end. I certainly intend to.

I should be pleased really, that she's gone. Excited that I can carry on where I left off, free to poke about again, to roam where I please. I found some trousers today. Left out on the bed. Leather! Well, well, I had her down as a goody two-shoes, but it seems Miss Buttercups and Daisies has a secret side. Leather! Who'd have thought it? Hidden depths, after all. But she didn't take them with her, did she? Leaving that side of herself in the big bad city, draped sluttishly over someone else's bed.

But it's not the same. Since she left – the so-called actress – the edge has gone off it, the thrill nowhere near the same if she isn't here for me to torment. Visiting an empty flat, without the *scent of her, the echo of her, does nothing, fulfils nothing . . . It's just curiosity, and that's not what this is supposed to be about.*

I await her return with . . . anticipation, is that the right word? Or expectation. Of the games to come. Of knowing there can be only one winner this time around. Me.

But there are only so many tricks I can play, only so many objects I can move, or steal. I'm getting bored. I've toyed with her long enough, but it's not working. I thought she'd be so scared by now, terrified even, but cancer's hard to compete with when it comes to fear.

She doesn't know about me. I'm sure about that. That solicitor came, but he didn't see her. He won't have told her anyway. Confidentiality, and all that. It's not as if he actually told me. Not all of it. Not about her. Well, not intentionally anyway. And he's long gone. Job done. Back to his gazumping and his divorce cases, spreading his misery and charging the earth for the privilege. If she'd figured it out, I'd know. But she hasn't. Not a clue.

So, if the cancer wasn't able to do it for me – and where would be the satisfaction in that? – perhaps it's time I did it myself. Finished it. Finished her.

I could do it, couldn't I? Finish this thing properly. An eye for an eye. Or is that just a fantasy scenario? One I can take pleasure from, but could never really do? Still, what's the worst that could happen? They could catch me. Unlikely, but possible. But who's going to suspect me? No one, that's who.

It's a risk, but it could be worth it. After all, I don't have much of a life left to lose. But she does.

Chapter 28

MADI

Faith's old oak dining table had been extended, its central section brought into play to accommodate the many dishes of food and to make room for the extra chairs. Sian and Ralph, along with his dad Ken, had been invited to join Madi and the family for dinner, and from the moment Faith had manoeuvred her into the chair next to Ken, it had become more and more obvious that there was more than a hint of matchmaking going on.

Madi liked Ken. She had enjoyed his company the night they'd first met in the pub, but she was absolutely not in the market for a man, no matter how amenable he might be.

'No Tom tonight?' Ralph said, between mouthfuls of cauliflower cheese. Whether he really believed that she and Tom were linked in some way other than simply as next-door neighbours, or whether he was just trying to help her throw Ken off the scent, she could not be sure. Either way, it certainly made Ken pull back a little as he poured her a second glass of the over-sweet apple wine he had brought with him.

'I didn't think to ask him,' Faith cut in. 'I didn't want to overwhelm Madi with too big a crowd, so I thought we should stick to family and close friends tonight, and you know that always includes you, Ralph. I'm just sorry you can't stay for long.'

'Well, someone has to go back to the surgery and check on Flo and I'm sure Prue would much prefer to have her dad and Sian here to chat to rather than me on her first proper evening back.'

'Still, seven is an odd number at the table, so maybe I should have invited Tom to join us,' Faith went on, as if she hadn't heard a word. 'But since the business with Flo, I wasn't sure that . . .'

'Oh, Mum, don't be silly.' Prue looked quite shocked. 'I'm not angry with Tom for what happened to Flo. It was 'an accident. And seven's fine. There are only so many mouths a chicken can feed, even a big one like this.'

'All the more for the rest of us,' Stuart said, patting his wife on the hand. 'Lovely gravy, as ever, by the way.'

'So, have you seen that errant son of mine since you got back?' Ken had half-turned away from Madi now and was talking across the table to Prue. He placed a hand on Ralph's arm, to the other side of him. 'The other one, I mean.'

'No. No, not yet. How is Joe?'

'How should I know? Since he moved back, I hardly see him. Bloody stupid, if you ask me, when he had a perfectly good home with us. And I'm sure you weren't the only one to think he'd be moving in with you soon enough.'

Madi couldn't help looking at Prue, seeing the embarrassment that flooded her face.

'We never talked about that, Mr Barton. He hadn't made me any promises.'

'Oh, I know. Enough said. That boy's never been one to talk much, has he? To share his feelings, or his plans. Bottles things up, that one. The sensitive type, as his mother used to say. But he's flown the nest now and I don't have any say in what he gets up to. Not any more. I'm just his father, after all.'

By the time they had all eaten the pie, finished the wine and downed the coffee, Madi was quite surprised when she glanced at her watch to realise it was almost ten o'clock. Ralph had left earlier, promising to phone if there was anything to report from Flo's sick bed, but no call had come so she assumed all was well. Still, Prue decided to take a walk down to check on her before bed, and Madi walked along with her as far as the cottage.

'You're sure it's all right me staying on here? Only, your mother has offered to put me up if . . .'

'It's fine, Madi, really.' They stood for a few moments at Prue's gate, the road dark ahead of them where the sparse line of streetlights petered out, and Prue fiddled in her bag for her phone so she could use its inbuilt torch to help her navigate the narrow lane leading up to the surgery.

'Hello, Prue. Miss Cardew . . .' The voice came out of nowhere, making Madi jump. It was followed by a slow-moving figure dressed in jeans and a black jacket, coming along the pavement, heading in the direction from which they had just come.

'Joe!' Prue's voice wobbled, the single word coming out in a strangled kind of croak.

'Sorry if I startled you. Just on my way back from the pub.' Madi had left the porch light on when she'd left earlier, so she would be able to see her way up the garden path and find the lock for her key, and the glow just about reached far enough now for her to get an impression of Joe Barton's pale face as he hovered a couple of feet away, as if unsure of whether to make conversation or hurry on by.

'We've been up at Orchard House for dinner.' Prue had lifted her head and was staring at him in the dim light. Madi could see she was struggling for something to say. Well, how was a girl meant to talk to the man she had hoped to marry, knowing now that that was never going to happen?

'That's nice. Always did put on a good spread, your mum.'

'Yes.' Prue hesitated. 'So, how are you?'

'Good. You?'

'Yes, okay, thanks. I've been away.'

'I noticed.'

'Sorry, Joe. I need to get on. I have to visit Flo.'

'Yes, I heard about that. Is she all right?'

'She will be. Thanks to my dad, and Ralph, of course.'

'Ah, yes. My brother, the miracle worker.'

'Yes, he is actually. And there's you, as jealous as ever.'

'Not jealous, Prue. It was never about jealousy. Just about fairness, that's all. It's always been about clever old Ralph and his big career and his wedding plans. But I needed to find my own way, and branch out on my own, just as much as my brother ever did . . .'

'Right, well, you've certainly done that now, haven't you?'

'I'm sorry, Prue, for letting you down. We've been friends for such a long time, and I miss that. I never meant for you to get hurt.'

'I know. My own stupid fault for assuming too much. But, as I said, I'm in a hurry, so . . .'

'Ah, okay. Bye then.' He hesitated for a moment before walking on. 'See you around, I expect.'

'Not if I see you first,' Prue muttered under her breath as he walked away.

'Well, that felt a bit awkward,' Madi said. 'He does seem to have a chip on his shoulder, doesn't he? A troubled soul, I'd say. But at least he apologised. Are you okay, Prue? Like to come in for a coffee, or to talk about it?'

'Thank you, Madi, but I really do want to see Flo before Ralph locks up for the night, and I'm a bit shaky but I'll live. It had to happen sooner or later, didn't it? The difficult first meeting. Hopefully it will be easier next time, now that's over with. One thing it has done though is prove what a lucky escape I've had. He's never going to let it go, about Ralph, his dad's so-called favourite. And it's so untrue. There's a bitterness about Joe that I was too blind or too stupid or too love-struck to see clearly before. And he doesn't make me laugh, Madi. I need more laughter in my life, more fun, and to widen my horizons beyond this tiny village and stop clinging so tightly to the things that feel safe. Meeting Aaron's shown me that.'

'Oh, I didn't realise that you and Aaron were . . .'

'Oh, no! Nothing like that. We're mates. Soulmates even! But he's too young for me, and there is definitely no romance.

He just understands me. Makes me realise there's a big wide world out there, and I'm not in any hurry but somewhere, some day, I'll meet the right person. The one who's meant to be. And Joe will too, I hope. I don't bear him any grudge, and it may have already happened for all I know. Still,' Prue gave a half-hearted laugh, 'God help whoever he ends up with . . .'

'Do you think that was why he turned you down?'

'What? That he might have met somebody else? No idea. It might explain the shock when I foolishly proposed that night. God, I must have had too much to drink. What was I thinking? But if he has found someone else already, or had someone all along, then she's welcome to him.'

Or *he* is, Madi thought, as the two new friends parted company and Madi stepped back inside the cottage and closed the door. But it wasn't her place to put Prue straight. If Madi was right in her assumptions, Prue would no doubt find out soon enough.

Donny had brought a whole gang of mates along with him to the first rehearsal on Saturday. One was carrying an old guitar in a tatty case, two or three had scraps of paper with scribbled jokes or poems or half-written songs on them, and one of the girls had found a microphone and stand at the back of her dad's garage and was dragging it along behind her as if it was a long-handled broom.

Tom was soon busily writing names in his notebook.

'Okay,' he shouted at last, putting down his pen, trying to restore some order as everyone milled about, chatting at full volume. 'Let's have some hush, shall we? Come and sit down, everyone, and if there aren't enough chairs, use the floor. Your bums are younger than mine.'

That seemed to get their attention.

'And put that cigarette out, Ricky Flynn. You're much too young to be taking up such filthy habits, and I just might feel obliged to have a word with your mother. Right, guys and gals, I'm not calling this an audition. As far as I'm concerned, whoever wants to be in is in. It's your show, not mine. Now, so far we have two solo singers, one with guitar, one without, a girl band, a rock group, three comedians, a performance poet and a magician. Plus, Josie here would like to have a go at training her dog to do a few tricks, Pudsey style. We'll keep an open mind on that one for now and see how it goes. So, all in all, I do think we have the basis for a show. A sort of *Shelling's Got Talent* but without the public vote. What do you think? Two songs each, a five-minute slot for the non-singers, and some kind of group finale? With an interval for refreshments, we should be able to fill a couple of hours, eh?'

There were enthusiastic nods all round.

'We appear to have a mike and a guitar at least. The rest of the props, scenery, costumes and all, we can work on, so what do you say we have a listen to our girl band today, assuming you're ready, girls?'

Madi saw the smallest of the girls, who she now knew was called Chantelle, look across at Donny adoringly, and Donny give her a reassuring nod, his cheeks reddening when he realised Madi had seen.

'Just give us one song for now,' Tom went on, oblivious to the mini-romance blossoming right in front of his eyes. 'And our soloist with guitar can follow on. Gerry, that's you. And then our poet maybe. But keep it light, eh? It's an entertainment show, so no doom-and-gloom stuff. That should give us a flavour of what's to come, and highlight any areas that might need work.'

Madi sat at the back of the hall and smiled. This took her back. The first day of rehearsals, a cast getting together for the first time, a new play to look forward to, with all the excitement and anticipation that went with it. Would they gel? Would there be backstage fallings out, costume malfunctions, problems with the scenery changes, an understudy having to step up at the last minute? Or would it all run like clockwork, with a full house, appreciative audiences, rave reviews? She had to admit she missed it. All of it. The good and the bad.

A steady stream of willing parents had been in and out, bringing clothes they thought might make good costumes, dropping off forgotten lunchboxes and volunteering their services for everything from make-up and refreshments to ticket production and sales. Choosing a Saturday to get the ball rolling had been a good idea. Most people had time on their hands and there was no rush to get finished and out of the hall quickly.

Madi's hand went instinctively to her side, slipping in beneath her open coat, over her jumper, feeling gently up and under her breast, and then moving tentatively to the other side, running her fingers along the line of her scar. She was healing. There was no pain now as she reached for something, carried something, turned awkwardly in bed. Just a soreness, and that nagging sense of loss that still reminded her of the emotional pain which she knew would take longer to heal than the physical. But this was it now. The breast was gone and, hopefully, it had taken the cancer with it. She had to be grateful for that.

As she watched the three girls take to the stage, saw the eagerness in their faces and the nervousness in their eyes, she knew exactly how they felt, caught up in the magic and the thrill of it all. Without a doubt, in that moment, she knew that she would go back to acting. How could she not? It was all she knew, all she had ever wanted to do, and she couldn't allow a disease to stop her, especially now it had buggered off back where it came from. Cancer, exit stage left . . .

She laughed to herself. Only George mattered as much as – no, more than – her career and, try as she knew she must to rebuild her relationship with her son, there was absolutely no reason she couldn't have both. Work and family. It's what millions of other women managed to combine happily, successfully, every day. George wasn't a child any more, far from it. He had his own life. He could look after himself. All she had to do was listen, offer support, do all the things he had accused her of *not* doing for so long. Yes, they had argued, not been there for each other in their times of need, not that he even knew she had had a time of need. And she still had no idea what had happened in his life, his marriage, to make him so bitter, so angry, and lead them to this awful distance that hung between them, this prolonged and ridiculous silence. The mistakes she had made in the long distant past could not be altered, but if he could find it in his heart to understand, and to forgive, then she could certainly do the same.

It was time to mend things, to build bridges, do whatever it took to get her son back. When she went home, they would talk. Face to face, not on the phone, and certainly not by text or email. She would tell him about the cancer, and he would tell her what had happened between him and Jessica, and if it could be fixed.

'Baby love, my baby love. I need ya, oh how I need ya . . .' the girls on the stage sang, their voices blending together, the words digging their way straight into Madi's heart. And it was true. She did need him. So badly. He might be nearly forty, but George would always be her baby.

Chapter 29

PRUE

Seeing Joe again had not been as traumatic as she had expected it to be. It had been less than a month since that humiliating evening in the pub, but she had taken huge strides in that short time, proving to herself that she could survive, and thrive, without him, and the pain she had expected to feel just hadn't happened. No broken heart, no pangs of loss, no desperate urge to throw herself at him and beg him to change his mind. If anything, the strongest emotion to hit her as she'd watched him walk away into the darkness was relief.

'He really wasn't worth it, you know.' Sian had caught up with her on her way to the surgery. She switched on the big torch she was carrying as they turned off the road and into the narrow lane. 'Never was.'

'I thought you were still happily swigging the last of the coffee back at my mum's.'

'No, any more of that and I'd be awake all night on some sort of caffeine high, which is fine when I need to stay up for

271

the patients, but tonight, assuming they're okay, I am looking forward to an early night with my very own Barton boy.'

'You definitely picked the right one!'

'Don't I know it? God, I love that man.'

'Who's that then?' Ralph said as they stumbled into the dimly lit waiting room, his voice carrying through from the staff area behind the counter where they found him sitting in one of the armchairs, with his feet up on the other, a mug of tea in his hand.

'You, you daft thing. How's Flo? And what are you doing sitting here drinking tea when you should be out the back administering your own special brand of TLC?'

'For those without medical training, Prue,' Ralph said, smiling up at them, 'that's short for Tickles, Licks and Cuddles. The animals do the licking, of my fingers mostly, and I do the rest. Works every time, better than any medicine.'

'I'm sure it does.' Prue laughed out loud. 'You know, I am so glad it's you caring for Flo. And Dad, of course. I'd hate to think of her with strangers when she's feeling poorly.'

'She's not so poorly now. In fact, she's doing really well. Fast asleep last time I looked, which is why I'm out here taking a sneaky rest. By all means go through, Prue, if you want to.'

Prue looked from Sian to Ralph. They both looked tired, and it was enough to know Flo was okay without keeping either of them here any longer. 'It's fine. I'll visit her tomorrow. Night, you guys . . .'

'Here, Prue, take the torch. I can share Ralph's.'

'Thanks. The light on my phone isn't really up to the job.'

She slipped the phone into her pocket and headed back towards her mum's, and the prospect of a warm inviting bed.

Madi was still up, the light on behind the curtains at the cottage as she passed, but it was all dark at Tom Bishop's next door. It was only as she approached Orchard House that she saw another light, the one shining over the porch door of the annex, its side entrance once the way into the old vet's surgery at the back. It still felt odd knowing that Joe was living in it, his bedroom where the operating theatre had once been, the waiting area now converted into a small lounge.

She stopped suddenly, in the shadows between lampposts, and switched off her torch. Was that movement ahead, someone walking towards Joe's door? Surely he should be inside by now. It had been a good quarter of an hour since she'd spoken to him in the street, on his way back from the pub. But no, that wasn't Joe's shape, or the way he walked. And, even in that long, black coat, this person was noticeably shorter, and thinner. After all these years, she would recognise Joe anywhere, in any light, and this wasn't him. It was a bit late for visitors. An intruder then? It wouldn't be the first time, even in a sleepy village like Shelling. She stood stock still, watching in silence, one hand gripping the phone in her pocket in case she had to call 999.

And then the door opened, before the mysterious figure had even knocked, and she saw Joe's face illuminated by the yellowy porch light, and the look of happiness reflected there as he opened his arms and welcomed his visitor inside.

* * *

It had been several days since Prue had fired up her laptop and checked her emails. She hovered over one from her boss before opening it, dreading being pulled back, before she was ready, into the day-to-day banality of her job at the paper. She was pleasantly surprised to see that it was just a nice, friendly message checking that she was okay and confirming her return date. He had even signed it off with a kiss. She had always got on well with Fred, who had known her dad for ages and treated her like a surrogate daughter. If she was going to do this, she knew he would support her and wish her well, despite his constant assurances that there was no better photographer for miles around and the paper couldn't do without her. It was doing without her now though, wasn't it? And if it could manage for a month, it could manage for longer. Maybe even for ever.

She minimised her email screen and opened up Google. She had started looking at courses on her last day in London, before she'd had to dash home for Flo and the whole thing had been left on hold. The sheer volume of information had overwhelmed her, and scared her too, if she was honest about it. Now it was time to start researching in earnest. Yes, she was a good basic photographer. She knew the mechanics, she had a good eye, and some of her images had been really quite outstanding, or so people were always telling her. Good enough to frame and mount on walls, from her own hallway to the vets' surgery and even the pub. But Shelling was hardly a gallery to the world, was it? And there was still so much she could learn.

It was the end of March now. Would all the best places for

September starts have been snapped up already? There was just so much to look into, so much to consider. Then there was where to choose. London was definitely calling to her. She had tasted life there now, and wanted more of it, but staying as local as possible would allow her to stay living at home. Still, where was the adventure in that? She should be going wherever the best courses took her, striking out on her own, like any new student, applying for grants, living in halls. There would be fees and living expenses, and the bills for the cottage still coming in, whether she was living in it or not. And how did any of the financial side of studying work when she was twenty-four and had been earning her own money, not eighteen and still dependent on her parents as most students were?

Only one way to find out. Prue took a deep breath and ploughed in, typing the words *Photography courses* into the search bar again. There were pages and pages of them.

Online distance learning. Study at home, at your own pace, in your own time . . . No, that was not what she wanted. That sounded far too much like she'd be treating photography as a hobby, something to fit into the gaps in an otherwise busy life. Maybe if she had commitments, a husband, children to consider, but that was not the way she wanted to go.

Day courses, evening classes, part-time . . . *Short specialist courses, taught by professional photographers* . . . *Combine creativity and technical skills* . . . *Develop a portfolio* . . . *Build a professional career* . . . There was so much choice, but none of them appealed to her. And besides, she was already a professional photographer, wasn't she? Well, she had a job that paid her to take photos, so she must be. But weddings, holes in the road, people proudly holding their prizes or their pets . . . she had taken enough pictures of those to last her a lifetime. Is that what she wanted? To carry on in the job, and study in the evenings? No, anything part-time would feel half-hearted and take too long. It wouldn't feel like she really meant it, really wanted it. No, it had to be all or nothing now. A breakaway, a fresh start, a determined effort to stretch herself, expand her knowledge, make something of her talent while she was still young enough, keen enough, bursting with ideas and enthusiasm. She had to channel that talent in the right direction, even if she wasn't yet sure what that direction might be.

Bachelor's and Master's degrees . . . Now, that was more like it. A proper, full-time course of study, a chance to immerse herself in her art, and with real qualifications at the end of it. They even did them in Norwich, but no. She needed to get away, and London had so much to offer, so London it had to be. She grabbed a notepad and started making notes. Studio and artificial lighting, portraits, food and product placement, moving image and interactive media, photojournalism, editing and visual effects, live projects, testing boundaries, professional career guidance . . . there were so many choices, so much to think about. She could feel her excitement mounting, along-side a flicker of panic. What did some of it even mean? Could she really do this?

'Prue? Do you want any lunch?' Her mum was knocking gently on her bedroom door. 'You do know it's almost two o'clock?'

'Is it? God, I had no idea. Yes, a sandwich would be nice. I'll be down in a minute.'

She dragged her eyes away from the screen and straightened up, stretching her aching back. Where had the morning gone? After a quick bowl of porridge and a flying visit to Flo, who was looking much more like her old self, she had been shut away in her room for more than four hours!

'I didn't like to disturb you,' Faith said, putting a big fat doorstop of a brown bread and cheese sandwich and a mug of tea in front of her. 'And Madi tells me you saw Joe last night, so I thought you might be a bit upset, or in contemplative mood, shall we say? I just happened to bump into her at Patty's and asked if she got home okay . . .'

'Well, clearly she did, not that much was likely to happen to stop her. We're not known for our axe murderers in Shelling.'

'No need to be sarcastic, Prue. I was just checking she was all right. And that you are. That's all.'

'I'm sorry. No need. But I did see a stranger wandering about last night actually, calling on Joe. Does he often have callers late at night?'

'I have no idea. Not up to me to monitor his visitors, is it? Pretty, was she?'

'I have no idea. I couldn't even tell if it was a he or a she. There was a car though, parked just along the road. I didn't notice it in the dark, but I spotted it this morning, from the window. Not a local, because it was parked right under the tree.'

'Ha, ha! Covered in pigeon poo then?'

'Oh yes. Roof and windscreen utterly splattered! It must have been there all night.'

'And you think it belongs to Joe's visitor?'

'Bound to.'

'And does that bother you, love?'

'No, not at all. I'm just curious, that's all. Joe can see who he likes, and do what he likes. He's not my problem any more.'

'Is that what he was, Prue? A problem?'

'I didn't think so while I was with him, but life with Joe was never going to be exactly thrilling, was it? Or fulfilling? It was all very embarrassing, the way it ended, but I'm glad now. That it's over, I mean.'

'Good. So, what's next? Are you going to stay, or scurry back off to London? Your little swapping arrangement with Madi hasn't actually ended yet, has it? Her place is still empty, and she's obviously not in any hurry to go home. She's fallen in love with the village, I can see that now.'

'Yes, and, to answer your question, I am thinking about going back to London, but maybe a little more long-term.'

'What, stay longer you mean? I don't know what Fred will say about that. Taking a whole month's leave at once was bad enough, but . . .'

'No, Mum,' Prue interrupted her. 'I meant staying there, and leaving my job altogether.'

Faith's hand flew up to her face in surprise, cupping her open mouth. 'Oh. I didn't see that coming. This isn't just to get away from Joe, is it? Because it does seem a bit drastic.'

'No, Mum. This has nothing to do with Joe, and everything to do with me. My life, my future. My . . . dreams, I suppose.'

'You'd better tell me all about it then, hadn't you? Not just slope off without a word like last time.'

'Well, I won't do that again. Head held high from now on, I promise. This time I'm going to do what I should have done ages ago, something you've been telling me I should do . . .'

'Well, whatever's going on, you'd best spit it out.'

'Come on then, come and take a look at something on the computer. I think you'll be pleased. Proud too, maybe.'

'I'm always proud of you, silly girl. How could I not be? But you've got me intrigued now, so hurry up and let me have a look.' Her mum crouched down in front of the laptop and Prue smiled.

'I'm actually looking at photography courses, proper full-time courses at university.'

'Oooh, lighting, creative skills, digital techniques, film production, working in TV . . . This looks really interesting, and right up your street, love,' Faith said, peering at the list of course contents on the screen. 'And food placement. What's that when it's at home?'

'No idea, Mum,' Prue said, 'but I fully intend to find out.'

Chapter 30

MADI

Madi woke up with a start. Someone was banging, loudly, on the front door.

She climbed out of bed and switched on the light, pulling on her dressing gown as she ran down the stairs.

'Miss Cardew, Miss Cardew . . .' It sounded like young Donny. What on earth could be so urgent? She stopped in the hall to check herself in the mirror, noting the rumpled nightie, the lack of make-up and the stubbly hair that reminded her she had left her wig upstairs by the bed. Still, what did any of that matter if there was some emergency requiring her attention?

That evening's second rehearsal had been a busy and productive one, as she and Patty had worked away at the back of the hall, altering and embellishing various donated dresses and waistcoats to make costumes, hemming the old stage curtains where some of the stitching had come undone, and clapping the burgeoning acts as they each took their turn on stage. She had come home exhausted and gone to bed early.

The clock on the wall in the kitchen told her now that it was not yet ten o'clock. She could only have been asleep for half an hour. She flicked on the porch light, yawning, and opened the door.

'Miss Cardew, come quick. There's a fire.'

'A fire? Where?'

'In the village hall, Miss. There's smoke and flames and everything.'

'Has anyone dialled 999?'

'Yes, and they're on their way.' He sounded excited, as only a schoolboy faced with the prospect of blue lights and sirens can be. 'I was first to see it. Mr Bishop's already gone running down there, and he said to come and tell you. Our stuff's in there, from the rehearsals. The microphone and the costumes . . .'

'But no people, Donny? Costumes can be replaced but . . .'

'No, everyone's out, Miss. We all left at the same time, soon after you did, when Mr Bishop locked up just after nine.'

'Thank God for that.' Madi felt a shiver run through her. She was still in her nightie, her feet bare, so it wasn't surprising she felt cold, but this was more than that. It was a shiver of fear. Tom! What was he thinking, running towards a fire, when any sensible person would make sure they ran away? But then she remembered he had been a fireman. At least he would know how to stay safe. He wouldn't take any risks, and perhaps there was something he could do, before the fire engines arrived, to help put out the flames.

'Right. Let me quickly get dressed and I'll be out. You keep well back from the fire now, Donny. No heroics, you hear me?'

'Yes, Miss.'

282

'What were you doing out at this time of night anyway? Why didn't you go straight off home?'

A definite shifty look passed across the boy's face, and he mumbled some sort of excuse about hanging around to look at the moon. Madi wasn't buying it, but this wasn't the time to stop and question him. For now, all that mattered was getting herself down to the hall and making sure that Tom was all right.

By the time she emerged into the street a few minutes later, the sky was lit with a bright orange glow that hovered above the line of trees like a bright and rather beautiful sunset. The smoke, carried by the wind, was drifting through the night air, catching in her throat. She could see the tips of the flames reaching for the sky before she turned the corner and saw the old wooden hall itself, or what was left of it.

Tom was doing his best with a garden hose, connected to the outside tap in the nearest garden, but the hose was not long enough and the trickle of water emerging from it was doing nothing but wet the pavement. A couple of the other men were running back and forth from their homes with buckets.

Everyone else was outside in the street, standing around in groups, watching in near silence as if they could hardly believe what they were witnessing. Some of them had come out in their dressing gowns and slippers, one or two wielding their phones and taking pictures, capturing the moment as the last walls succumbed to the flames and their cherished hall finally lost its battle for survival.

By the time the fire engines came roaring in, it was obvious that it was too late to do anything much but douse the flames.

* * *

'Well, that's it then.' Tom sat in Prue's kitchen clutching a warming cup of cocoa and shaking his head. 'That's the end of the show. Hall burnt to the ground. Costumes all gone . . .'

'If only we'd carried them down to store them overnight in Prue's shed as we'd planned.'

'But we didn't, Madi. My fault. I'm supposed to be the one in charge, and I left them there, at the mercy of the flames. All that flammable material. You hear about it, don't you? Cheap Halloween costumes catching alight . . .'

'These weren't cheap fancy dress, Tom. They were ordinary clothes, tarted up with sequins. The costumes aren't to blame. *You're* not to blame.'

'We don't know that. I'm an ex-firefighter, for God's sake. How on earth can this have happened?'

'Let's wait and see what the investigation turns up, shall we? And in the meantime, we can ask for more donations and make new costumes.'

'What's the point? We'd hardly got started anyway. And with no hall, we have nowhere to rehearse and, more importantly, nowhere to hold the actual show. No, it's over, Madi. It's a crying shame, but I've let those kids down.'

He went home to bed soon after, leaving Madi sitting alone at the table, suddenly wide awake.

She had been thinking, over the last couple of days, about going home herself. Her planned month in Shelling would be over soon, and her agent had emailed, asking when she might be ready to return to work. The rigours of touring still felt a little beyond her, but a small part, close to home, might be okay. A way to ease herself back in gently. It was so easy to get left behind or forgotten altogether in this business. And then there was George. If he had seen her missed call he had not responded to it, and she knew now it was going to be up to her to make the first move as soon as she was back in London.

She pulled her diary from her handbag, realising for the first time that it was April the first. A day for childish jokes and trying to fool people with fake spiders and eggs that bounce when you drop them. She'd had more than her share of silly backstage tricks in her time, but it was not really the right day for a devastating fire. She just hoped that, whatever had happened at the hall tonight, it had been an accident and not something to do with one of the kids playing some silly prank.

Where once her diary would have been filled with meetings, rehearsal and performance dates, the pages were ominously blank. In fact, looking back to the start of the year, the only things she had written in were her hospital appointments, and the start and end dates for her visit to Shelling.

She would talk to Prue in the morning and find out if she had any plans to go back to London in the next few days. If not, then she could see no reason to stay here any longer. All she had done since she'd arrived was lead the local teenagers into a project that was now totally dead in the water, set the rumours going about herself and a married man, and get herself involved in running over and almost killing a much-loved cat. This village would be a darn sight better off without her in it, that was for sure. And now that Prue was back in Shelling, it really didn't feel right to keep her out of her own cottage. No, they might as well officially swap back sooner than expected.

'I still can't believe it.' Faith stood outside the burnt-out hall, now cordoned off by a line of tape. 'This old hall's been here as long as I have. And it's been at the heart of things ever since. The W.I., the Brownies, the library . . . Oh, no. The library! All the books will have been lost. Oh, Madi, it's just too awful. And your wonderful show as well. I was so looking forward to that.'

'Yes, it's a great shame.'

'I'm assuming it was insured, so it will be rebuilt eventually, but these things take time, don't they? And you can bet the Council will argue over plans and try to make the replacement all modern and cover it in solar panels or fill it with all this wi-fi nonsense. And, while we're waiting, people are being deprived of their books. I wonder if we could put out an appeal? You know, asking for donations. Everyone's got books tucked away that they're never going to read again. The big library in town might even have some they don't need any more. I bet they throw them away when they get a bit bent or no one's borrowed them in a while, and that will never do. I'll ring them. Right now. And we'll need somewhere to store them, of course, somewhere people can come to browse. Ah, my dad's old darkroom! That never gets used these days. I'll ask Prue. I'm sure she won't mind . . .'

Madi smiled to herself as Faith bustled away in the direction of Orchard House. No doubt she would have roped Patty into her schemes before the day was out. If you want something done, ask a busy person, that's what they say, and when it came to those two, Madi knew the old saying was spot-on. If a problem needed solving, they were the ones to get on

286

with the job. She had no doubt the hall and all its activities would be back up and running as soon as was humanly possible, and probably better than ever.

She watched Faith stop as she bumped into her daughter further along the street, a few words passing between them before they parted ways and Prue came ambling towards her.

'Ah, Prue, I was just on my way to see you.'

'Morning, Madi.' Prue stopped and gazed at the hall. 'Terrible, isn't it? Have they any idea how it started?'

'Not that I've heard, but I expect Tom will be the first to find out. The dear man feels awful about it. I saw him first thing, on his way to visit his wife, but we've agreed to meet up this afternoon. I'll let you know if I hear anything. Now, there was something I wanted to talk to you about.'

'Okay. Walk with me if you like. I was just on my way to the shop for bread, and then I'm going to see Flo. Ralph says she might be able to come home later today.'

'Home, already? Oh, Prue, I'm so glad, but she'll need the familiarity of her own place, won't she? It really is time I went, so you and Flo can have your cottage back. That's what I wanted to ask you actually. About a date to swap back.'

'But that's all set for next Wednesday, isn't it? Flo will be fine at my mum's. It's always been like a home from home for her, and Mum will make a huge fuss of her. Now I don't have to worry about her, I was hoping to catch a train back this evening, so I can make the most of my last few days in London. I never did get to an art gallery, and there are a couple of other places I'd like to go and check out while I have the chance. I'd really like to see if there's been any progress with the plans for the garden and say a proper goodbye to Aaron too. Is that all right with you?'

'Of course.' They had reached the shop already and Madi wanted to avoid going in. If she did, she knew Patty would keep her talking for ages, and she wasn't really in the mood. 'We had an agreement and I have no intention of breaking it. If you want to go back, then go. I might even be able to get you a free ticket to a show somewhere. Let me try pulling a few strings and I'll let you know. And, as for staying in Shelling, I'm sure I can amuse myself for a while longer, especially now the weather's picking up.'

'It's not that far to the beach, you know,' Prue said, one hand on the shop door. 'And it won't be crowded this time of the year. Have you been?'

'No, I haven't. I kept meaning to, but I've been lazy, not been out and about much at all. I still need my rest . . .'

'Of course you do. I'm sorry. You just seem so lively, so . . . well, normal, I suppose . . . that it's easy to forget you've been so ill. Seawater's good for you though. Even if you only have a paddle.'

'I might just do that. And, if I don't see you again before you go, I just wanted to say thank you. This swap has been wonderful, and I would happily do it again. Shelling is a lovely place, full of lovely people.' She reached forward and pulled Prue into a hug. 'Maybe it could become an annual event? A holiday home away from home. Good for both of us.'

'That's not a bad idea, but I'm not sure where I'll be this time next year.'

'Oh?' Madi looked at her curiously but Prue did not elaborate.

'I'd love to keep in touch though. And thank you too, Madi. Your flat is gorgeous. Like a top class hotel! And the residents of Belle Vue are . . .'

'Unique?'

'I was going to say interesting, but yes, unique pretty much sums them up! Bye, Madi. Have a safe journey home next week. We'll probably pass each other somewhere in the middle!'

'You too, dear.'

Madi strolled back to Snowdrop Cottage and made herself a cup of tea. Her disturbed sleep last night had left her feeling tired and the fire had unsettled her. As she and Tom had been the last to use the hall, it was impossible not to feel . . . guilty was too strong a word, but certainly concerned. Was it something they had done? Something they hadn't spotted but should have? All those young people in their care, and the ending could so easily have been far more tragic. It didn't bear thinking about. And why was young Donny still hanging about the village after the others had all gone home? She shook away her silly suspicions. Donny, more than anybody, wanted the show to succeed, and the hall was a vital part of that. And if he hadn't been out so late, there might not have been anyone to raise the alarm.

She shuddered at the memory of the lit-up sky and the smell of the smoke that still lingered in her clothes. Well, at least there was something she could do about that, as she gathered up the things she had been wearing and bundled them into the washing machine. She'd have to strip the bed when she left next week and wash the covers, and all the towels, before she set off for home. Still, waiting for them to dry would give her time to say her goodbyes. And, even after just a month here, there would be quite a few of those.

When Madi opened her eyes, the washing had finished, the rain was pounding at the windows, and her neck ached. She must have nodded off on the sofa, with one leg tucked up beneath her and her head flopped over to one side. She stretched her limbs out and wriggled her head around a few times to loosen the stiffness, then glanced at her watch. She was surprised to see it was already a quarter past one. She really must have been tired.

Tom! She had agreed to meet him in the pub for a drink and a spot of lunch at one and she was not only already late but hadn't even changed out of her jeans. Which would he prefer? For her to run down there now, just as she was, and be only twenty minutes late, or to take the time to dress up and apply her make-up and keep him waiting for an hour? She knew the answer to that question. That was the beauty of their friendship. He accepted her for exactly who she was, warts and all, and probably actually preferred her that way. Knowing Tom, he'd be champing at the bit with his mouth watering at the thought of one of The Brown Cow's speciality pies, so who was she to keep him waiting? She grabbed her bag and her keys, slipped her coat and the nearest pair of shoes on and hurried out into the rain to meet him.

Chapter 31

Prue sat in the quiet carriage of the train and closed her eyes. Flo was safely ensconced at Orchard House and had already made herself at home on her parents' bed, the spectre that was Joe Barton had been faced and conquered, and there was a list of London colleges in her pocket, each of which she fully intended to go and take a look at, from the outside at least, before the weekend was up. Life was looking good.

She thought of ringing Aaron to let him know she was on her way back, but mobiles were frowned upon in the quiet carriage, and besides, you never knew with Aaron when he might be trying to sleep. His shifts at the supermarket didn't follow a regular pattern and she would hate to wake him unnecessarily. Anyway, it would be good to surprise him. With a bit of luck, over the last few days, he might have seen Simon and made some headway with the garden. In any case, she was going to call on Emily to see where things were with the cake, and she had promised to arrange a photoshoot too if Simon's mate was up for it. It would all help them to acquire the materials they needed, and perhaps a few hours of labour, if Simon had a couple of free days. She might not be around to see it completed but she liked to think it would build its own momentum once everyone saw how easy it was to do and that it wasn't going to cost them any real hard cash. It would be a lovely way to thank Madi for her stay too. She knew full well that, if she was Madi, going back to that tatty patch of land would not be so easy once she'd tasted the spacious green delights of Norfolk.

She was still smiling as she stepped from the train. The rain had not followed her from Norfolk. The air was quite warm, and the streets so well lit she could almost forget it was evening. How amazing it was that in just a short train ride it was possible to move between two such different worlds. Could she really leave the quiet little village she had lived in all her life and make London her home? Study here? Live here? Forge a new life for herself? It was certainly worth serious consideration. Flo would be quite content at Orchard House, and her cottage would still be there waiting for her when she returned. She could even think about renting it out to bring in some money and help pay her fees.

She stopped for a moment and looked at the list of colleges she had scribbled down. Most of them held open days and taster days, nearer to the start of the academic year, where she could see inside, ask questions and meet existing students, but she was feeling impatient. The nearest was only a couple of tube stops away, and she only had a small, light bag with her, most of her stuff having been left behind at Madi's flat when she'd departed in such a hurry a week ago. It was not as if she had any other plans. Why not go there now? She could take a look at the campus, the general area, get a feel for the place. Her camera swung on its strap and bounced on her chest as if it too was eager to take a peek at the future. 'You're right, Camilla,' she muttered, 'no time like the present,' as she swung her bag up onto her shoulder and headed back towards the underground.

With Easter only a week or so away, the term must have already ended, because there were very few people milling about. No obvious students anyway. Prue gazed up at the tall, modern buildings, so unlike the small, old-fashioned schools she had attended, and took photos of anything and everything that caught her eye. There was a noticeable lack of parking, which was to be expected in central London, so if she came here – or anywhere similar – she would have to leave her little Mini at home. Having managed without it for almost four weeks, that suddenly didn't seem like much of a hardship, and actually getting rid of it could save her quite a bit in insurance, road tax, petrol and repairs. She could get a bike! Just as the thought popped into her head, one rode by, the young girl on top of it speeding along faster than any of the passing cars.

'Oh, sorry.' A man had bumped into her. He stopped and held out a hand to steady her. 'My fault, for not looking where I was going.'

Prue was about to argue, knowing full well that she had been the one to stop dead in her tracks as the bike caught her attention, when she realised who he was.

'Simon?'

He looked at her for a moment, apparently confused, before the light dawned. 'You're the girl from Belle Vue. Prue! Whatever are you doing here?'

'Just wandering really. You?'

'I was meant to be meeting someone, but she bailed . . .'

'A date, you mean?'

'Oh, nothing heavy. Just someone from one of those dating apps. I've never actually met her. She must have looked at my profile picture again and changed her mind. And who can blame her?' He laughed. 'But that does mean I'm all dressed up with nowhere to go. I don't suppose you . . .? No, daft of me.'

'No.' Prue hesitated. 'I mean, no, not daft. Not no, I won't . . . Oh, you know what I mean. Do you fancy a drink somewhere?'

'You're only saying that so I'll build you a patio!'

'Of course I'm not, but I would like the chance to talk about the garden, if you've got the time.'

'All the time in the world. There's a little wine bar not far from here, and they do food too. Have you eaten?'

'I'm just back from Norfolk. I had a sandwich on the train.'

'That's a no then. Come on, I need proper food, and once you've seen the burgers in this place you won't be able to resist!'

They walked along side by side, not saying very much. Prue took a sideways peek at him as they waited to cross a road and decided she liked what she saw. He was taller than she remembered, and it looked as if he'd had a haircut since she'd last seen him, although it was still a bit too long at the front, but he was certainly good-looking and easy to get along with, in that Jack-the-Lad sort of way.

'You never called,' he said, as they settled into seats at a corner table. 'I bet you washed it off, didn't you? My number, that I wrote on your arm that day.'

'Of course I washed it off! But not before I transferred it to my phone. You can check if you like.'

'So, why . . .?'

'I had to go back to Norfolk. Long story, but it ended well, and I only got back today. You were actually quite high on my list of people to contact.'

'Not at the top then?'

'Almost. I was going to call you tomorrow, to see if you still wanted that anniversary cake, so I could pass on some details to the lady who offered to make it. And to ask you about the possibility of the photo shoot.'

'You know, it's a really strange coincidence, isn't it? Us meeting like this. As if fate was trying to tell us something.'

'What? That it's a small world and London's not such a big place after all?'

'You want the truth?' He lowered his gaze. 'I was meant to be meeting my so-called date in this pub she suggested, you know, a public place so she was sure I wasn't some evil kidnapper or a weirdo or something. It's just over the road there. Nothing great really, and too crowded for my liking. I'd been waiting almost an hour. Anyway, I'd just got the text to say she wasn't coming when I saw you through the window, so I watched you for a while, wandering about, and when it looked like you might be about to walk away, I nipped out and sort of accidentally on purpose bumped into you. Thus proving that I probably am some sort of weirdo stalker after all!'

'So why pretend?'

'Maybe I liked the fate-bringing-us-together idea better. Which it did, in a way. I mean, what are the chances . . .'

'Well, whatever brought you here, I think the drinks are definitely on you.'

'Of course. What would you like? Red or white?'

'Red please. And I'm sorry about your date. Or non-date, I should say.'

'I'm not. I told you. It's fate. There I was, alone, dumped, abandoned, and along you came, as if by magic. I needed you to make my evening complete.'

'And I needed you to help me make a garden.'

'I guess I'd better do it then. And it's a yes, to the anniversary cake. And my carpenter mate does want some photos done. His gran's got her ninetieth coming up, and they want a big family portrait. All the generations together. Are you up for that?'

'Yes! Whatever they want. If it gets us the benches we need, they can have it done in the nude if they like!'

'Prue, she's ninety. Think of all those wrinkles.'

'Oh, maybe not then.'

'Chips with your burger?'

'Of course. And ketchup. Can't have chips without ketchup.'

'Now there's a girl after my own heart. Back in a sec.'

She watched him walk to the bar, his smart jeans tight

across his bottom, his clean white shirt gleaming as if it was brand new and straight out of the packet, which it probably was. He really was quite sexy. Now she had the idea of nudity in her head, it didn't seem to be a ninety-year-old's body that sprang instantly into her mind. She must have flicked through a few too many naughty bits in that book on the train. It was giving her ideas.

And, if she wasn't mistaken, that was a definite tingle that shot through her as he turned and smiled, his floppy blonde fringe falling seductively over one eye. They say these things often happen when you're not expecting them. Not even looking, in fact. Maybe it was true after all. Fate really was trying to tell her something. That there might now be even more reason for her to consider moving to London.

'Let me see you home.'

'It's okay. No need. London doesn't scare me any more.'

'I didn't know it ever did.'

'It did at first. I wasn't used to it. The noise, the bustle, the fact that it never ever stops.'

He helped her into her coat and they went out into the street. 'Well, whatever you might think, it can still be a dangerous place. Especially for a girl on her own at night. I'm coming to your front door at least. It's not far out of my way. Any further than the door would be presumptuous!'

'Asking you in for coffee, you mean?'

'If that's what you want to call it.'

'On our first date? I don't think so.'

'So, this was a date then?'

'I don't know, Simon. You tell me.'

'It was, yes.' He took her hand in his. 'You're cold.'

There it was again. The tingle, the shiver, as soon as his skin touched hers.

'It is a bit chilly. It's getting late.'

'Come on then. Let's get you safely home.' They walked towards the tube, still holding hands. 'So, all we've talked about is the garden. I haven't found out very much about you. What were you doing here tonight, for a start? Walking about by yourself with your camera? You never did say.'

'Deciding.'

'Go on.'

'I'm thinking of going to uni, doing a degree.'

'That's brilliant. Here in London?'

'Could be. It's one of a few options. But there's a lot to consider, about fees and where to live and everything. I've got plenty of time to work things out. Term doesn't start until September.'

'Clever girl. You won't want to go out with me again then – a lowly builder of very little brain – not if you're getting letters after your name.'

'Who says?'

'Will you then? See me again?' He stopped and turned her towards him. 'Not just to sort out the garden, which I will do. Obviously, I will. But see me, like go out with me? Because I would like it a lot if you did.'

She could see his face moving closer, his eyes going very slightly out of focus as she gazed into them, and then they were kissing. She wasn't sure who had kissed who first, but it didn't seem to matter. The tingle had escalated into a full-on shudder as he pulled her towards him, his arms wrapping around her so tightly, his lips so wonderfully locked onto hers, that she thought she would never breathe again. If fireworks had started exploding above their heads she would not have been at all surprised.

'Wow!' That was all he said when they eventually pulled apart, but she couldn't have said it better herself. This was nothing like kissing Joe Barton. This was something totally different. This really was just . . . wow.

The automatic light clicked on in the hallway, throwing a dim halo across the floor. She waved goodbye to Simon, standing below her on the bottom step, and blew him a final kiss, then closed the door quietly behind her. It was well after midnight and she didn't want to wake anybody else in the block. The pink pushchair was in its usual place against the wall, and a scattering of junk leaflets scrunched underfoot as she stepped onto the mat. Nobody had bothered to gather them up and deal with them, so why should she? She peered into Madi's post tray. There was a small pile of letters, which she picked up although it wouldn't be worth forwarding them as Madi would be back next week.

The stairs creaked beneath her feet as she walked up to the top floor. She was glad to be back at last, fully intending to make these final days count before having to face returning to work and telling Fred she was thinking of leaving.

She turned the key in the lock and stepped inside the flat, putting her bag and camera down at her feet, flipping the light on in the small lobby area and slipping out of her coat. It might be late but she felt chilly and she fancied a hot drink before bed. Besides, her thoughts were swirling around like a whirlwind and she wasn't sure she would be able to contemplate sleep for a while. Simon! The kiss. Their hands locked together all the way home. The desperate urge to pull him through the door and up the stairs with her. Where had those feelings come from? She hardly knew him and it would be wrong to rush into anything so soon after Joe, but that was her sensible head talking. Somewhere deep inside her there was something else, something instinctive, telling her to go for it, to grab a bit of lustful fun. She took a big breath and smiled to herself. Really, how on earth had she managed to resist them?

She padded her way through the semi-darkness to the kitchen, dropped Madi's post on the table and leant back against the wall tiles as she waited for the kettle to boil. Its blue light mesmerised her as she watched the water start to bubble through the glass. She closed her eyes. She could still run after him. Or call him. She had his number in her phone. No, Prue. Take it slow. He'll wait. You know he will. She felt another of those unexpected shivers ripple through her. A shiver of anticipation, a promise of what was to come. And then . . .

She heard it before she saw anything. A faint noise, like a drawer closing. Her eyes flew open and she turned towards the open kitchen doorway and the darkened room beyond. A rustle of clothing, slow footsteps, a floorboard creaking, someone breathing. Who? Where? In the bedroom? No, the living room. Coming closer. Someone she couldn't yet see, but she knew they were there.

She felt her pulse quicken, her heart banging in her chest. There wasn't time to look for a rolling pin or take a knife from the drawer, so she grabbed the first thing to hand. The kettle. Hot. Steaming. Heavy. She lifted it from its base, clutched at the handle, held it in front of her, ready to throw it, hit out with it, protect herself.

Creak.

Now! It had to be now. She let out a loud scream, part cry for help, part battle cry, as she lunged through the doorway and into the space between them. But she was too late. The blow came quickly, from the side, sending her reeling backwards into instant blackness. Her head thumped hard into the kitchen cabinet on her way down as the kettle flew from her hands, a cascade of boiling water tumbling out of the top and down her arm, and spreading out around her on the kitchen floor.

Chapter 32

*O*h, no. What have I done? As she lies there, silent and still, I know I've made a terrible mistake.

It wasn't her voice, not her scream. It isn't her. Not who I had expected it to be at all. This isn't the actress. It should have been the actress. The other one, the young girl, had gone, and the place was empty again. Had been for days. Untidy, messy, but empty. She'd gone. I was sure she had. But I was wrong.

What was she doing, creeping in here so late at night? Like some kind of thief or intruder. What did she have to do that for? She shouldn't have been here. She wasn't coming back. I didn't mean her any harm. She was an inconvenience, that was all. Gone back where she came from, not part of my story. Our story. She was irrelevant, a nobody. But a nobody who was standing between me and the door, in the way, stopping my escape.

I thought it was the actress. I really did. I heard her come in, I tried to get out, but she sensed me, knew I was there, because she stopped, waited . . . What could I do? I had to do something. It was me or her. Just as it always has been. The game was so nearly up. And I didn't have time to think, to plan. Action. Reaction. Instinct. A way to finish it, once and for all. And with

303

her own award too. Justice. That was all it was. And poetic justice, at that. But it wasn't her.

And now her stupid, shiny statuette is in my hands, still clutched tightly despite the trembling, and she's lying on the floor at my feet – her, the other one – and I don't even know if she's alive or dead.

I should do something. What should I do? Bend down. Touch her. Check her. Call for help. The police. Ambulance. Or run? Should I run? Just go, hide, leave her to her fate? I know I should. It's my only hope. But I also know I shouldn't.

I put it down, slowly, on the carpet. The award she won. The weapon. Should I wipe it with something? Remove my fingerprints? Ah, but they'll be everywhere, won't they? On all the things I've touched. Not just tonight. All those other nights.

My toe meets something hard as I move towards her. Hard and hot. The floor is so wet my foot slides and I almost fall. I bend down, shaking, scared. The kettle is lying beside her. I push it away, touch her, and she is wet too. Her face. Her hair. I put my wet fingers to my lips. Not water. Blood.

I can't do it. Can't think. Can't move. Can't decide.

In the end, I just stand and pick up the statue thing and go, slowly, carefully, and as silently as I can.

I leave the door open, onto the landing. Someone will find her. Someone will help her. But it's not going to be me.

Chapter 33

MADI

'This was a lovely idea, Madi. I haven't had a day out at the beach for ages. Not since Barb went away.'

'Well, you should. Do it more often, I mean. The walking's good for you, and the sea air.'

'Just not the sort of thing I ever imagined doing on my own, I suppose. I thought she'd always be there. Still, it's certainly brought the colour back into your cheeks.'

'I'm loving it. I haven't had waves rippling over my bare toes for years! But I am feeling a bit tired now. Do you mind if we sit for a while?'

'Of course not. You should have said.' Tom took the rolled-up mac from under his arm and spread it out on the sand. 'There! Not sure why I brought it really, as there's hardly a cloud in sight. After yesterday's downpour, I guess we've been lucky, but at least the old mac's come in handy for something.'

'It's so empty here,' Madi said, sitting down and adjusting her pose to avoid a large pebble, which was digging into the back of her leg. 'Peaceful.'

'The families don't tend to come spilling out until the afternoon, when school finishes. The Easter holidays are nearly upon us though, and everywhere will be much more packed then, whatever the weather. Otherwise, it's just the dog walkers at this time of day.'

'Have you ever thought of getting a dog yourself? It'd be company for you, and the perfect reason to force yourself out for a bit of exercise every day.'

'Are you saying I'm in need of exercise, young lady?' Tom put both hands around the flesh above his waistband and wobbled it.

'I didn't mean you were fat!'

'No, I know you didn't. Only teasing. And, yes, I have thought about it. Getting a pet. A little elderly cat like Flo from one of those rescue places, or a budgie or something. But a dog's a big commitment . . .'

'Any pet is a commitment, Tom. That's why I don't have one, with my lifestyle. It wouldn't be fair. But you . . .'

'I know, but the other worry, for me, is what happens if, or when, I can't look after it any more? If I end up a few years down the line incapacitated, or unable to go out walking, or dead even? Animals can live a good few years. A pet could outlive me, and who'd take care of it then? I'm happy to leave my daughters all my worldly goods, but I don't want to lumber them with costs and responsibilities . . .'

'Oh, please, stop being so morbid. You're in your sixties, not your eighties! You've got years of good active life in you yet.'

'We can't know that, Madi. Look at my Barbara . . .'

'What about her? Her illness was a nasty trick of fate,

unforeseeable, sad, but there's no reason to suppose it's going to happen to you too. And is this what she would want? You putting your own life on hold, putting your own dreams and plans aside, just in case?'

'Probably not. And they were *our* dreams, not just mine. We didn't really need four bedrooms once the girls had gone. We always used to say that, when we retired, we'd think about leaving Shelling and moving into a smaller house. Oh, still in Norfolk, obviously, but somewhere we could see the sea from the window, listen to it at night, take moonlit walks on the shore, you know. That's not going to happen now though, is it? And we'd get a spaniel. A little girl. Barb wanted to call her Flush, like the one the Brownings had.'

'The Brownings?'

'Robert. Elizabeth Barrett. You know, the poets. She was into all that love poetry stuff, was my Barb. *How do I love thee, Let me count the ways*, and all that. Could recite so many of those old verses off by heart. She had a lovely reading voice. I doubt if she'd even recognise one of those poems now if she heard it, let alone be able to remember the words. No, it's all gone. The poetry, the retirement, the dog . . .'

Madi reached for his hand. 'I don't know what to say.'

'Don't say anything. No need.' He shook her off and rummaged in the small shoulder bag he had brought with him, pulling out a thermos flask and cups. 'Time for a cuppa, I think, don't you? And one of your favourite custard creams.'

Madi laughed. 'I wondered what you were hiding in that bag. I won't say no though . . . Do you think the tide is coming in or going out?'

307

'Can't say I've noticed really. Not been here long enough to spot the difference. Why?'

'Just making sure we're not going to find ourselves knee-deep in water all of a sudden.'

'Madi, I was a firefighter. If needs must, I will pick you up and sling you over my shoulder, if only to keep you dry.'

'Well, thank you, kind sir, but I'm sure that won't be necessary.'

'Is that your phone ringing?'

'I don't know. Is it?' Madi thrust her hand into the depths of her handbag. 'It's hard to hear it over the sounds of the sea.'

'Ignore it anyway. Whoever it is can wait. This is meant to be our getting-away-from-it-all day.'

'No, I can't do that. It might be important. It might be George.'

Tom raised his eyebrows. 'Really?'

'You never know.' Madi found the phone and peered at the screen. 'That's odd. It's Faith. What on earth can she want?'

'You'd better answer it and find out. Probably another invitation to tea, although she did know we were coming here this morning, so it could have waited . . .'

'Hello?'

Tom watched as Madi listened to the voice at the other end of the line, her face turning pale, her expression suddenly deadly serious.

'Right. I'll be there as soon as I can.'

'What's happened? You look like you've just seen a ghost.'

'It's Prue. She's been found unconscious, in my flat. Looks like someone attacked her and then just left. Faith and Stuart are already in their car on their way up to London.'

'My God! Is it bad? How is she?'

'She was hit over the head apparently. No obvious weapon left behind. But she's in hospital and having some kind of scan so they can see what's what. Faith was very upset, a bit garbled, but she says the police will be in touch, that they want me home. It may have been a burglary, someone Prue disturbed, and they'll need me to check if anything's missing. And to give them my fingerprints.'

'Oh, Madi, how awful. Poor kid, all on her own, and so far from home too.'

'Not for long. Stuart's driving like the wind from what I can gather. So long as they don't get stopped for speeding, they'll be with her soon. Come on, let's get back. The car's got enough petrol, and I need to get packed up, so I can leave today. I can't believe this happened in my flat, Tom. *Mine.*'

'Yes, it did, but that doesn't make it your fault.'

'No, it doesn't, but what if . . .?'

'What if what?'

'I know it sounds silly, over-dramatic even, but what it wasn't some random attack by a stranger?'

'Why would anyone go after Prue? She wouldn't hurt a fly.'

'No, she wouldn't. But what if it wasn't Prue they were after? Who even knew she was there? Hardly anyone. Maybe what happened . . . was actually meant for me?'

'Why would anyone target you?'

'I have no idea, but I've been away a long time. They might have known that, known I have nice things, jewellery, thought the place was empty. Or it could have been . . . No, I'm just being stupid.'

'What?' Tom was grasping her hand now, concern written all over his face.

'Well, I'd had the feeling for a while before I left that someone was watching me. I think I told you, I'd even started to think I was losing my memory, my mind . . . that something wasn't . . . right. That's the only way I can describe it. I've told myself it was the illness, the drugs, the worry of it all . . . But what if it wasn't that?'

'You think someone was after you? Deliberately trying to upset you?'

'No. Yes. Oh, I don't know. I'm probably wrong, but I have to find out. Who got into my flat. Why. And how. I ignored it, Tom. I did nothing. I let Prue walk into God knows what was going on there, and now she's . . .'

'Stop it, Madi.' Tom helped her to her feet and bundled up his mac and flask, tipping the dregs of their tea onto the sand. 'That sort of talk isn't going to help anyone. Best get you back to Shelling pronto, okay?'

Madi stood on the doorstep at Snowdrop Cottage and looked back at it for the last time. She'd packed hurriedly, stripped the bed and bundled everything into the washing machine but she really didn't have time to wait until it was finished so she could dry it. Her plan to take a leisurely stroll around the village and say her goodbyes had fallen by the wayside now. All that mattered was getting back home and finding out what was happening at Belle Vue Court. What state her flat was in, what state Prue was in . . .

Tom came out into the street at the first sight of her, as if he had been waiting at the window watching out for her to emerge, and picked up the various bags and bundles gathered at her feet. 'You should have called me to help you, lugging this lot down the stairs by yourself.'

'It's fine, really. Most of it was scattered about downstairs anyway. I've left things as tidy as I can. Ideally I should have run the vacuum round and emptied the bins and I haven't put any of the washing out to dry . . .'

'Oh, stop it, woman. I can nip in and sort all that out. Just leave me the keys and I'll pop them back to young Sian when I'm done.'

He lifted the bags one by one into the boot of Madi's car, and waited for her to close it. 'All in? Nothing you've left behind? Want to do a final check?'

'No, all good.' She yawned, trying to stifle it with the back of her hand. 'I should be going.'

'Oh, Madi, look at you. You're tired before you even set off. Are you sure I shouldn't drive you?'

'And leave my car here? That wouldn't work, would it?'

'We could go in yours.'

'And then you'd have all the hassle of getting a train back. Thank you, Tom, really, but I'll be all right.'

They hovered for a moment, neither of them quite sure how to manage the goodbye, until he stepped forward and pulled her into a gentle hug. 'I'll miss you, you know.'

'You too.'

'Will you come back, do you think?'

'I hope so. Maybe next year, if Prue's up for another swap. If she's . . .'

311

'She'll be okay, Madi. She's a tough young thing. It will take more than some lowlife burglar to bring her down.'

'Let's hope you're right. No doubt I'll find out soon enough.'

'Keep in touch. You promised me a backstage theatre visit one day, don't forget.'

'Of course. As soon as I'm working again. A front-row seat too, if I can arrange it. And if you find out any more about the fire, do let me know. I'd hate to think it was anything we did, or the kids . . . Still, that's not important now. Give my love to Barbara. And think about getting that dog. It's what she wanted, remember?'

'And you make peace with that son of yours. Family's what counts. Those you love. Not much else comes close in the end.'

Chapter 34

I haven't eaten. I haven't slept. I haven't been out.

I've listened though. Heard the comings and goings. The ambulance arriving, the banging on the front door, the hurried footsteps on the stairs. That horrible siren wailing as they drove her away. People moving about, talking in shocked voices. Stan rubbernecking in the hall and stirring things, like he always does, going on about security and hooligans and hanging. And later, policemen, or that's who I think it must have been, ringing on my bell. On everyone's bells. I ignored it, sat in silence, pretended I wasn't in. They'll be back though. I know it.

Is she alive or dead? I shouldn't care. I hardly knew the girl. Still, I need to know, don't I? I have to know. But I can't ask anyone. Can't look like I'm interested, like it's anything to do with me. Best to just stay here, say nothing, do nothing, let it all blow over.

This will bring her home now, I'm sure. The actress. Wherever it is she's been, she'll come crawling out of the woodwork soon enough. There will be police everywhere, poking their noses in, asking questions. And she'll be the centre of attention again. Acting out her part, as always.

313

Maybe I can do something to make it look like it was her. Using her key, coming in in the dark, thinking there was an intruder, bashing the girl over the head . . . It would get her arrested, locked up. Wouldn't that be the perfect end to it all? But, even as I think it, I know it won't happen that way. She wasn't here. She'll have some alibi. And she knew the girl was in there, had invited her. She had no reason to do it. Whereas I . . .

It's quieter now the hullabaloo has died down. Having a real-life crime happen on your doorstep has a way of hushing people, stunning them into a shocked silence. Nobody goes out. Nobody comes in. Only the police, their radios whistling, their big boots tramping up the stairs. All I can hear in here is the clock ticking on the dresser. Tick. Tock. Tick. Tock.

I should get rid of it. The weapon. Wipe her blood off it. Throw it in the river. But to do that I'd have to go out, and I can't do that. They'll work it out soon anyway, with or without it. I know they will. Who I am. Why I wanted her gone. It can only be a matter of time.

Chapter 35

Faith sat in the one good armchair next to Prue's bed, chewing her fingernails and staring, sightlessly, out of the fourth-floor window.

'Hours! Hours they say she might have been lying there. I dread to think what might have happened if that neighbour hadn't found her when she did. I mean, how long can a person survive like that, on their own, with no medical help? Oh, God, we could have lost her, Stu. We still could . . .'

'It will be all right, love.' Stuart perched on the edge of a red plastic stacking chair he'd dragged into the room from the corridor outside and reached for his wife's hand. 'The scan showed there's no obvious brain injury. No need to worry yourself into a lather. She will be okay, I promise you.'

'How can you do that? How can you possibly promise? Because you don't know for sure, do you? Our daughter isn't someone's favourite pet or some prize farm animal you're treating. It's different when it's a human being . . .'

'Would you like me to go and find you a drink or something to eat? Or you take a break and I'll sit here for a while.'

'I don't want food. I just want Prue to be all right.'

They sat in silence for a while. Stuart had picked up a magazine from a table in the relatives' room on one of his frequent can't-sit-here-doing-nothing wanders, and started thumbing through it. It was one of those country living glossies that in no way resembled the country life he was familiar with, but it wasn't easy to concentrate anyway so he put it down again. 'Well, I think I might pop out and find a vending machine. Or a shop. There must be one downstairs. I'm in need of a strong coffee, and maybe a sandwich. Are you sure I can't get you anything? Starving yourself until you faint won't really be of any help to Prue when she comes round, will it?'

'Oh, suit yourself.'

It was very quiet when he'd gone. The minute hand on the clock on the wall clicked with every movement as it made its way rhythmically round the big white face, there was a hum of passing traffic from the street down below, and various pieces of machinery buzzed and beeped both inside and outside the room. But, above them all, was the slow, reassuring sound of Prue's breathing. Not one of those ventilator machines doing it for her. She was breathing for herself. Faith closed her eyes and thanked God for that.

Her mobile vibrated in her bag, making her jump. She had switched it to silent, worried that if it were to ring some officious member of staff might point to the warning signs on the walls and tell her to turn it off altogether. She pulled it out and looked at the screen. It was Joe Barton. Just a month or so ago he would have been the first person she would have called as soon as this terrible thing had happened. He was one of Prue's oldest friends long before he had become her boyfriend, and he'd been the little boy Faith had always been so fond of and felt so protective of once his own mother had died, but now . . . Whatever hopes Prue had had for their future had been cruelly dashed and Prue had been left humiliated and heart-broken.

Faith hesitated for a moment before answering. Their spat wasn't her business. Joe and his father were old family friends. His brother was Stuart's business partner. She couldn't ignore him. The poor boy would be worried. Of course he would. The least she could do was update him, put him out of his misery.

'Joe?' She kept her voice low to avoid getting told off by some passing nurse. 'Yes, we're at the hospital now. They're keeping her sedated for a while, so she's sleeping, but they say she'll be okay. Oh, God, I hope they're right. Her head's all bandaged up and she's got some minor burns on her stomach and her arm. I don't know. Hot water, so they say. The police are staying close by, waiting to talk to her as soon as she's awake. No, no idea who did it, or why. Yes, okay, if you're sure. You do know that she might not want to see you? Right. See you later then. We'll be here. We're not planning on going anywhere. Now, just hang on while I give you the address of the hospital, and which ward . . .'

She wondered if she had done the right thing, agreeing to let him visit. It was so hard sometimes, dealing with other people's mess, to know what the right thing was. Still, Prue could always send him away again, couldn't she? Or who knew? This could be the big moment of revelation that proved to Joe just how wrong he had been and how much he loved her, the tearful reunion that sent them flying back into each other's arms.

'I got you a tea, and a cheese and pickle.' Stuart crept back into the room, cautiously. Faith wasn't too sure if it was in deference to Prue lying there so silently or for fear of getting his head bitten off by a distressed wife.

'Thank you,' she said, holding out her hand, not to take the food but to wrap her fingers around his own. 'You do know I couldn't do this without you, don't you?'

'Likewise, love.'

Prue opened her eyes. She didn't know where she was, or why the light above her was so bright, or where all the strange noises were coming from. This wasn't her room, not her bed.

She struggled to pull her thoughts together, but her head didn't feel right. Muzzy, muddled, like the worst kind of headache. What was going on? Had she been drinking? No. The last thing she remembered was being in the kitchen at Madi's, filling the kettle, boiling it, picking it up . . .

'Prue? Prue? Can you hear me?'

Who was that? Simon. Had he come home with her after all? She had wanted him to, so badly, but she didn't remember chasing after him. Had she? Still, he was here now. But why did she feel so sleepy? Had they . . .?

'Si . . .?'

'Don't try to talk, Prue. Do you know where you are? What happened to you?'

It wasn't Simon. It sounded like . . .

She turned her head, slowly, but it hurt. Her whole body hurt.

'Joe?'

'You're in hospital, Prue. Everything's okay. Take it easy now. Don't try to move.'

Another voice. From somewhere further away. One she didn't recognise at all. A woman.

'My name's Carol, and I'm a nurse. Your mum and dad are here, Prue, and Joe. You've had a little knock on the head. Nothing to worry about. Come back to us in your own time.'

'Oh, Prue, I've been so scared.' That was her mum. Unmistakeable. She tried to focus on the face that had loomed in over her, blocking out everyone else. Kisses landing frantically on her cheek, the smell an odd combination of cheese and eau de cologne and fear . . .

'Can we all just give her a bit of space now please?'

Prue closed her eyes and let the darkness wash back over her. Too much to take in. Too many questions. She let them all drift into the distance, just a fuzz of voices mingling together into one, and all so far away.

Chapter 36

MADI

It was after five o'clock when Madi pulled into her usual residents' parking spot along the road from the flats. She had stopped only once, for a quick snack, a visit to the Ladies, and to call Faith's mobile for an update and to invite them to stay at the flat later. She knew they wouldn't want to be too far away while Prue was still in hospital. Now she was exhausted. Her bags could wait. The first thing was to go in, check out any damage and make herself some tea.

As soon as she opened the front door she could hear raised voices coming from upstairs.

'Yes, I have keys, but I never use them. It wouldn't be right. They're simply for emergencies, to deal with leaking water, that sort of thing, especially with us living directly beneath. And I certainly didn't use them last night, if that's what you're thinking.'

'I am not thinking anything, Madam. Just checking the facts. There was no sign of a break-in, so it's fair to assume that whoever did this was either invited in or had a key.'

'Well, I don't know anything about that, do I?'

Madi walked tentatively up to the first floor. Aaron and Suzy's door was open and she could see two men standing just inside, one in uniform, one in plain clothes but still very obviously a policeman, both with their backs to her. She got the impression, from the tone of Suzy's voice, that she was not about to invite them in to sit down.

'Perhaps not, but we understand from another of the residents that you may have recently become the owner of Miss Cardew's flat, which makes you her landlord. Or landlady, if you prefer the term. Is that correct?'

'No, that's not correct.' Madi stepped forward, unable to help herself. 'Don't be ridiculous.'

The police officers turned. 'Inspector Fletcher,' the older one said, flashing his card. 'And you are . . .?'

'I'm Madalyn Cardew. And I can assure you that this lady here has nothing to do with my flat. So I would certainly like to know why she says she has keys, emergency or no emergency.'

'Perhaps we could take this inside?' the officer said, beckoning Madi forward. 'For a little privacy?'

'Or perhaps not,' Suzy said. 'I don't want her coming in here. If you want to talk to her, can't you do it upstairs?'

Madi was shocked by Suzy's animosity. 'Suzy, I don't know what this is all about, but I think we should get to the bottom of it, don't you? Helping the police with their enquiries just might give them some sort of a clue about who did this, who hurt Prue.'

'Well, it wasn't me.'

'I'm sure nobody thinks it was. But the keys . . .?'

'They're right. I do have keys.' Suzy spat the words out, contemptuously. 'I presume it was that Stan opening his big gob again. Got his nose into everything, that one.'

'Ladies. I hardly think . . .'

They both ignored the police officer as he attempted to bring the conversation back under his control.

'Mum? What's going on?' A bedraggled-looking Aaron emerged from a bedroom, looking only half awake, wiping the sleep from his eyes. 'What's all the yelling about? Is there news about Prue? Oh, hello, Mrs Cardew.'

'*Miss!*' Suzy snapped. 'She's not married, and we know why, don't we?'

'Pardon?' Madi looked from one to the other. 'I'm sorry, Aaron, but I seem to have upset your mum. Maybe you can explain what this is all about? They say she has keys to my flat, that she's the landlord?'

'Well, yes,' Aaron yawned. 'Grandad used to own the whole block, bought it as an investment years ago. Some have been sold off but Mum owns the rest now. Didn't you know?'

'Your grandad? Owned the block?' Madi was feeling suddenly faint. She was tired from the journey and she needed to sit down. No, that couldn't be right. The flats had been Jeremy's. He'd given her one to live in, as soon as he knew about the baby. Security, a home for life, he'd said. A cheap rent, no increases, for as long as she needed it. For ever, if that's what it took to keep her happy. And quiet. There was a special clause, an agreement, and it was still in existence, long after he'd died. A management company handled everything now. 'What was your grandad's name, Aaron?' she asked, although she already suspected now exactly what the answer was going to be.

'Jeremy Cave. He was an actor too, actually, just like you. Mainly theatre, but TV too, a few films . . . I think he was quite famous in his day, although he died years ago so I never met him, of course. Went by the stage name of Jeremy Cavendish. You might have heard of him. Why do you want to know?'

Madi looked straight at Suzy, as if she might see a trace of his face in hers. 'Is that true? You're Suzanne Cave? Jeremy's daughter?'

'So what if I am? Or was? It's been a long time since I've used that name. I've been Suzy Jones ever since I married Aaron's dad, and what a mistake that turned out to be. Men and their affairs . . . Yes, my dad too. And *you*. Don't try to deny it, because I know. I've tried to not let it bother me, tried to just keep my distance, but you're here, right here, living above me. How could you, Madalyn? You knew he already had a wife, and a daughter, but that still didn't stop you, did it?'

'I didn't . . .'

'Didn't what? Didn't think? Didn't care?'

Madi could feel her hands starting to shake, the police officer's eyes on her, taking it all in. She wouldn't be surprised if he took out his notebook and started writing it all down. This sudden link to her past, thrown in her face. His wife and child. Nancy and Suzanne. She knew their names, but they had just been shadowy figures, hardly mentioned. An inconvenience, keeping her and Jeremy apart. And Suzy was right. She had never thought about them as real people, with feelings. Only about herself. Her needs, her child . . .

'He didn't leave us though, did he?' Suzy said. 'Not for you, or for any of the others. He might have bought you all off with your posh flats, but he didn't want to live with you, did he? Any of you. His little harem, all under one roof, where he could keep an eye on you, control you, buy your silence.'

'What . . .?'

'But you were flings, the lot of you, and bloody expensive ones too,' Suzy went on, hardly stopping to draw breath. 'If you'd met someone else and got married, you'd have had to leave, wouldn't you? Or buy the place. You wouldn't have been allowed to keep on renting it then. All part of the legal stuff he tied us all up in, so I'm told, but oh no, you didn't even do that, did you, *Miss* Cardew? No marriage for you, while you could stay on here for as long as you liked. What man would be worth giving up all this, eh? Best flat in the block, and you know it. Still bloodsucking all these years later. Do you have any idea how much I could make if only I was allowed to sell? But I'm not allowed. Only to you, but oh no, you didn't want to buy, did you? Well, why would you, with the rock-bottom rent you pay?' She was crying properly now, the frustration and pain so evident in her screwed-up face that Madi had no idea what to say.

'Of all the stupid short-sighted mistakes he made . . . but it's not about the money. That's not what hurts, not really. He was my dad. He brought me back presents every time he went away, sat me on his knee, read me stories, dressed up as Santa at Christmas. He was only fifty-five when he died, and I was just twelve. A late baby, after years of thinking it would never happen, and he doted on me. Would have done anything for me. I still remember the smell of him all these years later, his soap, his aftershave, his big hands ruffling my hair, the feel of his stubble when I touched his face. He wasn't some famous actor to me, he was just my dad, and I wish I could always remember him that way. Not as this womanising . . .'

'I had no idea.' Madi was stunned, not sure how she was managing to stay on her feet.

'Well, guess what. Neither did I,' Suzy went on, sobbing quietly. 'Not about the women, or the flats. I never understood why Mum didn't sell the lot when he died and just walk away. Not until the solicitor spelt it all out to me, years later, after she died. What I had inherited, special clauses and sitting tenants and all. Oh, she knew about his affairs all right, my mum. Whether she knew while he was still alive and turned a blind eye – hah, the irony! – or only found out afterwards I don't know, and I never will know now, will I? What she had to put up with. My poor mum. But she kept quiet about it. Never said a word, in all these years. Just left it all for me to read after she'd gone, in a letter. She kept his sordid secrets, and her own dignity, and tried to protect me from it all, right to the end. She even bloody well apologised, for having to break it to me. The truth, at last. As if she had anything to apologise for. And now I've lost her too.'

'Your mother, the lady who lived here with you for a time, that was Nancy?' Madi said, still standing just a few feet away on the landing. 'Jeremy's Nancy? And all this time I was paying my rent to that management company, it was really going to her? And now to you?' She stood, swaying, trying to take it in.

Suzy sniffed, finally pulling herself together as Aaron came forward and put his arm around her shoulders. 'Someone came, from the solicitors. Tried your door after he'd spoken to me. You weren't about. Working, or sick or something. Didn't they write to you?'

'I don't read all that stuff. Not properly. All the jargon. I thought it was just routine, the same thing being sent to all the residents, the owner wanting to sell. I didn't think it applied to me, and I couldn't afford to buy the place, even if I wanted to. Oh, my God, I just thought some faceless company owned the place now. Not his family, not . . . *you*. I'm sorry, Suzy. I am so sorry, but I think I need to get back upstairs now. I can't . . .'

'Are you all right, Miss Cardew?' The older police officer looked concerned. 'This all seems to have come as a shock to you, and I'm not sure if it has anything to do with the assault on Miss Harris, but I certainly intend to find out. Now, allow me to accompany you back to your flat. We will need to ask you a few questions, and get you to take a look around for anything obviously missing. Perhaps after a nice strong cup of tea?' He had hold of her elbow now and was edging her away towards the stairs. 'I will be back to talk to you again later, Mrs Jones. Mr Jones too. Please let me know if you plan on going out.'

'My shift at work . . .' Aaron started to say. 'No, actually, I'm going to call in sick. I can't face it, not after what's happened

327

here. I've hardly had any sleep, and I'd like to try to visit Prue later, if she's up to it. How is she, do you know?'

'Her parents are with her, Mr Jones. And, for the moment, I don't think that you going anywhere near her would be appropriate . . .'

'What? Am I a suspect? She was – *is* – my friend. I wouldn't hurt her.'

'Our investigations are ongoing, sir. We do need to talk to everyone who had access to the building and to Miss Cardew's flat. We'll take statements either here or down at the station, so it might be wise to get dressed. Just remain at home for now.'

Madi walked slowly up the last staircase. The door to her flat was already open, a line of police tape stretched across the doorway to stop anyone going in.

Others? What had Suzy meant about others? She had truly believed she had been Jeremy's one and only lover, the one he had fallen head over heels for, no matter how briefly, before returning, tail between his legs, to his wife the moment the reality of her pregnancy and what it could do to his precious career had hit home. Could she have been that naïve, that wrong, that stupid? Just one in a line of other women, one of a string of casual, meaningless affairs?

And if Jeremy really had kept them all here in some kind of sick harem as Suzy had implied, just who exactly were they? Which of her neighbours had also fallen for the charms of Jeremy Cavendish and were still living on his generosity long after his death? It wasn't surprising that Suzy was so bitter, so angry at the world. Having to live with her blindness and the recent loss of her mother was bad enough, but it can't have been easy to discover the truth about her parents' marriage, the kind of man her father had been, and then to have to live here, reminded of it every day, her hands tied by some forever clause and unable to do anything about it. She felt sorry for her, sad for her. The poor woman was Jeremy's daughter . . .

Her neighbour, Betty Bloomfield, was hovering on the top landing, almost leaning over the banisters. She must have heard every word. She was still wearing her library name badge, pinned to her navy suit, so she could not have been home long. 'Madi, you're back,' she said. 'Terrible business. It was me who found her, you know, when I opened my door early this morning. Oh, you do look awfully pale, dear. Is everything all right? Anything I can do?'

'Not now, Betty. Please, not now . . .'

'Are you ready, Miss Cardew?' The police officer pulled one end of the tape aside and signalled for her to step inside her own flat. But it wasn't hers, was it? It never really had been.

'The only thing I can definitely see is missing from here is my gold locket. It's not particularly valuable, just nine carat, and I'm not sure why anyone would take that and leave some of my other pieces behind. This pearl, and the silver bracelet, are worth more, and quite obviously so. And the locket only had a photo of my son inside. Not of any interest to anyone else really.'

'No cash? Cards? Anything like that?'

They sidestepped round the young woman who was dusting

everything for fingerprints, the policeman adjusting his gloves so he didn't contaminate anything with his own hands.

'No, whatever cash I had was with me in Norfolk, in my purse, not that I ever carry a lot of it. And I only use one credit card, and that was with me too.'

'How about the other rooms, Miss Cardew? Anything gone? Disturbed? Out of place?'

'It's so hard to say. Lately I've found I move things about and can't even remember doing it, so nothing really has its own rightful place any more. A bit of brain fog. Stress, probably.' Even as she said it, the nagging feeling was there again. What if it was more than that? 'Because of my illness, you see.'

'Illness?'

'Cancer. Oh, it's gone now, dealt with, with a lot of help from chemotherapy, which made me feel very tired, a bit confused, sorry for myself. The truth is, I'm even more confused now. About the flat, about Suzy and her mother owning it now, having keys . . . I knew nothing about any of that.'

'Take a moment. No hurry. It's all been a shock, I'm sure.'

'But you do know that Prue has been living here for the last few weeks, not me? You'll find her fingerprints everywhere, I'm sure, and those of any visitors she might have had in here. And the place has a lot of her things still in it too. She might well have moved some of my belongings out of the way, tucked them out of sight, maybe.'

'Out of sight? Why would she do that?'

'I only meant if anything wasn't to her taste. The picture of my son staring at her from next to the bed, for instance.

A bit off-putting when you don't know the person. And my award too. I can see it's not in its place on the mantelpiece.'

'And what award would that be?'

'Just something I won years ago, as a young actress. I'm proud of it but I have to admit it is rather ugly. Big and heavy. Made to look like gold, but not, of course. Brass, I think. Maybe she didn't like it looking at her. It had a habit of doing that, or it could feel that way. The face on it, the eyes seeming to follow you round the room, you know . . .'

'Could you take a look for it, please? While you're checking the cupboards and their contents. Only we don't yet have a weapon, and your award is starting to sound very much like a possibility.'

* * *

'No, it's not here.' Madi had turned the flat upside down but there was no sign of the award. Or of her locket. Two things that had meant so much to her, for their sentimental value rather than any monetary one, and both gone.

'Thank you, Miss Cardew. I think we have all we need here for the moment. We'll be off and leave you in peace. Oh, and I've heard that Miss Harris has just woken up, you'll be pleased to know. I'm going to see her now, so hopefully we'll have more information soon, assuming her memory is intact. Don't hesitate to call me if you find anything or think of anything that might help us with our investigation.'

'I will. Just one question though . . . Do you think it was a targeted attack? As so little was taken, it can't have been a random burglary, can it? There's no mess, no drawers pulled out, no vandalism. And no sign of a break-in. Either she let them in or someone must have had a key. Was the attacker after Prue, do you think? Or could they have been looking for me?'

He couldn't answer that. Nobody could. But it was a worrying thought, that she – or poor, sweet Prue – might have enemies, someone who wished them harm.

Madi watched as the tape was removed and the flat reverted from a crime scene to a home. She closed the door after them all and sat down, finally allowing herself to close her eyes and breathe. Her thoughts were taking her to places she really did not want to go. It was all too much to take in. That she had been living here, right above Jeremy's family, without knowing who they were.

They had a key to her flat. And Suzy was so upset, so hurt. She really seemed to hate her. Enough to have done this, maybe? Invaded her space, stolen from her, hurt an innocent girl who just happened to be in the wrong place at the wrong time?

No, she mustn't jump to conclusions. Suzy was upset, but that didn't make her violent or a would-be killer. And she was blind, for heaven's sake. No, she must let the police do their job. They had heard the conversation, all of it, and they would be asking questions, the right questions, not just guessing at things the way she was. Besides, there were other keys to her flat. Too many, when she thought about it. George still had one, even though he'd not used it in years, and that surely meant that his wife had access to it as well – the wife he had fallen out with not so long ago. And Prue had a key, of course. And there was a spare too, that Madi kept in a kitchen drawer. Betty from next door had borrowed that key when Madi had first come home from the hospital after her mastectomy and had just wanted to sleep. Betty had used it to let herself in, not wanting to disturb the patient, when she'd been out to get Madi some shopping or to pick up her prescriptions from the chemist. Had she ever returned it? Madi couldn't remember. She went into the kitchen to check, and yes, it was there in the drawer where it belonged.

She really must stop trying to be some kind of amateur sleuth. The police would get to the bottom of things soon enough. For now, she had other things to be getting on with. Faith and Stuart would be here soon and she still needed to make up their bed, and change the sheets on her own. Madi just hoped they would be bringing good news with them because it was Prue who mattered the most right now.

Chapter 37

PRUE

'**P**rue?'

When she opened her eyes, she felt a lot better, clearer in the head. Joe was sitting beside her, holding her hand.

'Still here?'

'Of course.'

'What time is it?'

'Ten past eight. Visiting hours are over.'

'So how come . . .?'

'I sweet-talked the nurse, told her I'd come a long way, promised I'd be quiet. Your mum and dad have just gone. They didn't want to wake you, but they needed a change of clothes and a bit of sleep, now that they know you're okay. Miss Cardew said they could stay at hers. Your mum's shattered. It's been hard for her, seeing you so poorly. They'll be back first thing.'

'Great. Could you pass me a glass of water, please?'

He poured some from the big plastic jug on the tray at the foot of the bed, and held the tumbler to her lips.

335

'What exactly . . .?'

'Happened to you? Look, I know this is a lot to take in, but the police are doing their best to find out who did this. It was someone at the flat where you were staying, some sort of intruder. Someone you let in, or who was already there. Maybe you disturbed him, and he hit you. You've already told the police that you don't remember anything about it.'

'Have I? I don't even remember doing that.'

'Just an hour or so ago, but you were still very groggy. They'll be back again once you've rested.'

'Am I all right? Not going to die or anything?'

'A head wound, bruises, concussion, scalded skin in places. You were holding a boiling kettle, apparently. You've been very lucky it wasn't a lot worse, but I can assure you you're not going to die. A tough cookie like you . . . it'll take more than a bump on the head. And do you really think your parents would have left you here alone if that was on the cards?' He attempted a laugh but it came out more like a sob.

'Why are you here, Joe?'

'I had to come. I care about you.'

'Care about me? What exactly does that mean?'

'We're friends, aren't we? Good friends. That counts for a lot. To me anyway. We've known each other for ever, Prue. Been through so much together, good times and bad. You're like the sister I never had, the one I wish I'd had.'

'I know. Same here. About you being like a brother, I mean. Shame we confused it with something else, isn't it?'

'I do love you, you know. Always have. But just . . . not like *that*, if you know what I mean.'

'I'm beginning to.'

'Maybe this isn't the time to talk about this?'

'Why not? We've put it off long enough, don't you think? The big conversation. The why you never loved me *like that*. Why we're not meant to live happily ever after . . .'

'I'm not sure you'd really want to hear it.'

'Try me.'

'Maybe not now. You're tired, hurt . . .'

'Yes, now. And this is only physical hurt. It will heal. What you caused me was more like mental hurt, emotional hurt. Have you any idea how badly my confidence has been knocked over the last few years? For heaven's sake, Joe, I had a boyfriend who went off to uni and then worked miles away and who seemed really reluctant to come back, one who hardly touched me when he did. It didn't feel like love, not proper love. You weren't ripping my clothes off or looking like you wanted to. And when we did . . . you know . . . where were those fluttery feelings I knew we were supposed to feel? They weren't there, were they?'

'I'm sorry.'

'All I really wanted was . . . what Sian had.'

'Ralph, you mean? You wanted my brother?'

'Oh, don't be ridiculous. Stop comparing yourself with Ralph. It's not about Ralph. None of it is. No, what I wanted was romance, passion, lust! It was never really there, was it? I needed you to really want me. Fancy me. Have trouble keeping your hands off me. But you didn't. And in my head that had to be my fault. I wasn't pretty enough, sexy enough, maybe even clever enough, especially once you'd gone and got

337

your degree. I was just plain old Prue, country girl, and coming back to be with me wasn't enough for you. *I* wasn't enough for you . . .'

Joe gripped her hand, pulling it up to his lips and holding it there. He closed his eyes. 'So, how was proposing meant to help? Did you think a wedding ring on your finger – and on *my* finger – would change all that?'

'I don't know what I thought. That it might change *you*, I suppose. But I was just burying my head in the sand. Pretending. Trying to make you be someone you're not. I just wanted to shake you into doing something. Anything. So, tell me. What went wrong with us? Why was it a "no"? Why was it always only ever going to be a "no"?'

'Because . . . oh, this is so hard.'

'Just tell me, Joe. I'm tired now. Tell me, or go.'

'All right. All right. It was going to uni. Suddenly feeling free of my old life, free to do what I wanted without being watched or judged. It was like a light being switched on. I could be me. For the first time. The real me. And that was because of Jake.'

'Jake? Your flatmate?'

'More than that, Prue. Jake was . . . is . . . much more than that. We grew close, spent a lot of time together. It just sort of came out of that really.'

'What did? Do you mean that you and Jake . . .?'

'Are you shocked? Look, Prue, you're the first person I've told. The only person. And I'm not finding it easy.'

'You and Jake? Well, I didn't see that coming. But I'm not shocked exactly. Surprised, though. Go on, you've started now, so tell me. All of it. I'm not going to get upset, believe me. If that's who you are, what you want . . .'

'It is, and I am so sorry.'

'Don't be. It's a relief really. That the not fancying me stuff had a reason. That it wasn't me being . . . inadequate.'

'Don't be daft. You're gorgeous. Just not my sort of gorgeous, if you know what I mean.'

'Okay . . .'

'So, after uni, Jake went back home, up to Leeds. I wanted to be with him. I found a job up there, to be near him, but I was so scared to bring him home to Shelling, to introduce him to my dad, to have to tell him . . . and you. I was in denial. Hiding. I didn't know how to admit the strength of what I was feeling, to anyone. Even to me. And in the end Jake just had enough of it. If I couldn't walk down the street holding his hand, if I couldn't come out and tell my family who he was, and who *I* was, then we were over. So I chucked my job in and I came home to Shelling, and tried to fit back into my old life, and back in with you.'

'That was never going to work, was it?'

'Probably not, but I thought if I tried . . . Jake's not like me, you see. He knows what he wants. He's very upfront, very open. Nothing scares him. And everything . . . everything scares me.'

'Oh, Joe, you idiot. You could have saved us both so much aggro if you'd just told me. Been honest with me. And is it over, with Jake?'

'I thought it was, but I couldn't get him out of my head. We've met up again a couple of times recently. He's been staying in Norwich, on a work thing, and he's been over to my place once or twice. I think there might still be a chance, you know. Because it's still there, Prue. The spark . . .'

Prue's mind flickered to Simon and, yes, she did know.

'Then get out of this hospital and go get him! It doesn't matter what your dad thinks, or your brother, or me. If you love this guy, you have to tell him. You've got a lot of friends who care. And a dad who loves you, even if you're both too stubborn to sort out your petty differences.'

'So, you're not heartbroken then? About us? Or there not being an us?'

'Honestly? No. I think we both have a great future to look forward to, but separately, eh? We were brilliant as mates, just not so hot at pretending to be anything else.'

'Hello?'

They both turned towards the door and Prue felt her pulse speed up a notch just at the sound of the voice. Simon! As if just thinking about him had conjured him up.

'Is it all right to come in? The nurse says I can only have five minutes. Visiting's over, apparently.'

'Of course.'

'I'll leave you to it.' Joe stood up, looking awkward.

'Thanks for coming, Joe. I love you, you do know that?'

He came closer to the bed and leant down to kiss her goodbye. 'Love you too.'

'Simon, this is Joe, one of my oldest and dearest friends. And Joe, this is Simon, my . . .'

'Boyfriend?' Simon said, holding out his hand to shake Joe's and looking at Prue inquisitively. 'If she'll have me, that is.'

340

Oh, I'll have you, all right, Prue thought, gazing at Simon as those wonderfully unfamiliar butterflies flipped around in her tummy again, nineteen to the dozen. Just as soon as I'm out of this hospital bed, I'm definitely going to have you . . .

Chapter 38

MADI

When Prue's parents arrived, they both looked shattered. 'Oh, Faith, I am so sorry,' Madi said, pulling her friend in for a hug as Stuart dumped their hastily packed overnight bag on the floor and sank into a chair.

'She looks so pale, Madi, but she's going to be okay. No lasting damage, brain-wise anyway, although the burns might leave some superficial scars. She did wake up a couple of times, briefly, so we've spoken to her, which puts my mind at rest no end. The police have been too, but she doesn't remember much about what happened. She just needs time now, and plenty of sleep. As do I! We've left Joe with her. Poor boy drove straight up when he heard. He wanted to hang around as long as they'd let him, but I don't suppose she'll even know he's there. He was talking about a B&B if he didn't get to talk to her tonight, so he can see her again tomorrow. He's a good lad.'

'Do you think she'll want to see him, after . . .'

'Failed romance or not, Madi, they've known each other since

343

school. She won't turn him away. Which reminds me, I need to let Sian know what's happening too. She'll be worried sick.'

'A cup of tea first though, eh? And I've only been home a matter of hours myself so I have no idea what I can offer you in the way of food. Whatever Prue's left behind, I suppose, or something from my freezer.'

'Don't go to any trouble, Madi. We're all tired. Maybe there's a takeaway or something we could order in? Our treat, for putting us up.' She followed Madi into the kitchen. 'Is that . . . the kettle that was . . .'

Madi hadn't given it a thought as she'd filled it with water and flicked the switch on. 'Oh, I suppose it must be. It's the only one I've got.'

'I would have thought they might have taken it away, as evidence or something.'

They both stared at it as it began to boil, its blue light highlighting the bubbles as they bounced around inside.

'I just don't understand how this has happened. Or why.' Faith stood leaning against the wall, her arms folded tightly around herself. 'My Prue wouldn't hurt a fly . . .'

'I know.' Madi pushed down the awful thought that it was all her fault, that she should never have let Prue stay here when there was some maniac about, someone whose anger was more than likely aimed at Madi, not at Prue. 'Poor kid.'

'And she only came back here yesterday to have a last bit of fun, to finish her adventure. If only she'd stayed at home with us, where she belongs.'

'We can't tie our kids down, Faith.' She swallowed the lump

in her throat as she thought of George and just how much she needed him right now. 'They have to live their own lives.'

'Oh, I know. I'm just having one of those what-if moments. What if she'd never come to London . . . and now she's talking about moving here full-time, studying here. Doing a photography course. I shall worry myself sick the whole time, especially now.'

'I didn't know that. But she does have talent. Surely, if it's for her career . . .?'

'Yes, and I won't try to stop her, obviously. Doesn't stop me fretting though, does it? Now, come on, let's have that cuppa and ring Sian. Then you can fish out a takeaway menu if you have one.'

Madi remembered the piles of them that constantly built up in the hall downstairs. 'Oh, I think I can manage that,' she said.

'Mum! Are you all right?'

Madi stood at the door early the next morning, still wearing her pyjamas, and looked into the face of her son.

'George?' Was it really him? It was as if her longing to see him had actually conjured him up. She had to blink a few times to convince herself she wasn't dreaming. 'What are you doing here?'

'It's all over the papers.'

'What is?'

'The attack on that young girl, right here at Belle Vue Court.'

'Oh, it's just so awful.' She could hear the sob in her voice, but it wasn't for Prue. It was for George, whom she had so badly wanted to see.

'They didn't say which flat, but it didn't take a genius to work it out. A top-floor flat. Staying at the home of an actress. How do they get access to all this stuff?'

'I have no idea. No reporters have been here as far as I know. Unless . . .'

'What?'

'Stan. That old busybody downstairs would sell his own mother given half the chance. He has his nose into everything. He'd have seen the police, the ambulance, probably even watched poor Prue being carried out. You can bet your life he'd be more than happy to talk.'

'Well, I hope they didn't pay him anything, the bloody ghoul! But what's been going on here, Mum? Who was this girl and why was she here?'

'Oh, it's so good to see you, but come on in, George. Please. Let's not give Stan any more to gossip about. He's probably down there right now, listening up the stairs with his notebook out!'

It felt strange having her son back, large as life, in her living room. He had lived here as a child, in between long stays with his grandparents, but he had moved out as a young man, and she couldn't remember the last time he had visited. It must be at least a year ago. It felt even stranger when he stepped forward and wrapped his arms around her. But nice. Oh, so nice . . .

'I was so worried. Are you sure you're okay? You feel thinner. You haven't been dieting for a part?'

'No. Not everything in my life is for a part. I'm just thinner, that's all.'

He pulled back and looked at her more closely. 'What aren't you telling me?'

346

'I could say the same to you. Not a word in months. I have no idea what's been happening in your life either. And Jessica? You said she'd left. Are you . . .?'

'We're working on it, Mum. And she came back, which is what counts.'

'Not divorcing then?'

'Oh, God, no. I love her, Mum. And she loves me. It's just the baby-making thing, you know. Hospitals, tests, embryos, failure . . . all the stress of it, not to mention the cost. It took its toll. On both of us. Some days I just wanted to bury my head under the covers and never come out.'

'IVF, do you mean? I didn't know you'd taken things that far.'

'You didn't ask.'

'That's not fair. It's private, isn't it? Infertility, and all that sort of thing. You tell people when you're ready, and maybe you weren't.'

'Maybe not. But you know now. And we're going to have another go. At our marriage, and at the treatment. But I didn't come here to relive all that. I came here for you. To make sure you're all right. Come on. I know something's up, and it's not just this attack business.'

'Well . . . I've had my share of hospitals lately too.'

'You're ill? And you didn't tell me?'

'I did try to call.'

'Yeah. Once. I saw the missed call, but you didn't leave a message, did you? Or try again? If it had been really important . . .'

The door to the spare room opened then, stopping their conversation dead, and Stuart came out, rubbing his eyes.

'Oh, sorry, Madi. Don't mean to intrude. Just going to put the kettle on and make Faith a cuppa, if that's okay?'

Madi nodded. 'Of course.'

'We'll be out of your hair soon, back to the hospital.'

'No rush. This is my son, George. George, this is Stuart, Prue's dad. You know, the poor girl who was attacked.'

'Right. Morning, Stuart. Horrible business. I hope she's better soon.' George sank back into his chair and waited until Stuart had made two mugs of tea and disappeared back into the spare room and closed the door.

'Who exactly are these people, Mum? Why are they here? Why was their daughter here?'

'It's a long story.'

'Well, I'm not going anywhere.' He leaned forward and took hold of her hand. 'Start at the beginning, and don't leave anything out.'

'So, my dad was her dad too? This Suzy? I have a big sister you've never thought to mention?'

'*Half*-sister. And what would have been the point? He didn't want us. He saw us as an inconvenience, a potential stain on his reputation. He wanted to hide us away. And his other women too, apparently, whoever they might have been. I hardly think his wife and daughter would have been keen to welcome any of us into the family, do you?'

'And now?'

'You should have seen her, George. As far as Suzy's concerned, I'm public enemy number one.'

'Well, you have no reason to hate her back, do you? And

I certainly don't. Since we lost Gran and Grandad, apart from Jess, I've only had you, and you have to admit our relationship hasn't always been as close as it could have been. Not your fault, I know you did your best for me, but, God, Mum, you could have died from your cancer and I would never have even had the chance to say goodbye. What on earth were you thinking, keeping that from me? I would have had no one then, would I? Even Jess had left me. But now she's back, you're recovering and, right out of the blue, I have another family. A sister, and a nephew, living right here. It's a lot to take in. Weird. I mean, do they know I even exist?'

'I don't suppose they do. Your father was keen to keep us under wraps, so he won't have told them I was pregnant. Or told anyone at all, for that matter.'

'Do they look anything like Dad? Or like me?'

'I haven't really had time to think about that, or to notice . . .'

'Family ties matter, Mum. What's in our genes, our blood. Thinking I might never have children of my own has shown me that. I'd like to meet them.'

Madi closed her eyes. When she'd left Norfolk at lunchtime yesterday, she'd had no idea all this was waiting for her. It was too much to take in. 'I'd have to tell them about you first. It will come as just as big a shock to them as it has to you, I expect. And you'd have to be prepared for them to say no.'

'Okay, they probably need time to absorb it all, but they'll come round. Curiosity, if nothing else. And I can be stubborn.'

'Don't I know it!' She laughed then. 'Oh, George, I am sorry, really sorry, for letting things drift like this, for not talking to you.'

'It takes two, and I was just as bad, but we can sort things out now, can't we? Who knows, you might even be a grandma soon, if the treatment works out. Imagine that!'

'I'm trying to.' Madi gripped his hand and ran her fingers over his wedding ring. 'God, it makes me sound old, but I have to admit I like the idea of it. I may even have to learn to knit! But you're right. Family matters. I'll try to introduce you to young Aaron. I think he'll be an easier fish to fry than his mother at the moment. And then we'll just have to take it from there, won't we? See what happens . . .'

'Morning, Madi.' Faith emerged from the spare room, dressed but still bleary-eyed.

'Hello, Faith. This is George, as Stuart's probably told you. George . . . Faith.'

They nodded to each other.

'Did you manage to sleep?'

'Not well. I just keep thinking about Prue and what might have happened. We could so easily have lost her.'

'But you didn't.' Madi stood up and put an arm around Faith's shoulders. 'Now, I'm going to rustle up some breakfast. Only cereal and toast, I'm afraid, until I can get some shopping in, and I know you'll be anxious to get to the hospital, but you'll need something inside you.'

'I've already rung, on my mobile. They say she's doing well. A peaceful night. They might even let her go home later today. So quick, when you think how badly she was hurt, but I guess they need the bed, don't they? And I think that going home has to mean going home with us. She's not fit enough to stay on here, and now that you're back . . .'

'Of course. She'll need looking after, and who better to do that than her own mum? Shall I help you pack up her things? There are some clothes lying around, things in the bathroom, some shopping bags of things I don't think she's even worn yet . . .'

'Thank you, yes. I really wouldn't know which were yours and which were hers. If we could get that done this morning before we set off, we won't need to come back and trouble you later.'

'It's no trouble, Faith, you know that. And if they decide to keep her for longer you can always sleep here again tonight if you need to.'

'Thank you, Madi, but I really hope we won't have to take you up on that. I just want her home now, and to get back to the village and crawl into my own bed. But we'll stay in touch, won't we? Well, there'll be the police investigation anyway, so I'm sure we'll all need to be kept up to speed on that. You're welcome to come down to see us in Shelling anytime, you know. And Tom's been asking after you, according to Sian. She popped round there early, before work, and he was putting Flo's food down and giving her a cuddle. Oh, and he said to let you know they think the fire was started by a cigarette. Dropped into a wastepaper bin, apparently. He has his suspicions about who the culprit might be but he wouldn't say. Still, I thought you'd like to know.'

'Fire?' George asked. 'It's one drama after another around here. What else haven't you told me about? And who on earth is Tom?'

* * *

It was eleven o'clock by the time everyone had finally gone, George insisting it didn't matter if he was late to work and having one last cup of coffee before following Faith and Stuart out of the door. Madi sat for a few moments and enjoyed the silence. Despite all that had happened here, this was her home and she was glad to be back in it. There were sheets and towels to change, food to buy, post to open, but first she was going to call Tom. He'd be worrying, and she'd left in such a rush . . .

Besides, she needed to hear about the fire. If it had started because of a cigarette, and they both knew who had been caught smoking, who had been told off for it. Donny's mate, Ricky Flynn. But should they tell anyone? The police, the fire brigade, the lad's parents? What good would it do? It had obviously been an accident. Not deliberate, not arson, just a careless mistake. Madi sighed. Why did life have to be so complicated? So cruel? The boy would be feeling bad enough, without the world pointing the finger. Still, nobody had died. It was a building, that was all. And buildings can be rebuilt.

She smiled to herself. George was back, and they were on the way to rebuilding something too. A wave of determination ran through her. Sod stupid bloody arguments over nothing. She should never have let him go, never have lost touch for so long. She could have lost him, and he her. Sod the evil that was cancer. It had taken a piece of her flesh, but what remained was just as strong as ever, or would be, given time. Sod anonymous cowardly attackers who creep about in the dark. They would catch whoever it was, she was sure of it. What mattered above all else was that she was alive, and so was Prue. Hope had triumphed, and that made her feel glad. Optimistic. Surely, things could only get better now?

Chapter 39

*I*t's no good. I can't do it. Can't lie here in bed, in the dark, knowing what I've done, pretending everything is all right, that none of it matters. This wasn't the plan. Not that I had one really, but whatever I had expected to do, wanted to do, dreamed of doing, it was all about her. It was meant for her. Not the young girl. Why did she have to get in the way?

Her visitors are leaving, banging and crashing bags on the stairs. Aaron is down in the hall, going out for a walk, stopping them to ask after the girl, asking how she is, asking if he can visit. So many questions. I can't even hear the answers, hard as I try. I assume she must still be alive, and I am glad, relieved, but beyond that who knows? Bangs on the head can be tricky things. There will be consequences.

It's only a matter of time before the police come back and then there will be even more questions. Don't they know that I have questions too? All the whens and wheres and whys. It was all so long ago, of course, losing him so suddenly, that feeling that my heart might actually break into a million pieces, but I had come to terms with it all, put it behind me, moved on. And *then there was her. And she was here, and had been all along, here within reach . . .*

I pick up the phone. Call for a taxi. I have to get out of here before they come. I don't want them to take me. I want to leave under my own steam. I may not have had much say in what happened to me in life, but I want to write my own ending.

Chapter 40

PRUE

'Everything's packed up and in the car, so we can drive you back home as soon as the doctors say you can go.'

Prue managed a weak smile. 'Thanks, Mum.' She pushed her lunch around on its plate. Twelve o'clock felt much too early to be eating lunch but hospital routines had to be stuck to.

'I can go and find you a sandwich from the shop if you prefer,' her dad said, turning his nose up at the pale dollop of mush that was supposed to be macaroni cheese. 'And some chocolate?'

'No, I'm okay. I'm not even hungry really.'

'You have to eat something, Prudence, to keep your strength up.' Her mum only ever called her Prudence when she was in strict dishing-out-orders mode, and this was one of those occasions.

Prue pushed a forkful into her mouth, more so she wouldn't have to talk than anything else. Home. She didn't really want to go back to Shelling, but there was little choice. Madi had reclaimed her flat, and it was clear Prue would need some

357

help looking after herself over the next week or so as her bruising and burns started to recover. But there was so much left unfinished here . . .

'There was a boy asking after you.'

Prue's heart leapt. Simon?

'Aaron, he said his name was.'

'Ah, that's nice. I got on really well with Aaron. What did you tell him?'

'That you're doing well, but going back to Norfolk. He said to get well soon, and not to worry about the garden. That he'll sort it. Does that make sense?'

'It does.'

Prue finished her lunch and closed her eyes. She still felt so tired, and her head ached.

'We'll leave you to have a little sleep, love,' Stuart said, touching her arm and guiding his wife out of the door.

'Thanks, Dad. See you later.'

Prue lay in the silence and tried to gather her thoughts. Her memory of that evening was still hazy. She'd walked home with Simon, they'd kissed on the step, and she'd watched him start to walk away. That bit was clear as day, and just remembering the kiss sent a shiver through her. And after that . . . going into the flat, only putting the one light on, padding through to the kitchen in the semi-darkness to make herself a drink. No, she hadn't got that far, had she? There had been no drink. Just a noise, a movement, someone there. She had reached for a weapon. The kettle. Blue lights and bubbles. Held it up. Held her breath. But then there was nothing. Just a deep darkness that had slowly unravelled itself into hospital lights and strange beeping noises and pain. Voices. A bed. A story about being attacked. It was as if that part – the attack part – had happened to someone else. She couldn't recall it at all. Being hit. Lying on the floor. The hot water. How long had she been there? It could have been hours. It felt like seconds.

She drifted off into sleep. A happy sleep, awash with dreams. Of a beautiful garden, the warmth of the sun, the scent of herbs, the feel of big strong arms wrapped around her.

When she heard the tap on the door it was as if it was all part of the dream. A foot tapping against a new wooden bench, a woodpecker tapping at the bark of a tree, the rhythmic back and forth creak of a swing. No, there was no swing. She'd decided not to have a swing. This wasn't her garden, not her plan. The tapping stopped and the door opened. It wasn't the door to the garden. It was the door to her hospital room. A voice broke into her dwindling dream and blew it all away. 'Miss Harris? Prue? Are you awake?'

She opened her eyes and turned her head towards the door.

'Inspector Fletcher. We spoke yesterday. I'm sorry to disturb you again, but there's been a development. I thought you should know.'

'Come in. It's okay, I'm awake now. Have you seen my parents? Are they . . .?'

'Here, love.' Her dad followed the policeman into the room, her mum just a pace behind. 'We've had a lovely coffee and a cake, and we're back.'

'That's good. I can speak to you all together.' The inspector stood at the end of the bed, as if unsure whether he should pull up a chair. 'I'm pleased to report that we believe we now know who was responsible for the attack.'

'Thank God for that.' Stuart slumped down onto the bedcovers at Prue's feet. 'And I hope you'll be keeping them locked up and throwing away the key.'

'The person in question is not in police custody, sir.'

'Why the hell not? If you know who it is . . .'

'I'm sorry to say that we retrieved a body earlier today, from the railway line. It looks very much like a suicide. And there was a note. Well, more of a letter, I suppose. A full confession, in fact. Suffice it to say, we will not be looking for anyone else in regard to our enquiries, Miss Harris.'

'Oh, my God. You mean it was the person who attacked me? And that they've . . . been hit by a train? Killed themselves?'

The police officer lowered his eyes and nodded. 'I'm afraid so, yes.'

'But, why? Why would anyone do that? To me? To themselves?' Prue shuddered. 'I can't imagine . . . Oh, it's just horrible.'

'It is indeed. A horrible business. For the rail staff and the ambulance crew who had to deal with the incident especially. Not a pretty sight, when something like that happens on the tracks.'

'And can you tell us who it was?' Faith had a hand to her mouth as if she was about to be sick. 'And why . . .'

'I can assure you that your daughter was not the assailant's target, Mrs Harris. The person in question was known to Miss Cardew, and it was Miss Cardew who was the intended victim. I'm sorry, Prue, but you were very much in the wrong place at the wrong time, it seems. It could have been much worse, of course, and we must be grateful that she didn't manage to inflict a great deal more harm.'

'*She?*' They all said it together.

'Yes. A fellow resident of Belle Vue Court, apparently. I have officers there now. We need to inform the next of kin, you'll understand, so I can't say a lot more right now. I just thought you should know that the danger has passed, there is no assailant waiting out there to try again. That you are safe. And that there will be no need for a court case, obviously. No need for you to have to testify.'

'Thank you.'

'I'll leave you in peace now. And, if I don't see you again, I wish you a speedy recovery and a safe journey home. Goodbye, Miss Harris . . . Mr and Mrs Harris.'

Chapter 41

MADI

The police were back. There were two cars parked outside, right on the double yellow lines, three uniformed officers down in the hall, and the same policeman she had met before – Inspector Fletcher – was shaking the rain from his mac as Madi came in after them, a folded newspaper clutched in her hand. She had been curious to read the reports George had mentioned that morning and had been lucky to pick up the last copy of the paper in the shop. Now she got the distinct impression that whatever it said was going to be old news. It was clear from the level of activity here and now that something else had happened.

'Miss Cardew, may we have a word?'

'Of course. Do you want to come up to the flat?'

'I think that might be best.'

She led the way up to the top floor and let him in, one of the constables close behind.

'Would you like to sit down?' She pushed the pile of freshly washed towels out of the way and pointed to the sofa. From the window she could see someone out in the back yard, unloading pots and plants and a pile of shiny garden tools from a big wheelbarrow, despite the drizzling rain. 'Tea?'

'Tea would be very welcome, thank you. I'm afraid I have news that you may find distressing, so please get yourself a drink too, something a tad stronger if you think you might need it, and then we'll sit and have a little chat.'

'A little chat? I'm not sure I like the sound of that.'

'I'm afraid we recovered a body earlier today, from the railway line.'

'Oh, no. No!'

'One of your neighbours . . .'

Madi could feel herself start to shake, the blood draining from her face until she was sure she was going to faint. It was Suzy, she just knew it. It had to be. Suzy had seemed so troubled, so angry, but she had not expected this. An arrest, maybe, but not this. Never this. Madi closed her eyes and tried hard to control the long, anguished sob that was threatening to burst out from somewhere deep inside her.

'And in her pocket we found a written confession, I'm afraid. You were the intended victim, as we had feared. Not Miss Harris.'

'She hated me enough to want to bash me over the head, maybe even kill me?' Madi's voice wavered, the tears trickling unbidden down her face. 'Didn't she realise I had no idea who she was until yesterday? She was just a child back then. I was young, caught up in a foolish love affair. I didn't think about anyone else. Who I might be hurting . . .' Madi put her head down into her hands and breathed deeply, trying to stop herself from passing out. This was her fault. All her fault. What had happened to Prue, and now to Suzy. 'Oh, but what about Aaron? That poor boy. Does he know? Has he been told?'

'Aaron Jones, you mean?' The officer looked confused. 'Does he know what, exactly?'

'That his mother's dead. She was very upset, I realise that. All alone in that flat a lot of the time, and she was blind, for heaven's sake. What an awful way to live. And then to have to find out about her father . . . and me. But she didn't deserve any of this.'

The inspector put his cup down. 'Miss Cardew, I'm not sure what you think has happened here, but I can assure you it does not involve Mrs Jones or her son. The neighbour I am referring to, the person who attacked Miss Harris and has now sadly taken her own life, was not Suzy Jones. It was a Miss Emily Parker.'

Chapter 42

To Whom It May Concern

I, Miss Emily Jane Parker of Flat 3, Belle Vue Court, do hereby confess my sins. I am not a religious woman, but I do have a conscience, and I have done wrong. The punishment of the law frightens me. I am old, too old for life in a prison cell. I prefer to deal with my guilt in my own way, but I do apologise to those who find me, and for the inevitable mess. That worries me now, above all else. I like to be tidy. Neat. Clean. I like a job to be well done. I am a perfectionist. I like to finish what I begin, tie up the ends.

In recent months I have allowed my hatred for another woman to take over my thoughts, my daily life, my very existence. I had all but forgotten about her, the usurper from my past, until I discovered she had been here all along, the two of us living only floors apart. And then, suddenly, she had a name and a face, and she was real again, and old feelings came flooding back. Feelings of betrayal, abandonment, grief. A desire for revenge.

I wanted only to hurt her as she had once hurt me. To confuse her, unsettle her, make her feel she was going out of her mind, as she once caused me to lose my own mind for a while. To that end, I have been entering her flat in her absence and interfering with her possessions, moving them, hiding them, taking them away. I took some pleasure from it, and there has been precious little of that these last years. I did not want, or expect, to cause her physical harm. I may have fantasised about doing just that, but the courage escaped me.

You will find her locket and her statuette in my bedroom. There will be blood on the latter, which I am sure will come as no surprise. There will be no need to break the door down. The key is here in my pocket, alongside this letter. Unless it has been dislodged by the impact of the train, in which case I am sure you will recover it from the track.

The keys to her flat. You will be wanting to know about those too. How I obtained them. How I got in. We can blame Betty Bloomfield for that. A more scatty woman you would be unlikely ever to meet. I do not know how she holds down a perfectly respectable and responsible job at the local lending library when she has the attention span of a goldfish. In and out of the place, being a Good Samaritan, leaving the keys dangling in the door. So easy to slip them out and have a copy made. She never missed them. Not until she found them lying on her own doormat later that day and thought she'd simply dropped them. The woman is a fool.

As for my nemesis, the true target of my vitriol, I would never have known it was her if it wasn't for that damn fool solicitor. Or solicitor's boy, I prefer to call him. Hardly out of school, still wet behind the ears, bumbling about, dropping papers and spilling secrets he had no business to even know, let alone tell.

Living here, he'd said. On the same special terms. Protected tenancies. Reduced rents. Two other women, one since dead. It was that skinny dancer from number 6, where the new family now lived. Jeremy's family. His daughter, his grandson. Even his widow, for a while. How could I not have known who they were? But the dancer . . . I had never known much about her, never wanted to. She had been the one before me. Of no importance. She had been his past, and I was to be his future. I got some satisfaction from that. A small victory at least and, besides, it was much too late to deal with her now.

And then there was Miss Madalyn Cardew, at number 9. The one who came after me, the one he left me for. Right there under my nose, all those years. The one who had destroyed my life, and taken him away from me.

We met when he came into my café, Jeremy and I. It was 1976. A hot summer. I remember it as if it was yesterday. The place was empty, everyone outside soaking up the sun. We chatted as he drank his tea. I refilled his cup. He smiled and I smiled back. He took a rose from his lapel and handed it to me as he left. I pressed its petals inside a book. I have it still. There is nothing quite so romantic as a rose.

He came again the following week, and the one after. He would stay and chat when it was quiet, compliment me on my cakes, kiss my hand as he left. I was unused to male attention. I am not a woman of beauty. I never was. I was already forty and had never married. His charm, his easy manner, drew me in, enchanted me. Something in me must have appealed to him too, and for that I was grateful. Slowly, we developed an understanding, a closeness. I made no demands. I allowed him to

369

shuffle off his fame and just be himself. Fed him, held him, listened to him. He would call in whenever he was rehearsing nearby, or when he was in a London play. Sometimes weeks would pass, but he always came back. We were like magnets, Jeremy and I. He was the north to my south. We were pulled together. He made me feel special, beautiful, desired, as no one else did, or had, or could. I gave myself to him willingly. I loved him, and I believed that he loved me. I like to believe it still.

When he ended things, I was devastated. He had met another woman. Younger, prettier, someone in the same business, and he had fallen in love with her. He told me her name was Lyn. Just Lyn. I never knew her full name. Just that he was sorry if he'd led me on.

It turns out that she – Madalyn Cardew – is Lyn. Some silly, shortened nickname he used, but it's her. I know that now. Jeremy's Lyn. Oh, I hate even thinking of her in that way. Jeremy's Lyn. His Lyn. His! No, I was his, and he was mine.

I had accepted that he had a wife. Insipid, insignificant, but necessary. He had an image to maintain, a standing within his career, his world. And there was a daughter, still very young. He could not contemplate the possibility of a divorce and its conse-quences. I accepted too that there had been others before me, that liaisons were inevitable when a marriage was unhappy, a man unfulfilled. But somehow they didn't count. The wife, the lovers, the confidantes. I could not let them enter my thoughts. They were there before me, and the past is, sadly, unchangeable. What's done is done. But once we had found each other, I truly believed we would be together for ever. I never expected there to be anyone after me, instead of me . . .

He looked after me in his own way, gave me a flat to live in, made sure I felt grateful enough not to tell, but I never saw him again. Once, on stage, from my seat at the back of the stalls, but he did not know I was there. And on TV from time to time, my breath caught in my throat at the sudden sight of him there in my own home. But never to speak to, never to touch.

I gave up the café. He was everywhere there, in its walls and its windows, and I could not cope with that. I did write to him some months later, a last attempt to hang on, to grab back at least his friendship if not his heart, to recapture something at any price, even if it meant having to share him, but he did not reply. I knew then that he was utterly lost to me. To say that it broke me would not be entirely true, but it certainly hardened me, changed me, and not, I know now, for the better.

I thought it was her – Lyn – in her flat that night. I thought she had come back, caught me snooping, trespassing, that she would report me to the police, shame me. I let my temper, my anger, my jealousy, get the better of me. Some primal instinct rose up in me, to protect myself, to escape, to survive. And I hit her. I hit her hard, and I left her there, bleeding. But it was not her. It was the wrong woman.

I don't know if the girl will live. Perhaps it is better I die not knowing. If I am a murderer, I prefer not to know it. Either way, how am I supposed to live with what I have done? She was a sweet girl, with a good heart. She wanted to help others, to make a difference. I hope I have not broken that in her.

If she lives, tell her I am sorry. I wish I could have seen her garden, sat in it in the sun, seen out my days in peace, surrounded by roses. But now I never will.

I hate you, Madalyn Cardew, even now. And that bastard son of yours, the one I used to see running up and down the stairs from time to time, playing in the hall, holding your hand. I had no idea then who you were, or who he was. That Jeremy had given you a child, the one thing I craved above all else. My own child was stripped from me before it had a chance. That pregnancy was the beginning of the end, as far as Jeremy was concerned. I didn't have your determination, your willpower, your fight. Two hundred pounds he paid to have it taken from me. And abortion was not a pretty thing, not an easy thing, not back then. Never is, I suppose. I gave in too easily, to please him. To keep him. It didn't work, did it? I let my baby go, and I never had another.

This is what love does to a person. It takes away your sense of self, your reason, your soul. It breaks not only the heart and the mind but everything else in between. And yet, I would not have been without it. Its memory keeps me warm.

At least now I will be with him again. My Jeremy. The love of my life. And maybe with my baby too. I am not a religious woman, as I have said, so I don't know if I really believe that, but there is nothing left to me now but hope.

I have a niece, Sandra, who lives in Canada. Nobody else. Give whatever I have to her. And a quiet cremation please. No ceremony. No flowers. I do not deserve them.

Believe me, I am sorry. I don't quite know what I wanted to happen but it was never this.

Emily Parker

Chapter 43

PRUE

Three months later

'This long-distance-dating thing is a bummer.' Simon sneaked a kiss while nobody seemed to be looking.

Prue laughed. 'Not for much longer. I'll be back here properly in September.'

'Ah, but you'll be so wrapped up in your uni course, not to mention all those intelligent creative types you'll be mixing with. Will you still have time for me?'

She squeezed his hand. 'I'll make time.'

'Ah, so this is where you've got to.' Madi was making her way across the grass towards them, balancing drinks on a tray. She handed them each a glass of wine, kept hold of one for herself and put the empty tray down on the ground, gesturing for them to budge up a bit so she could join them on the shiny new bench beneath the tree.

'You've done a wonderful job, Simon. And Aaron too, of

course. The furniture, the paths, and now that all the plants are in, it looks really lovely.'

'And smells lovely too.' Suzy had joined them, clinging to Aaron's arm as they finished a tour of the flower and herb beds. 'Such a good idea of yours, Prue, to think of the sensory side of things. I love the noises it all makes too. The wind chimes, the crunchy gravel, the rustling of the grasses . . .'

'Here, take my seat.' Simon jumped up and laid his hand gently on Suzy's elbow.

'Nonsense. I'm blind, not crippled! I'm perfectly happy to stand. In fact, I think I might take another walk around. It's so nice to get out into the sunshine. I like the warmth of it on my face. I've been cooped up inside for far too long.'

'Do you need me to come with you, Mum?' Aaron said.

'No, let me.' George broke away from the small group of residents standing behind the tree and took her hand.

Prue saw Suzy blush as she realised who had spoken. It was clear she was still not used to having this newly discovered brother in her life, but that she was definitely coming around to the idea.

'I'd like that.'

'Mind if my wife comes too?'

'Of course not. How are you feeling, Jessica? Morning sickness kicked in yet? I remember mine went on for months.'

Prue watched the three of them set off along the path, George stopping to rub a finger over a thyme leaf and hold it up to Suzy's nose, Suzy giggling almost girlishly as she breathed in its scent. It was amazing just how much George looked like his famous father. Tall, dark, handsome, with that twinkle of easy charm in his eyes. She wondered why she hadn't spotted it before, when she'd lain in Madi's bed night after night and seen his face looking down at her from the photo in its fancy frame. Maybe you just don't see what's right in front of your eyes sometimes, until you know exactly what it is you're looking for. Like Joe and his struggle with his sexuality. She should have spotted that too, but it wasn't what she had wanted to see, was it?

She shook her thoughts away and turned her attention back to the garden. Having an official 'grand opening' party, now it was finally finished, had been Aaron's idea, and a good one at that. It was a Friday evening, still light, and surprisingly warm. Every resident of the block was here, even miserable old Stan, who continued to find things to grumble about while simultaneously helping himself to free beer and sausage rolls. The little girl from the ground floor, whose name Prue couldn't remember but who was noticeably taller than the last time she'd seen her, was happily running around with an ice lolly in one hand and a doll in the other, not in the least bothered that there was no swing, and several people had brought guests and family members along, Madi's son and his newly pregnant wife included.

Being asked to cut the ribbon at the small opening ceremony had been an unexpected honour and one Prue felt she really did not deserve, but it had all been her idea, as so many kept reminding her, even if circumstances had prevented her from playing an active part in most of its construction. She had coiled the shiny red ribbon up afterwards and slipped it into her pocket. A keepsake, to look back on. She smiled as she realised it was almost the exact same shade of red as her new T-shirt, the one with all the zips that she'd bought in Oxford Street and still hadn't quite found the nerve to wear.

It must have been her being thumped over the head and the shocking news of Miss Parker's involvement, right here under their own roof, that had jolted so many of the other residents into backing the scheme and contributing a few pounds towards the costs. Either that, or Aaron shaking a bucket on their doorsteps until the guilt kicked in. She could just picture him, staring them in the eyes, not moving an inch until the coins, or better still notes, had landed. She had laughed when he'd told her about it, but it seemed to have got results.

One or two had even helped with the digging and carrying, so she'd been told. But she knew it was Suzy who had really made it all happen. She had finally agreed to sell Miss Parker's flat to Simon's uncle, and Simon had told her on the quiet that Suzy had made what was meant to be an anonymous, but considerable, donation to the garden fund, pushing a large wad of cash into his hand to buy supplies. Prue wouldn't let on that she knew, not if Suzy wanted to keep it a secret, but she felt immensely grateful, just the same.

There had been a huge change in Suzy since she had found out she had a brother. Prue had heard all about it from her many phone calls with both Madi and Aaron over the last few weeks, and seen it for herself whenever she came up to see Simon, with Madi letting her stay for a night or two in her spare room. Suzy had even invited her in for tea, saying with a laugh that her cakes were probably nowhere near as good as Emily Parker's, but to blame Mr Tesco if they weren't.

Whatever feelings Suzy had had about her father's affairs, and her understandable animosity towards his many mistresses, none of that had shown itself in her blossoming relationship with George. Believing yourself to have no family and then discovering that you did after all must be a strange notion to come to terms with, Prue thought, wondering how she herself would feel if an unknown brother or sister suddenly crept out of the woodwork. But it was different for Prue. She still had two living parents, and the possibility that either of them might harbour memories of long-distant affairs or have created secret children was quite frankly unthinkable.

'Penny for them.' Madi's voice broke into her thoughts.

'Oh, sorry. Miles away there!'

'So, what do you think? Is it how you imagined it?'

'Even better.' Prue stood up, with Camilla the camera bouncing on its strap against her chest. 'And that is why I am now going to take so many photos that I'll be busy for a week trying to edit them!'

Madi put her hand out and stopped her from walking away. 'I am sorry, Prue. I know I've said it before. But if it wasn't for me, you would never have been living her, never have had that evil woman attacking you like that . . .'

'If it wasn't for you, I would not be standing in this beautiful garden, surrounded by new friends, with a wonderful new London life to look forward to. And I wouldn't have met Simon. Don't beat yourself up about things that were never your fault, Madi. How could you possibly have known what was going to happen? And, in the end, only good has come out of the whole thing.'

'Are you sure you won't move in with me while you're doing your course?'

'For three whole years? A month, we said. There's no way I am going to impose on you for any longer, and besides . . . I hear there's a flat going spare.'

'Here?'

'Emily Parker's. Suzy's made it a condition of the sale that I get it for the first year, if I want it. Special rent. She says it's her family mess that led to me being hurt and she wants to make amends. A year suits me fine. After that, who knows? I might move into student halls, or find someone I'd like to share with . . .'

'I think you probably already have.' Madi's gaze turned towards Simon, who had moved away to chat to someone about doing some building work in their mother's house in Ealing.

'Early days, Madi. I'm not going to rush it, not after the whole Joe thing, but I'm hopeful. I really am.'

'I'm glad. And thank you for inviting me down to Shelling for the weekend. I'm so looking forward to seeing everyone again.'

'We're glad of the lift back. Simon's bringing so much stuff I would have dreaded lugging it all home on the train. And they say it's us women who can't go away without packing everything but the kitchen sink!'

Chapter 44

MADI

On Saturday afternoon, Madi pulled the car into the kerb outside Prue's cottage. How different it looked now in the summer sunshine, the dead daffodils replaced by vibrant red dahlias that matched the colour of the front door, and the old wooden gate that had creaked and dragged against the path now replaced by a new one, also painted in bright shiny pillar-box red.

'Glad to be home?' Madi asked, turning in her seat to talk to Prue and Simon, huddled cosily side by side in the back seat.

'Always.'

'Won't you miss it when you move to London?'

'Maybe, but it will always be here to come back to, won't it? I've decided I'm going to let Sian and Ralph live here while I'm gone. They were lucky his dad let them stay with him once they got engaged, but they need their privacy, their own space, and there's been nowhere suitable without them having to drive miles in and out of town. My cottage is so near to the surgery, and I feel I owe them . . .'

'You'll charge them rent though?'

'Yes, but not too much. And they'll take on all the bills. The rent will top up my student loan and help me pay my way in London, Mum will happily give me a room to sleep in when I'm home in the holidays, and they can all fight over Flo. She can stay here or move to Mum's, or live between both homes if she chooses. They all love her just as much as I do. No, selling the place was never really an option. Not when it was my gran's . . .'

'It looks really quaint.'

'Oh, Simon, have you not been here before?' Madi said, opening the door and swinging her legs out of the car.

'No, first time. The cottage, the village . . . and meeting Prue's parents on their home territory. It's all a bit scary, to tell you the truth.'

'It will be fine, believe me.' She stood up and stretched, the two of them following her out of the car. 'Shelling could not be a more welcoming . . .'

Before she had even finished her sentence, the door of the neighbouring house flew open and a small chestnut-brown dog came running down the path, its ears bouncing up and down like little furry flaps.

'Madi, you're back!' Tom, hurrying out of his gate just a pace or two behind the dog, opened his arms and engulfed her in them, almost pulling her off her feet.

'Hello, Tom.' She pulled back, taking in his familiar face and excited eyes, before kissing him warmly on the cheek. 'And who is this little beauty?'

'This,' Tom said, reaching down to pick up the little dog and nuzzle its neck, 'is Flush. She is four months old, an absolute bundle of energy, and she's keeping me very much on my toes.'

'She's adorable.' Madi held out her hand to be licked, which Flush did with great enthusiasm.

'You've made a friend there, Madi,' Prue said, opening her gate as Simon took their bags from the car and carried them to the step. 'Flo's not been quite so keen. In fact, she's kept well out of her way since she arrived, but she'll get used to her. I mean, who couldn't fall in love with a furry little angel face like that? Even a cat would have trouble resisting.'

'I see she has you in the palm of her hand, Tom.'

'Or paw!' Tom said, moving towards Madi's car and insisting on carrying what was left of the luggage.

'Oh, no, not into Prue's! I'll be staying with Faith and Stuart while I'm here.'

'Of course. We'll leave your stuff where it is then and I'll come up there with you later to help carry. But, for now, come on into my place and have a cuppa. All of you, obviously. You've had a long journey. Everything's ready, and it will be so much easier for you, until you've unpacked and settled in.'

'I've only been in London since Thursday, Mr Bishop!' Prue said. 'There's milk still in the fridge, and it's July, so I don't need to light the fire to warm the place up!'

'Even so . . .'

'No, you go,' Prue said, grinning at Madi. 'Honestly. Don't worry about us. I'd like to show Simon the cottage before I take him along to Mum and Dad's, and I'm sure you two have a lot of catching up to do. We'll see you later, Madi. And thanks for the lift.'

Madi stood on the pavement until Prue's front door closed behind them.

'Aah,' she said, smiling. 'I bet they've been dying for some time alone together.'

'Oops, sorry, I didn't get the hint. I'm sure you're right though. They won't want two old fogeys like us cramping their style.'

'Not so much of the old. Now, I'm sure I heard you mention tea.'

'And I have custard creams and Jaffa Cakes. Take your pick, or push the boat out and have both.'

'Oh, Tom, you know me so well!'

'I like to think so. And thank you, Madi, for putting the idea of getting a dog into my head.'

'I thought it was Barbara who did that?'

'Well, yes, she did, when things were different, when we had planned our future together. But you were right. Life doesn't stand still. Plans don't have to stop just because things change. It's good to have someone to look after again, someone to share my life with, someone to love.'

'Even if it is just a dog?'

'*Just* a dog? Don't let her hear you say that!' Tom tried to cover the dog's ears with his hands but they didn't stay still long enough. 'You're looking well, by the way. And not wearing the wig any more?'

'No need.' Madi put her hand to her hair. 'It's a little greyer than it was, but I intend to do something about that when I've decided on a colour. Purple maybe, or a nice shade of blue . . .'

'Heaven forbid!'

Madi laughed. 'Only joking. It's a lot shorter than I'm used to, but it will grow. The important thing is that it's the real deal. All my own, every last strand of it. And since the Emily Parker business, I know I wasn't actually losing my memory, or my mind, so I'm starting to feel like my old self again. I've got a job lined up too. I've been turning work down but I'm ready now. It's time. Just a small part, with rehearsals starting next month, but it will get me back out there again, where I belong. And I haven't forgotten my promise to get you a ticket, and a backstage tour.'

'Thank you, and I'm glad things are working out for you. I may not have known the old you but I'm looking forward to getting to know her now! Let's start by having a chat over that tea, shall we, Grandma!'

Madi swiped at his arm. 'Cheeky! Not for a few months yet, I'm not. And it all happened so quickly, the IVF treatment, only their second go at it, and the miracle of it working, that I've hardly had time to get used to the idea.'

'A good feeling though? Hair, and work, and having your son back in your life? And a new little arrival to look forward to?'

Madi followed Tom up the path, Flush licking at his ear. 'Oh, yes. The best feeling in the world.'

'So, where exactly are you taking me?'

Tom held the passenger door open and ushered her towards his car, Flush jumping about excitedly from behind a wire barrier set up in the back.

Madi had slept amazingly well in one of Faith's cosily

decorated spare rooms, surrounded by flowery fabrics and enveloped in a thick duck down duvet and fat feather pillows. She was still feeling heavy from eating one of the village pub's famous pie dinners last night, where she had met up again with Patty and lots of the other villagers keen to remake her acquaintance and talk about the 'awful incident' they'd read about in the papers. And then, at around ten o'clock this morning, finally emerging from her room, she had been presented with a huge farmhouse-style egg and bacon breakfast. Now she still felt full to the brim, despite the fact she had eaten it more than three hours earlier.

'Please tell me we're not going somewhere for lunch? I couldn't manage a mouthful.'

'Not lunch, no.'

'Then where?'

'Never you mind. It's a surprise. Now, come on. Your carriage awaits.'

The car sped along the narrow tree-lined country lanes she remembered so well. They all looked surprisingly similar and her sense of direction had left her somewhere at the end of the village street. She had no idea at all where they were headed.

'So, how are the plans to rebuild the village hall? And you never did tell me what came of the enquiry.'

'Wheels turn slowly, Madi. You must know that. The fire was declared an accident. The insurance is paying out, but it will be a while until we have a usable hall again.'

'Such a shame. Especially for all those kids who were so keen to put on a show. How is young Donny, by the way? Still ringing the bells?'

'Ha! No, it seems he has something more interesting to do in the evenings these days.'

'Oh?'

'You remember little Chantelle, one of the singers in the girl group? It would appear he's sweet on her. Has been for a while. In fact, I rather suspect that was why he was still hanging around on the night of the fire instead of scooting straight off home. A bit of courting behind the bike sheds, if you know what I mean!'

'Well, it was obvious they liked each other.'

'Was it?'

'When it comes to romance, you men never seem to see what's right in front of your eyes! The blushes were a dead giveaway. Anyway, the hall didn't have any bike sheds, did it?'

'Metaphorically speaking, Madi. A bit of innocent teenage hanky-panky was going on, that's all I meant. Or I hope it's innocent, seeing as they're barely fourteen. You must remember what it felt like though? All the sneaking about, and the hand-holding, and kissing the back of your own hand for practice. We all did it, didn't we, back in the day? Young love, it's like no other, eh?'

Madi laughed. 'If you say so, Tom.'

As Tom pulled in through a set of iron gates and squeezed the car into the last available parking space, Madi realised where they were.

'We're visiting Barbara?'

'I thought she'd like to see you. And that you might like to see her again? I talk to her about you quite a lot, and she does remember. Sometimes . . .'

The three of them clambered out and Tom clipped a lead onto Flush's collar.

'They won't mind her coming in?'

'Oh, no. Pets are very therapeutic, you know. All the residents love her. They queue up for a pat and a cuddle, and some of them slip her little treats from their pockets when they think I'm not looking. Flush loves it all, being made such a fuss of, and making friends. But Barbara knows she'll get the most attention. Flush is our dog, after all.'

Madi smiled at that. Barbara might not be able to live at home any more but Tom made sure she was included in everything. It was still *their* house, *their* dog . . .

'Come on, let's get inside, shall we? They'll hopefully have cleared away the remains of Sunday lunch by now. They eat early, but regularly, just like in hospitals. You sure you don't fancy a bit of cold beef and a yorkie? There's bound to be some left in the kitchen.'

'You must be joking. Nothing for me until at least six o'clock.'

'Not even a slice of Olive's fruit cake?'

'Definitely not a slice of Olive's fruit cake! Oh . . .' Madi stopped in her tracks.

'Surprise!' A chorus of voices rose up as Tom and Madi entered the lounge. Madi looked around. The soft high-backed chairs had been rearranged into a long row, with lots of extra smaller stacking-style chairs lined up in front, and people of all ages were sitting in them, all heads turned her way. Was that Prue and Simon in the corner? And Patty, with Sian and her husband-to-be, the vet? And there were Faith and Stuart, whom she had seen only an hour or two ago. What was going on?

The more she looked, the more familiar faces she saw, laced in between the unfamiliar ones she realised must be the residents of the care home. And the whole area in front of the big floor-to-ceiling windows had been cleared to resemble . . .

'A stage?'

'May I show you to your seat, Madam?' Tom produced a small torch from his jacket and was pretending to shine it along the front row as he eased her into the centre of it and gently pushed her down into a chair. Flush leapt eagerly into the lap of a woman sitting to her right, who she could see now was Barbara. 'And here is your programme.' Tom handed her a small booklet before settling into the seat to her left. The lights slowly dimmed and she registered for the first time that all the curtains around the room were closed. Flush gave a contented little sigh and lowered her head against her mistress's shoulder, and silence fell.

'And now that our guest of honour is here,' said a voice she recognised as young Donny's, booming through a speaker somewhere close by, 'let the show begin!'

'You didn't think I'd let the little matter of a fire stop me, did you?' Tom whispered into her ear as Chantelle and her girl band stepped nervously into the spotlight. 'You would never have forgiven me if I'd just given up. The show must go on, as you actors like to say.'

And so must life, Madi thought, settling back into her chair and trying to peer at her programme through a sudden, unexpected blur of tears. Whatever it throws at you, life goes on. And sometimes, if you're really lucky, it can still find ways to surprise you.

THE END

Acknowledgements

This book is set in 2020, in the months immediately following 29th February, known as 'Leap Day', when women get their once-every-four-years chance to propose. When I was writing it, none of us had any idea of the imminent coronavirus crisis that was looming or the huge changes it would make to our everyday lives. So, the real 2020 ended up looking a lot different from the one played out in these pages. But it's fiction, and that means we are allowed a little make-believe!

Writing about a marriage proposal couldn't fail but bring back memories of the day that Paul and I spent in Hampshire in April 2014, first wandering around Birdworld looking at parrots and penguins, and then taking an evening ride on the Real Ale steam train on the Watercress Line, with Paul strangely keen to get on board quickly at Alton and secure us an empty carriage. Before we had even set off down the track, I found out why! He produced a ring he'd had hidden away in his pocket all day, and had just proposed and slipped the ring onto my finger when another couple decided to join us in the carriage. It didn't feel right to share our special moment with total strangers, so we acted as normally as we

389

could, made idle chit-chat, drank a few beers and said nothing about it, waiting until the first stop at Alresford to get out and find a spot where he could do it privately and 'properly', down on one knee on the station forecourt! Sadly, Prue's Leap Day proposal didn't turn out so well, but I hope you enjoyed the ending I chose to give her instead. All's well that ends well, as they say, and let's hope this very unusual 2020 turns out well too, with all our family, friends, and everyone we know and love coming out of it safely at the other end. A big thank you to all of mine, just for being around, even if it's had to be at a two metre distance!

A sadly neglected and little-used shared garden area features in this book, and I realise now just how many blocks of flats, especially in city areas, have similarly inadequate outside space, or none at all, so I am very grateful in these worrying times to have a garden of my own to relax in, complete with lumpy lawn, flowers, trees and the occasional squirrel. While our jobbing gardener has been unable to visit as frequently as usual, I have found out just how much work goes into keeping it neat and weed-free. So, a big thank you to him and to all those people who help to keep our lives ticking over but rarely get acknowledged – from the binmen to the hair-dressers to the postmen and delivery drivers, and to the many actors (just like Madi) and behind-the-scenes crew whose livelihoods will have been so badly affected by the closure of theatres and the halting of filming. It sometimes takes a crisis to realise how important a role they all play.

This summer I have really missed my pub lunches with writer friends, garden barbecues, trips out to concerts and theme parks, regular strolls round the clothes shops and, most importantly of all, spending time with my grandchildren, but thank heavens for my two cats, Pixie and Dixie, who I have been allowed to cuddle as much as I like, and to a never-ending supply of wonderful e-books which have done so much to keep me entertained and distract my thoughts away from reality and into the fictional happy-ever-after world I love best.

A very important aspect of a writer's life, apart from all that reading, is keeping in touch with other writers. In normal times, the summer of 2020 would have seen me attending fortnightly meetings of my local writers' group Phrase Writers, listening to author talks in my local library, spending a lovely weekend at the Romantic Novelists' Association's annual conference in Telford, and enjoying a special lunch and presentation at the House of Lords with fellow members of the Society of Women Writers and Journalists. Of course, none of that happened. Still, I would like to thank those wonderful organisations, and so many others, including my own publishers, for keeping in touch with everyone via email, newsletters, phone calls, online book clubs, e-learning opportunities, videos, social media, Zoom and all manner of technological meet-up platforms that many of us had never used before. The friendship, support and sharing of all things book-related may have felt different this year but are as much appreciated as ever, if not more so.

I must also take this opportunity to thank Charlotte Ledger, Bethan Morgan and everyone at One More Chapter, who have managed to edit the manuscript, design a cover and generally work so hard to get this book out, despite the inevitable obstacles that working from their own homes must have thrown in their way. Thanks too, to copy editor Fran Fabriczki for doing such a good job of pointing out all those tiny little errors it is so easy to miss when reading one's own story for what feels like the hundredth time!

Lastly, but by no means least, thank you to all my readers who continue to beg, borrow or buy my novels. I hope you enjoyed this one and might consider doing me a small favour now that you've finished reading it by writing a short review on Amazon or Goodreads. Reviews and 'star' ratings are so important in helping other readers to choose which book to read next, and in warming the hearts of writers who just love to know our words have done their work and left their mark.